TWENTY-
DAYS OF A
NEURASTHENIC

OCTAVE MIRBEAU

TWENTY-ONE DAYS OF A NEURASTHENIC

A NOVEL

TRANSLATED FROM THE FRENCH
BY JUSTIN VICARI

DALKEY ARCHIVE PRESS

Originally published in French as *Les 21 jours d'un neurasthénique*
by Bibliothèque-Charpentier, Eugène Fasquelle, Paris, 1901

Translation copyright © 2014 by Justin Vicari
First Edition, 2015

Library of Congress Cataloging-in-Publication Data
Mirbeau, Octave, 1848-1917, author.
  [Vingt-et-un jours d'un neurasthénique. English]
  21 days of a neurasthesnic / by Octave Mirbeau ; Translated by
Justin Vicari. -- First Edition.
     pages cm
  "Originally published in French as Les Vingt-et-un jours
d'un neurasthénique by Charpentier-Fasquelle, 1901."
  ISBN 978-1-62897-030-2 (pbk. : alk. paper)
  1. Mirbeau, Octave, 1848-1917--Translation into English.
I. Vicari, Justin, 1968- translator. II. Title.
III. Title: 21 jours d'un neurasthénique.
  PQ2364.M7V613 2015
  843'.8--dc23
                        2014037663

Partially funded by the Illinois Arts Council, a state agency
and the University of Illinois at Urbana-Champaign

The Publisher acknowledges the financial assistance of Ireland
Literature Exchange (translation fund), Dublin, Ireland
www.irelandliterature.com
info@irelandliterature.com

www.dalkeyarchive.com
Victoria, TX / London / Dublin

Cover: Typography and layout by Arnold Kotra
Composition by Jeffrey Higgins
Art by Nathan Parks

Typesetting: Mikhail Iliatov

Printed on permanent/durable acid-free paper

TABLE OF CONTENTS

Translator's Preface

I have been indebted to the Éditions du Boucher-Société Octave Mirbeau reprint of *Les 21 Jours d'un Neurasthènique*, edited by Pierre Michel and published in 2003. The copious and well-researched explanatory notes illuminated many obscure, esoteric references. In some cases, a decision was made to build the explanation of the references into the text, so as to preserve the immediate impact of Mirbeau's meaning and satirical humor. Rather than present the book to American audiences as a kind of scholarly artifact, a hybrid of fiction and research, or a puzzle to be decoded, with the reader flipping back and forth between the body of the novel and the end notes, I was intrigued to see if *Twenty-One Days of a Neurasthenic* could stand on its own, almost as a contemporary work. Thus, many references which Mirbeau's French readership would have read and understood (and probably laughed at) in stride, have been made accessible to contemporary English-speaking readers.

Some end notes, however, have been retained, in situations where a given reference could not be concisely explained within the text; where the reference itself was historically fascinating, and gained from further elucidation; or where the reference tells us something about Mirbeau's own life and opinions. The Notes that are here, therefore, should be seen as enhancing the text without overshadowing it. In some cases, my tendency to eschew scholarly notes wherever possible has meant adding some new material to the original; hopefully this has been done smoothly, and in the author's spirit. Additionally, some proper names that would be meaningless *without* an explanatory note have been omitted altogether and replaced with the generic type that they are meant to call to mind—i.e., "M. Goblet" has been rendered as "the reform candidate."

Again, some decisions have been made for the sake of the book's humor, which is rich, if ultimately bleak and very dark.

("Sick" things, extreme things, always tend to make me laugh.)
When Mirbeau states that a ham theater-actor had to give up
wig making as a side career because his shaking hands produced bad wigs, I have not been able to resist describing the
anomalous hairpieces in slightly more detail than Mirbeau did.
In general, English seems to thrive on a descriptive specificity
(with a stubborn mania for physical evidence and things of all
sorts) which French is often comfortable forgoing. A number
of times, Mirbeau has a character perform a "geste," or gesture,
which he does not describe, except, occasionally, with an abstract noun; I have attempted to define what such "gestes"
might look like: a "geste d'ennui," for example, has been translated as a yawn. Some of Mirbeau's invented character-names
look forward to Beckett in their punning or absurd allusive-
ness. "Clara Fistule" has become "Clara Fistula." The quack
doctor "Fardeau-Fardat" (literally "Burden-Burdened") has become "Cumberburden." An unsavory notary, who doubles as a
would-be pimp, is named "Claude Barbot" in the original—
"barbot" is a sputter, or the noise a duck makes—hence
"Claude Splutterduck" in the translation.

Mirbeau is allegorical enough to warrant the use of such
broad character names. He was a polemicist, perhaps nowhere
as full-throttle as in this episodic roman-à-clef, in which he
"names names," including a good many of his friends, enemies
and all-around targets. Politically, Mirbeau was left-wing, certainly not orthodox with current leftism in all of his views, but
definitely anti-war, anti-business and anti-rich enough to reso-
nate strongly with many of our own contemporary issues. That
being said, however, he is hardly a humanist: he is not squea-
mish when it comes to ridiculing a public figure (or fictional
character—or both, inter alia) for stupidity, or for physical ugliness and infirmity; nor when it comes to torturing a character
purely for the sake of impressing on the reader that the world is
bad, fate is cruel, and life is cheap. He could be scatological,
and ecstatically profane. He belongs to a small group of sati-
rists who made a point of being prickly and at times difficult to

like: Aristophanes, Jonathan Swift, Louis-Ferdinand Céline, and William S. Burroughs all come to mind when one reads Mirbeau. Indeed, these lines of Aristophanes' could serve as a motto for this novel's hero and narrator, Georges Vasseur:

> What heaps of things have bitten me to the heart!
> A small few pleased me, very few, just four;
> But those that vexed me were sand-dune-hundredfold.
> (*Acharnians*, trans. B. B. Rogers)

Or, in Vasseur's case, *mountain*-hundredfold. I feel as though much could be said about the way the Pyrenees—as intrusive, invasive presences—are linked with the people who bully and annoy Vasseur throughout the book, and who awaken his sense of impotence. And so we have the irony at the heart of the book: a man driven mad by mountains, sent to the mountains to relax! Any misanthrope will recognize the turn of the screw in this metaphor—people are all one has to help cure one's dislike of them.

Mirbeau looked at turn-of-the-century France and found many reasons to quarrel with the bourgeoisie of his time: among other things, rampant imperialism, and rabid xenophobia, and anti-Semitism. This was the era of the Dreyfus Affair—Mirbeau was outspokenly pro-Dreyfus, and made a number of enemies by being so—and Dreyfus becomes a motif of this book, if not a kind of shadow character, popping up now and then as a test case for the other characters' intolerance, like a red cape waved in front of a crazed bull. Mirbeau was also dismayed by the proliferation of a corrupt oligarchy masquerading as democracy, and a hypocritical morality that preferred to ban subversive or erotic books and art rather than take a stand against the ruthless exploitation of the poor. Priests and bureaucrats take frequent turns at the whipping post. As a writer, Mirbeau is often as grim as he is funny, and offers more disturbing insights into the eternal mechanisms of corruption and exploitation than he does solutions. And yet, much of my enthusiasm for Mirbeau, and for *Twenty-One Days of a Neuras-thenic*, stems from my conviction that we could use more writers like him today.

This book bears a complex relation to modern psychology and psychoanalytic theory. "Neurasthenia" is a diagnosis not widely in use anymore; essentially, it encompasses nervous disorders, neurological symptoms, anxiety, paranoia, and other types of neurosis. Much like TB, it seems to have been treated largely with extended rest-cures at supposedly therapeutic spas. The word has been kept for title recognition and also because there is no modern equivalent which touches on as many different kinds of mental, emotional and physiological distress. However, other, more fleeting references have been updated, only because it would have seemed strange to contemporary readers *not* to identify the classic anxiety-dreams described by the narrator in Chapter XV as "recurring dreams," or to use words like "depression" and "depressed" to denote a kind of inchoate, chronic melancholy that is, in fact, pathological and clinical. Writing about neurosis in 1901 made Mirbeau an astute pioneer; but most people today are fluent in the names that have been given to the landscape he explored when it was still, for the most part, a terra incognita.

Finally, I like the phrase "when all is said and done" in relation to this book, and I have used it often, usually for the French "*enfin.*" "When all is said and done" seems to me to encode many of Mirbeau's concerns—for one thing, that decadence and world-weariness of the narrator and other characters, who have seen too much. Also, perhaps somewhat conversely, the phrase speaks to the anarchist leanings of Mirbeau, who believed that the individual should be allowed as much unrestricted freedom as possible, to "say and do" "everything," although he did not naively shrink from the fact that such freedom can lead to difficult, painful situations. One man's meat, as it were, is so often another man's poison in this book. Nonetheless, Mirbeau's sympathies always lie with those who feel helplessly compelled to lift the brutal veil of life, in acts of murder and violation, and those who have fallen through the system's many cracks—prostitutes, convicts, the homeless, etc. His sympathies never lie with those who manipulate power and wealth, or those who are cold-bloodedly (and ignorantly) racist and prejudiced. Is "neurasthenia," ultimately, the paranoid anxiety that comes from a lifetime of swimming against the current and living against the grain? The freedom claimed by Mirbeau's characters very often takes them straight to the doorstep of some ruinous, murderous hell—but whose fault is this? In societies that cling to guilt and damnation, and which justify widespread exploitation with all manner of orchestrated terror, individual freedom is likely to always appear as a case of "going too far." For Mirbeau's characters, going too far merely marks the beginning of the journey.

Justin Vicari

TWENTY-ONE DAYS OF A NEURASTHENIC

I.

Summer, fashion, and health (which is just another kind of fashion) dictate that one travel. If you are a bourgeois member of the leisure class, highly conformist, respectful of social customs, you must travel for the entire month of August, abandon your hobbies, your pleasures, your comfortable idleness, your close friends, to go away without really understanding why, and plunge into the world at large (usually that of France). According to the anodyne language of news magazines and the elite people who consume them, this is called "getting away," a far less poetic term than "voyage," but so much more accurate . . . ! Of course, the heart seldom gets away, you could even say it almost never does; still, you must sacrifice your friends, your enemies, your shopkeepers, your servants, around whom you must always maintain an air of superiority, for traveling requires money, and money requires that you at least appear superior.

Therefore, I am traveling, which bores me tremendously, and I am traveling in the Pyrenees, which turns my general boredom of travel into a heightened form of torture. What I loathe most about the Pyrenees is that they are mountains . . . Now, I have a wild, boundless and poetic appreciation for mountains, as much as the next man; nonetheless, they represent for me everything the universe can possibly bear of incurable melancholia, hopeless discouragement, an unbreatheable, deadly air . . . I admire their grandiose shapes, their changing light. But their inner life terrifies me . . . I feel as though the land of the dead must be nothing but mountains upon mountains, just like these which I am staring at now, as I write. Perhaps that is why so many people flock to them.

The defining nature of this city I am in, and whose "sublime idyllic beauty" the first-rate Baedeker, in deadpan German, praises with extravagant odes, is precisely this: it's not a city at all. Generally, a city consists of streets, the streets of houses, the houses of occupants. In X, however, there are nei-ther streets, nor houses, nor native occupants, only hotels, sev-enty-five hotels, mammoth structures resembling barracks or madhouses, receding one after the next, indefinitely, along a single line, at the bottom of a black and foggy gorge, where a paltry stream, like a bronchitic old man, ceaselessly coughs and splutters. Here and there: displays outside the hotel lobbies, bookstalls, racks of illustrated postcards, photographic views of waterfalls, mountains and lakes, arrays of alpenstocks and ev-erything else a tourist needs. Then, a few villas embedded in the foothills . . . and deep down in a hole, the hot spring that dates from Roman times . . . Ah, yes, the Romans . . . ! And that's it. Facing you, a tall, gloomy mountain . . . To the right, a mountain with a lake sleeping at its feet; to the left, yet another mountain, yet another lake . . . And no sky, never any sky above you! Only dense clouds dragging their bloated, milky bulk from one peak to the next . . .

If the mountains are foreboding, what can I say about the lakes — oh, these lakes! — whose false, cruel blue (neither ocean-blue, nor sky-blue, nor blue-blue) does not match any-thing around them or reflected in them . . . ? They seem paint-ed — oh, Nature! — by M. Guillaume Dubufe, whenever that artiste, so beloved by M. Leygues, worked himself up to epic compositions, symbolic and religious . . .

And yet, I might be able to excuse the mountains for being mountains and the lakes for being lakes if they did not com-pound their general, natural insult with the injury of being the pretext for hideous assortments of every human specimen to gather in their rocky gorges and along their groaning shores.

In X, for example, all seventy-five hotels are crawling with tourists. Just finding a single room for myself was a fantastic ordeal. Everyone's here, the English, the Germans, the Spanish, the Russians, even the French. These throngs do not come here to cure their liver problems, or their dyspeptic stomachs, or their dermatitis . . . They come — just listen to this — for fun!

And from morning to night you see them in taciturn groups or mournful single file, parallel to the row of hotels: clustering around the displays, lingering in one spot for ages, squinting through enormous lorgnettes at some renowned, snow-capped peak which they are certain is there, and which is indeed there, but can never be spotted behind the thick upper reaches of the wall of clouds eternally enshrouding it . . .

Everyone here is ugly beyond belief, with that ugliness endemic to seaside towns. Surrounded by all these leathery mugs and potbellies, I am lucky if once a day I have the pleasant surprise of a pretty face and a fit body. Even the children are like little old men. A depressing spectacle, since you soon realize that the middle class is dying out everywhere, and every person you meet (even the children, those wretched spawns of the putrid swamps of marriage) is already extinct!

Yesterday evening, I dined on the hotel terrace. At the table next to mine, a gentleman was braying: "Ascensions? You want to talk about ascensions . . . ? I've done them all, let me tell you . . . and without a guide! This place is a joke . . . The Pyrenees, they're nothing to speak of . . . Not real mountains . . . Now, Switzerland, I'll have you know . . . ! I scaled Mont Blanc three times . . . as if I'd never left my armchair . . . in five hours flat. That's right, five hours, dear sir."

Dear Sir said nothing, he just kept eating, his nose in his plate. The other one started up again: "I don't mean Mont Rose . . . or Mont Bleu . . . or Mont Jaune . . . Don't get any fancy ideas. And you haven't heard anything yet, let me tell you, one year on the peaks of the imposing Sarah Bernhardt, I rescued three Englishmen trapped in an avalanche. Ah! If only I had seen Fashoda coming . . . those Brits would never have dared to take it from us . . ."

He said some other things I could not hear very well, but which featured "I! I! I!" as a constant theme. Then he cursed the waiter, sent back the dishes, haggled over the price of a wine, and turned again to his companion: "So, up we go, then, up we go . . . ! I've tackled far worse. I rowed across Lake

Geneva in four hours flat, from Territet all the way to Geneva
... That's right, I ... I ... I!!"

Do I even need to tell you that this gentleman was an actual
Frenchman, from France?

My attention wavered at the sound of gypsy music, for
there was gypsy music playing, too ... You see, the scene was
complete.

On the other hand, how better could I spend my time than in-
troducing you to some of my friends, some of the people with
whom I rub elbows here, all day long? They're like most people, some grotesque, others merely repugnant; in short, perfect
scum whom I would not recommend young ladies to read
about. I know perfectly well what you must think of me: "This
gentleman knows some very strange people," but I know others who are not strange at all, and whom I never talk about, because I cherish them infinitely. But I beg you, dear readers, and
you as well, demure female readers, do not label me with that
celebrated proverb: "*Birds of a feather* ..." For the souls whose
often ugly physiognomies I am going to reveal, about whom I
am going to tell you the most unedifying stories and propose
that they are nearly always scandalous—I do not "flock together" with them, as the proverb goes ... I simply stumble
upon them now and then (an entirely different matter), and do
not mislead them into believing I care about them at all, then I
commit these encounters to paper for your amusement and
mine ... Mainly mine!

What a preamble, just to explain to you that my friend
Robert Hagueman is not really my friend. He's just someone I
met once, someone who is on familiar terms with me and
whom I am on familiar terms with; a person I run into from
time to time, always by accident and never with pleasure.

Besides, you know him too. My friend is not an individual
but a herd. Gray fedora with a wide brim, black jacket, pink
shirt with a white collar, white trousers with crisply creased
pleats, white patent leather shoes, they're on all the beaches

and in all the mountains; at this very moment, there are 30,000 Robert Haguemans, whose clothes and souls you would think the exact same tailor had fashioned—bargain-basement souls, it goes without saying, for they are haphazardly cut from a cloth worth next to nothing.

This morning, as I left the café, I spotted my friend Robert Hagueman. His early morning grooming was impeccable, and did not shock the admirable plane trees along the lane, eminently philosophical trees who have seen countless others since the Romans, those builders of elegant baths and channelers of community hot-springs. I immediately feigned an intense interest in the movements of a road worker who, armed with only a saucepan, bailed water out of the stream and then emptied it into the middle of the street, under the fallaciously municipal pretext of watering it ... And, in order to give my friend time to slip by unnoticed, I even engaged this worker in a conversation about the pre-aedilitian strangeness of his equipment, but Robert Hagueman had also noticed me.

"Ah! Speak of the devil!" he said. He came up to me, overflowing with effusions and holding out his hands in white leather gloves. "How is it possible? Can it be you? What are you doing here?"

There is nothing I detest more than confiding my minor infirmities to people. I replied, "I'm just here to stretch my legs ... And you?"

"Oh! Me ...? I'm here on a course of treatment. My doctor sent me here ... Slight case of exhaustion, you see ..."

The conversation suddenly took a banal turn. Robert talked about Paul Deschanel, arriving the following day; about the Casino, not very lively this year; about the pigeon shooting, not going very well, etc. "But no women, buddy-boy, no women!" he concluded. "Where are they this year? No one knows ... Hell of a season, you understand ...!"

"But just look at that mountain!" I cried with sarcastic enthusiasm. "It's so awe-inspiring here ... Why, it's paradise on

earth. Look at all this plant life ... these phlox, these leucan-
themias that grow as tall as beech trees ... and those gigantic
roses, which seem to have been transplanted from God knows
what dreamland, in the chapeau of M. de Jussieu!"

"What a simpering child you are!"

I exulted, "And the streams, and the glaciers ... So, none of
this speaks to you at all ...?"

"Don't make me laugh," Robert replied. "Do I really seem
like the kind of chump who climbs into boats like those? To
get tossed around by those choppy currents ...? And what's so
amazing about that mountain ...? It's Mont Valérien, it's tall,
so what? Anyway, it's hollow inside ..."

"You prefer the sea, then?"

"The sea ...? Now you're really pushing your luck ...! My
boy, for fifteen years now I've spent every summer at Trouville
... You know, if I had one wish, it would be ... to never have
to look at the sea again ... It turns my stomach ... No ...! I
think I'd rather do anything else in the world than go around
stunning myself with what you call the spectacle of nature ...
I've had it up to here, understand?"

"Okay, but didn't you say you came here for your health?
Are you following the treatment at least?"

"Stringently," Robert said. "Where would I be without it!"

"What do you do?"

"For the treatment?"

"Yes."

"Well, it's simple, really ... I get up at nine ... Stroll
through the garden around the café ... Meet up with a gentleman here, a lady there ... We relax a bit ... We talk about how
we're all bored stiff ... We complain about the toilets ... That
takes me right up to lunchtime. After lunch, a poker party at
Gaston's ... Casino at five ... A half-hearted spot at the baccarat table ... A few fistfuls of coins, a promissory note ... Din-
nertime ... Re-Casino ... And that's it ... And the next day, it
starts all over again ... Now and then, a little interlude with a
Lais of Toulouse, or a Phrynna of Bordeaux ... Ooh, la, la,

buddy-boy! Ah, well, would you believe it? This resort, praised throughout the world for curing every ill ... It's produced no effect on me at all ... I'm just as exhausted as when I arrived ... What a laugh—thermal waters ..."

He sniffed the air and said, "And that stench again ...! Can't you smell it ...? It's putrid ..." An odor of hyposulfite, escaping from the café, wafted among the plane trees ...

My friend started again, "It smells like ... Christ, I hate to think about it ...! It smells like the Marquise's house." He guffawed uproariously. "Picture this ... One evening, the Marquise de Turnbridge and I had plans to dine at a restaurant ... You remember the Marquise, that statuesque blonde I spent two years with ...? No ...? You really don't remember ...? But, buddy-boy, everyone in Paris knows all about that. Anyway, who cares ...!"

"What was this Marquise like?"

"A very fashionable woman, my old buddy-boy ... A former laundress from Concarneau, she had become, thanks to someone whose name I've forgotten, a marquise, and the Marquise de Turnbridge no less ... And an intellectual, I didn't tell you that ...! Anyway, instead of dining at the restaurant as planned, the Marquise—on a whim—decided we'd dine at her house ... But before we had even closed the door, an appalling odor choked us in the antechamber: 'For Christ's sake,' said the Marquise, 'it's my mother again ...! When will she kick off already ...?' And she stalked toward the kitchen in a rage. There was the sainted mother, boiling a cauldron of cabbage soup ... 'I don't want you to make cabbage soup in my house ... I've told you twenty times ... It stinks up the whole place ... And if I had brought home some man other than my lover, what impression would I have made, with this outhouse stench ...? Have I finally made myself clear?' And turning back to me, she added: 'For Christ's sake! It's as if a whole troop of Cossacks burst in here and farted ...'"

He grew very wistful over this memory, and sighed. "All the same, she was a splendid woman ... you understand ...? And so fashionable ...!" Then he reiterated, "Well, this stench, hovering all around us here, reminds me of Mother Turnbridge's cabbage soup ... It's exactly the same ..."

"Thinking about the Marquise must help take your mind off it somewhat," I said, then I held out my hand to him. "I have to go, hope you're feeling better ... I'm interrupting your treatment ..."

"Wait a minute—wait!" Robert called out.

But I had dashed into the garden, and placed the width of an enormous Wellingtonia between my friend and me.

II.

This evening I went to the Casino. Actually, I forced myself to go ... I have to kill time somewhere, before bed ...

While I was there, slumped on a bench in the garden, watching people, a fat greasy man, who had been staring at me for some time, suddenly came up to me. "Am I mistaken?" he said. "Aren't you Georges Vasseur?"

"Yes ..."

"And me ...? You don't recognize me?"

"No ..."

"Clara Fistula, old buddy ..."

"I can't quite recall ..."

"But yes ... yes ... Ah, how wonderful to see you again ...!" He squeezed my hand as if to break it. "What's this? You really don't know ...? I'm a bigshot around here ... I'm public relations director ... No kidding, old buddy ... At your disposal, sapristi ...!"

With a friendly enthusiasm that left me cold, he offered me his services: free admission to the Casino and the theater, credit at the club, the best table at the restaurant, and young girls ...

"Ah, we're going to have fun here!" he exclaimed. "You know, I can't believe my eyes ... Goddamned Georges, what do you say ...? I'll be damned if this isn't just what I've been waiting for ...!"

I thanked him profusely. In order to feign interest, I asked, "And you ...? Have you been here long?"

"As an invalid ... ten years," he replied. "As a spa employee ... four ..."

"And are you happy?"

"You have no idea ...!"

But before going any further, I want you to meet Clara Fistula . . . Here, then, is a portrait of him which I found among my
notes:

"Today I had a visit from Clara Fistula.

"Clara Fistula is not a woman, though you might be led to
believe this from his first name. He is not, strictly speaking, a
man either; he is a kind of missing link between man and God;
an Interman, as Nietzsche would have called him. A poet, it
goes without saying. But he is more than a poet, he is a sculptor, musician, philosopher, painter, architect, he is everything
. . . 'I totalize, within myself, the multiple intellectualities of
the universe,' he declares, 'but it is extremely exhausting, and I
have to bear the crushing weight of my genius all by myself.'
Clara Fistula is not yet seventeen, and (oh prodigy!) he has already spent so much time deep at the depths of everything. He
knows all the secret wellsprings, all the mysteries of the abyss.
One hell satisfies another.

"Doubtless you picture him oddly lanky and pale, with a
brow misshapen from the earthquakes of thought, and eyelids singed by dreams. Nothing of the kind; Clara Fistula is
a fat, stout, thick-set boy, with the stocky build of an Auverg-
nat whose red blood simmers from playing sports. He does not
acknowledge the material solidity of his body and believes he
has willed himself 'incorporeal.' Although he preaches asexu-
alism and flutters about everywhere proclaiming 'the horror
of being male' and 'the obscenity of being female,' he clandes-
tinely impregnates all the nubiles in his neighborhood. Surely
you have seen, in exhibitions of paintings at the Bodinière and
the Oeuvre, a creature garbed in a long, pearl-gray waistcoat-
girdle, the bosom squeezed into a vest of copper-colored fur,
and the head, with its long plaited hair, coiffed with a wide-
brimmed, black felt hat, a Presbyterian hat around which is
wound a cord snake with seven tassels, in tribute to the seven
ordeals of woman. That's Clara Fistula. As you see, he's a real

mishmash. But you mustn't expect logic from seventeen-year-old geniuses who have seen everything, felt everything, understood everything.

"I received Clara Fistula in my study. The first thing he did was to sneer at all the decorations on my walls, the ingenious arrangement of my library, my drawings . . . I waited for some compliment.

"'Oh, my,' he said, 'things like that do not interest me in the least. I see only in the abstract.'

"'Really . . . ?' I replied, slightly piqued. 'That must trip you up at times . . .'

"'Not at all, dear sir. The materiality of furniture, the misbegotten crudeness of wall decorations, always offended me . . . What's more, I have managed to liberate myself from contingencies . . . I eschew ambiance . . . I abolish the material world . . . My furniture, my walls are merely projections of my being . . . I live in a house built from my thoughts alone, and decorated with nothing but the sunbeams of my soul . . . But that's not why I am here . . . I came about graver matters.'

"Clara Fistula deigned, nonetheless, to take the seat which I offered him, and which I asked his forgiveness for offering him, knowing it was so little in harmony with the sunbeams of his ethereal ass.

"'My dear sir,' he said to me, after a somewhat haughty gesture of condescension, 'I have invented a new method of human reproduction.'

"'You don't say!'

"'It's called "Stellogenesis" . . . This method of conception is very close to my heart . . . I cannot bear the idea that I . . . Clara Fistula . . . I was engendered from the bestiality of a man and the prostitutional indulgences of a woman . . . Moreover, I never wanted to recognize as such those two pitiful creatures which civil law calls: my parents.'

"'That does you credit,' I said approvingly . . .

"'Doesn't it . . . ? See, dear sir, it is unacceptable for a being

of superior intelligence, as am I, for an all-spiritual being, as
am I, for a being finally godlike enough to have retained only
the most strictly necessary vestiges of a human body, alas! in a
society as imperfect as ours, it is unacceptable, as I said, for
such a being to be forced to emerge from hideous organs
which, for being instruments of love, are no less nauseating
and excrementitious . . . If I were convinced that I owed my life
to such a commingling of horrors, I could never survive that
original shame for one instant . . . But I believe I was born
from a star . . .'

"'Oh, I think so, too . . .'

"'I believe it all the more because, at night sometimes, in
my room, I give off a distinct glow . . .'

"'More power to you . . .'

"'Well, sir, to put an end once and for all to this psychological error of men being reproduced from other men . . . I have
composed an extraordinary and electrifying work which I call
Cosmogonic Virtualities . . . It is, if I dare say so, a triptych in
which I employ three different forms of expression to make my
meaning as clear as possible: sculpture, literature and music . . .
With sculpture, I use geometric lines and paralleloid curves to
show the trajectory of the stellar egg at the precise, earth-shak-
ing moment when, touched by the telluric pollen, it exploded
into human shape . . . The book is the metrical paraphrase of
this explosion, and the music its condensation . . . orchestrated
or with condensed orchestration. You see that, different from
mere speech, this work is constructed from the concept and
continuity of a symbol . . . However, I cannot find anyone to
publish it. In other words . . . would you lend me twenty
francs?'"

That is the end of my notes on Clara Fistula.

Due to my lending him twenty francs, which he never paid
back, we became friends . . . And then, one beautiful day, I lost
touch with him completely . . .

How could he have fallen from such lofty ambitions into the drab reality where I have told you I found him? I expressed my astonishment.

"Oh, you think I've changed . . . ?" he said to me. "It's true . . . And it's quite a story . . . Would you like me to tell it?" And without waiting for my consent, here is the strange account he gave me . . . "Ten years ago, when I was ailing, I was sent to X . . . Surely, when it comes to its reputation as a great healer, X deserves it more than all the other resorts of its type, for, during the six consecutive years when I sought a cure from its waters, its climate, its doctors' treatments, not once did I hear of a single patient dying. Yes, indeed, death seemed to have been outlawed in this corner of the French world . . . In actual fact, it happened every day that a number of people suddenly disappeared . . . And if you asked, you were invariably told: 'They checked out yesterday' . . . One day, dining with the spa director, the mayor of the city, and the manager of the Casino, I marveled at this ongoing miracle, not, however, without admitting to some doubts about its veracity.

"'Rest assured,' they spoke in chorus . . . 'It's been over twenty years since we've seen a burial here . . . And because these omens have smiled upon us, dear sir, we turned the staff of the funeral home into our bath-house attendants . . . our croupiers . . . our nightclub singers . . . And now we dream of transforming our cemetery into a marvelous shooting gallery, with pigeons . . .'

"It wasn't until the final year of my treatment that I learned the secret of that extraordinary immortality . . . It happened like this. One night, when I was returning home very late, and the entire contented, immortal town seemed fast asleep, I noticed, coming out of a side street to the main one where I was walking, eerie noises, hushed, breathless voices, thudding footfalls, thunderous clangs that seemed to crash against each other . . . I turned down the street, dimly lit at the other end by the faint and flickering glow of a single streetlight. And before I could make out what was happening, I distinctly heard this: 'For Christ's sake, keep it down . . . ! You'll wake the tourists . . . ! And if they took a notion to come out and see what we're doing . . . well, we'd all get the ax.'

"I crept closer, and here is the strange, surprising, morbid spectacle I witnessed: ten coffins, each carried by four men, ten coffins in single file . . . a processional receding into the shadows . . . In a city where no one ever died, I had stumbled on an embarrassment of coffins . . . The irony of it could have knocked me over!

"Then I understood why they had never seen a burial at X for twenty years . . . They bury the bodies on the sly . . . !

"Furious at having been hoodwinked by the municipal and Casino bigwigs, I questioned one of those pallbearers whose face glistened with sweat in that Shakespearean night. 'Hey there, friend . . . ! How do you explain those?' I asked, pointing to the coffins.

"'Those?' he said . . . 'They're steamer trunks . . . the trunks of the tourists who are checking out.'

"'Trunks . . . ? Ha, ha, ha . . . !'

"'Yes, trunks . . . We carry them to the train station . . . the central station.'

"A local police chief, who was supervising the operation, came up to me. 'Please stand aside, sir,' he begged, on his best behavior . . . 'You are blocking these men . . . They are losing time . . . These trunks—and that's really all they are, trunks— are very heavy . . . And the train won't wait . . .'

"'The train . . . ? Ha . . . ha . . . ha . . . ! And where is it bound for, this train?'

"'But . . .'

"'It's bound for the Great Beyond, right?'

"'The Great Beyond?' the chief said coldly. 'I've never heard of that country . . .'

"The next day, you can bet I frightened the mayor, the director and the Casino manager with that little scene I'd witnessed . . . I threatened to unmask everything . . . They calmed me down by offering me a considerable sum of money, and hiring me, in a shrewd codicil, as their exclusive public relations director . . . And here I am . . . !"

Beaming with deep, inner satisfaction, he slapped me on the knee. "Good one, eh . . . ?" he said. "By the way . . . do you have a doctor?"

"Yes."

"Cumberburden?"

"No . . . Triceps . . . My friend Doctor Triceps . . ."

"Ah, too bad . . . ! Because Doctor Cumberburden . . . Wait! . . . I haven't even told you that story yet. Ah, this place is full of characters . . . ! There's never a dull moment."

And Clara Fistula launched into a new tale: "So I was sent to X . . . The same day I got here, I went to the home of Doctor Cumberburden, to whom I had been specially recommended . . . A charming little man, vivacious and spirited, given to exuberant speech and silly little gestures, but who nonetheless inspired confidence.

"He greeted me with a fussy, somewhat generic cordiality, and after giving me a cursory glance from head to toe, he said, 'Ah-ha! So . . . Bad blood . . . ? Weak lungs . . . ? Neurasthenic . . . ? Alcoholic . . . ? Syphilitic . . . ? Happens to the best of them . . . Let's see, let's see . . . Have a seat . . .'

"Then, while he rummaged for God knows what in the chaos of his desk, he interrogated me with a gleeful half-smile, and without giving me time to respond: 'Genetic abnormality . . . ? Family history of TB . . . ? How about syphilis . . . ? On the father's side . . . ? On the mother's side . . . ? Married . . . ? Celibate . . . ? What about women . . . those whores! Ah, Paris! Paris . . . !'

"Finally finding what he had been searching for, he began again to grill me for a long time, more probingly, listening to my heart and lungs at great length, measuring my chest with the gestures of a tailor, testing my muscle strength with a dynamometer, and jotting down, in a little notebook, my responses and my comments; then, abruptly, with a jovial air: 'Now, the most important thing . . . one question, if I may . . . ? In the event of your death while on these premises . . . do you wish to be embalmed?'

"I jumped out of my chair. 'But, Doctor . . . ?'

"'It's not going to happen anytime soon,' the amiable practitioner corrected himself . . . 'But what the hell . . . ! If it *happens* to happen . . .'

"'But I had the impression . . .' I said, a bit frightened, 'I had the impression that no one ever died at X?'

"'Of course . . . of course . . . In theory, no one ever dies here . . . But over the long haul . . . an accident . . . a stroke of bad luck . . . an exception . . . Surely you are aware that there are always exceptions . . . ? You have a ninety-nine percent chance of not dying here . . . That's a statistical fact . . . So . . . ?'

"'So . . . it's pointless to talk about this, doctor . . .'

"'Excuse me . . . on the contrary, it's extremely to the point . . . in terms of the treatment . . . oh, damn it all!'

"'Well, then, Doctor, if by an extraordinary and one-time-only event I should happen to die here . . . no, I do not wish to be embalmed.'

"'Ah!' the doctor exclaimed . . . 'That's where you're wrong . . . because we have the most amazing embalmer . . . the best in the world . . . so friendly . . . A once in a lifetime opportunity, dear sir . . . He does such excellent work . . . simply perfection. When you get embalmed by him . . . you feel as though you have come back to life . . . one hundred percent back to life . . . to scream . . . now that's an embalmer . . . that's an embalmer!!!'

"Then, since I continued to vigorously shake my head no, he said, 'You really don't want to . . . ? So be it . . . After all, we can't force you to get embalmed . . .'

"On the notebook page where he recorded all of his observations pertaining to my condition, he scrawled in red pencil, in enormous letters: 'DO NOT EMBALM,' then he began to write out an endless prescription while looking up at me with the following words: 'Okay, then . . . Intensive treatment . . . I will come to see you every day, even twice a day.' Then, warmly squeezing my hands: 'Okay ...! All things considered ... you're doing very well ... Till tomorrow ...'

"I have to admit, little by little I came to appreciate his ingenious and devoted care. His originality, his unswerving, spontaneous and at times slightly morbid cheerfulness, won me over. We became firm and loyal friends.

"Six years later, when he was dining at my house one evening, he explained to me that I was definitively cured, with a joyous affection that touched me to the bottom of my heart.

"'And you know something?' he said to me. 'You've come a long, long way, my friend ... Ah, sapristi!'

"'I was very, very ill, wasn't I?'

"'Yes ... but that's not what I mean ... Do you remember when I insisted so strongly that you get embalmed?'

"'Of course ...'

"'Well, if you had said yes, dear friend ... you'd be dead now ...'

"'Really ...!? Why is that?'

"'Because ...' He suddenly fell silent ... and looked solemn and worried for a few seconds ... Then, he broke into his usual smile again: 'Because ... money was tight then ... and we had to turn a profit ... If we had embalmed you, then, with those other poor chaps, who, today, would be ... alive like you and me ...! What did you expect ...? One fellow's death means life for the others ...'

"And he lit a cigar."

Clara Fistula fell silent ... Since his confession left me speechless, he went on to say, "A charming fellow, I assure you ... Doctor Cumberburden ... it's just that ... you understand ... you are never entirely sure where you stand with him ... he embalms ... he embalms ... well, it doesn't matter ... So you really think I've changed?"

"One hundred percent!" I replied. "So, no more *Cosmogonic Virtualities* ...? No more "Stellogenesis" ...?"

"You said it . . . !" Clara Fistula exclaimed. "Childish hobby-horses . . . Ah, it seems so long ago now . . ."

I had a devil of a time that evening getting rid of my friend, who wanted to drag me off to the Casino and introduce me to some "fantastically chic" young girls . . . "I'll call you some-time . . . !"

III.

Of course, Doctor Triceps is hardly much better than Doctor Cumberburden . . . but Triceps is a friend (I've known him for ages!), and since he is here . . . since, after all of his adventures, he has ended up here, in this resort town . . . better him than some stranger . . . Death gives doctors a wide berth . . .
Another character, that one, as Clara Fistula would say.

He is a very short man, average, ambitious, fussy and obstinate. He dabbles in everything, performing with equal competency in all disciplines. He was the one who, at the 1897 Convention of Folrath (in Hungary), proposed that poverty was a nervous disorder. In 1898 he delivered a famous address to the Biology Club, in which he recommended the practice of incest as a means of repopulating the human race. The following year, he helped me during a somewhat strange episode, which gave me confidence in his diagnostic skills . . .

One day, I went down to the cellar (searching for God knows what), and discovered . . . down in the bottom of an ancient mason jar from the grocery store, under a thick bed of fine straw leftover from the packing . . . I discovered . . . what . . . ? A hedgehog. Curled in a ball, he was asleep in there, deep in a terrible, comatose hibernation whose morphology our learned scholars have never been able to explain to us— can it even be explained? This animal's presence in a mason jar did not surprise me one bit. The hedgehog is a shrewd, highly resourceful quadruped. Instead of seeking out a winter sanctuary closer to hand, under a risky, unsecured drift of leaves or in the hollow of some dead ancient tree trunk, this one had decided he'd be safer in a basement—not to mention warmer, for, as a further guarantee of creature comfort, he had chosen to hibernate inside this mason jar precisely because it sat against the wall right below the current from a heating duct. In this, I noted one of the well-documented traits of hedgehogs, who are not stupid enough to let themselves freeze to death, like vulgar rats.

As I gradually awakened him with cautious caresses, the animal did not seem unduly startled at the presence of a man in the cellar, leaning over the jar and staring at him. He uncoiled slowly and cautiously, then he stood up on his hind paws and stretched himself like a cat, scratching the ground with his claws. An extraordinary thing: when I picked him up and held him in my hand, not only did he not roll into a ball, he did not stick out a single one of his quills, and he never once pricked me with the barbed-wire pleats around his little cranium. On the contrary, by the way in which he grunted and chattered his jaw—by the way, too, in which his tiny snout wriggled—I observed that he was conveying joy, trust and ... appetite. Poor little bastard! He was pale and, as it were, wilted, like a salad sitting out for too long in some musty corner. His jet-black eyes kindled with a strange luster I recognized from the eyes of anemics; indeed, his eyelids, slightly damp with sweat, revealed to my trained etiologist's eye an advanced case of anemia.

I carried him up to the kitchen, and he immediately astonished us all by his friendliness and the ease with which he made himself at home. Like a starving man, he sniffed at the pommes frites simmering on the stove, and his nostrils inhaled, with delicious desperation, the aromas of sauces wafting through the air.

I poured him some milk right away, and he drank it down. After that, I tempted him with a morsel of meat, and he hurled himself upon it voraciously, as soon as he smelled it, like a tiger on its prey. With his two front paws crossed over the meat, as a sign of absolute ownership, he tore it to shreds with the corner of his growling mouth, and his black pinpoint eyes sparkled in fierce flashes. Thin red fibers dangled from his jaw, and his snout dripped with sauce. In a matter of seconds, the meat was all gone. It was the same story with the potatoes; a bunch of grapes, too, disappeared the instant it was offered. He slurped a bowl of coffee in big resounding gulps . . . Afterwards, sated, he dropped onto his serving dish and fell asleep.

By the following day, the hedgehog was as tame as a puppy. I made a very warm bed for him in my room, and whenever I came in, he leapt up, overjoyed, and ran straight to me, contented only when I picked him up. Then, as I stroked his back (his quills were so deeply retracted that they were as soft as the fur of a kitten), he spoke in brief, low cries, which soon settled into a continuous, sleepy drone, like a purr.

Yes, it is important for naturalists to know this: hedgehogs purr.

Since he gave me so much pleasure, and since I was falling in love with him, I gave him the honor of allowing him to sit at my table. They set his dish next to mine, and he ate every bite; it was amusing to see him huff in peevish annoyance when he watched them taking away a plate from which he had not been allowed to sample anything. I've never met an animal less finicky in his eating habits: meats, vegetables, pickles, desserts, fruit, he ate everything. But his favorite was rabbit. He could always smell it cooking; on those days he went mad, and could not get enough. On three occasions, he suffered severe attacks of indigestion from eating too much rabbit, and he might have died, the frail thing, if I had not acted quickly to administer potent laxatives.

It was a stroke of bad luck that I, out of human weakness, perhaps out of perversity, got him used to alcohol. After drinking liquor, he stubbornly refused to drink anything else. Like a connoisseur, he took his daily glass of the finest champagne. There were no bad side effects, no problems, no signs of inebriation. A hard drinker, he held his booze like an old sea captain. He became addicted to absinthe, too, and it seemed to do him good. His fur got darker, his eyes dried out, and all symptoms of anemia disappeared. Now and then I caught him staring off into space, as if preoccupied, with something like faint glimmers of lust in his eyes. Certain he would find his way back home, I turned him loose in the woods on warm, lovely nights to seek the companionship of female hedgehogs, and in the morning, right at the crack of dawn, there he was by the door, waiting to be let in. He slept like the dead the whole next day, recovering from his nocturnal orgies.

One morning, I found him stretched out on his bed. He did not leap up when I approached. I called to him. He did not move. I picked him up; he was cold. Nonetheless, his body still palpitated ... Oh, his tiny eye, and that look he gave me, with all the strength he could muster! I will never forget it ... that almost human look, filled with astonishment, pain, tenderness, and so many profound mysteries I longed to understand ... He took one more breath ... a kind of faint rattle, like the gurgle of a bottle being drained ... then two shudders, a spasm, a cry, another spasm ... Then he was dead.

I nearly cried ...

I stared at him in my hand, uncomprehending. There was no sign of a wound anywhere on his body, crumpled, now, like a rag; no visible symptom of disease revealed itself. The night before, he had not gone to the woods, and that evening he had richly, heartily savored his glass of fine champagne. What could have killed him? Why this sudden turn?

I sent the cadaver to Triceps for an autopsy. And here is the brief letter I received, three days later:

Dear friend,
Total alcoholic inebriation. Cause of death: dropsy.
An unprecedented case among hedgehogs.
Yours,
ALEXIS TRICEPS, M.D.

From this, you can clearly see that my friend Triceps is not a total brute.

Noble Triceps!

Ah, that trip I made to X, on family business! It's so long

ago now! After I'd settled my affairs, I remembered that a friend was incarcerated in the asylum for foreigners. This friend was none other than Triceps. I resolved to pay him a visit. The weather was beastly that day . . . The air was icy; fierce north-westerly blasts flayed the skin from my cheeks. Instead of taking shelter in a café, I hailed a fiacre and went to the madhouse.

The fiacre rode through commercial districts and teeming slums. It rolled through dismal suburbs, past vast empty lots enclosed by tarmac-covered fences, and now and then the sudden apparition of sprawling black buildings, hospitals, military barracks, prisons, some topped with crosses wobbling in the wind, others made taller by massive flood-lit spires, around which yellow-beaked crows shrieked and wailed. Then, the fiacre turned between two towering walls, billowing with smoke and made of thick, dreary, suffocating stone, pierced here and there by small frosted panes with iron bars, letting out a stink of misery, damnation and death. In front of a vaulted door, painted dingy gray and hammered with huge bulbous nails in all four corners, we finally came to a stop.

"Those are the crazies . . . We're here," said the driver.

I hesitated for a few moments before crossing that intimidating threshold. At first, I was all set to go right inside, for the sake of my friend, locked up for making indiscreet requests and solicitations of every kind; but then, I remembered I could never stand the eyes of madmen. Looking into madmen's eyes terrifies me as if they were contagious, and the sight of their long gnarled fingers, their grimacing mouths, turns my stomach. My own mind immediately falls prey to their delirium; their dementia communicates itself instantaneously throughout my entire nervous system; and in the soles of my feet I feel a painful, agonizing, tickling sensation, which makes me jump along the madhouse corridors like a turkey whom sadistic boys force to walk upon a sheet of white-hot steel.

Nonetheless, I did go in. The porter handed me over to a guard, who led me through courtyards, courtyards, and still more courtyards, by some stroke of luck deserted at that hour; took me down hallways and made me climb staircase after staircase. From time to time, on the landings, glass doors were left ajar on cavernous rooms, white-walled vaults, and I noticed cotton nightcaps strangely askew on ashen, knitted brows. But I forced myself to stare only at the walls and the ceiling, across which the shadows of wringing hands seemed to flutter in the intermittent patches of light. I don't know how I ended up in an extremely bright room. My friend Triceps threw his arms around me and said: "Ah, speak of the devil ...! Speak of the devil ...! Is it really you ...? Ah, it's good to see you ... you couldn't have arrived at a better time ... What a chic idea ...!"

And, without any other words of welcome, he launched into the following: "Listen ... you can do a favor for me, can't you ...? See, I'm just putting the finishing touches on a little research into 'surgical dilettantes' ... Perhaps you've never heard of that ...? No ...? It's a new form of mental illness they've just discovered ... Guys who chop up old ladies into pieces ... they're not killers anymore ... they are surgical dilettantes. Instead of giving them a whack on the neck with the guillotine, they shower them with praises ... All of the men here have been taken out of the executioner's care and entrusted to mine ... And that's what I'm doing here ... A pretty good joke, eh ...? Why, it's hilarious ...! But for me, it's like hitting the jackpot ... I wrote a famous dissertation on surgical dilettantes, you know ... I have even—but just as a lark—I have even discovered the exact mental defect corresponding to this mania ... see ...? So, naturally, I am going to present this dissertation to the Academy of Medicine in Paris ... Well, you have to wangle me a prize ... an impressive prize ... and academic laurels ... I'm counting on you ... You shall go and meet with Lancereaux, Pozzi, Bouchard, Robin, Dumontpallier ... See all of them ... I'm counting on you, understand ...? I'll send you all the details, later, via letter ... Ah, dear boy, you came at the perfect time . . . no, truly . . . it's a stroke of luck . . ."

I watched him while he spoke. It seemed to me his waist was much thinner, his skull much more exposed, his beard much more pointy. With his velvet skullcap, his taupe linen shirt which puffed him up like a balloon, his staccato gestures, he resembled a child's doll, the kind you see in side-street boutiques.

"So, what do you think of my room?" he asked abruptly. "It's nice here, isn't it . . . ? I'm not doing too badly for myself, am I . . . ? And this? . . . what do you think of this?"

That was when he opened the window and pointed to the view: "Those trees, right there, and those little white machines, that's the cemetery . . . There . . . those big black buildings on the right, that's the hospital . . . On your left . . . look where I'm pointing . . . there . . . the marine barracks . . . You can't see the prison very well . . . but in the courtyard, very soon, I'll show you everything . . . See? You get fresh air here . . . it's quiet . . . it's peaceful . . . Let's go outside . . . I'll give you the grand tour."

In fact, we did go outside. We could hear church bells chiming.

"Well, here we are . . . !" Triceps says to me. "These are the crazies who are allowed in the courtyards . . ."

And so, we go into a courtyard.

Some of the lunatics stroll under the trees, sad-looking, or haggard; some sit on benches, motionless and seething. Against the walls, in the corners, a few of the lunatics lie prone. Some moan; others stay more silent, more insensate, more dead than cadavers.

The courtyard is enclosed on all four sides by monstrous black buildings — even their windows seem to stare at you with psychotic eyes. Overhead, no available refuge of liberty and joy; always the same block of empty sky. And you hear a dull lamento of muffled screams, muzzled howls coming from

God knows what torture chambers, God knows what unseen tombs and hidden limbos ... An old man hops on his withered, trembling legs, his body hunched over, his elbows folded tightly at his hips. Some of the madmen pace back and forth very quickly, drawn toward what blind destinations? Others talk to themselves, angrily.

When they notice us, the lunatics fidget, huddle, whisper, deliberate, debate, casting sideways glances, devious and mistrustful, in our direction. Soon, we see their hands rise defensively and flurry in the air, very livid hands resembling flights of startled birds. Guards pass through the groups, gruffly exhorting them to calm down. Little symposiums take place.

"Is that the prefect?"

"Go ahead ..."

"No, you ..."

"He never understands me when I talk."

"He never listens to me."

"Nonetheless, we have to ask him to stop serving toads in our soup."

"Nonetheless, we have to get them to promise to take us for a little outing in the country."

"You go ahead ... And be direct, the way men speak to each other."

"No, you ..."

"I will ..."

A few lunatics step out from their groups, venture toward Triceps, voice reasonable or incomprehensible complaints about the food, the conduct of the guards, the unfairness with which they are treated. Faces glow, necks stick out. Their pitiful eyes are like the eyes of frightened children, where glimmers of vague hope flicker on and off; meanwhile, the old man, indifferent to everything, continues to hop on his withered legs, and a young man leaps forward, his eyes burning with rapture, his arms outstretched, opening and closing his long bony hands to clutch at the air. To all of the complaints, Triceps responds: "It's being taken care of . . . it's being taken care of . . ."

He says to me, "These devils are on their best behavior . . . a bit sedated . . . Have no fear."

I reply, "But they don't seem any crazier than other people . . . They remind me of something . . . I think they resemble the House of Representatives, only more colorful."

"And more pleasant . . . And then, as you'll see, my friend, it can be quite entertaining . . . Sometimes you just can't imagine what gets into these poor wretches . . ." He stops a passing lunatic, and questions him: "Why aren't you demanding anything today?"

Pale, thin, extremely morose, the madman shrugs. "What good would it do?" he says.

"Are you angry? . . . Out of your head?"

"I'm not angry . . . I feel bad."

"There's no reason to feel bad . . . Your conditions here are genuinely awful . . . Will you tell us your name?"

"Excuse me?"

"Your name . . . Tell us your name."

With a sheepish look on his face, the lunatic gently rebuked Triceps: "It isn't right to taunt a poor man. You know, better than anyone, that I do not have a name anymore . . . May I say something about this, sir . . . ? This gentleman is the prefect?" And, after a nod from Triceps: "Well, I am very glad to hear that . . . You see, Mr. Prefect . . . I do have a name, like everybody else . . . It's my natural right, isn't it? It seems to me that isn't asking too much, wouldn't you agree . . . ? But when they put me in this place, this gentleman here took away my name . . ."

"You don't know what you're saying."

"Excuse me, excuse me, I do know what I'm saying." And, speaking to me: "What did he do with my name . . . ? I don't know . . . Did he lose it somewhere . . . ? It's possible . . . I've complained to him about it a thousand times or more . . . Because, when all is said and done, I need my name ... He never wanted me to get it back ... It's very sad ... And I don't believe the gentleman even has any right to take my name ... It strikes me as a real abuse of power ... You must understand, Mr. Prefect, how disturbing this is for me ... I don't know who I am anymore ... I am—not only to the others but to myself—a stranger ... In fact, I no longer exist ... Just think that, for a long time, all of the newspapers have been clamoring for my life story ... But how can it happen now ...? Whose life story ...? Whose, I ask ...? I no longer have a name ... I am famous, extremely famous, everyone in Europe knows me ... But what good is this fame to me now, since it has become anonymous ...? Isn't there any way for me to get my name back once and for all ...?"

I reassure him, "Certainly ... certainly ... I will take the matter under advisement ..."

"Oh, thank you! And since you are so kind as to show an interest in me, Mr. Prefect, may I ask another favor of you ...? For, the truth is, I am the victim of uncanny things, things which I myself would not even believe, if they had happened to anyone else but me ..."

"Speak, my friend."

Then, he whispers confidingly: "I was a poet, Mr. Prefect, and I owed some money to a tailor of mine ... He used to make me the most beautiful clothes, when I frequented the home of the Marquise d'Espard, in the house of Mme. Béauséant, and before I married Mlle. Clotilde de Grandlieu ... This episode is detailed at great length in Balzac ... So you see I'm not lying ... This wicked tailor harassed me constantly ... He used to threaten me and demand his money ... I was flat broke ... One day he came over, more threatening than ever, and I offered to let him take anything he wanted from my house, in lieu of payment ... A clock—I had a very beautiful clock—a family heirloom ... That was what he really wanted ... But do you know what he ended up taking ...? I still can't believe it ... He took my mind ... Yes, Mr. Prefect, my mind ... just as, later on, the gentleman took my name ... Did I ever really have a chance ...? And what would a tailor want with my mind?"

"But how did you come to realize that this tailor had taken your mind?" I ask him.

"How? Why, I saw it in his hands, Mr. Prefect ... He had it in his hands at the moment he took it from me."

"What did it look like?"

The madman looks at me with admiration, but also good-natured condescension. "It looked, Mr. Prefect, like a small yellow butterfly, very pretty, very fragile, fluttering its wings; a small butterfly, like you see hovering above roses, in gardens, on sunny days ... I begged that evil tailor to give me back my mind ... He had fat fingers, stubby and clumsy, brutal fingers, and I was afraid he would crush it, it was so light, so delicate ... He stuffed it in his pocket and ran away, snickering ..."

"Indeed, that's inconceivable."

"Isn't it ...? The first thing I did was to write to the tailor, demanding my mind back, dead or alive ... He never answered ... I went to see the police commissioner, who threw me out of his office and treated me like a crazy person ... Finally, one evening, some bad men broke into my house and dragged me here ... I've been here for six months ... forced to live, Mr. Prefect, among rude, demented people who do irrational and terrifying things ... How could you expect me to be happy?"

From his shirt pocket he takes a little notebook carefully wrapped in paper, and holds it out to me: "Please, take this ... I have written down all of the unlucky things that have happened to me ... After you read this, you can determine whatever course of justice you deem fit ..."

"I understand ..."

"But I should tell you, I don't hold out hope ... These disasters are so uncanny, and so much stronger than the will of man, that no one could possibly reverse them." "Yes ... yes ... I give you my word ..."

After a brief silence, he says, "Would you like me to tell you something, just between you and me?"

"Please do!"

"It's very strange."

He whispers very softly, "A small butterfly comes here sometimes ... I can't understand why, because there are no flowers here, and it's bothered me for a long time now ... A small yellow butterfly, it's here sometimes ... It's exactly like the one I saw that terrible day, in the tailor's fat, clumsy hands ... It's just as delicate, fragile and pretty ... And it flies so gracefully ... It's delightful, watching it fly around ... But it's not always yellow ... Sometimes it's blue, sometimes white, sometimes purple, sometimes red ... it depends on the day ... For instance, it's only red when I'm crying ... That doesn't seem right to me ... And I truly believe ... yes, I am convinced to my soul that this tiny butterfly ..." He leaned in close to me, and said mysteriously, with his lips nearly pressed against my ear, "It's my mind ... Shush ... !"

"You think so?"

"Shush ... ! It's looking for me ... It's been searching for me for six months. Don't say anything about this ... don't say anything about this to anyone ... Ah, what a journey, that poor unfortunate thing ... ! It's probably crossed oceans, mountains, deserts, frozen tundras, just to find this place ... It breaks my heart ... But how do you expect it to find me, since I no longer have a name? It doesn't recognize me anymore ... I tried to call it, but it flew away from me ... It's obvious ... And what would you do if you were it? So away it flies, gone ... That's why I'm not myself sometimes." Abruptly, he regains his composure. "But wait, do you see that ... over there ... above the trees?"

"I don't see anything."

"You don't see anything ... ? Wait ... over there ... it's landing." The poor madman points toward an imaginary spot in empty space. "It's purple today, solid mauve ... I recognize its diaphanous and unerring flight ... It's searching for me ...

and we will never meet again . . . May I?"

He waves, turns away, and walks toward the imaginary spot. For several moments he chases an invisible butterfly, runs, turns around, points in the other direction and runs back, slicing the air with his arms. Then he collapses, out of breath, exhausted, sweating, at the foot of a tree.

Triceps smiles and shrugs. "Basta . . . ! Maybe he's no crazier—maybe he's much saner, who knows?—than other poets, poets in free society who pretend to have gardens inside their souls, avenues inside their brains, who compare the hair of their chimerical mistresses with the masts of ships . . . and to whom they award prizes, and erect statues . . . When all is said and done!"

But the lives of these pathetic creatures depress me. I beg Triceps to take me away from this awful scene . . . We cross courtyard after courtyard after all-white cloisters, and come out on a sort of terrace where a few scrawny flowers sprout, where two cherry trees wither away behind long resin tears. From there, we can view the whole tragic landscape of black walls, shaded windows, barred-out daylight, graying shrubs, that whole landscape of communal dread, lamentations and tortures, where you feel an entire poor and imprisoned race of people suffer, groan, and die . . . My heart clutched tight, an anguish strangling my throat, I remain silent, with the sensation, all over my body, of something inexpressibly heavy, inexpressibly insane.

Then, like a dwarf mountebank in his black velvet skullcap and ballooning shirt, Triceps shouts at me: "Look to your left . . . the prison, old boy . . . Quite chic, you know . . . the latest design . . ." And, while dragging me away to who knows where, he concludes: "You see . . . things are nice here . . . flowers, the horizon, greenery . . . It's just like being in the country . . . !"

And here and there, below gray walls, below black walls, in front of invisible exits, invisible soldiers parade the fierce lightning of their bayonets . . .

IV.

I am in the hotel garden, waiting for the restaurant to open for dinner ... And I am dying of sadness! That agonizing, lugubrious sadness over nothing, that's just it, over nothing at all. Was it brought on by thoughts of that madhouse, the disquieting, uncanny faces of those unfortunate lunatics ...? No ... because I've been sad ever since I got here ... To know why you feel sad is something close to bliss ... But when you cannot even guess the cause of your melancholy, there's nothing more excruciating ...

I am almost convinced that the mountains are making me sad. The mountains weigh on me, crush me, infect me with disease. In the words of Triceps, whom I just chatted with at his home a few minutes ago, I suffer from a phobia: mountainphobia. How ironic ...! To come here in search of health and find only neurosis ...! And how can I possibly escape it ...? In front of me, behind me, above me, there are always walls, walls and still more walls sealing me off from life ...! Never a sunbeam, no view of the horizon, no flight toward any other place—no birds ...! Even if I was prone to sentiment, I could not distract myself by singing

> Timid swallow
> Flapping at the window
> Of the convict ...

for I'm far more unhappy than Silvio Pellico, who at least composed some of his best verses during the years of his false imprisonment!

No, there is nothing but these black, gloomy walls my eyes smash into, without being able to penetrate them, and where my thoughts shatter, unable to transcend them ... And no sky anymore; never any sky ...! Have you ever felt such panic ...? Dense, suffocating clouds, falling, falling, blanketing the mountain peaks, seeping down into the valleys, creeping across the dunes, which are also swallowed up, just like the peaks ... These are limbos ... this is the void ... No amount of dreamy gazing ever opens up this sky, more solid than granite and schist; it drives me out of my mind ... It speaks to me of nothing but despair, brings me only constant warnings of death ... Suicide hovers over every inch of this landscape, the way, in other places, joy hovers over meadows and parks ... And I feel as if I've been buried alive, not in a prison but in a crypt ...

"You must conquer this," Triceps tells me. "Go walking, walking ... sapristi!"

I am intrigued by his advice ... But where can I walk ...? Walk toward what goal ...? In search of what ...?

The more I walk, the more the walls close in, the clouds thicken and descend, descend until they touch the top of my head, like a low ceiling ... And I become short of breath, my legs buckle and refuse to carry me, my ears buzz ...

I ask my guide, "Why are there so many crickets here ...? They're getting on my nerves ... Can't you shut them up?"

"Those aren't crickets," the guide replies. "That, sir, is the singing of your blood ...!"

And it's true ... What is singing, all around me, is my own internal cricket; fever's frightful cricket ... Yes, I know that, now ...

"Well, you just shut up, then ... stupid creep!"

And it sings on, louder ... filling my ears with its high-pitched buzzing, which only grows stronger every time I try to block it out ...

Phobia and fever ...! What more do I need?

Ever since Triceps told me to walk, I have been walking, I have been doing nothing but walking ... The narrow gorge has become a track, and the track a fissure into solid rock ... For hours and hours, on my right, there is a seeping glacial wall, so

high I cannot see the top; a paltry stream groans on my left . . .
It's irritating, that little stream . . . I feel as though I am listening to an old man, clearing his throat and grumbling . . . Ah,
here is a bridge, at last . . . Maybe things are about to change
. . . I cross the bridge . . . And indeed, there is some change, for
now the seeping wall is on my left, and the little grumbling
stream on my right . . . I keep walking . . . I keep walking . . .
and that's what I do all day long.

From time to time, the guide points out scenic landmarks:
"That spot is called Hell's Alley . . ."
Or:
"That spot is the Devil's Hole . . ."
Or:
"That spot is Death's Doorway . . ."
He rattles off the names of peaks, passes and caverns. And
every single one of those names has something to do with dam-
nation and evil. Here and there, little wooden crosses, to re-
mind hikers of the memory of someone buried under snow or
rocks.

"On this spot, nine ironworkers perished on the journey
back to Spain," the guide tells me, because he sees how miserable I am, and knows he must distract me a little.

"But the peaks . . .? What about the peaks . . .? I want to
reach the peaks . . ."

"There are no peaks . . ."

And he's right, this guide. There are never any peaks . . . Just
when you think you have reached a peak, you find that you are
still stuck inside a prison, a crypt . . . In front of you: the even
more terrible, even blacker walls of yet another mountain . . .
You climb from one mountaintop to another, only to get that
much closer to death . . .

I look at the guide. He is short, stocky and squat . . . But he,
too, is sad . . . There is no sky in his eyes—only the dim, looming, hopeless reflection of these walls we are trapped inside.

Ah, let's turn back, let's turn back . . .

So I decided, in the end, never to leave the hotel garden again
... This garden is surrounded by walls, and the walls have windows in them, and, now and then, through these windows I
glimpse something that reassures me and almost resembles
life ... Yes, sometimes there are faces in these windows ...
Now and then, I notice a gentleman twirling his mustache, another putting on his smoking jacket ... And here, to the left, a
maid fastens her mistress' corset ... I cling to these faces, these
images ... I cling to the passersby who stroll in the garden, to
the clumps of sickly geraniums, to the banana trees shivering
on the lawn, to yellow slippers and white bathrobes and the
obsequious uniforms of the waiters ... I cling to all of this so as
to prove to myself that I'm surrounded by life here, and that
I'm not dead ...

But I am gripped by a new melancholy, the melancholy of all
resort towns, all these disparate existences flung together far
from home ... Where do they come from? Where are they going ...? I don't know ... and neither do they ... While trying
to figure it out, they drag around the leashes of their boredom,
trotting in circles, poor blind beasts ...

    Now the clock strikes ... Night is falling ... rooms light up
... People arrive, people I do not know ... But really, I know
them all too well, they are strangers to me only insofar as I've
never met them ...

    "Are you going to the Casino tonight?"

    "Where else?! Are you?"

    "Sigh ...!"

    Ah, if only all these mountains were gone ...! Wasteland,
wasteland, wasteland!

V.

M. Isidor-Joseph Tarabustin, a high-school teacher from Montauban, has brought his family to spend the season at X. M. Tarabustin suffers from a catarrh of the Eustachian tube; Mme. Rose Tarabustin from water on the knee; the son, Louis-Pilate Tarabustin, from rickets: an ultra-modern family, as you can see. On top of these infirmities (openly admitted and respectable enough), they have others dating from birth and before. For both husband and wife were spawned from corrupted bloodlines, incestuous passions, furtive, greedy perversions and other marital cesspools—M. and Mme. Tarabustin were born to produce, and end in, this ultimate spectacle of human deformity, this rancid, scrofulous abortion known as young Louis-Pilate. With his muddy, wrinkled complexion, his zigzag spine, his pretzel legs, his soft, spongy bones, this child seems to be seventy years old. He looks for all the world like a little old man, withered and maniacal. To spend any time around him is to be tortured by a frustrated urge to kill him. When I first saw the collected Tarabustins, I wanted to go up to them and scream: "Why have you come here to spoil the pristine splendor of the mountains and the purity of the springs with your triple presence, your undying triple presence . . . ? Go back home . . . You know perfectly well that no waters, miraculous as they are, could ever wash away the age-old rot of your organs, not to mention the moral decay that gave birth to you . . ." But I think M. Isidor-Joseph would have keeled over on the spot from such strong language; certainly, he would never have obeyed their Homeric injunction.

Every morning, like clockwork, along the paths or in the Quincunxes, you see M. Isidor-Joseph Tarabustin returning from the baths, solemn, methodical, scattering words and gestures to the high wind, airing his stubby legs, his bubonic face, and his ailing belly. He is always with his family, and now and then, a friend from the cabin next door, a teacher like him, whose sickly, pasty skin makes him look exactly like a sad clown caked in flour make-up. Nothing is as mesmerizing as watching them walk around the lake and talk to the swans, while young Louis-Pilate throws rocks at them . . . Perfect!

"I'd really like to know why they call these birds 'swans,'" M. Isidor-Joseph Tarabustin demands.

To which the friend whines in reply, "They're just geese who had their necks pulled, that's all . . . Everything's fake."

Every evening, before bedtime, M. Tarabustin strolls majestically on the Spanish Way, to see "the last gaslight in France." He says, swelling his voice: "Let's go and look at the last gaslight in France!" His wife walks behind him, limping painfully, flabby, smeared with yellow grease, and followed by her son, who deliberately steps on the largest cow-pies, the biggest mounds of horse dung, which are everywhere at this hour, since endless teams of cattle and horses clomp up and down this road all day long . . . When he finally arrives in front of the last gaslight in France, M. Tarabustin freezes, meditates for an eternity, or, according to the mood he is in, tosses off sermons, heady philosophical pensées for his family's edification. Then, he plods back toward town, and returns to his room, which has no air or light, and which he has rented in a cramped, sweltering, disease-infested boarding house, darkened, even on the sunniest days, by a double row of trees. And all three slumber in adjacent beds, their chests breathing in and out, family style, the triple poison of their commingled air . . . Sometimes, while their son is snoring, they toil away at hideous lovemaking, and rend the peaceful silence of the night with their lip-smacking kisses . . .

Yesterday, on the Spanish Way, I saw M. Isidor-Joseph Tarabustin, frozen at the foot of the last gaslight in France. His wife stood on his right, his son on his left. And, against the backdrop of the mountains, in moon-silvered twilight, it made for an uncanny passion play: Calvary as clown show.

There was no one else on the road, neither animal nor hu-

man. In the chasm of the narrow valley, the stream bubbled between rocky landslides, dislodging stray pebbles with the
squawking sound of a harmonica. The moon slid slowly across
the sky, into the V between two mountains, which grew less
and less black with every second, though remaining shrouded
in mauve mists.

Sensing that M. Isidor-Joseph Tarabustin was about to prof-
fer some definitive statement, and wishing to hear it, I hid behind the bend of the road, so as not to scare away his eloquence.

"Rose," M. Tarabustin abruptly commanded, "and you,
Louis-Pilate . . . look, both of you, at that instrument . . . of
illumination."

And, with a sweeping gesture, he pointed to the streetlight,
which, due to a shrewd stinginess, the municipality had not
bothered to light, since the moon was full that night.

"Look at that instrument," the teacher repeated, "and tell
me what it is."

Louis-Pilate shrugged his shoulders. Rose rubbed her sick
knee and replied, "It's a gaslight, my friend."

"A gaslight . . . a gaslight . . .! Well, of course, it's a gaslight
. . . But it is no ordinary gaslight . . . It is something very unique and, I daresay, highly symbolic . . . When you look at it . . .
see, my dear Rose, and you, Louis-Pilate, if it doesn't give you a
sensation . . . an emotion . . . a shiver . . . of the strongest, most
powerful kind . . . religious . . . or, to give it its true name . . .
patriotic . . .? Think hard for once, Rose . . . Louis-Pilate, look
deep within your soul . . . Well, don't you have anything to
say . . .?"

Nearly at the point of tears, Rose sighed. "But why, Isidor-
Joseph, do you want me to feel things for this streetlight that I
wouldn't feel for any other?"

"Because this streetlight, dear wife, represents an idea . . . a
sacred idea . . . an idea of motherhood . . . a mystery . . . which
no other streetlight represents . . . because . . . listen to me carefully, now . . . because this gaslight is the very last gaslight in

France, because, after this ... there is only the mountain ... Spain ... the great unknown ... do you understand ...? In a word, *foreigners* ... Because this beacon is the shining light of the Fatherland, every single night, shining for love, for our grateful hearts, as if to say to us: 'If you love me, you will not cross this border!' That is the meaning of this gaslight ..."

Mme. Tarabustin stared up at the gaslight for a long time, shaking and seething with the effort of feeling that divine revelation. Then, overwhelmed with sorrow at not being able to feel the same noble sentiments that swelled her husband's bosom, she moaned, "I'm just not as intelligent as you, my friend ... And I can't see such beautiful things in a simple streetlight ... It's a shame ... For me, a gaslight is always just a gaslight, even if it is the last gaslight in France ..."

M. Tarabustin's voice was tinged with sadness. "Alas!" he said. "You are only a woman ... Unlike me, you have not penetrated the world's depths ... The world, my poor friend, is only a veil of illusion covering certain eternal symbols ... Stupid people see only the illusion ... Only noble beings, such as myself, can uncover the symbols beneath the veil ... when all is said and done!"

They stopped speaking.

The Tarabustins breathed through their open mouths, profaning the pure and bracing evening air with their noxious triple breath. A scent of wild carnation wafted toward them, but was repelled, and dissipated across the valley. Crickets fell into a hush, stunned by the grating discordance of the teacher's voice: "And how about you, Louis-Pilate?"

But the child was occupied with crushing a glowworm, which had lit up in the grass, under the sole of his shoe, and did not respond.

Discouraged, M. Isidor-Joseph turned his rapturous eyes once more on the last gaslight in France. Then he went away, followed by his wife, limping painfully again, and by his son, who deliberately squashed every cow-pie and every mound of horse dung along the way.

VI.

Today, in the Casino garden, while the orchestra, under a tent, played the overture to *Semiramis* (oh, that overture to *Semiramis*, so throbbing and oppressive!), I watched a ton of people walking around, all types of people, ones I knew and recognized, all the different figureheads of Parisian high life: M. Georges Leygues with his provincial courtliness; M. du Buit, Esquire, the famous attorney for the Worldwide Metals Corporation; M. Émile Ollivier; as well as actors, poets, dentists, great divas and debutantes, every one of them freakish and thoroughly depressing . . . ! And I cannot get enough of watching them. I impose a life story on each of their faces: memories which manage, for a day at least, to tear me away from my ennui and its gloomy shadows. And then there is General Archinard, who defeated Dahomey; the Marquise de Parabola; Colonel Sheepsalt, and more, more, always more . . .

But I am especially fond of M. Georges Leygues, for he inspires nothing but delight in me.

I have a boundless love for M. Georges Leygues, and his beautiful southern-style directness, and his ease with people, such a rare gift in politicians, especially to the high degree that he possesses it. You could love M. Georges Leygues with your eyes closed; in fact, that's the best way to love him so as to avoid any disillusionments . . . For me, it is always a pleasure — a pleasure both genteel and overpowering, always new, and, so to speak, distinctly patriotic — whenever I find myself anywhere in his company. I admire the way that being the Secretary of so many government departments has gradually made him the very soul of tact and eclecticism, to whose protean charm you surrender in spite of yourself . . .

One evening, backstage at the Paris Opera, he started to tell one of his stories, which always began the same way: "Back in those days—I was not yet Secretary . . ."

"No, not those days!" M. Gailhard demanded. As Director of the Paris Opera, he had a right to be demanding.

"So be it!" M. Leygues smiled, and began again. "Back in *those* days—I was *already* Secretary and Chief Bailiff in Tarn-et-Garonne."

And so he told his story.

The definition of banal, yet inexhaustible in its rhetoric, his conversation always yanks this one praising exclamation from the lips of all who hear him: "What a smooth talker!" And indeed, this mesmerizing character can talk about all things with equal skill. I don't believe I've ever in my life met a man so well-versed in every subject. But aesthetics are his unquestioned domain . . . If you have never heard him speak about the decorative feeling in Flameng, you have never heard anything . . . And when he gets going on the edifying beauties of operettas . . . ah, what a wonder!

One day I flattered him—a cheap whore's trick—about his self-evident expertise.

"No," M. Leygues replied modestly. "I'm not an expert on *anything*."

"Oh, but Mr. Secretary . . . !"

"I'm an expert on *everything*."

"Well, of course you are."

"But not all at once, you see . . . I master subjects successively . . . according to whichever department I'm directing at the time."

"And since you have directed all of them, Mr. Secretary . . . ?" I said, with my head bowed very low.

"You said it, I didn't!" M. Leygues exclaimed, with a delightful pirouette that showed his hamstrings were as supple as his mind.

He's a charmer . . .

Whenever I dine with him at friends' homes, and I study his pate of polished ivory, his imperial mustache, it makes me proud to be a taxpaying member of society. And I daydream:

"To think that that's the man who set the fire that burned
down the Comédie-Française, and who will surely burn down
the Louvre next . . . ! And yet he's so humble . . . just an average
man . . . !"

And one day, giving verbal flesh to his unexpressed
thoughts, I spoke up in a loud voice: "After all, one day soon,
the Louvre *will* burn—right?"

It was a few weeks after the catastrophe at the Théâtre-Fran-
çais. M. Leygues modestly replied, "As far as what happened at
the Comédie, we received warnings, but I—you must believe
me—placed no stock in them. Such terroristic threats, not unlike the masterpieces of our classical literature, always conform
to certain traditions. They simply do not happen randomly,
dear sir. Hell . . . ! They obey certain laws, or, if you prefer, pe-
riodic cycles, like epidemics, World's Fairs, Ice Ages, great rev-
olutions, and great wars: cycles whose internal logic we cannot
know, but which nonetheless begin and end, and whose irrup-
tions are timed, almost mathematically, nearly to the month.
So, now, we have many years of law and order to look forward
to."

"I'll drink to that . . . !"

"We must also take into account," M. Georges Leygues
continued, "purely materialistic reasons, in which I place, it
goes without saying, far less stock, but which do play their own
small but pivotal role . . . And a political role at that, insofar as
you can ever ascribe any political significance to reasons that
are exclusively materialist, therefore unstable and relative by
their very nature."

"And what are these reasons, my dear Secretary?"

Charmingly—for his charm is as inexhaustible as it is famous—M. Georges Leygues replied, "After any disaster, you
always see the following measures: stringent surveillance; more
firemen hired; an almost daily testing of our unbreachable national security; massive relief efforts; heat-seeking missiles;
communication lines, and who knows what else . . . ? All the el-
ements of a no-nonsense emergency plan, to put the bigwigs at

ease. For how could you explain to the bigwigs about ineffable laws of nature, cosmic cycles, or any other kind? They would laugh you right out of their boardrooms. People like us, meditative, idealistic people, who think profound thoughts as second nature, who understand that everything comes down to the vast harmonics of the universe—the only thing that truly sets us at ease, regarding the matter of whether or not the next big disaster will occur, comes down to, I repeat, laws, cycles, and traditions. Now, tradition—call it by whatever name you like—marshalls all of its implacable forces around the looming idea of another conflagration. The Odéon, perhaps . . . ? And yet, it's so far away! It certainly doesn't fall easily into the cyclical territory in question. But relax, dear sir, let's change the subject."

"You see, Mr. Secretary," I replied, "whenever we find ourselves reeling from the blows of some great personal misfortune, when, for example, we have lost someone dear to us, or a lot of money, or our homes, we fall prey to the habit of thinking too much, remembering too much, of going over our conscience with a fine-toothed comb . . . and finally vowing to lead a new and improved life . . ."

"*Arriving at the crossroads, he reevaluated his life*, as the psychological novelists always put it . . ."

"You said it . . . ! Ah, well, isn't it true that the Comédie-Française, as well, tried to reevalute and improve itself but simply failed to do so? I can see its good points . . . It has real class . . . real elegance . . . even an extremely subtle self-loathing, all of which are highly respectable, and to which, for my part, I am certainly not indifferent . . . But it freezes the fire of masterpieces and makes them static . . . It turns the whole array of humanity it portrays into mannequins. Oh, pretty enough, I grant you, and well-mannered . . . but mannequins all the same, drained of life . . . Even in moments of intense and frenzied passion, it retains the typical stiffness of its overacting; it cannot do without, not even for a moment, that declamatory rhetoric, that stilted diction, so anachronistic, which paralyzes the spirit, kills the emotions and, by extension, art . . ."

"But that is the mark of high art," M. Leygues interject-
ed . . .

"There is no high or low art . . . no old-fashioned or youthful art . . . There is only art . . ." After declaring this article of
faith, I continued: "There's never anything spontaneous, anything anarchic at the Comédie-Française . . . Never any of that
unpredictability which facial expressions, gestures, exclamations take on in real life . . . Always the same rote tragic grimace, the same stock comic grin . . . You never have the sensation—overwhelming, necessary, cathartic—that these men
and women are truly alive, walking around, weeping, agonizing, or laughing, amid the lavish sets, but instead statues whose
voices—for these are talking statues—are as cold and polished as the marble from which they are carved. Does it all
come down to a question of asking you to choose one style of
acting over another? Of course, and I know that the theater
lives and dies on its stylization. But couldn't all of this stylization be made even more rigorous and more beautiful, by bringing it as close as possible to nature and life, without which
there can be no art at all . . . without which nothing at all can
exist . . .? No," I insisted, cutting off a vague gesture from
M. Leygues, "the Comédie-Française isn't really a theater; it's a
museum . . . I admit that all of those actors have enormous talent . . . And if they fail to apply it more maturely, it's the fault
of the early training they receive . . ."

"Well, then, let's burn down the Conservatory while we're
at it!" M. Leygues roared with delight.

"No, my dear Secretary, I'm not asking you to burn down
the Conservatory. But if you could close it somehow, and permanently . . .? See, just that name, 'Conservatory' . . . notice
how redolent it is of old moribund things, antiquated abandoned forms, old dead dust . . ."

M. Leygues thought for a moment. Inside him, a violent
struggle raged between the two rival halves of his personality.
He said, "As a man, I agree with you. I might even go further

than you do ... For I like the striking boldness ... of violent, revolutionary, anarchistic opinions ... But the man is only half of my being; I am also Secretary. And as Secretary, I am unable to endorse the opinions I profess as a man ... Not only can I not endorse them, I must actively fight against them ... And it is, take my word for this, a very wistful and, at the same time, a very funny thing, this struggle to the death between man and Secretary within the selfsame person ... Never forget that I represent the State, that I am the State ... and that the State, if it wants to remain the State, can only tolerate art up to a certain point, cannot permit art to truly flourish, nor permit genuis to exist in the contemporary world ... As far as the State is concerned, genius cannot be labeled officially 'genius' until it is hallowed by the centuries ... Where genius has not yet been hallowed by the centuries, the State regards it as an enemy ... To summarize ... For all these reasons, I will rebuild the Comédie-Française on the very same spot and in the very same spirit. For it's obvious, isn't it, that in this Homeric conflict I have just described to you, the Secretary always beats the man ... If not, the man would not be Secretary anymore ... And then, what on earth would I do ...?"

All this gloomy second-guessing chilled me to the bone, and, thinking of all the great things a man like him could still accomplish, I voiced my fears that his staff could not be trusted, and I argued that the ruination of so many important plans came from getting cold feet ...

"As for me," M. Leygues said indifferently, "those things do not matter at all. They absolutely bore me stiff ..."

"But why?" I cried. "Don't you mind being at odds with your department?"

"I'm in agreement with every department," the Secretary briskly retorted. "And being in line with all of them in general, I am allied with none in particular. This is what places me in the unique and somewhat comical situation of being the Eternal Secretary that I am ... Other Secretaries come and go ... I am here to stay ... Some are radicals ... others are corrupt ...

some are nationalistic . . . still others are socialists . . . I am here
to stay . . . The others come and go, whether they are anti-na-
tionalist and anti-cleric radicals, pro-business protectionists,
center-leftists, independent socialists, right-wing populists . . .
it makes no difference . . . I am here to stay."

And, with crowning logic, he added: "Thus, the Louvre
could never burn under any other authority but mine . . ."

After a brief silence, in which my neighing admiration
chomped at the bit, I cried, "Ah, Mr. Secretary! It will be no
small task, you know, to burn down the Louvre . . ."

To which M. Leygues solemnly replied, "There are never
any small tasks . . . only small Secretaries." And he shot back a
drink of champagne.

We rose from the table. Later, I found M. Leygues again, in
the smoking room. Although he was surrounded on all sides by
people to whom he was gallantly handing out crosses from the
Legion of Honor, I managed to draw him into a corner, where
I said to him, "I cannot stop thinking about what you said
during dinner. Indeed, I have complete faith in your Secretarial
permanence; I am convinced that your spirit is resourceful
enough, and your heart independent enough, not to let a
straightforward matter of political or social opinion become an
impediment to . . . how shall I put this? . . . to your Secretarial
immortality."

"Of course! I am gifted with a sort of moral levitation which
lifts me up and lets me soar above petty, trivial things . . ."

"Of this I have no doubt. But, finally, in human events a
man must always take the unforeseeable into account. What if
some kind of fluke occurred—a long shot, to be sure, but possible, after all—in which you were no longer Secretary . . . ?
Just now, you yourself expressed such a fear."

"Just an ironic figure of speech, dear sir . . . The fact is, such
a fluke could never come to pass, I wouldn't allow it . . . Christ!
I'd become an under-clerk first . . . But as it happens, you see
. . . I'm the number one man in this new government . . . I've
got a plan for education reform all ready to go, in my desk

drawer ... It's quite an achievement."

"I do not doubt it."

"It's quite an achievement because I give absolute and exclusive monopoly on education to the Jesuits ... And yet, I also have a second plan ready, whereby, in case of a republican victory ... I give this same absolute and exclusive monopoly to the Freemasons ... for I have it on good authority that the Freemasons really do exist ... So, what do you say to that ...? You can clearly see that the 'fluke' you mentioned will never come to pass ..."

"A man must plan for everything, Mr. Secretary ... A man as wise and farsighted as you must plan for everything ..."

"Well?"

"Well, like you, just now, I am often beset by anxiety, I am not lying, by depression even, at the thought that you might no longer be, by whatever fluke or freak occurrence, Secretary ..."

I saw a cloud pass across M. Leygues' brow. And when it had passed, he said, "But what else could I be ...?"

"Right ... right ... Absolutely right!"

Raising his voice, his arms akimbo, his mustache more pointy than ever before, he said majestically, "A poet ...! *That* would be *really* beautiful ..."

At that instant, I heard something shatter in the room. It was a bust of Victor Hugo, who, at the Secretary's words, tumbled from its pedestal and rolled along the mantel, onto the floor, where it smashed into a thousand bursts—of laughter.

VII.

And now for M. du Buit, Esquire.

Sometimes M. du Buit takes his bath in the cabin next to mine ... I hear him talking to the boy ... "It's not my jurisdiction ... People with more authority than I ... And I must add ... my bath is cold ... and I must also add ... it needs more sulfur ... We're at a turning point in history ... and, if you will permit me this expression ... at a dangerous crossroads of human civilization ... Military honor ... Bétolaud ... Damn writers ... They are an eternal burden ..."

He says many other things, just as noteworthy ... Even while engaged in the basest bodily functions of his basest organs, he is still an orator ... and acquits himself eloquently ...

A memory from long ago still haunts me ... It was the ballyhoo trial of Worldwide Metals, a trial that has been forgotten, because everything gets forgotten these days. M. du Buit, a formidable attorney, whose spreading bald spot ringed by gray tufts of hair was as imposing as his name itself, was defending, as I recall, M. Sécretan. And here is the speech:

M. DU BUIT, ESQUIRE: Gentlemen, they reproach us — let's not mince words — they accuse us of cornering the copper market ... Copper, gentlemen! (*Sardonically:*) Truly an outrageous accusation. (*He turns toward the public prosecutor and gives him a nasty look.*) And a heartless one, wouldn't you agree ...? But gentlemen, I will, with one word, one single word (*he shakes his folder stuffed with legal documents*), I will, I say, with one word, crumble to dust (*he pounds on the bar with his fist*), decimate ... and destroy our opponents' worthless arguments ... their so-called mathematical calculations ... their so-called evidence, cooked up on a whim by the office of the public prosecutor ... (*Calms down suddenly, only for a moment.*) A cursory examination will suffice ... (*Pause. He half-turns and quickly straightens out the folds of his flounced sleeve, which has gotten bunched up in his armpit, then he points his index finger up toward the ceiling, while leaning across the bar until his whole body is doubled over, a Guignol gesture.*) Gentlemen ... (*In an insinuating whisper:*) A laborer ... (*In a firmer, more righteous tone:*) A farmer ... (*In ringing tones:*) A peasant ... (*Pause. He whirls his raised index finger in the air, gives a dramatic shudder, stops, then, an instant later, yanks himself fully upright again*) Who planted his wheat ... (*Gradually raising his voice:*) Who mowed his wheat ... who harvested his wheat ... who threshed his wheat ... who stored his wheat (*the voice crescendos to its maximum intensity—then it weakens and falls back, as if broken, into lower registers*). Yes, gentlemen, would anyone dare say ... (*the same vocal play as before*) that this aforesaid peasant ... this grower ... this farmer ... this laborer (*same vocal play again*) who planted this wheat ... who mowed this wheat ... who harvested this wheat ... who stored this wheat ... Yes, I ask of all clean consciences ... would anyone dare say that this grower in question ... this farmer ... this laborer ... this peasant ... *cornered* the wheat that he planted ... that he mowed ... that he harvested ... that he stored ...? The wheat that is his very sweat, and allow me to say, here, without any hesitation and without any equivocation—his very blood? No, gentlemen ... (*The index finger folds back down into the fist, and the arm rises and falls, rises and falls, pounding the desk with regular blows like a steam-hammer.*) You cannot say it ... you must not say it ... you will not say it ...! (*Another pause, during which he lightly mops his brow, then he takes a step back, folding his arms and splaying his fingers across his chest.*) Because, hear me well, gentlemen ... judicially, civilly, morally, and, I will add, legally ... yes, Mr. Public Prosecutor, legally, this

peasant ... this grower ... this laborer ... this farmer ...
who merely planted his wheat ...

And so M. du Buit, Esquire, went on and on in this same vein
for two straight days ... And his eloquence was so powerful
that that hypothetical *peasant ... laborer ... farmer ... grower*
became a real living, breathing figure ... All by himself, he
filled the hall with his undeniable, all-consuming presence.
You could not take your eyes off of him. And the copper re-
serves themselves seemed to have vanished.

The judges were spellbound. During courtroom breaks, excited attorneys filled the corridors, crying their admiration.
You heard conversations like this one:

"No, it's truly amazing ... Did you ever hear a more brilliant argument?"

"Never ... This takes me back to the heyday of Berryer ...
to the epic battles of Jules Favre ..."

"You hit the nail on the head! Gosh ...! And yet, the public
prosecutor ...? Did you see him, huh ...? Do you think he's
amused?"

And emboldened defendants suddenly began to sneer at the
world with the imperious looks of their accusers ...

A few weeks later, M. du Buit, Esquire, was named President of the Bar, by a unanimous cheer.

VIII.

I used to have nightmares about M. Émile Ollivier, always so smugly self-satisfied, always grinning ... But his satisfaction and his grin no longer frighten me, since I now know their cause ... since their secret was revealed to me ...

It was four years ago ...

Naturally, it was in a train car ... With a plaid quilt draped across his knees, and a Scottish tam-o'-shanter pulled down around his ears so that it resembled an upsidedown bedpan, M. Émile Ollivier was in the middle of one of his aimless, hopeless pilgrimages, without a destination. Or at least that was how I liked to think of them.

This forlorn image of Émile Ollivier in self-exile, wandering all over the world without ever stopping anywhere, despised everywhere he went; Émile Ollivier crossing prairies, mountains, forests, seas, getting off trains and boarding trams, getting off trams and boarding steamers, trading steamers for camels, camels for dogsleds, forever searching for an impossible silence and an even more impossible oblivion: this image (at very first sight, I swear) entranced my patriotic soul, thirsty for retribution—the souls of patriots are always thirsty for something—and I found myself daydreaming about Alsace-Lorraine with a sad and swollen heart!

He must have been preoccupied by the same thing, and how obsessively, the poor bastard! He was extremely pale, his eyelids puffy from insomnia, his face frozen by a grim mask of despair. It was as if his outsides had turned entirely to stone, just as I imagined his soul had always been, and I could not help but get choked up, for I am one of those patriots—a bit delusional, I admit, though never sappy—in whom patriotic fervor has managed to completely smother all compassion to-

ward my fellowmen and all feelings of human pity. Yes, that
man — for isn't the type always a man, after all? — moved me.
For thirty years he has traveled without rest, without respite,
here, there and everywhere, under the most maddening suns,
across the most merciless Arctics, nearly shipwrecked on the
ill-fated Ananké, back and forth from the North Pole to the
South again and again, until the end of time . . . Could anyone
devise a more hellish torture? Is there a more agonizing fate
anywhere on earth . . . ? Ah, poor bastard . . . !

My imagination, which has always controlled me more
than anything else, worked itself into a frenzy, until I was willing to extend the most indulgent excuses, the fullest pardons,
to M. Émile Ollivier. I wished, for his sake, for the final shudder to come, the last gasp: the sweet death that finally set Bazaine free. And I fervently prayed to whatever nonexistent
God, who, of course, didn't hear me: "He has been running
long enough, dragging his threadbare rags through the dust of
the earth long enough. By your grace, let him finally come to
rest someplace, it doesn't matter where, even if it's only under
the shade of a weeping willow, in the corner of some forgotten
graveyard . . ."

A trifling dispute about the window of the train car (two
travelers were arguing about whether it should be left open or
closed; we had to intervene) caused us to become fast, firm al-
lies. And, without any further ceremony, we introduced ourselves. Ah, life!

"An honor, sir . . ."

"Likewise. Truly . . ."

"Sir!"

"Sir!"

But in spite of these friendly greetings, it was not possible
for us to speak freely, because those two travelers, already in a
bad enough mood, still hovered around us, listening in. Out of
good manners more than pity, I did not want to expose him to
the coarse insults of those rubes, those French rubes, and perhaps to their mindless rage as well (it's likely he sent half their

sons to the battlefield, after all) — that bedraggled figure in the tam-o'-shanter, that sad, vulnerable pariah, that tragic "Wandering Jew of Eternal Guilt," whose safety it seemed I had chivalrously decided to protect, and who commanded my undying respect. And even after shaking off those nosy fellow-travelers, who had started eavesdropping on our conversation and giving openly nasty looks to my unlucky friend, I felt I had to keep up the pretense of calling him by an alias, "Mr. Lightheart," repeating it again and again as loudly as I could. I even gave him the provisional cover of a champagne vintner, asking him all about the harvesting of grapes: a ruse which his baffled expression told me did not please him at all; on the contrary.

A few stations later, the two travelers disembarked. We were alone after that, and we spent hours and hours, whole nights, rolling on the rails past oblivious countrysides. Eventually, by smiling at him constantly and being generally deferential, I succeeded in getting M. Émile Ollivier to open up and talk freely, and, my soul overflowing with sympathy, I encouraged him to go even further: "Speak, poor man, and unburden your heart, unburden it completely . . . Nothing brings such sweet relief in our times of pain . . . And if you feel like weeping, weep . . . Ah, please do . . . ! I am not the sort of man who scoffs at tears!"

But did he pay any attention to my fervent, whispered plea? No, he paid no attention at all, for this is what he said: "Sir, I read the papers this morning . . . Anyway, that's just the tip of the iceberg . . . The sickness runs as deep as it can go . . . We have no government at all . . . We are more lawless than the most naked savages in the heart of the African continent . . . And, when it comes down to it, I don't even know . . . correct that, I don't dare to wonder, I don't want to know where we are headed . . . France has no principles anymore, sir, no traditions, no morality, no respect for the law, no patriotic feeling, nothing, nothing, nothing . . . It's monstrous . . . !"

"Who knows?" I said, feeling suddenly put off by his tirade, which was the last thing I expected to come from his lips.

M. Émile Ollivier continued: "It's monstrous ...! A government of chaos and ineptitude, elected from the filthiest provincial scum; a Parliament of pirates, besides, who have virtually taken France hostage; and communist influence undermining everything, with its murders, its riots, its strikes, all of its extremist violence enshrined as law ...! That's what we're up against today ... If only there was some kind of back-up, a rearguard among the men of State ... a few men such as I ...? Ah, yes ...! Everywhere, scum intent on nothing but their own private gain, answerable to nothing but their own bank accounts and their fat bellies—the kind of scum who spit on the memory of Lamartine... It's abominable; I've never seen the likes of it before, and I can't fathom how France has put up with it for so long... No, indeed, France's tolerance enrages and disgusts me ... It drives me to despair, drives me out of my mind... Your own complacency truly astonishes me ..."

Since I said nothing, rendered mute by shock, he went on berating me. "You really can't see what these common thieves are doing? They're digging a hole that we'll never get out of ... A few more weeks of this regime, a few more months at most, and we'll be ... Do you know where we'll be?"

"Couldn't venture a guess!" I said, growing more and more irritated.

"Well, we'll be bankrupt, that's what, my dear, blind sir, and furthermore—listen to me now with both your ears wide open, and never forget what I am about to say—the Fatherland itself will be sold off ... The *Fah-Ther-Land* ...! Do I make myself clear?"

"You take a dark view of things, M. Émile Ollivier."

That name I had just uttered, Émile Ollivier, right at the end of his sentence "the Fatherland itself will be sold off," which he (Oh warmonger! Oh shameless!) had just spat out with venomous emphasis—that name resounded throughout the train car like a tragic echo from the past. And I shuddered, from head to toe, at the exact moment it left my lips, for within that name I heard clearly, distinctly, and, so to speak, symphonically, jingoistic slogans shouted in rage, widows sobbing, mothers cursing bitterly, the dying screams of massacred soldiers and civilians.

But, just as he'd paid no attention to the way I had begged him to humbly confess, so Émile Ollivier heard no echo in his own name when it was abruptly tossed into his face—none except his own vanity and his delusional pride. In fact, he smiled at his name, gazed into it as into a flattering mirror, found it beautiful, and categorically denied all charges. "No, not a dark view ... a wise and judicious one, that's all, and a patriotic one ... I have a sixth sense about politics, among deputies I'm a clairvoyant, who has shaped the great lessons of history, and the epic wars of our time where I earned my reputation ... I know people, my dear sir, and how to conquer and rule them ... and I also know what Europe is like, its unchecked ambitions, its dirty backroom deals, what it hopes to achieve with our obscene books, our putrid art, what it hopes to profit from our decadence and our willingness to look the other way ... And this is why I tell you: 'The Fatherland is going to be taken over and sold off ... The *Fah-Ther-Land* ...!'"

In a magnificent dramatic gesture, he doffed his tam-o'-shanter, which landed among the newspapers and train schedules on the seat cushions, and he continued: "The deal's been made among the ruling powers ... the concessions agreed upon ... And even though I know, I can do nothing to stop it ... I did what I could ... But what can I do without a mandate? I am nothing now ... I have lost everything but my eloquence and my political genius ... They refused to listen to me ... Today, they are deaf to political genius, and eloquence is sneered at ... So, it's all been decided ... Ah, how my heart bleeds ...! Spain will annex the Pyrenees; Italy will take Nice, the Savoy, and the headlands of the Rhône; Germany will get Alsace, Lorraine, and Champagne ... As for England, insatiable England ... naturally, she will grab up ..." And he waved his hand as if to sweep away the entire world ...

I stopped listening; I looked at him ... No, indeed, he did

not appear to be joking with me, nor with himself; his dark global conspiracy was no sarcasm. His prediction of the future annexation of Alsace-Lorraine by Germany was not intended as a provocative witticism. He was devout and sincere and no doubt red-bloodedly patriotic in his mystifying paranoia. And he continued to pontificate with a real and fiery anger, the mad gleam of a prophet in his eyes. He pontificated on everything, passed judgment over everything, condemned everything, all men and all things, without mercy, without pity, his rash words whipping his murderous cynicism into a frenzy. In spite of myself, I was struck by this sentence: "In politics, you do not have the right to be wrong . . . Error is a crime, error is *treason* . . ."

I was so stupefied by this that it did not occur to me for one instant to disagree, or to remind him of the blood on his own hands, to point out to him that he was lucky to have avoided a prison term, forgotten, if not forgiven, for the past thirty years. And why on earth would it have occurred to me? What good would it have done . . . ? Since, only a minute before, M. Émile Ollivier had not shuddered in shame, nor chattered his teeth in fright, to hear his own name spoken aloud; since he had not hidden his head under his blankets; and since he had not taken it upon himself to shatter his skull by leaping from the open window of the train, into the night . . .

Yes, what good would it really have done? For now I understood the terrible secret that made him speak the way he did; I knew the reason for his disturbing lack of conscience:

MONSIEUR ÉMILE OLLIVIER HAS AMNESIA!

Confronted with such an unusual pathological case, my anger suddenly abated; and in a gentle voice, the kind you use with sick people and far-gone maniacs, I said to him, "That's quite enough for now . . . It's late . . . Get under your blankets, stretch out and get comfortable . . . most of all, don't say another word . . . and go right to sleep!"

Yesterday, I followed M. Émile Ollivier down the garden paths
at X, where he strolled with M. d'Haussonville . . . He was beside himself . . . And I heard him once more prophesying
France's hellish doom . . . "I tell you, my esteemed colleague . . .
it means, in short order, the selling-off of the Fatherland . . .
the *Fah* . . . *Ther* . . . *Land* . . ."

"We need a king," M. d'Haussonville suggested.

"No," M. Émile Ollivier quickly countered. "An emperor."

And M. d'Haussonville said, attempting to manufacture
consensus: "An emperor-king . . ."

And periodically—for I could not understand most of
what he said—I heard M. Émile Ollivier shriek with the shrill
caw of a hawk: "The . . . *Fah* . . . *Ther* . . . *Land*! The . . . *Fah* . . .
Ther . . . *Land*!"

IX.

A visit from Clara Fistula this morning. Among other gossip, he fills me in on how the Colonel, Baron Sheepsalt, spends all his days and nights here, at the baccarat table ... The Casino management tolerates the valiant Colonel losing his mind over that game with the little push-paddle ... With each deal, the croupier gives him one louis, which is immediately paid back to the house ...

"What do we need more than anything?" Clara Fistula explains to me. "The respect of the army ... And you know that doesn't come cheap ... it's all part of our overhead ..."

Yesterday, when he won his tableau, the intrepid Colonel quickly shoved a one hundred franc note across the felt table-top, and, when the croupier turned to him, the Colonel gaily declared, "Go bank!"

The croupier hesitated, not knowing what to do ... "But, Colonel ... ?" he muttered.

"What is it, man ... ? What is it ... ? Can't you see that's a hundred franc note ... for Christ's sake?"

At that point, the supervisor, who happened to be standing directly behind the heroic soldier, leaned over him, tapped him discreetly on the shoulder, and whispered in his ear, "Pay attention, Colonel ... you're exceeding your limit ... you're exceeding your limit ..."

"The hell you say ... !" the Colonel exploded. "Oh, damn it ... !" And, turning back to the croupier: "Just one louis, on my tab ... What a dishonor ..."

A true military man, as you can see ...

Now and then, at the height of the Dreyfus Affair, the Colonel used to come and see me in the mornings ... He stormed into my home, farting, spitting, cursing ... And our conversations always went like this:

"Well, Colonel?"

"Well, what ...? I'm becoming a bit more like my usual self, as you can see ... But I've had some rough times lately ... Oh, for Christ's sake!"

"Your patriotism ..."

"This is not about my patriotism ... it's about my rank ..."

"They're the same thing ..."

"You bet your life they're the same thing ..."

"Well, then?"

"Well ... I've been on tenterhooks these past two weeks, worrying they would strip me of my rank, those jackasses ... I'm not lying ...!"

"And what finally happened today ...? You decided to calm down?"

"Calm down ... calm down ...? When all is said and done ... you barely catch your breath, that's all ... I mean, can you believe it ... can you believe it, for Christ's sake ...!"

At this point, the Colonel grew meditative, and beneath the brushy squiggles of his eyebrows, his stare seemed to pierce the future itself ... I asked him point blank: "So, are you going to add 'wiping out the filthy pig vermin' to your daily agenda again ... and vow to stick your valiant sword through the guts of the cosmopolitans?"

"The hell you say ...! You don't know the first thing about it, you ...! First, I'm going to let the chips fall where they may ... If they land where they're supposed to, that's to say, if the government backs down ... ah, I tell you what—I will have a few direct orders to give to the cosmopolitans myself, right to their faces ..."

"And if they land badly, Colonel?"

"What have you heard about it ...?"

"I've heard that the government may get even more zealous than ever ... and if it should take serious defensive actions against these praetorian uprisings?"

"That's a duck of a different color ... Loose lips sink ships, right, son ...? Or then again, I might even take an oath of loyalty to this bitch of a government ... swear my obedience to the sacred cow of the Republic ... Am I a soldier, yes or no ...? So—attention, turn to the left ...!"

He added, wistfully: "Ah, it's certainly not all sunshine and peek-a-boo in the military profession ... You have to keep your sword in its sheath, Christ knows ... more often than you'd like ... But who gives a crap ...? What else can you do ...? Patriotism ..."

"Your rank of Colonel ..."

"They're the same thing ..."

"Well said ..."

The intrepid Colonel paced up and down the room, chomping on his cigar and drawing only little wisps of smoke ... Between each puff he repeated: "France is fucked, for Christ's sake ...! France is being raped by these damn cosmopolitans ...!"

"You use that word, 'cosmopolitans,' a lot ... Would it be rude to ask you exactly what you mean by it ...?"

"Cosmopolitans?"

"Please, Colonel, for me ..."

"How the hell should I know ...? Syphilitic pricks ... filthy traitorous pig vermin and anti-patriots ..."

"Of course ... but beyond that ...?"

"Turncoats ... Freemasons ... maggots ... *civilians* ... right?"

"Be precise, Colonel."

"Scumbag crooks, for Christ's sake!"

The Colonel relit his cigar, which had completely gone out under this furious tirade of philological definitions ... "And do you know what they're saying now ...? Galliffet is going to ban *uniforms* in the army ...! Did you hear that?"

"Good heavens, no ...!"

"They say it's going to start with the breeches, *ad libitum* for the July 14th parade ... White breeches, blue breeches, checkered breeches, breeches with velvet stripes down the side, even bicycle pants ... And for officers, top hat and tails will be mandatory ... No more white feathers ... no more flair ...? Fine ... Might as well get rid of the whole army, then, lock, stock and barrel ... I mean, what the hell is the army, after all ...? It's *flair*, for Christ's sake ...! How else could you tell the damn difference between a civilian and a soldier ...?"

"Aren't there many ways, Colonel, to tell civilians from soldiers ...?"

"And what's this we're still hearing in the papers ... about letting Dreyfus back in France ...?"

"Well, why not, Colonel?"

"Well, it's the last straw, that's why ...! It's too much ... Oh, it's just too much!"

"But ... since he's been found innocent?"

"Innocent ...? That Jew ... that filthy rat? The hell you say ...! And what will happen if they do this thing ...? What will it lead to ...? Where will we be, then ...? Innocent, my ass ...! What's next ...? That's not a reason ..."

"Come now ... Colonel ...!"

"No 'come now' ... Was Dreyfus condemned? Yes. By military judges? Yes. Is he a Jew? Yes ... So they can take a flying leap ... Ah, if only we had, instead of this cosmopolitan government, if only we had a government made up of real patriots, they'd send him scurrying back to his island, where he belongs, that rat ...! *Hup*, one ... *hup*, two ... It's the last straw ...! Innocent ...! First of all, any turd who would allow himself to be found innocent without formal orders from his superior officers is a no-good scumbag, do you hear me ...? A filthy prick ... a turncoat ... And how's he behaving now, that miserable turd of a traitor?"

"They said, above all, he seemed utterly transformed, and very sorry ..."

"Don't make me laugh! When is an innocent man ever *sorry*? Am *I* ever sorry? Give me a break ...! When a man has nothing to hide, he shouts it, he screams it, for Christ's sake! Hell, he doesn't hang his head and cower in the corner! He holds his head high ... just like a soldier."

"But that's just what Drefyus did, Colonel ... because the original report turned out to be false ... The truth is, Dreyfus seems firmly resolved, ready to fight ..."

"Oh, what, a deceiver, then ...? A two-faced charlatan ...? To hell with it ...! It's just like I said ... When a man is truly innocent, he doesn't strut and swagger around ... He waits to be vindicated, filled with sorrow, his head hanging down, his hands at his side, his mouth zipped up tight ... just like a soldier ... But that's not even half of it ... Innocent or guilty, he's been compromised ... He cannot come back here ... or France is super-fucked ... So, as for me, wait a second, here's what happened to me ... Some friends of mine, who own a few racetracks, had a derby the other day ... a derby to end all derbies, for Christ's sake ...! They picked me to be the judge, because my integrity is a matter of legend ... We go out to Maisons Lafitte ... The horses run ... What's going on? I've got no idea ... Did I go temporarily blind ...? Perhaps ... Anyway I awarded first place to the horse that came in last ... My friends swore up and down, ranted and raved, raised all kinds of hell ..."

"What happened, Colonel?"

"Well, son, I stood behind my judgment, ten thousand per-cent ... and I sent them all packing, saying: 'I'm wrong, okay, it's true ...' I shook my finger at them, like this ... 'I'm aware of it ... So fuck off ...! If I was a civilian, a filthy prick of a cosmopolitan, I would have given the prize to the horse that really won ... or else I would have reversed the decision ... But I am a soldier ... and I pass judgment as a soldier. Disci-pline and perfection ... I stand behind my decision ... Get lost ...!' And they got lost ..."

"Nevertheless, Colonel ... justice ..."

The brave Colonel shrugged, then, crossing his arms over his chest spangled with crosses, medals and other decorations, he said: "Justice ...? Look at me for a second ... Do I look like a filthy prick to you ...? For Christ's sake ...! Am I a soldier, or aren't I?"

"Ah, Colonel," I replied, "I'm afraid you are even greater than your rank."

"It's all the same!" yelled the valiant warrior, who began to march around the room, kicking over end tables, stabbing the armchairs with his sword ... and screaming at the top of his lungs, "Kill the Jews ...! Kill the Jews ...!"

This evening, the Colonel, Baron Sheepsalt, was the guest of honor at a banquet thrown by the colonials and patriots in treatment at X, and by General Archinard, "our illustrious host," as the *Internationals' Gazette* put it ... The event took place at the Casino restaurant. The spread was sumptuous, and how inflamed the toasts! As always, the Colonel was eloquent and succinct.

"Long live France, for Christ's sake!" he bellowed, raising his glass ...

If we did not immediately go out and conquer Egypt, chase the English out of Fashoda, the Germans out of Alsace-Lorraine, and the foreigners out of everywhere else ... don't blame the banqueters.

It was a few years ago that General Archinard, hungry for a little literary glory to add to the glory he already had as a soldier, published a series of articles in the European Gazette, laying out his plans for colonization. These plans were straightforward enough, yet grandiose nonetheless. I here reprint the following proposals:

"The more you strike down the guilty and the innocent, the more you will be admired."

And more:

"The sword and truncheon are worth more than all the peace treaties in the world."

And more:

"... by mercilessly slaughtering an astronomical number."

Finding these ideas by no means new but certainly interesting in themselves, I went to the home of that brave soldier, to perform the patriotic duty of an interviewer. It is never an easy task to get an audience with such an illustrious conqueror, and I had to parley with him for a long time. By a stroke of luck, I was forearmed by "friends in high places" with letters and references which impressed even a hero of his ill-temper. The General put up only a token resistance, just for show, and gentle enough, before finally welcoming me in ... God knows my heart was thumping out of my chest when I shook his hand.

I have to say, he greeted me with that charming brusqueness which passes for pleasantry in the homes of military gentlemen. Jovial, luxurious and cordial pleasantry in the manner of a Frenchman who has read the war stories of M. Georges d'Esparbès. Wearing a red burnoose, he sat on a tiger-skin and smoked a giant hookah in the Arab style. At his invitation, curt as a command, that I should—*hup*, one ...! *hup*, two ...!— take a seat on a simple sheep-skin opposite him, I could not prevent myself from feeling a surge of intense excitement, obeying his order. The hierarchical distinction between the types of fur he and I sat upon—their respective positions in the food chain—was not lost on me, though following the analogy to its ultimate philosophical conclusion was a cold comfort at best.

"Civilian ...? Soldier ...? What ...? What the hell are you ...?" Those were the questions which the General volleyed at me in quick succession.

"Reservist ...!" I replied, trying to find common ground.

A poo! or perhaps a poop! left his lips, in a belch of contempt, and because of that one word of mine, that attempt to be clever, I surely would have ended up with my head on the chopping block, as they say, if it had not been for a negro dwarf, dressed in exotic costume, who entered at that very moment carrying a tray on which countless bottles and glasses were arrayed ... It was the relaxing hour, when heroes get drunk.

I was delighted to have been lucky enough to come when absinthe was being served.

"Vermouth . . . ? Curaçao . . . ? What . . . ?" the noble soldier asked me curtly.

"Straight, General . . ."

He smiled in approval of my unequivocal declaration, and I realized I had won the benevolence and perhaps even the respect of the great conqueror who civilized the Sudanese at the point of a gun.

While the General poured the aperitifs according to meticulous rituals, I studied the room I was in. It was very dark. Oriental fabrics hung above the windows and doors in a decorative fetish slightly too antiquated, too Cairo Street, for my taste at least. On the walls, a vast collection of weaponry, intricate, Medieval weaponry, gleamed. Above the fireplace, between two tall vases that held bunches of human scalps made to look like flower bouquets, the stuffed head of a jaguar closed its fierce fangs around a glass ball, at whose heart a watch-face told the spellbound, transparent, endless hours. But what made my jaw drop the most were the walls themselves. They were entirely upholstered with leather, a very unusual kind of leather, an extremely smooth, fine-grained material whose greenish black color, with golden highlights here and there, exerted a profound influence over my mood and caused me to feel unspeakably depressed. A strange scent breathed from this leather, pungent and fleeting at the same time, which I could not manage to place. The scent was, as chemists say, *sui generis*.

"Ah-ha . . . ! You are looking at my leather . . ." said General Archinard, whose face suddenly lit up, while his wide-open nostrils inhaled, with visible pleasure, the double aroma given off by the leather and the undiluted absinthe.

"Yes, General . . ."

"Shocks you, that leather, huh . . . ?"

"It does, General."

"Well, son, it's the skin of negroes . . ."

"The skin of . . . ?"

"Negroes . . . That's right . . . Original idea, huh?"

I felt myself turn pale. My stomach, churned by a sudden

revulsion, heaved almost to the point of vomiting. But I hid this fleeting weakness as best I could. Besides, a swallow of absinthe quickly restored my system's equilibrium. "Original, indeed . . ." I agreed.

General Archinard expounded, "Used in this way, negroes will no longer be lifeless fodder, and our colonies will at least provide us with something worthwhile . . . But don't just take my word for it . . . Look at that, son, feel that . . . That is first-class leather right there . . . Huh . . . ? These negroes could put Córdoba out of business with their hides . . ."

We got up from our furs and toured the room, examining in minute detail the seamlessly joined swathes of leather that covered the walls. Every minute, the General repeated, "Original idea, huh . . . ? Feel that . . . Attractive . . . sturdy . . . durable . . . waterproof . . . A real goldmine, right, and cheap at the price!"

And I, pretending that I wanted to learn all about the benefits of this new tanning method, asked him technical questions. "How many negro skins, on average, would be needed to cover a room this size?"

"One hundred and nine, just slightly less . . . give or take a few . . . than the population of a small village. But, you must realize, not everything can be used . . . However, certain parts of the skin, especially the women's, are so soft and supple that they can be made into leather goods that are like works of art . . . luxury curios . . . wallets, for instance . . . luggage and travel kits . . . even gloves . . . funerary gloves . . . Ha, ha, ha . . . !"

I found myself laughing, too, though my clenched throat fought against that brand of anthropological and colonial humor.

After the detailed inspection, we took up our positions again on our respective furs. I asked the General to clarify his point of view for me, and he said, "Despite the fact that the only thing I despise more than newspapers are the journalists who write them, I am not displeased that you've come . . . because you will give a considerable boost to my system of colonization . . . Here's what it comes down to, in two words . . . As you know, I don't use long-winded arguments . . . I get straight to the point . . . Attention . . .! I know only one way of civilizing people: kill them . . . No matter what sort of yoke you place upon the necks of a conquered people . . . protection, annexation, etc. . . . there is always restlessness, upstarts who will not keep the peace . . . By slaughtering them all to the last man, woman and child, I avoid the problems that always crop up later . . . Is that clear . . .? It's just that, you see . . . so many corpses . . . Gets so you can't even move . . . And it's germy . . . Diseases can spread . . . So, I tan them . . . I turn them into leather . . . And you can see for yourself what quality leather you get from negroes. It's amazing . . .! But I digress . . . On the one hand, the suppression of uprisings . . . and on the other hand, the creation of a thriving commerce . . . That is my system . . . Everyone benefits . . . What do you say to that, huh?"

"I agree with you in theory," I objected, "about the skin . . . But the meat, General . . .? What do you do with that . . .? Do you eat it?"

The General thought for a few moments, then replied, "The meat . . .? Unfortunately, negro meat is not digestible; in some cases, it is even toxic . . . And yet, if you cured it . . . I suppose you might be able to make very good jerky out of the meat . . . strictly for the troops . . . It's worth looking into . . . Matter of fact, I am going to submit a proposal along those lines to the government . . . But it's too soft-hearted, this government . . ."

And here the General became more confiding. "What destroys us . . . make no mistake, son . . . is soft-heartedness . . . We're a race of wet hens and bleating lambs . . . We don't know how to take direct action anymore . . . With the negroes, my God . . .! Case in point . . . There's not much of an outcry when they're massacred . . . because, in the public imagination, negroes are not people, they're practically animals . . . But if we put even a scratch on one white person by accident—ooh, la la!—the bad press would never stop . . . I ask you, in all good conscience . . . Prisoners, convicts, for example, why not exterminate them as well ...? We have to feed them, house them, clothe them, they're a burden ...? Right ...? Do you want me to say it ...? You can't be in favor of running these penal colonies, jails and prisons like nice, cushy barracks ...? What leather we could get from the hides of the inmates ...! Leather made from criminals—well, all the anthropologists will tell you there's nothing better ... Ah, yes sir ...! But just try and lay your hands on a white person ...!"

"General, I have an idea," I interrupted. "This may sound like I'm making fun of you, but it's not meant to."

"Go on ...!"

"Perhaps you could paint white people black, in order to mislead national sentiment ..."

"Okay ... and then ...?"

"Then ... you could kill them ... and tan their hides ...!"

The General became solemn and uneasy. "No," he said, "no swindles ... That leather would not be true ... and I am a soldier, brave and true ... Now, run along ... I've got work to do ..."

I drained my glass of its remaining drops of absinthe and left.

All in all, I had a delightful visit, and it kindles my pride to see, from time to time, heroes like that ... who embody the very soul of the Fatherland.

X.

As everyone knows, the Marquise de Parabola has revolution-ized the entire country, not to mention the foreign colonies, with her style and her resplendent beauty . . . I knew her, knew her intimately, years ago—but quite innocently, quite respect-ably, as you shall see . . . Perhaps I might be able to get to know her again . . . The thought has crossed my mind . . . But what would be the point . . . ? I am at peace with the fact that my face—for I see her, mornings and evenings, in the lounge, in the garden, in the Casino—triggers absolutely no memory of our former intimacies, in her . . .

A divorcée after her first marriage, a widow after her sec-ond, I have only the vaguest idea what she is doing now, how she lives, and how she came to be called the Marquise de Pa-rabola . . . What I do and do not know about her hardly mat-ters at all . . . Here, she is always surrounded by a large and loy-al entourage . . . always at the parties and the picnics . . . and she leads a flock of admirers including every species the human animal can produce.

But notice how things happen at seaside resorts, the only places in the world where the actions of divine providence, so murky everywhere else, are writ clearly.

For the past few days, the hotel room next to mine has been occupied by a gentleman who is either very shy or extremely depressed . . . No matter that his hair is solid gray, gray as his face and his vest and, no doubt, his soul . . . no matter that his back is hunched and his legs wobbly, he does not seem to be very old . . . He does seem to be awkward, and insane . . . At dinner I have noticed him several times, in the hotel courtyard, on the promenade, staring at me with a nagging curiosity . . . This alarmed me, although, when I stared back at him, I saw no trace of personal hatred in his eyes . . . Nevertheless, I had made up my mind to put an end to his games once and for all, when, only yesterday, he suddenly burst into my room . . .

"Excuse me," he said, "but I could not hold myself back any longer . . . I must get something off my chest . . . You know the Marquise de Parabola personally . . . I have seen you talking with her often, all the time, at the theater . . . in the restaurant . . ."

"Yes, I knew her," I answered coldly. And I felt the need to add, idiotically: "Quite innocently . . . quite respectably . . ."

"Explanations are not necessary, sir." Then, after a brief silence, he introduced himself. "I am the Marquise's first husband . . ."

I bowed and, after this formality, looked at him with a distinctly quizzical expression.

"You see, sir . . . I am still in love with the Marquise . . . I follow her everywhere she goes . . . I don't dare speak to her, or write . . . So, I thought . . ."

"Thought what, sir?"

All at once, he seemed very embarrassed . . . And he groaned, "Oh, sir . . . ! My life is so absurd . . . Would you allow me to begin by telling you the strange story of my marriage?"

I nodded yes . . .

"When I married her, the Marquise was a young woman, pink and blonde, very striking, lively and charming, a very striking, lively and charming little June bug, who gamboled here and there, like a kid-goat in the Luzerne, and chattered like a woodland bird in spring. To tell the truth, she was not exactly a woman, not exactly a June bug, and certainly not a bird. There was something slightly robotic and very unusual about her— her noisiness, her wit, her mindless babble, her whirlwind moods, as well as her way of being the night to my day in all matters of taste, sensibility and love—which reminded me a little of all those creatures. The strangest thing about her was her soul: it was a very tiny soul, a mini-soul, a fly's soul, teasing, ticklish, and thrumming, ceaselessly fluttering all around me, in zigzags, and pinging against everything—ping, ping!—with screams and peals of laughter, driving itself, and everyone around it, crazy.

"Laure was my sixth wife . . . Yes, that's right, my sixth! Two died, I don't know what from; the others all up and left me, one fine day . . . Why? I never heard from any of them again. And what I still cannot figure out is why I felt so absolutely compelled to marry her, beyond all reason and hope, since I knew from the start exactly what was in store for me.

"My life, if I may say so, dear sir, is a web of contradictions . . . It is my belief that I am the most accommodating man in the world, I never sulk, brow-beat, or have bad moods. I have no will, or energy, except to please the woman I love. If she is unreasonable, I bow to all her whims. I never complain, argue, express an opinion, or issue a demand. I sacrifice myself—to the point of annihilating myself completely, silencing my own wishes, my own tastes—to whatever I believe will make my wife happy. Well, in spite of this Olympic skill at self-effacement, I cannot hold onto a woman for longer than three or four months. At the end of three months, brunette or blonde, short or tall, stout or willowy, I wear them out so much, they come to detest me—and then, one, two, three . . . poof! Some drop dead, others simply leave, without an explanation. Without an explanation, I say, or at least no other explanation except that, they being women and I being a man, we are, they and I, absolutely unable to see eye to eye when it comes to anything.

"Yes, yes, I know what people probably say about me . . . They say I keep playing with fire and then complain when I get burnt each time . . . But, you see . . . I hate being alone more than anything. Whenever I am alone, I feel completely lost, and I am overcome with panic and suicidal terrors, which plague me far worse than any woman. I need a familiar, daily background noise in my life. It doesn't matter whether it is music or caterwauling, provided that it's there and it dispels the silent ghosts of my gloom.

"What I'm going to tell you next is somewhat off-color. So please forgive me — I shall try to stick to the point and leave out the sordid details.

"My wedding night was the occasion of something strange and very unpleasant. I was having, er, communion with my wife, and the spirit was truly upon me, when, suddenly kneeing me in the groin, Laure wriggled out from under me and shoved me out of bed, yelling: 'My God, how forgetful I am! My God, my God . . . ! I completely forgot to say my prayer to Saint Joseph!'

"Without paying the slightest attention to my shock, or the way I was doubled up in pain, covering my poor, exposed parts, she got on her knees in the middle of the bed, and, with her hair all wild and her bare breasts bouncing, she crossed herself: 'Oh, oh, Saint Joseph,' she prayed, 'please bless and keep Daddy, Mommy, and Little Sissy-Sis . . . and let them lead long and happy lives . . . ! Please bless and keep Plume and Kiki, my sweet, wonderful cats, and also poor Nicolas (Nicolas was a parrot), who is getting so old now that he no longer talks very much, but still I can't stand to think that he might die one day . . . And last of all, bless and keep my wittle-wittle hubby, and see that he does not do anything to hurt me.'

"After this, she stretched out on her back again and smiled at me: 'Okay . . . all done . . . You can go back to what you were doing now . . .'

"But the mood was killed. It was impossible to get into the moment again. This seemed to make Laure angry at me; though she told me she wasn't, I could tell she was, because the corners of her lips were pursed for most of the night (it took us both a long time to fall asleep).

"The following day, we went to the country after lunch. She was charming and carefree, a little nutty, but just her usual nuttiness, nothing too alarming. She rolled around in the grass, talking gaily to the flowers, the birds, the insects, as if she herself were, by turns, a flower, a bird, an insect . . . Her little fly's soul whirled through the sunbeams, making the tiniest buzzing sound ... I kissed her in a grove of chestnut trees, since we were completely alone, just the two of us ... It was already late by the time it occurred to us to start walking back. She was a bit tired, and leaned on my arm as she walked. I myself was completely at peace, in seventh heaven ... silent, too, with that silence that makes words unnecessary; that silence, filled with the most beautiful music and the most dramatic thunder. All at once, she pushed my arm away and started to run along the main road, as fast as she could, but daintily, like a magpie skipping through dewy morning grass. She veered off to the right and started dashing down a footpath that led into the valley. I shouted, 'Laure! Where are you going ...? Why are you going down there ...?'

"'Our house is right over there, on the other side of the hill ... I'm taking a shortcut,' she said.

"And she continued to skip down the path, lightly, airily. I caught up to her. 'This path leads nowhere, my dear little soul ... It goes to the river ...'

Laure fired back, 'Well, if it goes to the river ... we're sure to find the bridge.'

"'But there is no bridge ...'

"'No bridge ...? Why do you say there's no bridge ...? Really, you're not being very nice to me ... Why on earth would there be a path here if there's no bridge ..? It would be pointless to have a path here at all ...'

"And, suddenly turning harsh, with her lips pursed, she said, 'I want to take the bridge—so there ...! Understand ...? Walk back through town, if that's what you feel like doing ...'

"I gently tried to dissuade her, but she told me to shut up in a tone so angry, so firm, so cutting, that I did not dare to argue with her anymore, and I followed Laure down the footpath, over big sharp rocks that hurt our feet and through thorn bushes that tore her dress ...

"At the bottom of the path, the river coursed along, deep and wide and sealed off on its far side by a thick curtain of willows and alders, whose reflection tinted the surface of the water a blackish green, the green of the abyss.

"'Now you see,' I said to her softly, without blame. 'There really is no bridge ... And you're going to be all worn out.'

"She pursed her lips very hard, not saying a word in reply, just standing there for a few moments, staring at the green water and the alders and the willows on the other side of the river. Then, we trudged back up the way we had come, both of us suddenly embarrassed by the awkwardness of the moment, both oppressed by the unexpected piece of bad luck that had overtaken us and made our pleasant little stroll as laborious and fateful as if we were climbing Calvary.

"When Laure rubbed her legs in exhaustion, I offered her the support of my arm, as I had so many times that day. She refused, point blank: 'No ... no ... I don't want your arm ... I don't want anything from you ... You are a bad man.'

"That evening, my wife did not come to dinner, and would not let me into her room (she had bolted the door). 'Go away,' she said to me, through the door. 'I am very ill ... I can't stand the sight of you ...'

"I begged and pleaded, to no avail ... With an eloquence I never knew I possessed, I begged her to forgive me, if I had inadvertently done anything to hurt her ... I even went so far as to apologize. All in vain. 'But yes, you were right!' I cried out, twisting the key ... inside the lock ... 'Yes, of course ... Of course there was a bridge ...'

"She remained inflexible, stubborn, repeating: 'No ... no ... it's over ... it's too late ...! I do not ever want to see you again ... Go away ...'

"So I went away and wept all night long. 'My God,' I said to myself, going into my room, 'I've lost another one ...! And why ...? What made her change ...? Can't she ever forgive me that there was no bridge across the river ...? I suppose not ... Clémence left me because it started raining one night when we were going to a party and her make-up streaked ... Or does she honestly think that I plotted to trick her, in some cruel, elaborate plan, or maybe that I simply forced her, as her big, strong brute of a husband, to go down that footpath, when it was already late and she was very tired, looking for a bridge that I knew did not exist . . . ? I'd like to know . . . Perhaps she doesn't even know.'

"I ask you, wasn't I unlucky the day I met her?"

He stopped talking.

"So," I asked, "you got divorced?"

"Six months later, yes . . . because I was going crazy . . ."

"And she remarried?"

"The very next year, to Joseph de Gardar, a very nice young man whom I knew well . . ." He added, after a pause: "He died . . ."

"No!"

"As I live and breathe—yes!"

"But how?"

"Oh, sir, in the silliest way!" He muffled a snicker. "Here is what happened . . ." he said.

"Eight days after their wedding, while they were having dinner together, just the two of them, Laure said to her husband: 'My friend, would you take a bath, for me . . . ?'

"Gardar's eyes grew wide with fright. 'A bath . . . ? Right now . . . ? Why on earth . . . ?'

"'Because I want you to, my friend.'

"'Am I that dirty?'

"'Oh, no . . . ! But even so, I want you to take a bath, right this moment.'

"'But that's insane . . . ! Later tonight, okay . . . But right this moment?'

"'Oh, yes . . . right this moment . . . right this very moment . . . !' Her hands were clasped together; her voice was cajoling.

"'Darling, it makes no sense for you to ask me to do that . . . Besides, I can tell you for a fact, it's dangerous . . .'

"'Oh, make me happy by doing this . . . I want you to so

much, my dear . . .' She went and sat on his lap, kissed him
sweetly, and murmured, 'I beg of you . . . right this moment!'

"They went into the bathroom. Laure wanted to run his
bath herself, and filled an end table with soaps, oils, scrub
brushes, horsehair gloves, pumice stones . . . 'And I myself will
scrub you . . . Get in now, it's ready.'

"Even while stripping stark naked, he kept arguing, repeating, 'What a crazy idea . . . ! And you know, it's very dangerous,
so soon . . . after eating dinner . . . People have died from doing
this . . .'

"But she let out a ringing laugh, carefree and bright. 'Oh,
what do people know . . . ! First off, no one man has ever died
from pleasing his little wifey . . .'

"He was determined, however. 'And also, I'm a guy with
regular habits . . . I took my bath this morning . . . I'm spotless-
ly clean.'

"'Come on, come on, don't upset me!'

"Dumbfounded, he stepped into the tub and sank into the
water.

"'There!' said Laure. 'Isn't that nice? Submerge yourself
completely, darling . . . There . . . ! Now do it again . . . !'

"After a few minutes, Joseph de Gardar felt strangely ill.
Though the water was boiling hot, he felt as if his legs had become ice-cold. At the same time, he could not catch his breath;
and his whole head, which had turned as red as a lobster, was
on fire . . . His ears rang, as if deafened by the clocks, which
were all chiming the hour.

"'Laure!' he cried, 'Laure . . . ! I feel ill . . . extremely ill . . .'

"Then, suddenly, his bulging eyes rolled back in his head
and the whites were streaked with broken blood vessels. He
tried to stand up, his hands thrashed in the water with impotent reflex movements, and he collapsed, sliding to the bottom
of the tub with one enormous burble.

"Laure, her lips slightly pursed, murmured, 'Oh, darling . . . ! You're not being very nice to me . . .' And, her feelings
hurt, she left the bathroom and went to lie down.

"The following day, the butler found his master drowned in the tub . . . naturally."

The gentleman shook his head and said, "Ever since then . . . the Devil knows what she's been up to . . . And by the Devil, I mean you, me . . . and everyone . . . everyone else . . ."

He fell silent again, still with a sort of twisted snicker stuck to his lips . . . And since he kept sitting there, without speaking or moving, I asked him, "So, what about it, sir?"

He replied, "What about it—yes, good question . . .! I don't need you to do that favor for me anymore. Talking about her has alleviated my longing . . . It's certainly an extraordinary thing that she would become so indifferent to me so abruptly. Forgive me, sir, and do not think too badly of me for paying you this awkward visit."

He stood up, and I walked him to the door, where he expressed once more his apologies and good wishes.

I spent the rest of the day lost in thought . . . in memories . . . Absurd memories and depressive thoughts . . . !

I knew the Marquise, because she was the mistress of my friend Lucien Pryant, a noble, attractive young man who has become famous, rich, and highly decorated today, after his stunning, meteoric rise in the world of military espionage.

From the very beginning, both Lucien and Laure took me into their confidence about their love affair, not from a spirit of friendship, as you might think, but because they thought I could be very useful to them . . . And then, I am uniquely suited to play the trusty go-between . . . in a farce . . .

Lucien was penniless in the days I am speaking of, having not yet had the opportunity to hand over secrets about our arms supplies, as well as the plans for our "immobilization"— open secrets, at any rate—to foreign powers. More to the point, he lived in a shabby little furnished room in a run-down hotel on Rue des Martyrs, a déclassé neighborhood not fit for love affairs of that sort . . .

"Look," Lucien said to me, "I really can't have my girlfriend
come over to my place ... My place is disgusting. Cheap furniture with garnet-colored upholstery, armchairs missing legs ...
And if you saw my bed ... if you saw my armoire ... As prissy
as she is, so accustomed to luxury—every kind of luxury—
she'd dump me in a second ... Love can only take place on a
beautiful stage set ...! Just think, my friend, I don't even own
a piano, and the artwork that decorates my walls is nothing but
cheap chromos: *Return of the Seafarer, The Curtains Close
Again, A Rabbit Tied Up By One Foot,* nothing that would appeal to the refined, transcendent soul of a woman who owns
Maurice Denis paintings—she's a nut for religion, you
know—and who is having her own portrait done by Boldo-
ni—for she is so very ... perfect ...! It's stupid not to have a
cozy, heated apartment, with wallpaper and rose-tinted lamp-
shades ... and carpets that won't turn the heels of her little
bare feet black with soot ...! And if you knew how many
once-in-a-lifetime opportunities, how many glorious one-night
stands with married women, I've had to miss out on ... because of this crappy room!"

"But," I replied, "your girlfriend is a widow and lives
alone ... Why can't she host you at her place?"

"She can't, my friend ... because of her servants ... Also,
she's a rising star in Catholic circles ... She knows Mun and
Mackau ... She runs a booth at the Charity Bazaar ..."

Then he started whining: "Your apartment is so nice ...!
Tudor and Louis XVI, like hers ... and so cozy ... so romantic ...! How great it would be to make love in a place like
that ...! I've got it all worked out, just listen—I will tell my
girlfriend that I cannot have her over to my place ... because
my father lives there, along with my sister and my two paralyzed aunts ... It's such a shame ...! Are you really going to
make me lose out on this opportunity ...? Oh, it's all in your
hands ...!"

Sick of listening to these pleas, I agreed. Three times a week
I turned my apartment over to the sexual needs of Lucien and

his mistress. I set the scene nicely for them. I lent Lucien my Oriental slippers, my nightshirts, my cologne, the key to my forbidden library. I even used my good taste to cater their love meetings for them, gourmet snacks, stamina-building and substantial: sandwiches, gingerbread cakes, port, tea, etc . . . Thus, I was in on all their pleasures.

"What a lovely apartment you have!" the Marquise told me every evening, at the restaurant, at the theater, in the car—in spite of Mun and Mackau, and right in the middle of the Charity Bazaar. "We don't ever want to leave it . . . Such exquisite taste . . . ! It's perfect for lovemaking . . . !"

"Indeed, it is . . . ! I am glad you like it . . . You are very nice to say so . . ."

"Well, but, on the other hand, your bathroom . . ."

"You don't like that!"

"It's not that . . . ! It's just that . . . well, couldn't you show a bit more modesty, with those lewd paintings . . . ?"

"Couldn't *you* . . . ?"

"It's like your books . . . What a nightmare . . . !"

"So you read them, then . . . ?"

"When all is said and done, you do have good taste . . . !"

Thus we spent our evenings in the discussion of refined and edifying matters.

The affair went on for three months. Then, one day, Lucien, looking pale, haggard, his eyes full of tears, came to tell me that everything was broken, finished. She had deceived him . . . They'd had a terrible, knock-down-drag-out fight . . . ! In the course of explaining things, he had to break three of my mirrors and a number of very expensive miniature figurines . . . Then, he gave me back the key to my apartment, and left.

I did not see him again for several years, and just as suddenly, I lost track of the Marquise de Parabola.

I ran into her again one evening at a friend's house, the home of an Austrian woman from Galata, who collected strange people and sang Schumann, badly. What made things entertaining was that no one knew each other at this woman's house, since the guests were constantly changing, recruited mainly from the foreign colonies, not to mention the most fashionable prisons in all of Paris.

I walked right up to Madame de Parabola. She was still youthful, beautiful, crazy, seductive, passionate, and slightly more blonde than before.

"Ah, what a long time it's been ...!" I cried. "And what have you been doing ... since the big break-up ...?"

Madame de Parabola stared at me, her brow furrowed by a violent effort to remember me. "What big break-up?" she asked.

"Aren't you Madame de Parabola?"

"Of course ... And who, sir, are you?"

"Georges Vasseur," I announced, bowing. "You don't remember ...?"

"Not at all ...!"

"And Lucien Pryant?"

"Lucien Pryant ...? Who's Lucien Pryant ...? Oh, wait ... Short and blond?"

"No, Madame, tall and dark ..."

"I don't remember him at all!"

"A tall, dark-haired man whom you made love to passionately ... three times a week, for three months ... in my home ... in my apartment ... my lovely apartment ...?"

Madame de Parabola collected her thoughts, scanned all her memories, counted off all of her lovers one by one ... her lovers' apartments ... Then, with regretful and evident sincerity, she said, "No, indeed ... tall and dark ... in your apartment ... I don't remember that at all ... And I think you're mad, sir ...!"

Eight days later, I ran into her again, at the home of a different friend, a Chilean woman from Canada, who sang Schubert with the voice (and the black gloves) of Yvette Guilbert ... This time, *she* approached *me* right away, flirtatious and smiling. "You must have thought I was crazy ... the other evening ...? But I remember everything perfectly now ...

Lucien Pryant ...! Of course ...! God, what an idiot he was, that poor boy ...! And how we cheated on him, you and I!"

"*I* cheated on him?" I jumped. "But with whom ...?"

"With me, of course ... Our kisses ... our love bites ... and my hair! So you've forgotten everything already, you ungrateful wretch?"

It was my turn to be dumbfounded. "Madame, you are mistaken ... You did not cheat on my friend Lucien Pryant with me ..."

"With whom, then ...? Look ...! You were Lucien Pryant's best friend, weren't you ...?"

"Certainly!"

"So—whom else would I have cheated on him with, if not you ...?" She pouted adorably, her eyelashes fluttering with disbelief...

"Well, then, it's news to me ... You leave me absolutely speechless ..."

At that moment, a minor commotion broke out in the salon. They announced that the lady of the house was about to sing a love song by Schubert. When I turned back to her, Madame de Parabola had slipped away.

> I didn't see her again ...
> I didn't see her again, until now ...
> Perhaps I will try to talk to her, tomorrow ...

XI.

Before dinner, I strolled through the Quincunxes with Triceps. We encountered a woman, far too chic for words, leaving the bar. She smiled at Triceps and said, "Good evening, old man . . ."

"Good evening, kitten," Triceps replied.

She passed by in a swell of perfume . . .

"That's Snowball," Triceps explained to me, "the former mistress of old Baron Kropp . . . You know him . . . Died last year . . . Old Baron Kropp . . . You don't know him . . .? Ah, dear friend, it's hard to believe there was ever a man like that . . .! Just listen . . ."

And Triceps, happy he'd found a good story to tell, took my arm and said to me:

"One morning, the old Baron came to my house. And without any preamble, he asked me, 'Is it true, Doctor, that there's iron in the blood?'

"'That's right . . .'

"'Ah! I didn't dare believe it . . . How baffling nature is!'

"The old Baron's lips were trembling and he was drooling a little. His eyes were nearly dead . . . And the skin of his neck bunched like a loose cravat of flab below his chin. He thought for a moment, then asked, 'Is there very much . . . a lot?'

"'Oh, Christ!' I replied. 'It's not like there's a mine . . . not like the ones at Ariège . . .'

"'Well, exactly what are you saying . . .?'

"'I am saying, you couldn't extract enough iron from a man's bloodstream to—how can I put this?—to build a second Eiffel Tower, for instance . . . Get me?'

"'Yes . . .! Yes . . .! Yes . . .!'

"And the old Baron timed each of these 'yesses' with a deep nod of his head, as if to express both ready understanding and a profound sense of disappointment . . . He went on, 'Anyway,

I don't need that much ...' Then, after a brief silence: 'So, do you think you could actually extract some iron ... a little bit of iron ... from the blood ... from my blood ...?'

"'Eh ...! Why not ...?'

"'The Baron grinned, and asked another question. 'Is it also true that there's gold in the blood?'

"'Ah! Not gold, no ... Now you're pushing it, my Baron ... There is only gold in teeth ... Rotten ones.'

"'Unfortunately, Doctor, I don't have any teeth anymore, not even rotten ones,' groaned the old man. 'And if I did have any teeth, or any gold in them, that would just be foreign gold, not gold I manufactured myself—not gold that was part of my essence, in a word. Therefore, what good would it be? So you are absolutely certain there's no gold in my blood?'

"'Absolutely ...'

"The baron sighed. 'That's a shame ... And it really pains me ... Because, you see, I would have preferred gold much more than iron, for my ring ...'

"I did not pry, thinking the baron a bit senile. He went on to explain, clicking his tongue against his lips dripping with saliva, 'You don't know how much I love Snowball ... I've given her everything ... hotels, horses, jewels, lovers who make her scream with joy ... She has sheets that cost fifty thousand francs ... She has everything a woman could ever want or dream of ... Well, I'd like to give her something even more, something no woman has ever had ... Yes, to give her, all in one shot and in tangible, material form, everything that is left of my marrow and blood ... all of my essence, in a word, contained in a jewelry box inlaid with the most beautiful diamonds in the world ...! My death is a small price to pay ... Okay, but will I have enough blood for it?'

"'Anyone's got enough blood for that,' I replied casually. 'At any rate ... we'll get what we can ...'

"'Ah, Doctor ...! I don't feel well ...'

Worn out by the impotent strain his senile lust had placed upon him, the old Baron turned very pale and fainted. I laid him on a divan, elevating his feet, made him breathe the most pungent smelling salts I had, and whipped his face with the tip of a wet towel ... His swoon lasted several minutes. Then, when he came to, I ordered two of my servants to escort him, holding him up by each armpit, to the door of his car which was parked on the street ... He mumbled between his lips, which had difficulty staying closed: 'Ah ...! Snowball ...! Snowball ...! You shall have it ...'"

"And, collapsed in a heap on the seat cushions, his legs gone limp, his head rolling onto his chest, the old Baron stubbornly continued to talk in his sleep: 'Yes ... that's it ... all of my essence ... I will give you all of my ess ...'

"The following day, he went to the office of a chemist, very famous for his expertise. 'I would like to hire you,' he said, 'to draw enough blood from my veins to extract thirty-five grams of iron.'

"'Thirty-five grams?' said the chemist, who could not restrain his astonishment. 'Hell ...!'

"'Is that too much?' the Baron asked, uneasily.

"'It's a lot ...'

"'Money is no object ... And if you should need all my blood, take it ...'

"'It's just that,' the chemist objected, 'you are very old ...'

"'If I were young,' the Baron replied, 'I wouldn't be giving my blood to my beloved Snowball ... but a different fluid ...'

"After two months, the chemist delivered a small scrap of iron to the Baron.

"'It only weighs thirty grams ...' he said to him.

"'How tiny it is ...!' murmured the Baron, whose voice had become nothing more than a whisper, and whose face was whiter than a shroud ...

"'Christ! Baron, sir ... iron is dense, it doesn't have to be that big.'

"'How tiny it is ...! How tiny it is ...!'

"And, staring at the speck of metal between the tips of his trembling fingers, he sighed. 'So, that is my essence ...! It's not very pretty ... And yet, the entire immensity of my love is contained in this black dot ... How proud Snowball will feel to own such a gem ... a gem made from my marrow ... made from my blood ... made from my life ...! And how she will love me ...! And how her love for me will make her weep!'

"He whispered the final words, no longer possessing the strength to utter them aloud ... And after being asked to repeat himself, he said in a hush, 'It's so tiny ... And yet, in all the world, there is not, nor has there ever been, around the neck of a woman or on the finger of her hand, so great a jewel ...'

"He lapsed into a restless, nightmare-filled sleep.

"A few days later, the Baron was on his deathbed. Snowball sat with him, gazing at all the things around her with a look of boredom, a look which said: 'The old fart's really getting on my nerves ... Why can't he just hurry up and die ...? There's somewhere else I'd like to be ...'

"A servant brought in a jewelry box. 'What is that ...?' the Baron panted.

"'It is the ring ... Baron, sir.'

"Hearing that word, the dying old man got a smile on his lips and a twinkle in his eye ... 'Give it here ... And you, Snowball, come here, close to me ... and listen closely ...'

"With great effort, he creaked open the box, slid the ring onto one of Snowball's fingers, and said, through a constant stream of rales and rattles, 'Snowball ... look at this ring ... What you see here is made of iron ... This iron represents all of my blood. They opened and drained my veins to extract it ... I have killed myself so that you would have a ring that no other woman in the world has ever had ... Are you happy ...?'

"Snowball looked at the ring with an astonishment tinged with contempt, and said simply, 'Oh, well ... buddy-boy ... you know ... I would have rather had a pendant.'"

And Triceps ended his story with a burst of laughter. "No ...! What a wit that Snowball is ...! A natural ...!"

XII.

Today I made an important discovery about the immunity of hedgehogs to snake venom, and I ask your permission, readers of the future, to share my joy over this, with you.

Contrary to the beliefs of natural scientists, who cannot see beyond the points of their scalpels, this immunity is not due to specific physiological traits that render the hedgehog constitutionally impervious to the effects of snake venom. It comes solely from the astounding cunning with which nature endowed that little quadruped, and the miraculous ingenuity he employs in his struggle to survive. I will demonstrate this, soon enough.

If I refrain from submitting any part of this discovery to what is called the academic world, it is only because I know how unreceptive that world is to independent researchers, and how its own survival, as a closed system, depends on its open hostility to writers who make contributions to the field of science, which it considers its own exclusive domain. (And so much the worse for science, I daresay.) Nevertheless, my early work and subsequent investigations should furnish incontrovertible proof that I am no rank beginner when it comes to this area of human knowledge. Must I remind you that I was the one who expostulated the fascinating and unheard-of law of ambulatory movement in plant life? As for my findings on the bi-mentality and autocriminology of the spider, they altered our understanding of the physiology of that articulated arthropod so radically that Sir John Lubbock (to whom I dedicated them—written up in a glowing report) became so enraged that, had it not been for the diplomatic skill of Baron de Courcel, our London ambassador at that time, England would have surely rushed into Egypt to commit more follies.

It is fortunate, nevertheless, that simple poets sometimes correct the errors of trained specialists, and I don't even want to think about the terrible intellectual dark age we would still be plunged in, if we had only the so-called experts to explain to us the precious little we know of nature's secrets. Van Helmont, a very great scientist for his day, with a mind more obsessively intuitive than rigorously analytical, gave to science the theory of spontaneous generation. This is how he did it. One evening, he placed a few dried-up walnuts in his garden, beneath the hermetic seal of a flowerpot. The following day, he lifted the pot, and saw mice nibbling at the nuts. He immediately concluded that the mice hatched from the nuts in a miraculous instance of spontaneous generation, and he brought this good news to the enthused academies of Europe. Sadly, nearly all scientific discoveries are judged by the same standard: in the cauldrons of our present day no less than in the inscrutable athanors of the Middle Ages, they have perpetuated the outright lie (to say the least) that the Jesuits are the best teachers. In a few years, our sons will laugh at Pasteur's microbes the way we laugh at Van Helmont's spontaneous mice, and Doctor Charcot's brain-maps will become, perhaps, a joke even more outlandish than the homunculus of Arnaldus de Villanova (who searched for the philosopher's stone and got excommunicated) or the universal toads of Hennig Brandt (who searched for the philosopher's stone and discovered phosphorus instead). "Experience is deceptive," as old Hippocrates said.

This afternoon, I went walking with my friend Robert Hagueman in a forest ... really an abandoned, overgrown park in a valley several kilometers outside the city, in a spot where the valley, tired of being just a chasm in a mountain, widens until it almost looks like a small prairie ... Grown wild again, indeed nearly virgin, the forest is wonderfully cool and quiet. Many varieties of flowers thrive there, yellow, red, blue, and pink, and you can even see some sky between the branches.

Having walked for a long time, I sat down to rest at the edge of a clearing, my back against the trunk of a beech tree. Right beside me, starflowers opened their white-blossom parasols to the sun. Everywhere, St.John's wort decorated the shade with their golden stars ... And my mind was clear of all thoughts, except enjoying that respite of sweetness and light which nature offered me. Robert Hagueman was asleep on a bed of moss. Ah, if anyone had told me I was about to make an important biological discovery, I would not have believed him.

My attention was suddenly caught by something shiny slithering through the grass and lifting up, like a flash of silver lightning, the low leaves of the St. John's wort. I saw it was a snake, and I would be lying if I did not add, the most danger-ous variety. He did not see me, and frisked around, freely, lazi-ly, among the flowers. He disappeared and reappeared again — sometimes straight like the blade of a little knife, sometimes oval like a bracelet, and sometimes rippling through the moss like a trickle of clear water. But something else intrigued me even more. Not far from the playful snake, I spied a little pile of dry leaves. At first glance, it did not look like anything spe-cial; but peering at it more closely, I found it suspicious. The cluster actually seemed to be solid all over, and no breeze rus-tled it: the little grass blades, poking through, stayed perfectly still. It was as though someone had painted a clump of birch leaves on the ground. And yet, that clump of dry leaves was moving; a slight, but perceptible, breathing motion stirred it ... It was alive ... And because it was alive, that little ball of leaves frightened me beyond words ... I opened my eyes as wide as I could, to see it better, to stare my way through the cover of those leaves that apparently hid a mystery, one of those thousand crimes of the murderous forest. But which one?

The most dim-witted animals, the most vulnerable insects and the most ridiculous larvae are all gifted with incredible powers to battle or evade their own natural enemies. They are alert to the most oblique threat, with an intelligence that never fails them, even if it does not always save them. Whatever ene-my was hiding there, under the leaves, must not have posed a threat to the snake, or else he would not have appeared so non-chalant, so indolent, basking in his own voluptuously sinuous grace among the flowers and the silky moss. Surely I was mistaken; it was only my imagination that made me glimpse, just now, a hungry snout and two gleaming eyes beneath those innocent leaves. I decided to wait behind my tree, without making a sound, without making a single move, so as not to warn off the snake. Robert was still sleeping . . .

And all at once, at the instant the snake's slow crawl grazed the pile of leaves, I saw an astonishing spectacle, one of the most shocking dramas a man has ever been allowed to witness. The dry leaves flew to either side, and a fat hedgehog emerged, her quills out, her snout outstretched. Quickly, with a leaping attack whose nimbleness was impossible to believe in an animal so fat, the hedgehog hurled herself upon the snake, bit down on his tail very hard, then rolled herself into a ball, her body entirely protected by the thousand erect quills all over her skin, like the pointy tips of lances. And she held this position in perfect stillness.

Then, the snake began to pant horribly. With vigorous writhing movements that made him stiffen out, straight and blinding as a cut from a knife, he tried to free himself from the hedgehog's clutches. In vain. In vain, he tried to bite the hedgehog, thrusting his venom-dripping jaws into the quills of the cunning beast, and getting torn to shreds. Covered in blood, his tiny eyes bursting out of his head, he kept struggling, reaching to bite the monster's impenetrable armor, his fury raised to fever pitch by his wounds. This struggle lasted ten minutes. Finally, in his rage at being held captive, he impaled his head upon the unyielding needles, and fell back limp, thin gray ribbon stained with blood, beside the motionless ball.

The hedgehog waited for a few moments. Then, with a prudence, a truly admirable caution, she retracted her quills, took the risk of raising her snout, uncurled the upper half of her body, opened her two black little eyes, fierce and gloating, and unclasped her paws. Then, when she was completely certain the snake was dead, she ate him, grunting like a pig.

After which, bloated and oafish, she just waddled away on

her short legs, and, digging the ground with her snout, rolled herself back into a ball, on a pile of leaves where she soon disappeared completely . . .

On our way back, Robert, who was bored stiff by my account of the combat between the snake and the hedgehog, told me stories about women, gambling, horse races. I wasn't listening . . . When we were a few hundred meters from the city, he took me by the arm, and, pointing out a picturesque house, well-placed halfway up the hill, among terraces and sumptuous gardens, he asked me, "Do you know that house?"

"No . . ."

"That's the haunted villa, buddy-boy . . . I can't believe you haven't heard of it . . . A shocking story . . . Here is how I learned about it."

And my friend told the story:

"Two years ago, I was looking to rent a villa here . . . People told me to go and see one of the notaries, Claude Splutterduck, Esquire, who owned four of them, the four most beautiful and best situated villas in the region. That ministerial official received me with an overdone courtesy whose somewhat smarmy cheerfulness irritated me right away, and to my very last nerve.

"He was a short, bald man, with a round, fish-lipped face that seemed genderless; his belly bulged beneath a velvet vest with a flower print, whose fadedness made it seem even more out-of-date. Everything about him was as round as his face, everything about him was crassly cheerful, except his eyes, whose rheumy and worried-looking pupils, ringed with red and plunked into the greasy fat of his triple eyelids, oozed (can't think of a better way to say it!) a rather sinister expression. But I was accustomed to seeing that expression, or at least one very much like it, in the eyes of every businessman I've ever met, so I paid it only the most indifferent and cursory attention, no more than I would to the eyes of strangers passing me on the street. Besides, considerable interests were at stake in my negotiations with that resort-town lawyer. I was determined not to let him chisel me out of more than several louis at most, on the rent, provided the location of his villa was to my satisfaction.

"In a few short, succinct words, I explained to him the purpose of my visit.

"'Nicely, nicely!' he said, while splaying his chubby, hairy hands across his stubby thighs (for even though his cranium was completely devoid of hair, his hands sprouted thick tufts) . . . 'Nicely, nicely—so you'd like to vacation all summer long in the Pyrenees . . . ? A splendid idea . . . There is no better spot, there is nowhere more pleasant or more healthy . . .'

"'I hope so,' I declared idiotically, not knowing what to say.

"The notary emphasized the off-putting friendliness of his speech:

"'And you've decided . . . Nicely, nicely . . . ! And you've decided to ask yours truly here, Claude Splutterduck, Esquire, to rent you one of his little villas . . . ? I should think so . . . you bet! They truly are the nicest, with the best amenities . . .'

"'They have that reputation at least . . .'

"You see, whatever answers I gave only seemed to make things worse. Splutterduck, Esquire, grinned: 'And they have earned it . . . ! Well, it seems to me that we can take care of this matter . . . Yes, yes, we can definitely take care of this matter . . .' The notary folded his arms and rocked backwards in his chair. 'Let's see now . . . let's see now . . .' he said. 'Back to business . . . First question . . . Are you married?'

"'No.'

"'Ah . . . ! Not married . . . very good . . . very good . . . ! Second question . . . Do you have a roommate . . . ? I mean a companion, er, um, a mistress . . . to put it plainly . . . ?'

"And, with a wide smile to indicate he meant no harm, he added, 'My goodness gracious, we know all about life here . . . The provinces are not so backwards as is generally assumed . . . There are young people everywhere, after all . . . and here is no exception . . . And to heck with the formality of all this notary stuff . . . ! Nicely, nicely . . . !'

"Since I did not say anything, stunned and shocked at the turn the conversation had taken, Splutterduck, Esquire, explained, 'My goodness gracious . . . do forgive me for asking you these questions . . . It is so I can determine what your needs are . . . My concern is strictly that of a landlord . . . My four villas, dear sir, are furnished differently to meet the needs of different social situations . . . well-defined situations . . . or left undefined, by choice . . . do you understand . . . ? I have one for committed relationships: it's the worst one . . . another for temporary relationships, summer flings: it's a little better . . . another one for confirmed bachelors: that's a nice one, that one there, dear sir . . . And so forth and so on . . . You understand, the same sauce doesn't go with every type of meat . . . So, then, what category should I put you in . . . ?'

"'I am single,' I confirmed.

"'Good for you!' cheered Splutterduck, Esquire. 'You have chosen the right path in life . . . And now you are entitled to my most beautiful villa . . . You see how happy I am, because you have made me very happy . . . very, very happy . . .'

"I waved and nodded in a vague attempt to signal my thanks. The notary began again: 'Perhaps it surprises you that I reserve my most beautiful, most fully furnished, most luxurious and all-around nicest villa for single men . . . ? It was a brainstorm of mine, and I will explain it all to you shortly . . . when we see the place, if you do not mind . . .'

"And his eyes, still rheumy and worried, examined me, as if searching deep within me. I really felt that stare of his rub me up and down, weighing me, appraising my social, moral and retail worth. Being eyeballed by that man made me feel like a diamond in the palm of a Jew.

"At that moment, the office door opened and, in a flurry of silk and lace, with the unmistakable scent of a woman's body and flowers, I saw red hair, a red mouth, the blue lightning of two adorably bright eyes; a dazzling apparition, a miracle of

beauty, youth and love, who disappeared the instant she was
seen, with a cry of 'Excuse me!'

"'My wife . . .' Claude Splutterduck, Esquire, casually explained.

"'My compliments . . .!' I said, not yet recovered from the
shock I had been thrown into by that radiant creature's fleeting
apparition, barely glimpsed in the crack of the door, opened
quickly and just as quickly closed again . . ."

Robert fell silent for a moment. "Ah, buddy-boy," he sighed,
"whenever I think of her . . .! Those eyes . . .! Those lips . . .!"

Then, he began again.

"The villa pleased me. It was in the most picturesque spot on
the hillside, surrounded by gardens and massive trees, its ar-
chitecture was streamlined, clean — Splutterduck, Esquire, had
not exaggerated its merits. Inside the decoration was soothing
yet exciting, opulent yet tasteful, so as not to detract from the
magnificent view the villa commanded, of verdant countryside, mountains, and sky.

"I especially remember the bedroom, a yellow room with
white furnishings, bestowing an instant sense of well-being;
where flesh tones and the shapes of objects took on an extraordinary sensuous softness, suffused by the uncanny light of
dreams. Several lewd prints by Jules Romain adorned the walls,
along with others, frankly pornographic, by Félicien Rops, I
believe; here and there, on the mantle, the bookshelves, the
end tables, erotic figurines from Saxony added graceful touches
of charming sin . . .

"We were right in the middle of this bedroom — Splutterduck, Esquire, and I — when, my mind made up to rent the
villa, I asked him how much the rent was.

"'Fifty thousand francs, not a sou less,' he declared firmly.

"I jumped. But the notary invited me to take a seat, and
here is what he said to me, the whole time staring at me with
those ghastly eyes, spectral, mesmerizing: 'Fifty thousand

francs ... Offhand, that sounds expensive to you, I suppose? I understand ... But I am about to tell you everything you need to know ... This villa is haunted ...'

"'Haunted ...?' I stammered.

"'As haunted as can be ... Every night, a ghost appears ... Not a ghost with a skull for a head and a skeleton for a body, dragging shrouds, iron chains, and moonbeams through the hallways at the strike of midnight ... No ... This is a kind of ghost you do not often get to meet, even in dreams, an adorable, ravishing ghost, with the head and body of a woman, whose red hair, blue eyes, and radiant skin under her see-through, perfumed lingerie, could tempt a saint ... This ghost exists for one thing only: she knows every erotic trick in the book, and has even invented a few more, plus she is discreet, very discreet ... She comes when you want ... and goes the same way ... No one knows anything ... or sees anything ... In the end, she is yours to do with as you wish ... This ghost comes with the villa ... She's included in the rent ... But if you don't want her, it won't keep me awake at night ... No, it won't keep me awake at night at all, by Jove!'

"I looked at the notary. A cynical smile pursed his lips, and the red circles around his pupils oozed their bloody discharge with new force ... And I heard myself yelp: 'But, this ghost ... I know her, I've seen her ... She's ...'

"Splutterduck, Esquire, silenced me with this violent interruption: 'She's just a ghost, that's all ...! You don't know her, you've seen nothing ... She's just a ghost like any other ... We might as well go, then ... You can think it over on the way ...'

"And, shrugging his shoulders in an air of lofty disdain, he went on to say, 'Oh, only a moron would haggle over the price when it comes to having sex with a ghost ... an actual ghost ...! Ooh, la, la ...! How much is it worth, after all, to explore rare sensations, unexpurgated pleasures ...? Literary hacks ...! We might as well go then ...'"

Having finished his story, Robert suddenly asked me, as he

jumped out of the car: "And do you know ... who's living in
the haunted house this season? It's Dickson-Barnell, the American millionaire ... What's more, you know we're having dinner with him this evening ...? See you soon ...!"

A charming young man, that Dickson-Barnell ...
    After the introductions were made, and over a few cocktails,
we became the best of friends, even before the first course ...
    Moreover, he was a fun companion—at least, he struck me
this way at first sight—with a sense of fun that was spontaneous and sincere ... as sincere as gold. In the friendliest way, I
made a point of complimenting him on his bon vivant spirit.
    "A very rare virtue, dear sir, and one that is being lost, day
by day, in this country of ours," I said, with affected, dogma-
tic solemnity. "Anyway, no people are more fun than the Amer-
icans ..."
    Dickson-Barnell agreed. "Indeed," he said, "I am fun, so
much so that I'm actually an expert in having it. But
that doesn't mean I'm happy ... The sermonizers are right, you
see ... Rich people can't be happy ... Happiness is something
other than money ... In fact, I believe it's the exact opposite."
    When I expressed surprise at this string of depressing plati-
tudes, he sighed. "Ah! When you're as rich as I am, you see
through everything too quickly ... Life becomes hideously
monotonous, with no surprises ... Women, wine, horses, travel ... paintings, antiques, if you only knew how quickly you
start to feel disheartened ... an infinite disheartening ... infinite vanity ... vanity of vanities."
    I was determined to flatter this man in every possible way,
so I said, "You even talk like gold, dear sir."
    "Hell!" was all the millionaire said, with a shrug whose
crowning despair I will never forget. And, after a few moments
of silence, he brusquely asked me, "You smoke?"
    "Don't mind if I do ..."
    He handed me a cigar as long as an obelisk, glittering like a
solid gold pillar in the sun.

"I'll be damned!" I said in admiration.

Dickson-Barnell smiled the kind of disenchanted, sardonic grin that must have appeared often on the lips of the gloomy Preacher of Eccelesiastes. And he explained to me, "Yes, it's my own invention. This cigar is made entirely from leaves of stamped and certified gold. I have case after case of them— cases as long and as deep as the divans your Baudelaire talks about . . . It occurred to me that smoking gold would be the height of luxury . . . Well! It turns out it's the worst thing in the world, my dear sir . . . It's absolutely unsmokeable . . ."

Again, he shrugged in such a broadly demoralized way that the entire universe seemed to be collapsing around him . . . Then he said, sighing and dragging out every syllable in a tone whose deep misery cannot be adequately represented by words flatly printed on the page: "Everything—alas!—is unsmokeable . . ."

He continued, "It's like women . . . Ah, dear sir . . .! I can tell you I've had them all . . . and I can tell you I got absolutely nothing out of it, nothing but weariness and disgust . . . I wanted to make the poets' dream come true . . . I wanted to hold creatures of beauty and myth in my arms, the kind of extraterrestrial goddesses you read about in poems. I hired the most outstanding artists in the world to design women for me, women with hair of real gold, lips of pure coral, their skin the unmistakable pulp of lilies . . . breasts sculpted from actual snow, etc., etc. . . . Yes, dear sir . . . And you know what . . . ?"

"What, what . . . ?"

"It was unsmokeable . . ." He moaned, "Oh, being rich . . . being too rich . . . it's the death of a man . . .! And the terrifying thought that you can buy anything, right at the very moment you want it, anything . . . even literary genius . . . with money . . .! For I also possess literary genius . . . I am the author of a slew of plays written by a young man who accompanies me everywhere . . . The plays are long, and I can't make heads or tails of them . . . And the worst part is . . . I myself don't even know how rich I am . . . Every day, I can dip my toes in the vast ocean of my wealth, but I can never touch the bottom. Do you know about my gardens?"

"No . . . but I would love to know all about them!"

"They are fifty-hectare gardens, where all the flowers of all the flora are artificial, and hold tiny electric lights inside their calyxes. In the evening, when night falls, I flick a switch and all the flowers light up . . . It's magical, dear sir . . . and you've no idea how much it disgusts me . . . It disgusts me so much that, in all of my palaces, yachts, castles, and villas, I've replaced the electric lighting with smoky, archaic candlelight . . . Ah, the hell with it—never get rich, buddy . . ."

Dickson-Barnell sighed a long sigh. He twisted and turned on his seat cushions without being able to find a comfortable position. And he continued his lament. "I've tried my hand at science, philosophy, photography, and politics. I have read, read, and re-read books of all types and by everyone you can think of. In order to extract their ideas and pass them off as my own, I have tried to master the works of M. Paul Bourget, M. René Doumic, and M. Melchior de Vogüé, by the same laborious physical process of panning that was once used to dig for gold."

"Too bad!" I interrupted. "It's been quite a while since any of those books have measured up to anyone's gold standard, let alone your own. And they remain, even now, nothing but lifeless matter and deadweight."

"Didn't I tell you!" groaned the unfortunate Dickson-Barnell. "Everything is unsmokeable . . . And listen to this . . . ! I was in negotiations with the Belgian King—what a Greedy Gus he is, by the way!—to purchase Belgium from him . . . I wanted to reenact all the orgies and scandals of the Roman Emperors there . . . We'd nearly reached an agreement, Léopold the Second and I . . . when I saw *Quo Vadis* at the Porte Saint-Martin . . . That turned me off Neroism once and for all . . . Everything is unsmokeable . . ."

Dinner was like a funeral . . . Robert Hagueman was out of sorts . . . Dickson-Barnell drank like a deaf-mute, in total silence . . . his face crimson, his eyes bloodshot . . . In vain, Triceps tried to be as nimble as a squirrel . . . and only managed to hop around from one subject to another . . . As for me, I daydreamed about the combat, in that verdant clearing, between the snake and the hedgehog . . . As we got up from the table, I said to Dickson-Barnell: "Well . . . is the ghost of the haunted villa . . . ho, ho, ho . . . also unsmokeable . . . ?"

"Unsmokeable," stammered the American millionaire in a whisper. And, murmuring in his drunken haze, he added, "Everything . . . everything is unsmokeable . . ."

He tried to stand up like the others . . . His weak legs could not support the weight of his body . . . He fell back into his chair in a heap . . . while muttering with drunken stubborness, "Everything is unsmokeable . . . un - smoke - a - ble . . . !"

Then he passed out . . .

Robert Hagueman said, in the smoking room: "He's really changed, that poor Dickson-Barnell . . . He used to be scintillating . . . back when I knew him . . . First of all, he held his liquor like a steel safe . . . And then, he wasn't always moaning and groaning about life like some lyric poet . . ."

"Hell! Being so rich, so rich for so many years," Triceps said, "has left him, at the very least, a hopeless neurasthenic."

Robert went on, "I can't believe you haven't heard—it was the talk of the town in Paris—about what happened to him, one morning when he was coming home from a drive in his coach-and-four. His horses dragged the carriage right into his hotel's wrought-iron gate, you see. Dickson-Barnell was thrown from his seat like a parcel, damn the luck, and was dashed against the courtyard pavement—flat as a pancake. They found him unconscious and so grievously injured they thought he was dead. Indeed, it's impossible to believe he didn't die. His skull was fractured in two places, three ribs were cracked, both knees were dislocated, one leg was crushed, and the blood gushed out of him from a long gash in his stomach. With great difficulty, they managed to carry him to his bed. He left a trail

of blood all along the way, on the staircases and in the vesti-
bules, and the servants who carried him were red from head to
toe . . . The doctor, who had been summoned quickly and who
was a very close friend of Dickson-Barnell, came running up,
examined the wounds, frowned, and tried to stop the bleeding
with bandages and tourniquets, while waiting for the surgeon
whom he had immediately called as soon as he saw the injured
man. 'Is he dead?' asked Dickson-Barnell's valet, coming into
the room. 'Not yet!' answered the doctor, 'but . . .' And he
hung his head, as if to say: 'But he might as well be . . .' 'My
God! My God!' exclaimed the valet . . . To which the doctor replied, in a harsh tone: 'Come now, Winwhite . . . if your master
heard you, he would not be pleased . . .' Bandaged up, the
wounded man regained consciousness. He regarded the doctor
with that shrewd, direct, arresting look, the way he looked at
everyone in those days, for he saw his whole life much more
clearly then. He realized the seriousness of his condition, and,
in a dry voice, with that abrupt way of talking that he had, he
asked: 'Done for?' 'Most likely,' replied the doctor who, from
spending time with his friend, had picked up that same style of
cursory, telegram-like speech, in which all unnecessary words
and even most short ones were eschewed, or translated into the
most primitive verbal sign-language, so to speak. 'Very well,'
said Dickson-Barnell . . . And without any further concern for
himself, since he had been taught never to get upset about a
simple fact that you cannot do anything about, he drew a black
line crossing out his entire life like a bad debt . . . 'And yet,' the
doctor seemed to change his mind, 'I think we could perform
an operation . . . Are you up to it?' 'How?' asked Dickson-Barnell. 'Cut your stomach open . . . wash all the blood from your
intestines . . . stitch you up . . .' 'I see . . . I see . . .' the injured
man spoke up . . . Then he quickly asked: 'What are the chances, with the operation?' 'Two in ten.' 'Very good . . . What are
the chances without the operation?' 'None.' 'Operation.' This
was said without a gesture, without a complaint, without a
shudder of terror, with the same complete calm as if it was a

question of buying a loaf of bread or dumping worthless stock
at the exchange. But as brief as they were, the words exhausted
him, and he could no longer speak. For several minutes he remained silent, his face perfectly still below the bandages
wrapped around his skull ... The surgeon arrived and took his
turn attentively examining the injuries, and after a short con-
ference between the two doctors, Dickson-Barnell asked:
'Could you give me half an hour ... beforehand?' 'Of course,'
agreed the doctor ... 'That gives us the time we need to get
ready.' 'Good ...! Winwhite ...? My will, please ...' Winwhite opened a desk drawer and took out a large envelope
sealed with six red seals, which he began to break one by one.
And, while the doctors and their assistants hurriedly sterilized
the next room and prepared the torture rack, Dickson-Barnell
went over his will, crossing out some paragraphs and writing in
new heirs, with a firm, confident hand whose unfaltering purpose could not be swayed for a single minute by physical agony. When this was done, he asked his friend the doctor to at-
test to the will, that he was of sound mind and possessed of all
his mental faculties. He even saw to it that the two assistants
affix their signatures below the doctor's, to bear witness to the
will's unassailable authenticity. After which, the envelope closed again and resealed, he awaited the knife ... In the middle of
the night, after the operation, in the throes of high fever and
dying of thirst, Dickson-Barnell called out: 'Winwhite!' 'Sir?'
'A drink ... of water!' 'No, sir.' 'Five hundred dollars!' 'No, sir!'
'Two thousand dollars!' 'No, sir!' The doctor, who was sleeping in the room, stretched out on a chaise longue, woke up at
the sound of voices and came to the sick man's bedside: 'You
want something?' he asked. 'Yes ... A drink ... of water!' 'No.'
'Twenty thousand dollars!' 'No.' 'Fifty thousand dollars!' 'No.'
Then, taken aback by this resistance, Dickson-Barnell regarded
his friend with a searching look, a calculating look that seemed
to appraise the doctor's price ... 'One hundred thousand dollars!' he finally said, the final bid. 'No.' 'Very well ...' He
stopped insisting; but noticing his pince-nez on the table by

his bed, within reach of his hand, he picked it up and brought it to his lips. The coolness of the glass seemed to calm him a little, and he dozed off . . ."

When Robert finished talking, Triceps opened the door that separated the two rooms. And we saw Dickson-Barnell, his head rolling on his chest, his mouth agape, his arms hanging limp . . . still collapsed and snoring in his chair . . .

"It's a beautiful sight, a rich man," Triceps said.

He closed the door again, took an expensive cigar, lit it, and blew puffs of smoke into the air. "Everything is unsmokeable . . . !" he moaned, parodying the voice of poor Dickson-Barnell.

XIII.

Today I received a lengthy letter from my friend Ulric Barrier, who is traveling through Russia ... I have excerpted the most provocative pages from this bulky sheaf, and here they are:

"... In the larger cities, I've seen several handsome cavalry regiments. What is more, they love showing off for tourists, as if to say: 'Take that! We've got a fearsome, dazzling army ... If you're looking for trouble here, you will find it!' In fact, they aren't regiments of soldiers but clowns. I have attended a number of revues, and every time I felt like I was at the circus. These cavalrymen are astounding; they can perform a thousand feats of dexterity, equilibrium and acrobatics with perfect ease, on horses trained to do all kinds of tricks. And they glitter, they shimmer, they shine ... I'm sure they would be a big hit at Franconi & Son's Flying Big Top. In spite of the grandeur of these maneuvers, what sticks in my mind is an impression of constant, explosive energy, but like that of a theater show. I am afraid they have nothing to back up these lavish, multicolored trappings — and as a Frenchman I suppose I should be happy about that.

"Returning to my hotel this afternoon, near one of the taverns in town, I saw an elderly Jew sitting on a stone distance marker on the street corner. He had a hook-nose, his beard was forked, he was leering, covered in stinking rags, but in spite of all that, he was very handsome, warming his persecuted bones in the sun ... An officer came by, brandishing a large saber in the air. Seeing the Jew, he stopped right in front of him and began to insult him, without any provocation from the Jew, just to bully him for fun ... The old Jew did not seem to hear him. Enraged by the fact that the Jew was ignoring him (and not from fear but contempt), the officer struck the old man with his gloved hand, so hard the poor devil was knocked from his perch onto the ground, where he writhed like a rabbit brought down by a gunshot. A few bystanders, soon a whole crowd, eager for excitement, gathered around the fallen Jew, and went, 'Hoo! Hoo!' then they kicked him and spat on his beard, shamefully. The Jew got back on his feet with great difficulty, being elderly, weaker than a small child, and, without any trace of anger in his eyes, only stupefaction at such an inexplicable, senselessly brutal crime, he said: 'Why do you beat me ...? Have I wronged you in some way? Do you have some complaint against me ...? Do you even know me ...? It makes no sense to beat me ... Are you all insane, then?' The officer shrugged and went on his way, followed by the entire mob, proclaiming him a hero ... As for the old Jew, he calmly sat down again on his stone marker ... I asked him about what had happened: 'They are all like that,' he told me. 'They beat us for no reason. That officer knows not what he does. But he's not such a bad guy, after all ... He could have killed me ... No one would have blamed him ... On the contrary, they would have congratulated him ... And undoubtedly he would have gotten a promotion ... No, indeed, he wasn't such a bad guy ...'"

* *

"... The deeper you go into the countryside, far from the big hubs of industrialization, the less you see of anything but misery and blight. It makes your blood run cold. Everywhere, gaunt faces and hunched backs, stooped, pathetic, slavish spines. Something inexpressibly sad weighs on this wasteland, and on these men blind with hunger. It is as if a continuous death-wind blew over these desolate steppes. The dark forests filled with slumbering wolves are a sinister sight to behold, and the hamlets silent and mournful as cemeteries. Nowhere do you see any gleaming uniforms or dancing horses; gone are the cavalrymen with their clownish antics. I ask: 'What about the army ...? Where is that impressive fighting force?' They point out a few rag-tag characters, without weapons or boots, most of them drunk on vodka; they prowl the roads at night, shaking down the peasants and looting the churches; fearsome beggars, drifters in the deadly twilight. And someone whispered to me: '*That's* the real army. There is no other. Now and then, you see handsome regiments in the cities, dancing and playing music, but the real army is made up of these poor bastards ... They don't even want to be soldiers ... They aren't happy, and they are rarely fed.' Someone else confessed to me: 'They have no weapons, no ammunition, no provisions in their arsenals and storehouses ... They sell it all, the Devil knows to whom ... They sell everything ... That's how it is here.' What is more, I have seen this with my own eyes, as you shall see."

* *

"... For a few weeks now, I have been staying with Prince Karaguine as his guest ... His castle is something to see. It is an endless array of towering monuments, grand courtyards, royal terraces, and spectacular gardens. Life here is busy, exciting, noisy and bustling, like a big city. The stables are large enough for one hundred horses, while the serving staff operates with military precision, as gaudily dressed as a crowd of extras in a play. The food here is exquisite, the wines are rare, the women are beautiful and think only of love. The grounds surrounding the castle consist of fields and forests, and cover an area as large as a small kingdom. We hunt every day, and I do not believe there are any hunting grounds in France, not even on the estates of our most decadent bankers, that overflow with as many imaginable kinds of prey. Every day is a massacre, an imitation of mass extinction, red mounds of slaughtered animals everywhere. Every evening, balls, comedies, delirious flirtations, moonlit parties in the parks and gardens lit with Chinese lanterns ... And yet, I feel sad, sad, terribly sad. The pleasures I get from this whirlwind of elegance and luxury never last; they clash so bitterly with that whirlwind of misery which is right there, only two feet away from us. In spite of the gaiety, the ex-

hilarations that distract me from my own thoughts so violently, I always feel like I hear someone beside me, weeping ... I
cannot chase away the endless guilt I feel here, guilt at getting drunk again and again on the suffering of an entire race
... Yesterday, during the hunt, three peasants were accidental-
ly killed: what is more, it was an everyday incident that no one
even cared about. They simply left them where they lay. While
an army of servants conscientiously collected all the dead
game, the tragic corpses of the three peasants were left sprawling on the moss, exactly where the hunters' bullets struck them
down. They will not receive a burial. 'What's the point?' the
prince said to me ... in answer to a question I thought it appropriate to ask him. 'Wolves will come and devour them tonight ... What better tomb for riffraff like that?' And the subject was never brought up again ..."

* *

"... The day I arrived at the castle, after crossing triumphant
courtyards and walking under porticos, through colonnades,
and around marble basins, I noticed, at the foot of the grand
staircase—actually a monumental series of staircases orna-
mented with statues of red porphyry and balustrades of mala-
chite—I noticed an ugly stall, slapped together from un-
even boards and covered with a makeshift roof of birch twigs.
Against the beauty of the castle's façade, that stall was like a
canker on the face of a lovely woman. Seeing my surprise, the
prince told me: 'My entire fortune comes from that stall ...
That's where I sell vodka to my peasants ... All the wheat, all
the potatoes from my land are brought here and made into
alcohol ...' Then, he cheerfully added: 'Yes, you've come to
a land of drunks ...! There are no bigger souses than my
peasants ... Some days, every man, woman and child on my
land is inebriated ... It's a funny thing, truly a funny thing
to see ... But then, what more can I ask ...? The more they
drink, the richer I become ...' Now, as landlords go, the prince

is considered extremely liberal ... No, honestly, he has done a great deal for the peasants ... He is even suspected in high places of being a revolutionary ... If that is the case, what can the others be like?"

* *

"... One day, we realized there wasn't a single bullet left in the whole castle; and it upset us even more when we remembered the big hunt planned for the following day. It was out of the question to send someone to the city to fetch gunpowder, because it was very far away and a violent storm had washed out the roads during the previous night. Everyone was gloomy unto death itself.

"'I have an idea,' said the prince. 'Let's go to the arsenal ... Perhaps we can buy some gunpowder there ...'

"'How?' I cried, slightly stunned. 'The arsenal sells gunpowder?'

"'Of course, my friend ... Gunpowder, rifles, cannon, anything you want.'

"The arsenal was a few kilometers from the castle. We walked there after lunch. The officer on duty greeted us very graciously. In answer to the prince's question:

"'I am deeply sorry!' he excused himself. 'Just this morning we sold the little bit we had left.'

"'What about grenades ...? Mortar shells ...?'

"'Cleaned out, Prince ... Completely cleaned out ...'

"'Oh, that's annoying!'

"The officer thought for a moment. 'I have an idea,' he said. 'The men might have a few rounds left in their knapsacks.'

"'Well, please check and see,' the prince beseeched ...

"The officer left. He came back in a few minutes, followed by a soldier carrying a sort of basket in which he had collected nearly a hundred cartridges ... 'This is all we have left,' said the officer. 'I'm very sorry ...'

"The prince asked, 'How much, sir?'

"'Ten rubles, Prince.'

"'Gracious me! That's a little steep.'

"'Hell!' simpered the officer. 'You get nothing for nothing, here ...' And turning to the soldier, he ordered, 'Take these cartridges to Prince Karaguine's castle.'

"On our way home, the prince confessed to me: 'Charming country, isn't it? My friend, you could buy up all the artillery of our little father the Czar ... You could easily take it all back to France with you ...'

"I smiled. 'I'm sure that would be very expensive.'

"And the prince replied phlegmatically, 'Depends on the time of day.'"

* *

"... Princess Karaguine is a passionate, graceful woman, with very beautiful, savage eyes, and a special feeling for animals. She spends much of her time in the stables with the stallions, caressing their supple backs and their glistening, shuddering coats. Six giant white mastiffs follow her everywhere, strong and growling, like tigers ... This morning, I watched her dismount from her horse, after returning from her customary ride. The second that she touched the ground, quickly lifting up the hem of her dress and tucking her riding whip under her arm, she kissed the stallion on his snorting lips. And since a trace of the animal's saliva remained on her lips from this kiss, she swallowed it with a lick of her tongue, sensually savoring the treat, as it were. And I thought I saw her gleaming eye catch fire with Pasiphaë's wild lusts ..."

This evening, I dined at the Casino, at Clara Fistula's invitation. Among the guests was a Russian actor named Lubelski. Naturally, we spoke of his country. And since I was still very much under the spell of my friend Ulric Barrier's letter, I thought I should ask an actual expert, so I told a thousand stories. M. Lubelski said nothing. From time to time, he nodded or shook his head at what I was saying. After dinner, since he was very drunk, he said the following in answer to a question which Clara Fistula asked him:

"I knew Emperor Alexander III very well. He was a great man, as far as you can ever compare any emperor to a man, I mean an ordinary man, like you and me and everyone else. Hell! I would never be so bold. When all is said and done, he was a great emperor, a true son of his people, and I am not at all displeased that your Republic has seen fit to name a bridge in France after him. I am certain that bridge must serve to connect one uncanny, enigmatic place with another. To claim that Emperor Alexander III was my friend would be presuming too much. The truth is, he did me the honor of his kindness and, in the best of times, bestowed his generosity upon me. He gave me, not a snuffbox, but a silver cigarette case, engraved with my monogram and inlaid with extremely rare gemstones, the kind you find in the mines of the North Pole . . . It isn't worth very much, and it isn't particularly beautiful. He also gave me—I swear—a tinderbox, made from an unknown metal that smells like gasoline; but I cannot get it to actually light anything. And yet, the beauty of these imperial gifts does not reside merely in how much or how little they cost, how much or how little they are worth, but in the *souvenir* itself, *n'est-ce pas*?

"In Russia, at that time—I mean six years ago—I occupied a similar position to the one which your 'Frédéric the Great' held so gloriously during the reign of Napoléon III; similar, albeit far inferior, for there is no one else in the world like Frédéric Febvre! To say it in plain speech—I was an actor. Emperor Alexander had a keen appreciation for my talent, which consisted of a sort of haughty elegance, combined with the finest in make-up, which stayed on even when I did my famous crying scenes. I was something of a Russian Lafont, if you will. The emperor tried never to miss any of the thousands of roles I played, and although he was never a demonstrative man, he actually deigned to clap for me when I was really good. He was a refined soul, and—I am not boasting when I say this—he appreciated my stirring performances without any need to resort to phony formalities, which, anyway, do not suit the Russian character. I cannot count the occasions when His Majesty summoned me to appear before him, and congratulated me with that uniquely icy enthusiasm, the mark of an absolute monarch, who must hold his emotions in check regarding so many things. Russia, you know, is not the Riviera, and there is no more sunshine in our souls than in our wolf-infested forests of snow-covered pines. But who cares? The emperor loved me to the point where, not content with applauding me in public, he also wanted to consult with me on important matters, but (it goes without saying) only those which touched upon my craft. As I already said, there is no one else in the world like Febvre! They put me in charge of staging plays at the Winter Palace and other imperial residences, wherever the emperor was giving a party at the moment. And my reputation grew to such an extent that M. Raoul Gunsbourg began to give me the evil eye, and slander me to your late Sarcey, predicting that it was only a matter of time before I, too, ventured out on a French-Russian tour of France.

"Still, I was happy then, rich and famous, with many friends who either were influential or had the reputation of being influential, which is often better than the real thing, and every night before I went to sleep, I prayed to the icons that my life would continue like that, provided I was able to curb my ambitions and never hope for more than what I already enjoyed—ah, what I already enjoyed so completely!"

Here, the speaker's voice became grave, his eyes became wistful, and after remaining silent for a few moments, he continued: "Since my parents were dead and I was a bachelor, I lived with my sister, an adorable fifteen-year-old girl, the joy of my heart and the light of my life. I loved her more than anything in the world! Who couldn't love that delightful little creature, so sprightly and pretty, devout and mild, impetuous and generous, whose lips were constantly ringing with laughter, and who responded to everything beautiful, everything noble? Inside that carefree girl's delicate cocoon beat a passionate, profound, and independent heart. Back home, it's not at all rare for eruptions of our particular, national form of heroism to bloom in such circumstances. In the suffocating silence which oppresses our land, in the vast network of secret police who keep it bound up in paranoia, genius sometimes chooses to seek shelter, to hide inside that sacred refuge which the heart of a child or a young girl always represents. My sister truly was one of the chosen ones. Only one thing made me uneasy about her: the extreme frankness of her speech and the independence of her rebellious spirit made it impossible for her to hold her tongue and be discreet around anyone, even those around whom you must keep your tongue absolutely silent and your soul completely closed. But I reassured myself that, at her age, no one would hold such small slips against her—without realizing that, in our country, there has never been any age limit on injustice and misery.

"One day, returning from Moscow where I had gone to give a few performances, I found the house empty. My two old servants were crying on a bench in the foyer.

"'Where is my sister?' I asked.

"'Alas!' said the one, since the other never spoke, 'they came . . . and took her and the nanny away . . . God have mercy on us!'

"'I think you've gone mad,' I cried, 'or else you're both drunk . . . or what . . . ? Do you even know what you're saying . . . ? Come on already, tell me where my sister is!'

"The old man lifted his sad, bearded face toward the ceiling. 'I told you,' he muttered. 'They came . . . and took her away . . . and only the Devil knows where . . . !'

"I think I fainted from grief. But I managed to catch myself against the doorjamb and, hanging there, I screamed, 'Why . . . ? Tell me why . . . ! Did they say anything . . . ? They couldn't have taken her away for no reason . . . Did they say why ...?'

"And the old man, shaking his head, replied, 'They didn't say a word ... not a single word ... They came like ghosts, out of nowhere ... And when they left, we could only beat our heads against the wall and weep ...'

"'But what about her?' I pressed. 'Didn't she say something ...? Tell me ... did she put up a fight ...? Did she threaten them with me, with my friend the emperor ...? Didn't she say *anything* ...?'

"'What would you have liked her to say, dear soul ...? What on earth could she have said? She clasped her hands together, as if kneeling to the icons ... And that was that. Now, you, and the two of us, who loved her more than life itself ... we will have to spend the rest of our lives weeping ... For no one ever comes back from the place where they took her ... Blessings to God and our father the Czar!'

"I realized I would not get anything but resignation from those broken, slavish brutes, so I dashed out to the street, seeking information. I was sent from bureaucratic office to bureaucratic office, from department to department, from information desk to information desk, and everywhere I ran up against the same stony faces, dead-bolted souls, padlocked eyes, like prison doors ... No one knew ... No one knew anything ... They could not tell me what happened ... Some of them urged me to speak in a whisper, to say nothing, to go home with a smile on my face ... In my distress, I decided to ask for an audience with the emperor ... He was kind, he loved me. I would throw myself at his feet, beg for his mercy ... Then again, who knows ...? If he himself had given the orders for this sinister crime to be carried out, he would probably ignore me—yes, he would certainly ignore me ...!

"I had a few friends who were officials, and I went to them, asking their advice, but they quickly talked me out of this plan. 'You mustn't say *anything* about it ... You mustn't say anything about it ... This happens to everyone—even us! We, too, have sisters, girlfriends, who were taken to that place ... You mustn't say anything about it . . .'

"To take my mind off my sorrow, they invited me to go out with them that evening . . . We would drink ourselves senseless with champagne, hurl waiters through windows . . . We would tear the clothes off young women . . . 'Come with us . . . Dear friend, come with us . . .'

"To my noble friends!

"It was not until two days later that I could get an appointment with the chief of police. I knew him well. He often did me the honor of visiting me at the theater, in my dressing room. He was a charming man; I admired his friendly manners and edifying conversation. As soon as I mentioned anything about my sister, he became visibly upset and said, 'Hush! Just forget about it . . . Some things you should—you must—forget.'

"And, abruptly changing the subject, he pried me for extremely intimate details about a certain French soprano, who had received a standing ovation at the Opera the night before, and whom he was smitten with.

"Finally, eight days after those terrible events—it felt like a century, I assure you . . . ah, yes, a century of anguish, mortal agony and unspeakable tortures where I thought I was going mad!—the theater gave a command performance. The emperor sent an officer from his retinue to summon me. He was like usual, he was like always: serious, somewhat melancholy, with his slightly weary regal bearing and his slightly icy kindliness. I don't know why, but in the presence of that colossus (was it out of respect, fear, or the sudden realization that he held the power of life and death in his very hands?), I could not bring myself to utter a word, not a single word, especially that simple word 'amnesty!' which, just until then, had swelled my chest with nameless hopes, had quivered in my throat and burned upon my lips. I was truly paralyzed, as if empty, as if dead . . .

"'My compliments, sir,' he said to me. 'You performed like M. Guitry tonight . . .' After which, holding out his hand for me to kiss it, he dismissed me with his thanks."

TWENTY-ONE DAYS OF A NEURASTHENIC

The speaker looked at his watch, and compared its time with
the clock ticking on the end table next to him. Then, he began
again: "I'm getting to the end. And it's about time, since these
memories are eating my heart alive ... Two years dragged by,
and still I knew nothing. I had not managed to uncover a single thing about the terrifying mystery that had suddenly swept
away what I loved most in the whole world. Every time I questioned some functionary, I could get nothing out of him except that blood-chilling 'Hush!' which they used everywhere to
stonewall my most urgent pleas, the instant I brought up the
event. All the favors I tried to call in only served to make my
burden of worries heavier, and to thicken the shadows that had
tragically darkened the life of the poor darling child for whom
I wept ... You are probably wondering how I could still go onstage and say my lines, how I could still take part in that life of
phony emotion which I had once lived for. But, as excruciating
as it had become for me now, I never once thought of giving it
up. Thanks to my profession, I was in daily contact with important people throughout the Empire, and perhaps I would
find one, some day, whom I could persuade to help me with
the devastating fate that had befallen me. That was enough to
keep me going—vague, distant hopes that flickered on and
off, at the corner of my eye, just out of reach. As for the emper-
or, he treated me with the same glacial, high-handed kindliness. Sometimes, when I looked at him, I sensed that he, too,
was the victim of some gnawing, unspeakable torment, which
he bore with noble, silent resolve. Gazing into his eyes, I could
feel ... ah, I could feel, as if he was my twin brother, that he
didn't know, he didn't know anything, he was kept in the dark
as much as anyone, and that all the infinite sadness of his people combined in his sadness, and death gnawed away at him,
dragging his strong regal bearing and his chronic melancholy
deeper and deeper into the same grave. And my heart was
wrenched with unbearable love for him ... So, why didn't I
dare scream it at the top of my lungs—the cry that might have
saved my sister ...? Why ...? Alas, I do not know!

"After days and nights of unfathomable suffering, unable to go on living that way and determined to risk everything, I went to see the chief of police. 'Listen,' I declared firmly. 'I'm not here to waste words ... I'm not asking you to pardon my sister, I'm not even asking you where she is ... I only want to know if she is alive or dead ...'

"The police chief yawned. 'This again? Why can't you stop thinking about this, my friend ... You are not being very reasonable, I'd say ... And you're making yourself feel bad for no reason ... Look ... ! This was all such a long time ago now ... Just make-believe she is dead ...'

"'That is exactly what I want to know,' I insisted. 'This doubt is killing me ... Is she dead, or is she still alive ...? Tell me ...'

"'You are unbelievable, my friend ... How many times must I tell you—I know nothing about it ... What makes you think I would know ...?'

"'Please, find out ... It's my right, after all ...'

"'You want to know?'

"'Yes, yes, yes, I want to know!' I screamed.

"'Well, so be it ... ! I will find out, I give you my word ...' And he added casually, while playing with a solid gold penholder: 'Just one thing: in the future, my friend, I recommend that you not make such reckless assumptions regarding what your rights are ...'

"Six months after this conversation, at the theater one evening, in my dressing room, while I was getting into costume to go onstage, a policeman handed me a sealed letter ... I tore it open feverishly. The letter bore neither a date nor a signature, and contained these words scrawled in red pencil: '*Your sister is alive, but her hair is completely white.*'

"I saw the walls of the dressing room, and the vanity lights and the mirror go spinning, spinning, then disappear completely ... And I collapsed, like dead weight, on the rug ..."

The speaker stood up. He was slightly paler, and hunched over like a cripple ... And he was swaying ... blind with sadness, or perhaps with champagne, because nothing causes you to drink like emotional pain.

"That was five years ago," he concluded. "Today, the poor little girl would be just twenty-three ... The emperor is dead ... And we have a new emperor ... And nothing has changed ..."

After which, having shook our hands, he took leave of us ...

We did not know what to do with the feelings that overflowed our hearts. The evening had ended on too sad a note, so old Plançon, a theater manager who had dined with us, decided to cheer us up a little by singing some old songs from his youth ... He was from the school of happy endings, and he never wanted the curtain to fall, in the theater as well as in life, on tragic climaxes ...

Poor old Plançon ...! While he sang in a quavering voice, with movements that reminded you of a skeleton trying to dance ... the Casino director told me the following story about him:

"One day, old Plançon was called over by his director. 'Sit down, old Plançon,' the director said with a solemn expression. 'And let's chat a little, eh?'

"Old Plançon was a small and gentle man, wizened, wrinkled as a prune, bald, baby-faced, whose oversized clothes billowed on his scrawny frame like a curtain blowing at an open window. He always seemed wretched and defeated, but he felt at home on the stage, where he achieved a sort of grotesque dignity, an ironic importance that became his only place and purpose in the world—turning his misery into a kind of bleak comedy. Since he never earned much money at the theater, he had been picking up extra work for years; in addition to the noble calling of bit player, he was also a wig-maker. At first, he seemed to be good at this, and to bring an unusual degree of integrity to the manipulation of fake hair. But unfortunately, time revealed his wigs as threadbare and shoddy, and he was forced to give it up.

"'It's disgusting,' he complained. 'You can only get black hair now—Jewish hair to boot . . . There's no blond hair on the market anymore . . . no pure French hair . . . And you know, black hair, dyed hair, and foreign hair simply do not make first-class wigs . . . They're not shiny . . . not soft . . . not anything . . . ! The ladies won't wear my wigs anymore, and I have to say I wouldn't wear them either . . . They can't even properly be called "wigs" . . .'

"The truth was that his hands had begun to shake; he could not even feel the hair with his numb fingertips. He ruined all his wigs, which came out looking like flattened rattails. So, he went to work as an insurance agent. But he wasn't very good at insuring things, poor old Plançon. And he was still miserable.

"Old Plançon sat immediately opposite his director, according to strict rules of staging. Posing with his upper body leaning forward, his legs tucked gracefully to one side, his right elbow slightly raised and his hand flat on his thigh, he asked, 'Am I placed right, Mr. Director? Am I within the tradition?'

"'Perfect,' the director approved.

"'Okay, Mr. Director, I am listening to you.'

"So the director spoke: 'Old Plançon, it is exactly forty-two years ago today that you made your home at the Dramatic Athenaeum Theater. That doesn't say much for your age, buddy . . . or mine for that matter, not to mention the theater's . . . But what can we do . . . ? That's life, right . . . ? You are a noble, wonderful man, it's true . . . ! You have always fulfilled your duties with honor . . . Everyone likes you here . . . Finally, you are a voice of conscience, my old Plançon . . . Am I right or am I right . . . ?'

"'I have worked, Mr. Director,' the humble fellow declared. And that simple line, 'I have worked,' attained extraordinary lyric resonance in his mouth.

"The director became more effusive. 'Ah, yes, and how you have worked . . . ! You don't have to convince me . . . When it comes to your signature line, 'Madame is served,' no one has ever been, nor will ever be, your equal ... That's clear ... All the critics agree ... Even when you had no speaking lines, when you were just carrying a tray, turning off a lamp, dusting an armchair, ushering the Viscount into the Marquise's bedchamber, it was scintillating ... it was brilliant ... it was perfection! A great artiste, my old Plançon, to put it plainly ... Modest roles perhaps ... but a great artiste nonetheless—yes, you are a great artiste ... No mistaking that ...'

"'Nature, Mr. Director ... I have studied raw nature,' explained the old bit player—who, his chest swelling with pride at the director's compliments, began to straighten his bowed back. And he added, 'Nature, and the tradition ... that is my secret.'

"'Yes, yes ... Ah, domestics like you—they just don't make them anymore ... The mold has been broken in the theater no less than in this world of ours. Just try to get a young actor to play a butler today ...! Ah, no mistaking it, yes ...! So, here is what I have decided ... Next month we shall give your farewell performance ... We shall announce it: *Glory and Fatherland*, your greatest role ... That pleases you, eh ...? Tickles your ego ...?'

"Old Plançon could not help but look disappointed. But the director ignored this. 'But of course ... of course ...' the director insisted. 'It's raw natural talent ... Goddamned old Plançon! When you open the salon door in Act Two and toss off your 'Madame Countess is served!' it's really riveting, you know ... You *are* a butler ... You become the role, that's the only way of saying it ... You - become - the role.' And the director hammered his fist against his chest, where his heart was.

"But in spite of these memories of past glories, old Plançon had sunk into deep despair. He had never thought the day would come when he would have to give up the theater, the way he had had to give up making wigs. And the thought of it knocked him flat, not only because he did not know where he would go now, but because the theater was his reality, his only life, and he saw no horizon beyond the the-ater, only shadows and death. Shattered by his director's words, but remembering to employ dramatic gestures appropriate to the situation, he stammered, 'So ... next month? Am I dream-ing ...? So soon ...?'

"'What do you mean "so soon" ...? After forty-two years of work, of solid, loyal service—you call that "so soon?" Look, look, my old Plançon ... you will get two hundred francs for this performance ... Two hundred francs ... Ah-ha! That's nice, isn't it ...? And then, afterwards, goodbye friends ... freedom, rest, the country ... You will go and plant your cab-bages.'

"And he went on, cheerfully, 'How can you have any doubts about it, goddamned old Plançon ...? And in *Glory and Fatherland*, yet ... That was your crowning moment ... To retire at the height of your crowning moment, with two hundred smackers ... And yet, he still doesn't look happy ...! What more do you want, for Christ's sake?'

"The director paced back and forth in the auditorium, wav-ing his arms and repeating, 'What more can I do for him ...? Not a goddamned thing, but there he is, stubborn to the bitter end ... Ah, these goddamned great artistes ...! They're all the same ...'

"After a dramatic pause, when he tried to get the lump out of his throat, old Plançon said in a soft, resigned voice, 'Well, so be it, Mr. Director ... Just one thing, though ... I am going to ask you for a favor, one tiny favor, which you cannot refuse me ... On the day of my farewell performance ... I would like, oh, well, I'm just going to come out and say it ... I would like to play the Young Viscount ...'

"The director jumped. 'You're crazy, completely crazy,' he cried. 'That's impossible ... The Young Viscount ...? That's a rotten part, a joke, not worthy of your talent ... Never ... Not in a million years would I do that to you ... I want you to leave your public with an unforgettable impression ... do you understand, old Plançon ...? I want them to say in fifty, one hundred, three hundred years, no one but old Plançon could deliver the line, "Madame Countess is served!" I will defend your glory against even you if I must . . . Oh, the curs, the curs, the filthy curs . . . ! You bring them foolproof success, certain acclaim, ten, fifteen, twenty curtain calls . . . and money beyond the going rate . . . And they'd rather go off on some half-baked, crackpot whim . . . The Young Viscount! No . . . ! No, it's completely idiotic . . .'

"'Mr. Director . . . !'

"'No . . .'

"'Mr. Director, hear me!' begged the old bit player now standing there before him with his arms outstretched in rhythmic beats. 'I appoint you arbiter of my fate, Mr. Director, I consign my professional honor to your hands . . . Hear me, in heaven's name . . . I must confess to you . . . The Young Viscount, for more than ten years I have studied this part, memorized it, lived with it in secret every night . . . This part is only ten lines . . . But it's meaty, and I will give it everything I've got, everything . . . ! Ah, if you would only say yes . . . ! This will be the crowning glory of my career. The public will at last see one of the hidden sides of my talent revealed . . . Mr. Director, let me play the Young Viscount . . .'

"'No . . . no . . . a thousand times no . . . ! Is that clear enough . . . ?'

"'Mr. Director, I am begging you . . . !'

"'No, I tell you . . . ! There's absolutely nothing you can say . . .'

"'Mr. Director—I am prepared to forgo my two hundred francs . . .'

"'Oh, fuck off, old Plançon . . . ! You've pissed me off for the last time . . . Go, get out, out of my sight . . . !' And the director stormed away.

"Old Plançon was more unhappy than he had ever been. Every day he went to the theater and paced up and down onstage and off; anxious, silent, almost Hamlet-like. When his colleagues spoke to him, he scarcely responded. And he

kept up a continuous soliloquy in his mind: 'The Young Viscount . . . ! I just can't believe it . . . For me to be denied such a
small part, which would have been so beautiful, something
that would have brought me glory and been a revelation for
the theatergoing public and for Sarcey . . . What can I do about
this scumbag, this rotten scumbag who has lined his pockets
with my talent, my years of dedication . . . ? Ah, now I'll never
get the chance . . . ! And no one will ever know what I had inside me, here, inside this skull of mine . . .'

"He convinced himself it was the work of a cabal, a conspiracy against him, and he eyed everyone around him suspi-
ciously, with a look in which he strove in vain to combine un-
restrained malevolence with self-righteous vengeance. The
poor, sad fellow.

"Finally, opening night arrived. Deep down inside, old
Plançon had hoped for a miracle. And it was with a tortured
heart and tears in his eyes that he watched the curtain slowly
and implacably rise on Act One of *Glory and Fatherland*.

"The mild-mannered old man did not go on until the end
of Act Two. Hearing his cue, he stepped onstage majestically,
wearing a white wig and black stockings, pushing open the
swinging doors with great dignity and entering the dining
room set, which sparkled with the glittering reflections of the
spotlights on the glasses and silverware. And he announced in
that solemn, quavering voice of his: 'Madame Countess is
served!'

"At that very moment, his dreams all dead, his ambitions
crushed, every bitter pill he had been made to swallow rose up
gurgling in his soul. In a single instant, as if overwhelmed by a
furious wind inside him, he decided to take a stand against his
entire résumé of insignificant, non-speaking roles—and finally
make himself seem eloquent, imposing, charismatic, transcendent. Scraps of dialogue, urgent replies, bewildered asides, anguished vibratos, prisons and palaces, catacombs, daggers and
arabesques all came flooding back into his memory, in a del-
uge, pell-mell, lashing and torrential, like tidal waves. He felt

the spirits of his theatrical brethren—Frédéric Lemaître, Mélingue, Dumaine, Mounet-Sully, Coquelin—leap forward and bellow in his soul. He was also very drunk, to the point where he did not know what he was doing and did not feel that he had anything to lose. Thus, straightening the stooped bow he had adopted for the old butler, throwing back his head where the white wig flapped like an avenging angel of felt, with his bosom heaving and panting, his left hand beating his breast, and his right hand outstretched like a trusty sword, he turned and thundered at the Invited Guests, his voice breaking with the emotion of revealing himself, at long last, a hero to the mob: 'Yes, Madame Countess is served ...! But first, General, let me tell you flat out ... Any man who insults a woman is ... a coward!'

"Then he stepped off stage to let the dismayed Invited Guests make their entrance.

"A roar of applause broke out in the theater. Moved by the sublime vitality of old Plançon's exit, they went into a frenzy, calling him back for a curtain call. But the curtain remained stubbornly lowered, in spite of the shouts, the stamping feet, the enthusiastic shouts of 'bravo' that went on and on, drowning out some of the entr'acte.

"As for old Plançon, his colleagues mobbed him and spat insults at him. 'What were you thinking, old Plançon?' said the High-Class Coquette. 'Have you lost your mind ...? Or are you having a stroke ...?'

"'No, Madame Marquise,' old Plançon replied, looking down his nose at her. 'And never speak to me again about your so-called honor ... Honor does not obey a double standard ... It is only for people who are worthy of it ...'

"Then, after raising his finger defiantly, accusingly, straight up toward the wings, he stalked away and disappeared among the shadows of the backstage clutter ..."

Meanwhile, old Plançon was still singing ...

XIV.

After my lunch, I went to the club. And I was completely absorbed in reading the paper when a man suddenly came bustling along and, noticing me, gave a loud cry of joy . . .

"Parsifal . . . !" I cried back. "My old friend Parsifal . . . !"

"So . . . I have to come all the way to this place just to see you again, eh . . . ?" He embraced me affectionately. Parsifal isn't really such a bastard, when all is said and done . . . "And you've thought about me all this time?" he said, cutting short his effusions. "Let's add it up . . . How long has it been . . . ?"

He was right: it had been five years since I last saw him . . .

"You know . . . you're looking much worse for wear, old buddy," he added, raining happy little mock punches on my shoulder. "Truly a shame . . ."

Parsifal hadn't changed much at all . . . hadn't grown up much, either. "What are you doing now . . . ?" I asked him.

"Jack of all trades," he replied. "Whatever comes my way . . . I take ads for newspapers . . . I sell champagne . . . I'm company secretary for a velodrome . . . and Poidatz is letting me in on that popular theater scheme of his . . . None of that pays very well . . . My best and steadiest job is the one I got through Rouvier . . . our old friend Rouvier . . . I just started last month . . . correcting the epitaphs for the cemeteries of the Seine valley . . . Yes, friend . . . Real ages, real occupations—I'm the guy who makes you tell the truth on your tombstone . . . ! But what more could you ask for . . . ? It pays six thousand per annum . . . Death always pays well . . ."

"So you've gotten out of politics once and for all?"

"I was forced to . . . I got caught . . . caught . . . you see . . . ! That's what frustrates me the most . . . And yet . . ."

Comically, he turned his pockets inside out, and intoned: "As Chénier said on his way to the gallows—*I had something, once . . .* !" He let out a long sigh . . . "Ah, I was unlucky . . ."

"And your wife?" I asked, after a brief silence.

Parsifal looked deeply disturbed, as though he wanted to run away, far away . . . "My wife?" he scoffed. "Well, she's dead, old buddy . . . two years now. Consumption did her in . . . not soon enough, alas, since I owe all my troubles to her . . . She never understood politics . . ."

Doubtless, these memories saddened him . . . He sat down beside me, picked up a newspaper . . . and became very quiet . . .

Meanwhile, I thought about the past . . . Parsifal's past . . . and the heroic Parsifal of former times flashed before my eyes . . . For instance, that November morning when he came knocking on my door, white as a ghost, defeated, begging me to save his life . . . In those days he was the deputy of the North-North-west region . . . I greeted him amiably, as always, if not without a certain cynical smile, since his bouts of anxiety had become a familiar routine. "Another scandal, I bet," I said.

"What else," replied Parsifal, "would have me running over here at this ungodly hour?" "Let's have it, then! Go on, speak."

We never stood on ceremony with each other, though he was not, properly speaking, a friend of mine. No. He was something much worse. He had been willed to me by Gambetta through circumstances which I will explain; and you must understand, any legacy from Gambetta is a prized possession for me — by god!

When he was on his deathbed, Gambetta summoned me, and here is what he told me, in a voice that still carried as far as the grandstands, the last grandstand: "I am leaving Parsifal to you . . . Parsifal is not a dog, as you might think . . . He is a person, a deputy in my gang . . . He represents my political interests in the North-Northwest . . . I am telling you this because there is a lot you do not know about my current affairs, hah . . . !"

The illustrious statesman did not elaborate . . . I could feel his end was near . . . After a few seconds' pause, he began again, with a less pronounced southern accent, for death makes all voices sound the same. "I am leaving Parsifal to you ... Even though he's a big thug—like most of my friends were, alas ... All the same, deep down ... he's not really such a bastard ... Watch over him ... you will make me happy ... Besides, his wife is someone who ... someone who ..."

But the poor great man, unfortunately, died mid-sentence ...

What was he trying to tell me ...? For the life of me, I still don't know ... Anyway, when I went to claim my legacy, I immediately saw for myself that this Parsifal really was a big thug, and that his wife was ugly, bossy, always spoiling for a fight— hardly the kind of woman whose dying lover would whisper in your ear that she was *someone who ... someone who* ... No, she had nothing, nothing of those dreamy dangling charms that could make you fantasize about flings and frisks and naughty dalliances with men who ... men who ... Oh, I don't even want to picture it!

Still, according to the great man's dying wishes, I watched over Parsifal, and, on five separate occasions, thanks to certain relations, let us say of the carnal variety, which I was having with a senior magistrate's maid (a very dirty little maid!), I was luckily able to snatch Parsifal from the clutches of justice, each time right at the very moment when that intrepid legislator from the North-Northwest was about to be convicted for crimes as nefarious as they were various—even more nefarious, as it turned out, for they all carried a sentence of ten years in prison. Once I even rescued him from life in a penal colony: ah, I had to put in a lot of hard work for that one! My skillful behind-the-scenes maneuverings, invisibly guided by the great man's ghost, not only saw that Parsifal won back his political office each time, but that his power grew year by year, until the day when Parsifal, convinced he no longer needed my protection anymore and could "fly," after a manner of speech, on his own, promptly became persona non grata ...

When I asked Parsifal what the coup de grâce had been, he

said to me: "Well, those numbskulls are starting up again, you know ...? Arton's squealing again ... He talks too much ... He's even talking about me now ... The biggest problem is the 47,500 francs which that son of a bitch placed right in my hands, in two consecutive, equal payments ..."

"Yes, I'd say that is a big problem ..."

"How calmly you take the news of me getting shafted ... These self-righteous gossips get away with murder ... Don't you realize the mess this puts me in at home?"

"Your home life isn't what matters here," I said naively. "It's what the whole country will think of you—that's what's worrisome ..."

"Ah, the country ...! The country can go fuck itself," Parsifal said, and he did have a point there. "My wife is another matter ... My wife is not some meaningless entity, some abstraction, like the state ... And the shame, the scenes, the gossip ...? I feel like it will never end ..."

"But your wife," I argued, "can't be too much of a problem ... What can she say, after all ...? How could she blame you for a bribe which she herself benefited from, with expensive dresses, lavish furnishings, and the easier life that an unexpected windfall of 47,500 francs represents in a household like hers ...? She's as guilty as you are ..."

"You don't know anything, my poor friend. And you talk like an economist ... My wife hasn't seen a single sou ... Do you honestly think I'd be dumb enough to give my wife ... 47,500 francs ...? Have you seen her ...? I haven't given my wife a damn thing ... I spent all that money on women a good deal less dried-up than my wife ... And that's what she blames me for ... That's why she's so angry at me ..."

"So you actually admitted to pocketing that 47,500?"

"Hell ...! There's damning evidence ... I kept receipts, for one thing ... Everything will come out sooner or later."

"You're not seeing the bigger picture ... First of all, what makes you think anyone will believe Arton ..? No one's interested in yesterday's news, no one cares ... Secondly, what

makes you so sure Arton will really come forward? And finally,
you who are so smart, and who have never been caught in a lie
... why the hell did you admit it? Always deny—deny the evidence, deny the proof ... That gives you the benefit of the
doubt in people's minds, no matter what the evidence! Ah,
Parsifal ...! Parsifal ...! I'm disappointed in you ..."

"You're right ... But what could I do ...? No man can
think straight when a woman's screaming at him ... That's the
truth ...! Congresses, courtrooms—I've bent them all to my
will ... With the whole nation watching, with the law breathing down my neck, I've wriggled my way out of much stickier
situations ... But a woman—my wife ... Do you know what
I mean ...?"

"So ...?"

"So, after I admitted it, I played dumb, understand ...?
I told her I donated the whole amount to the poor, the striking
workers, that subscription to build a monument to Floquet ...
That didn't work, because Floquet wasn't even dead at the time,
and because he ... Ah, well, poor Floquet ...! And then
I told her I never could have lived with myself if I had brought
into my very proper, very respectable home that tainted money of my shame, of my bartered conscience, my dishonor ...
Anything before that ...! Ah, if you had seen the face my
wife made ... No, truly, the way women can see through lofty
sentiments ... it's terrifying, old buddy ... My wife seethed
with rage ... She screamed: 'Con artist! Thief! You took 47,500
francs ... you crook ... you traitor ... you spy ... and me, I
didn't see one centime of it ... no, not a single centime ...!
47,500 francs ... and I didn't get any of it ...! And I've been
cutting back on my hats, my dresses, the candles, the heat,
the butcher's ...! I turned down so many invitations ...!
I didn't go to the Elysées once ... or the Opera gala ... nowhere ...! I just sat here among my worn-out furniture like
some dumb animal, left in the corner ... Ah, the crook ...!
The crook ...! The rotten crook ... To think that for five years
now I've wanted an English parlor ... and he knew it, that

dirty rotten crook . . . ! And he couldn't bring himself to pay for it with the 47,500 francs he took . . . ! Ah, it's unbelievable . . . ! Well, it's prison for you, crook . . . it's the penal colony, convict . . . Yes, yes, the penal colony, do you hear me? And I'm the one who is going to send you to the penal colony!' So, you see, this is what happened . . . The mirrors, the figurines, the china, the framed portrait of Félix Faure, the bust of the Republic, the photograph of the Czar, and the ones of Méline and Madame Adam—everything's gone . . . The whole house looked like it had been ransacked . . . Fortunately, none of it was very valuable . . ." And, doing an about-face, he added in a wryly cheerful tone, "Nothing worth 47,500 francs, anyway! Hah!"

Parsifal's nature is so perverse that he wore a sweet, open smile while telling me about this tragedy, for in the end, he isn't really such a bastard. Gambetta had been right all along. "And that's not all!" he went on, puffing himself up and searching my eyes for a sign of approval. "Those 47,500 francs are all going to pay off my fines and, whatever's left is going to my wife, to keep her from finding out about all the other bribes I took, against my better judgment . . . I mean, what would happen if my wife ever learns that, during the fifteen years I've held office, I have taken . . . yes, old buddy . . . I have taken 259,000 francs . . . ? And Italy, Turkey, Russia, England, Bulgaria, Romania, the independent sovereignty of Monaco, etc., etc., have all made staggering monthly payments to me . . . and with all that money changing hands, not a centime . . . no, I swear to you . . . not even a two-sou bunch of violets . . . went to my wife . . . Do you think she'll just laugh that off . . . ? And why would I have brought a single centime into that house when I spent so little time there . . . when I ate there barely twice a week . . . when I didn't even entertain my friends there . . . ? Is that fair, I ask you?"

"And now what are you going to do . . . ? Get a divorce?"

"I can't . . . she won't give me one . . . And that's what makes my situation so complicated . . . My wife is furious . . . she hates me . . . yes . . . but deep down, she still loves me . . . She

loves me even more than she did before ... She said: 'Once a
crook, always a crook ... It's up to me to keep an eye on the
old glad-hander, to make sure he brings it all home to me.' Her
unstoppable anger, her threats, it's all window-dressing ...
Whenever she's done with her little charade, she'll just change
the dressing, that's all ... holding out her purse to be filled up."

"Well, then, nothing is lost ..."

"On the contrary, everything is lost ... My whole life is
over ... If I am ever offered 47,500 francs again, I will have to
share it with my wife ... Ah, no, never in a million years ...!
I'd rather take no bribes at all ..."

I did not know what to say to him, his situation seemed
hopeless. "Have lunch with me," I proposed. "Perhaps we will
come up with a plan over dessert."

And, with a divinely inspired finger, I pointed out to him
the portrait of Gambetta smiling down at us from the wall,
that handsome man who ... that handsome man who ...

Parsifal let the newspaper fall onto his knees, and I realized that
he, too, had been reliving the same memories that I was, because he said to me, with a sort of long sigh: "Ah, yes ...! In
spite of everything ... those were the good old days ..."

No, Parsifal is not really such a bastard ...

We left together and took a short stroll through the Casino
garden. All at once, in one of the lanes, I noticed an old man
chatting with a busboy from the restaurant. I recognized Jean-
Jules-Joseph Lagoffin ... and I started to shake all over as if I
had come down with sudden fever. "Let's get out of here," I
said to Parsifal. "Let's get out of here quickly ..."

"What is it?" he asked, not understanding why I had become so afraid. "Is Arton here?"

"Let's get out of here ..."

And I quickly dragged him to another lane, one which I
knew had a kind of exit ... into the open countryside ...

Parsifal's curiosity was piqued; he insisted on knowing what

had thrown me into such a panic ... I refused to tell him ...
but you will understand everything, dear readers, when I tell
you the story of Jean-Jules-Joseph Lagoffin ... Here it is:

Having suffered substantial losses in a business venture that
was, unfortunately, far less stable, though no more illegal, than
the Panama syndicate, the Southern railroad scam, and other
recent financial crises, I was eventually reduced to the point of
trying to squeeze blood, as they say, from a stone. I sold off
some of my houses and cut my staff of seven servants to as few
as was strictly necessary—a valet and a cook—which ended
up being less of a savings than I had thought, since those two
intrepid domestics immediately set about stealing from me, between them, as much as all five of the ones I had dismissed, put
together! I sold my horses and carriages, my art collection and
my Persian clayware, a portion of my wine cellar (alas!) and my
three greenhouses stocked with magnificent exotic plants.
Finally, I decided to rent out a little house, a charming little
house, separate from the main house where I lived, but on the
same grounds, furnished by me especially for illicit and expensive rendezvous, which I'd also had to forgo. With its isolated
spot inside the garden as well as its cozy amenities, that house
would have been extremely convenient for any pleasure-tripper
of either sex who wanted to break away from the celibate life
for the summer, or conceal an adulterous fling.

Lured by the strategically worded ads I had placed in certain adult magazines (and no doubt by the network of under-
ground word-of-mouth), many people—all foreigners, as it
turned out, and unusually ugly—made their way to see me.
Again and again I gave them my speech about the beauty and
the security of this retreat—its outside covered with virgin
vines, so that they could break as many rules as they wanted on
the inside (wink, wink) and live there exactly like a couple of
leaves on the vine, if not at all like virgins. But they were all so
picky about demanding the craziest renovations—they wanted the wine cellar in the attic instead of the basement, top was

bottom and no end was up — I could never close the deal with any of them. I despaired of ever renting the house — for it was nearly summer already — when, one afternoon, a short gentleman, his face shaved to the point of rawness, his back ramrodstraight, very polite, and well advanced in years, appeared at my door, his hat in his hand. His clothes were archaic and did not fit him very well; he wore a long watch chain that jangled with esoteric charms, and a moldy blond wig whose old-fashioned shape recalled the vilest, most despotic chapter of our Orléanist history.

This short gentleman found everything perfect ... perfect ...! He went into one ecstasy after another, complimenting everything so much that I was truly at a loss as to how to respond to him. When we got to the bathroom, and he saw all the erotic paintings adorning the wooden panels (wooden panels alternated with mirrored panels), his head was turned so fast that his wig had to do a little jump to stay on top of him — and nearly did not make it. And he said only, "Ah! Ah!"

"It's Fragonard," I explained, unsure whether his "Ah! Ah!" was meant as a shocked reproach or a sigh of pleasure. But I soon found out.

"Ah! Ah!" he repeated. "Fragonard ...? Really ...? Perfect!"

And I watched his tiny eyes make a strange, wincing squint, as if he were overcome by a physical reaction he could not conceal. After a brief silence, which he spent in detailed examination of the artwork, he said, "Well ... that settles it ... I am taking this perfect little house."

"And perfectly discreet," I added in a chummy, suggestive tone, and without needing to say another word, I pointed out, through the open window, the roof-high, matted, impenetrable curtain of vines surrounding us on all sides.

"Yes ... perfectly discreet!"

Seeing the submissive, seemingly half-wit eagerness of this prospective tenant, I felt it was practically my duty — using various improvised reasons, and without any objection from him — to raise the already exorbitant rent I had mentioned in the ads by a few hundred francs. But none of this really matters now, and if I bring it up at all, it's only to pay my respects to the perfect manners of that short gentleman, who flattered me, moreover, stating that he was "delighted" by my treatment of him.

We went into my house, where I quickly drew up an impromptu lease for him. Since we were both about to sign, I asked him his name and occupation. That was when I learned that he was Jean-Jules-Joseph Lagoffin, former notary of Montrouge. I further asked him, as a way of dotting the i's and crossing the t's on our agreement, to tell me whether he was married, widowed or single. He did not answer; instead, he piled several stacks of banknotes on the table in front of me, obliging me, without further ado, to relieve him of his money and my questions. "Evidently," I thought to myself, "he's married . . . but doesn't want to admit it, because of . . . Fragonard."

Then, I looked at him more closely. I looked at his eyes, which might have expressed happiness, if anything, or something like it. But they expressed nothing, in fact they seemed, at that moment, dead—dead as the surrounding skin of his brow and cheeks, slack, wrinkled, and solid gray, and which seemed to have been simmered over a low flame in boiling water, like overcooked meat.

After politely agreeing to toast our deal with a glass of orangeade, Jean-Jules-Joseph Lagoffin departed, with many thanks, blessings and good wishes, and letting me know he would move into the little house the very next day—if this wouldn't disturb me—and start living there at once. He asked for a key, and I gave him one.

But he didn't show up the next day, or the next day after that. One week, then two, went by—I heard nothing from him. It was odd, but I guessed there was some reason, after all. Perhaps he had come down with the flu. But surely he would have sent me a note, his precise standing on ceremony ensured that. Perhaps the roommate he planned to move with—perhaps she changed her mind at the last moment? This seemed more plausible to me, since I didn't doubt for a second that Jean-Jules-Jospeh Lagoffin had rented this nice, discreet pavillion for any other purpose except to be alone with some woman, the way he squinted at the dazzling sight of the Fragonards and the heaving movement of his wig presenting clear signs, to me, of his lustful intentions. I decided I didn't need to worry unduly over whether he would or would not come; after all, I had already been paid, and generously paid, paid beyond my wildest hopes.

One morning, I was airing out the rooms of the little house, which had been closed up ever since the day Jean-Jules-Joseph Lagoffin signed the lease. I went through the foyer, the dining room, and the living room, and as I opened the door of the study, I screamed in horror and jumped back.

On the floor, a nude body, the corpse of a little girl, lay in the middle of the room, alarmingly stiff, her arms and legs twisted, as if she had been tortured.

Yelling for help, yelling for my servants, yelling for anyone and everyone—that was the first thing I did, when suddenly, the initial shock worn off, I thought it would be better to start by examining things for myself, all alone, without witnesses. I even took the precaution of locking the front door again, with a triple lock.

It was, indeed, a little girl, barely twelve, with the skinny body of a young boy. She had red fingerprints around her throat, from being strangled; on her chest and stomach there were long, straight, deep slash marks, made by fingernails, or rather, razor-sharp claws. Her swollen face had turned completely black. On a chair, a few rags, a worn-out little dress, frayed and mud-splattered, and a tattered pair of underwear, were arranged almost ritualistically. And on the marble floor of the bathroom, I saw a serving tray with a smear of leftover pâté, two green apples (one of them gnawed by a mouse), and an empty bottle of champagne.

I inspected the other rooms one by one, but nothing had been touched in any of them. Every piece of furniture, every single thing was in its customary place.

Then, quickly, feverishly, my thoughts came in a jumble ...
"Call the police, the law ...? Never ... Investigators will come,
and I won't have any concrete information to give them ...
Turn in Jean-Jules-Joseph Lagoffin ...? Obviously, that man
did not give his real name, and I don't have to go all the way to
Montrouge to find out he never lived there ... What, then ...?
They'll never believe me ... They'll take it as a personal affront
... They'd never believe that some man carried out this horrible crime, only a few feet away from my home, inside a dwelling belonging to me, and I saw nothing, heard nothing ...
Give me a break ...! You simply cannot place faith in the law
at a time like this ... They'll get suspicious, and interrogate me
with the long, hungry looks of hyenas, and I'll end up falling
helplessly into the trap of their sleazy, leading questions ...
They'll dig up my entire life, every aspect of my life ... Fragonard himself will be used against me, Fragonard will scream
volumes about the brazen risks taken in my private life and the
inevitable guilt that attaches itself to the kind of pleasures I
pursue ... They'll want to know the names of everyone who
ever came here, everyone who might have come here, everyone
who never even set foot here ... And all the filthy stories told
by the maids I tried to seduce, that gardener I sacked, that baker I confronted about his thumb on the scale, that butcher
whose tainted meat I took back ... and everyone else who'll
come crawling out of the woodwork, huddling under the
judge's robes and sullying me with the mud of their revenge
and their grudges ... And finally, one fine day, they'll use my
uncertainty, my blushing testimony, my fear of scandal as the
very confession of guilt they need, to lock me up and throw
away the key ... Oh, no ... no detectives ... no magistrates
... no police here ...! Never ... Just a little dirt to cover this
poor little body, a little moss on top of the dirt, and silence, silence ... silence drowning out everything!

I took the frayed, mud-splattered dress, the tattered underwear, and used them like a shroud to wrap up the body of that

nameless little girl ... Then, after double checking that the whole house was hermetically sealed, off limits to my servants snooping around or stumbling onto anything, I left. For the rest of the day I walked around and around the house, waiting for nightfall.

That evening, there was a feast in town. I told my servants to go and have fun, and when I was alone, all by myself, I set about burying the little girl in the garden, six feet under the roots of a beech tree ...

Yes, yes, yes! Silence, silence, silence, covering everything ...!

Two months later, in Monceau Park, I ran into Jean-Jules-Joseph Lagoffin again. He still had the same slack skin, the same dead eyes, the same moldy blond wig. He was following a little flower girl, selling sunflowers to passersby. Near me, a cop waddled along, ogling a maid ... But the stupid look on his face made me turn around and slip away ... I sensed that, once I opened my mouth, unavoidable complications would arise ... but what ...? What were they ...?

"Who cares? Let them come digging!" I said to myself ... "They won't have anything on me ..."

And I fled from the cop, from Jean-Jules-Joseph Lagoffin and the little sunflower girl ... whom someone else might bury in his garden, under a beech tree, some night ...

We arrived at the door of the hotel in total silence, Parsifal and I. Parsifal had forgotten about my sudden fear ... He was preoccupied ... Without doubt he was preoccupied with the past, because, when he left me, he shook my hand and said, "Yes ... yes ... old buddy ... how true it is ... those were the good old days."

XV.

I have recurring dreams.

I'm in a train station, catching a train. The train stands there, growling right in front of me. Friends of mine, my traveling companions, leap aboard the cars so easily ... But I cannot move ... They call to me ... I cannot move; my feet are nailed to the ground. Train conductors rush past me, jostling and urging me: "All aboard! All aboard!" I cannot move ... Meanwhile, the train starts up, departs, disappears. Round windows, tires, manhole covers all laugh at my impotence; an electric clock mocks me. Another train arrives, then another ... Ten, twenty, fifty, one hundred trains appear just for me, open their doors to me one after the next ... I cannot move ... They go away, one after the next, and I have not even been able to reach the steps, the handle of the door. And there I am for eternity, nailed to the ground, paralyzed, seething, surrounded by crowds who come and go at will, weighing me down with a thousand mocking grins.

Or else I am hunting ... As I walk through the heather and alfalfa, young partridges flap up noisily into the air at every step ... I aim my rifle ... I shoot ... my rifle does not fire ... my rifle never fires ... I squeeze the trigger until my hand is shaking. Nothing happens ... It does not fire ... Again and again rabbits stop in their tracks and stare at me, wonderingly ... Even the partridges stop mid-flight, as if frozen in time, and stare at me, wonderingly ... I shoot ... I shoot ... My rifle does not fire; it never fires.

Or else I am standing at the bottom of a stairway ... This stairway is in front of my own house ... I am needed inside, I must go in. There are five flights of stairs. I lift one leg, then the other ... but I cannot climb ... I am held back by an un-stoppable force, and in spite of making the most violent efforts, I cannot even reach the first step ... I trudge, I trudge, I wear myself out with futile climbing motions. My legs kick at the air, one after the other, dizzyingly fast ... And I never get anywhere ... Sweat bathes my whole body ... I cannot breathe ... And I never get anywhere ... Then, I suddenly wake up, my heart pounding, my chest tight, fever racing through my veins where the nightmare still throbs ... and throbs.

Well, X is like one of those nightmares for me ... I made up my mind to leave at least twenty times, and I have not been able to. Some kind of demon has possessed me, so to speak, and his iron will buries me deeper and deeper in this loathsome place; he has me bound and chained ... The extinction of my personality is so complete that I feel incapable of making the slightest effort to snap my suitcase shut, jump onto the bus, and from the bus onto the train that would finally rescue me and take me out to the open plains ... the open plains, those wonderful plains where everything is alive and in motion: the grass, the trees, the vast wavy lines of the horizon; the little hamlets and the larger, more sprawling towns surrounded by greenery; the roads turning golden in the sun, and the gentle rivers that are not like the scary rapids here, always grumbling and wheezing ...

Here, the sky lays over me like lead, weighs upon my skull so heavily I feel the timeless, inexorable cosmic weight as a real physical burden ... As far as I can see, I have not found better health at X, by bathing in its waters and inhaling its sulphuric vapors, but instead, the utter false advertising of its hoax-like springs, and I have been thoroughly invaded and conquered by neurasthenia ... One by one I surrender to all the symptoms of nervous depression and mental collapse. Every face, every memory ceases to be a refuge, a distraction, an end to the ennui that devours me alive. I cannot work anymore. I cannot concentrate on a single book. Rabelais, Montagne, La Bruyère, Pascal ... and Tacitus, and Spinoza, and Diderot, and all the others ... whose sacred books I have lugged here with me and not even opened ... Not once have I asked their brilliance to comfort me and help me forget where I am ... Meanwhile, Triceps gets on my nerves with his manic agitation and his stories ... And every day, all day long, some people go and still others arrive ... And the same wan faces keep coming back, the same dead faces, the same lost souls and the same tics, the same alpenstocks, the same cameras and binoculars fixed on the same bloated clouds, behind which all those people eagerly wait to see the famous mountains whose "terrifying splendor" Baedeker describes, but which are never visible—it would truly be a wonderful irony if they did not actually exist, in spite of the fact that the false advertising of the hotel owners, guides and railroad companies has led entire generations to stream before this geographic conspiracy ... I'd love it if I turned out to be right about this! But unfortunately, it cannot be the case that so many incompetent Administrations could pull that off ...

Since this place is supposed to be so sweet and soothing to a sick person, full of bright, enthralling, ethereal things, bathed in silvery light, under big sun-swept skies as whimsical as they are infinite, skies where pleasant clouds drift, glide, disperse, and come together again like pleasant thoughts endlessly crossing the bright, whimsical, infinite sky of a tranquil mind ... Being sick—it cuts you off from any kind of happiness!—in a region like this, scorned by the Baedeker, a stranger among all the tourists, mountain climbers, and amateur strategists ... a region where there is nothing but (oh heaven on earth) scenic landmarks ...!

Scenic landmarks: is there anything more hair-raising, more promising of torture ...? Scenic landmarks, where you see the actual physical shape—whether formed into glacial crystallizations or ponderous stalactites—of the endless, repetitive, nonstop drivel of everyone who visits them. Consider this: once, in Douarnenez there was an old oak tree and, next to the old oak, an old, ruined, dried-up well ... In Douarnenez there also happened to be a breathtaking sea and an amazing natural light, even through the fogs that were tinted delightfully pink, or gold, or gray above the sea ... But no one ever went there to

look at the sea, since the sea was not a classic and highly recommended scenic landmark at Douarnenez ... Everyone
trooped in worshipful processions to the old oak and the old
well ... They said to each other: "Have you seen the amazing
scenic landmark at Douarnenez yet? Have you seen it ...?"
And of course, painters immortalized it: more than twenty
thousand sat down a few meters away from that old oak and
implacably painted it ... It was also seen in souvenir shops, reproduced on stones, on nacreous seashells, on bottles ... It
died, choking on its own glory, sick of hearing the same inani-
ties from everyone's mouth for fifty years ... At least oak trees
have the good taste to die ... Why not mountains?

It is only at evening time, in my room at the hotel, that I
begin to feel a little bit alive again, for the thin partition walls
come to life in the evening ... They talk ... They have voices,
human voices ... and these voices, suddenly resonant, speak to
me of passions, obsessions, secret lives, everything that matters
to me and makes me recognize the human soul ... Not man
standing in front of an invisible, sneaky mountain, but man
standing in front of himself ... The walls quiver with all the
humanity they shelter, which is somehow filtered to me,
stripped of its lies, its poses ... Precious hours which distract
me from my sadness, from my loneliness, and which wash me
all over again in that vast, fraternal absurdity of life ...!

It's ten o'clock. The gypsies have stopped scraping their
maudlin violins. Slowly the hotel dining room empties. They
turn down the lights, and the glow, now more yellow, suffus-
es the pattern of poppies on the modern-style wallpaper. Everyone goes back to his or her room. Ah, the pathetic cigaril-
los and colorful eye shadow of the elegant ladies of Toulouse,
Bordeaux or Leipzig! They walk in single file as at a funeral. If
their digestion has been morose and joyless, the night promises to be suffocating and loveless. They trudge to their beds to
sleep the way someone else would stay up with insomnia—
gloomily. In places like this, sleep has the airless, black weight
of mountains. For there is a mountain everywhere you look.

The mountain is inside your locked and shuttered room; the mountain is inside you, its shadowy mass fills your dreams ... And what stunted freaks will be conceived tonight inside the cramped wombs of this tourist race, dragging its terminal apathy from void to chaos?

In the hallways, exotic scents waft by, helping you discern, far more than the languages they speak, the nationalities of the women who come and go. The mountain climbers plod back to earth, back to their rooms, their doors click shut and lock, the floorboards creak, the buzzers for the servants bluster. Eventually, everyone settles in. And from floor to ceiling, the walls of my small cave start to whisper.

My neighbors on the right arrived only yesterday evening, and I have not seen them yet. By their cloying, sing-song accent, you can tell immediately they are from Geneva. To come all the way from Geneva and end up here is only trading the Alps for the Pyrenees ... I have no doubt they are husband and wife, they sound so hostile and ugly when they speak to each other. Their voices are no longer young; still, they are not old either. Forty-five-year-old voices, approximately, who have talked to each other every day now for so many years that everything they say comes out sounding harsh and unpleasant. They are as discordant as any real voices, unguarded voices that do not think they are being heard by anyone who matters. What absolute rancor in those voices!

At first I can not hear what they are saying, because there is still too much background noise throughout the hotel, a sort of dissonant buzz making the wall-voices less clear, less pronounced. My neighbors' room sounds like only a quiet droning, even a purring, continuous and inarticulate, accompanying the rustle of soft footsteps, suitcases being opened and closed, and God knows what porcelain figurine being shattered. Then, a few words stand out and register more distinctly in my ear. The wife is talking, talking, talking, as if she were telling a story, a grim one. She talks ... and talks ... and talks. From the tumult of her sentences (most of which escape me), her breathlessness, and the curses that slip out now and then, followed by abrupt stops—it must be a disturbing story. I feel as if I have heard this same tone of voice before, reading out loud from a police report. The Geneva accent drops out of its cadence, its drawling beat. Sour notes begin to creep in, modifying her lost sonority into a series of yelps. Bitterness freezes her words, anger makes them hiss. It is no longer a Geneva accent, but Everyman's. And her voice seems to sharpen, shoot, pinpoint and poke through the cracks in the partition directly to my ear.

I listen avidly. And I learn that this woman is furious with her chambermaid. From what I can make out of the tirade, which accelerates, huffing and puffing through the mad flight of her words, a terrible, unimaginable thing has happened to this lady: her maid was not there when she returned to her room to dress for dinner. She had to ask everyone, and no one knew where the maid was. She didn't come back until seven-thirty . . . ! And I hear words like "that *girl*," "that dirty slut!" and "that miserable bitch!" uttered in such a tone of disgust that you would not think they referred to a human being at all but a filthy animal, a pox, or a pile of excrement. And the voice says, as if responding to an objection I did not hear: "That's not true . . . I told her to be here at six. And even if it did slip my mind to tell her, isn't it her job to be here around the clock, every hour of the day and night, to wait on me? I don't understand how you could defend her, and that you can't see how insulting she's being . . . It's shameful . . . But then again, you . . ."

My neighbors have obviously moved to a more distant corner of their room, because I can no longer make out anything but confused things, murky, fuzzy. Finally, after a moment or two: "I agree . . . I agree . . ." says the voice of the husband, who seems to come back closer to the partition.

"Well, then," replies the wife's voice, "why did you say that? You implied I didn't know what I was talking about . . ."

I hear someone stomping the whole length of the wall, then getting further away . . . Then the husband's voice, but so muffled now it is only a sort of monotonous, drawn-out rattle, something like: *er-er-er-er-er* . . .

To which the wife answers in a voice that pierces the air like the noise of someone tearing up a bed sheet: "No, no, I can't stand it anymore . . . I don't want that slut in my house anymore, I don't want that filthy bitch in my home anymore. I'm throwing her out. She won't be here in the morning. When I think how I've been forced to mend . . . *I myself,* do you understand . . . my own garters! It's a form of torture . . ."

The husband's voice drifts away again, and at the same time I hear the sound of someone winding a watch: "*Er-er-er-er-er.*"

"What . . . ? What did you say . . . ? I think you've gone crazy . . ."

Though my ear is pressed against the wall, I cannot hear his response. Nonetheless, the ingratiating quaver in his voice tells me he is pleading to keep the maid. "*Er-er-er-er-er!*"

"No, no, a thousand times no . . ." the wife yelps. "She's going, tomorrow morning."

"*Er-er-er-er* . . ."

"What about her ticket? You're going to pay for her ticket? Don't even dream of it . . ."

"*Er-er-er-er* . . ."

"She'll find somewhere else to go. I'll just tell her she's fired . . . for the mistake she made, the very serious mistake . . . A girl like that will find lots of places she can go."

"*Er-er-er-er-er* . . ."

"Are you crazy? I don't want any excuses. I won't hear any excuses . . ."

"*Er-er-er-er-er* . . ."

"I'd like to see you try it!"

"*Er-er-er-er-er* . . ."

"Leave me alone . . . ! Shut up . . . ! Get into bed . . . !"

Now, a silence . . . and soon the sound of movement . . . silk garments falling . . . glasses clinking . . . decanters being drained . . . objects picked up and set down again on the marble bathroom sink.

But after a few minutes, in response to a new "er-er-er"
from her husband, the wife says, even more harshly, "Don't
waste your breath ... She's the worst thing in the world ... I
could be ill—do you think she'd be there to help me, morning
and night, waiting at the door? Huh?"

"*Er-er-er-er ...*"

"Sure ... Oh yes, sure ...!"

"*Er-er-er.*"

"And first off, I can't even believe you're sticking up for her.
How can you stick up for her?"

"*Er-er-er?*"

"Oh, you ... Use your brain for once!"

"*Er-er-er ... er-er?*"

"Yes, you ...! You bet your life on it ...! I've known all
about it for a long time now ... Well, you won't be able to do
those dirty little things to each other anymore ... At least, not
in my house ..."

"*Er-er-er.*"

"Leave me alone ... Don't say another word to me ... Get
out of those clothes ..."

"*Er-er!*"

"Damn! Shit!"

Another silence ... But the husband sounds as if he has
lapsed into a state of furious agitation ... He paces up and
down the room, moaning ...

Suddenly, the wife's voice: "Well, thanks a lot ...! It smells
like you haven't washed your feet in a week ... How lucky I
am, sharing my bed with a guy like you ...!"

"*Er-er-er ...*"

"No, I said, leave me alone ...!"

"*Er-er-er ...*"

"Leave me alone ...!"

Then, more pacing ... a chair pushed back, the bed squeak-
ing ... and silence ... a silence sadder than anything I've ever
heard.

Then, after a few minutes of this silence ... the wife's voice, less harsh ... more playful ... "No ... let go ... Not tonight ... you don't deserve it tonight ... Oh, your hands ... Stop ...!"

Then, muffled cries ... smooching kisses ... lip-smacking kisses ... panting ... him, then her ... then both of them panting together ... And the wife's voice, acquiescent now, very acquiescent, "Darling ... Oh, yes ...! Like that ...! Oh, God ...!"

Then, after a few more seconds, almost a scream ... and these words of desperate gratefulness: "My big daddy ... my big daddy ... my big daddy!"

XVI.

This morning, coming from my bath, I ran into Triceps, walking with a rather nervous, sickly-looking gentleman . . . He approached me. "Permit me to introduce you to Monsieur Jules Rouffat . . . one of my best patients, arrived here yesterday evening, on orders from my friend Dr. Huchard . . . This gentleman you see before you just got out of prison, where he spent the past seven years . . . by mistake . . . ! Yes, old boy . . . That certainly didn't do any wonders for him . . . Hell . . . !"

M. Rouffat smiled shyly. "And you . . . that surely must interest you, as a defender of people's rights? That is sort of your specialty, is it not . . ?"

I shook hands with Triceps' patient, and we exchanged a few basic pleasantries. In spite of his shyness and his nervousness, I noticed that M. Rouffat seemed to look down on everything around him, as if he thought himself superior to everyone else . . . Now that he was free, it was clear that it did not particularly bother him, having formerly been in prison. On the contrary, he seemed to be proud of it and to derive his identity from it. While bathers came and went all around us, M. Rouffat said, in a fussy, mannered drawl, making sure everyone heard him: "Yes, sir, I am the victim of a judiciary error. And I lived—*lived?*—inside prison walls for seven years . . . ! It is beyond comprehension . . ."

Then Triceps asked me, "Are you going back to the hotel?"

"Yes . . ."

"Well, let's go together . . . M. Rouffat will tell you his story . . . It's shocking, old boy . . . A readymade subject for an article . . ."

At the hotel, I ordered us a round of port and sandwiches . . . And after these light refreshments, M. Rouffat began: "One morning, while I was taking my customary stroll on Three Straws Road, I noticed, not without surprise, a group of peasants on the embankment, a few hundred meters away. Among them, a police officer was trying to keep them all back, and three gentlemen, dressed in black frock coats and very formal top hats, were waving their arms in the air. All of the people gathered around, craning their necks, leaning their heads toward something which I could not see. A carriage, a sort of hansom cab—quite an antique, the kind you only see in the sticks!—was parked on the road, facing the group. This unusual gathering piqued my interest, for normally the road was deserted, and you only saw wagons there, now and then, and ghostly cyclists. I chose that spot for my walks precisely because it was so isolated, and also because it was bordered by ancient elms, which, as hard as it is to believe, still grew there freely and were spared being hacked down thanks to public-works schemes. The closer I got to it, the more I could see the little mob pulsing in its frenzy. The driver of the carriage was in a tète-à-tète with the police officer.

"'No doubt some local land dispute,' I said to myself, 'or even an interrupted duel, perhaps?' And I approached the group, inwardly excited by the hope that the latter hypothesis would prove correct.

"I had been living in the village of Three Straws for only a brief time, and I had not met anyone there, being very shy by nature, and shunning, on principle, all social interaction, where I have never found anything but deception and despair. Apart from the walk I took every morning, I stayed shut in my house all day long, reading books I loved, or keeping myself busy by tilling the beds of my modest garden, which sheltered me from the neighbors' prying eyes with its high walls and its thick curtain of trees. Not only was I not popular in that area—to tell the truth, I was an absolute stranger there, to everyone but the mailman, with whom I was forced to maintain ongoing relations because he often needed me to sign for things, and also because he could not do his job without making endless mistakes. All of this background is only by way of explaining my story, please understand, and certainly not for the foolish vanity of talking about myself, or to stupidly praise myself for being this or that kind of person—merciful heavens, no!

"Thus, I approached that group in the same quiet, cautious manner that I have always performed even the most insignificant acts in my life; and, without being noticed by any of them—so extreme was my discretion and, I daresay, my stealth at mingling with them in my typical fashion—I made my way right into the middle of these strangers on the embankment, all looking at who knows what . . . And a terrifying sight, such as I had never imagined, presented itself to me . . . A dead body was stretched out in the grass, the body of a homeless man judging by the squalid rags which he used for clothes; his whole skull was nothing but a scarlet pulp, so squashed and mushy it resembled a strawberry pie. The grass was trampled, flattened down, in the spot where the corpse rested; along the slope of the embankment, bits of crimson brains quivered like thistle-buds.

"'Oh, my god!' I screamed. And so as not to fall into a faint—since I felt sure I would—I had to gather up the little strength I had left, and cling desperately to the police officer's sleeve.

"I am a sensitive man, and I cannot stand the sight of blood. My veins immediately drain of blood, my head spins, spins and buzzes; my ears hum as if they had flies trapped inside them; my weak legs buckle, and I see a million stars dancing around me, a million gnats with horns of flame; it is rare when these sieges do not end in fainting. When I was young, I did not even need to see blood, I only had to think about it, and I fainted dead away. The idea alone—no, not even the sight—the idea alone of a mutilating injury or a painful operation caused all my blood to suddenly freeze, a black-out, total loss of consciousness. Even today, I still faint whenever I think about a mysterious bird that was served to me in a restaurant one evening, the flesh disgusting and rotten.

"Standing before that corpse, it took a stiffening of my will,

a violent concentration of all my energy, not to faint completely. But I did turn very white; my temples, my hands and my
feet were glazed with the chill of death; and a heavy sweat
poured over my whole body. I wanted to get away from there.

"'Excuse me . . . ?' one of the men in black coats said to me,
clapping his hand rudely on my shoulder. 'Who are you?'

"I told him my name.

"'Where do you live?'

"'In Three Straws.'

"'And why did you come here . . . ? What are you doing
here?'

"'I was walking down the road, as I do every day . . . I saw a
group of people on the embankment . . . I wanted to know
why. But this is too much for me . . . I'm going home.'

"He pointed to the corpse. 'Do you know this man?'

"'Not at all,' I stammered. 'How would I know him . . . ?
I don't know anyone here . . . I've only lived here a short
time . . .'

"The man in black fixed me with a sidelong gaze, a blinding
gaze like a flash of lightning . . . 'You *don't* know this man?
And yet, you turned pale when you saw him . . . ? You nearly
fainted . . . ? And you think that's normal?'

"'I did . . . but it's not my fault . . . I can't stand to see blood,
or a dead body . . . I faint at anything and everything . . . It's a
purely physiological reaction . . .'

"The man in black snickered, and said, 'I've heard everything . . . Science, now . . . ! I never thought anyone would try
to use *that* as a defense . . . This case is open and shut . . . You
yourself have furnished the proof . . .'

"Then, he issued an order to the officer. 'Arrest this man . . .'

"To no avail, I tried to stammer a few protests, to wit: 'But
I am a good man, a sensitive man . . . I have never harmed anyone . . . I faint for no reason . . . no reason at all . . . I'm innocent . . .'

"My words went unheard. The man in black was staring
down at the corpse with a meaningful, vengeful look, and the

police officer, to get me to be quiet, punched the back of my head several times.

"Indeed, my case was open and shut. From that moment on, it was handled very quickly. Throughout the two months of the investigation, I could never explain to anyone's satisfaction my paleness and my disturbance at seeing the corpse. All the reasons I gave, it seemed, ran counter to the most fundamental theories of criminology. Far from helping me, they added new proofs to 'the dossier' of prior, hard, irrefutable evidence which they had about my crime ... My denials were used by the press and the court psychologists to show how hardened and unrepentant I was. They depicted me as craven, amoral, deranged and maladjusted; they said I was a common murderer and absolutely undeserving of sympathy. They clamored for my head every day.

"On the witness stand, the entire village of Three Straws testified against me. Each one spoke of my sleazy demeanor, my anti-socialness, my furtive morning walks, obviously a cover for all the crimes I must have committed with such well-concealed savagery. The mailman stated that I received numerous mysterious letters, unsavory-looking books, suspicious packages. A gasp of horror rippled through the judges' bench and the audience when the President himself announced that they had seized the following books from my home: *Crime and Punishment*, *Crime and Madness* ... the works of Goncourt, Flaubert, Zola, Tolstoy. But all of this would have been nothing, immaterial, circumstantial shreds, flimsy accusations, were it not for that grand confession: my fainting.

My fainting confessed to such unspeakable crimes, it confessed so loudly, that not even my attorney wanted to plead my innocence. He pleaded insanity, involuntary manslaughter; he swore that I was afflicted with every kind of dementia, that I was a mystic, a sex fiend, a sadist, a would-be writer. In a sublime piece of oratory, he adjured the judges not to sentence me to death, and he begged them — with a touching show of tears, very touching compassionate tears! — he begged them to lock up my dangerous mind forever in some nameless padded dungeon, and throw away the key!

"Everyone burst into applause when I was sentenced to death . . . But as it happened, the President decided to commute my sentence from the gallows to life in prison . . . And I would still be in that prison right now if the real killer, driven by remorse, had not publicly confessed his guilt and my innocence, just last year . . ."

Silent now, M. Rouffat gazed into the mirror admiringly . . . "Yes, indeed," he seemed to say to himself, "I am a very noble martyr . . . And such unusual events do not happen to most people . . ." Then, in a chastened tone but nonetheless expansive, he told us all about his seven years of torture.

I shed many tears for him. And, hoping to comfort him by linking his misfortunes with the misfortunes of all the unlucky victims of the justice system, I said, "Alas, sir . . . ! You are not the only one who has been attacked by a society that is founded on blindness, if not an outright principle of victimization . . . Poor Dreyfus has also had this terrifying experience . . ."

At that name, "Dreyfus," M. Rouffat's eyes gleamed with intense hatred. "Dreyfus!" he said harshly. "That's not the same thing at all . . ."

"Why not?"

"Because, sir, Dreyfus is a traitor . . . and because it is disgusting, and supremely criminal, that that animal has not had his throat cut, for the honor of justice, church and fatherland, as the final mercy of his so-called 'torture' . . . !"

Triceps shook with laughter in his armchair. "Ah, see!" he cried. "I told you so!"

M. Rouffat stood up. He glared at me with hostility, nearly the kind of look that duels are fought over . . . And he left, issuing the following statement: "Long live the army! Kill the Jews . . . !"

For a few moments after M. Rouffat left, we stared at each other, dumbfounded, Triceps and I.

"There goes a real scumbag ...!" I cried, unable to control any longer the indignation boiling up inside me ...

"No," said Triceps, "he's just crazy ... I'm certainly not pro-Dreyfus, and I have the right not to be ... because it makes my clientele more comfortable ... you see ...? But him ...? I'm telling you he's crazy ..."

And he started in on his favorite theme, insanity ... piling up observation after observation, case history after case history ... Here is one of the stories which Triceps told me, in order to demonstrate that M. Rouffat was insane, that I myself was insane, that everyone in the world was insane ...

"Jean Loqueteux, tired after walking for a long time, sat on an embankment by the side of the road, his head in the shade of a spreading elm, his feet in a ditch that was still cool and damp from a recent rain-shower. At that moment, the sun was beating hard on the drying road, and the heat was stifling. Jean Loqueteux unshouldered his knapsack, which was full of stones, and he counted these stones, setting them out in a row beside him in the grass. Then he put them back with solemnity and pride, and said, 'The count is good ... I still have my ten million ... but it's very strange ... I've been giving them away to so many people—because I'm not a mean rich man, not a miser ...! And yet I'm not missing a single one ... Ten million ... It's all there ...!'

"He hefted the knapsack, mopped his forehead, and groaned, 'How heavy it is, this ten million ... Both of my shoulders are sore, and cut, and my back is breaking ... If I still had my wife, she would help me, of course ...! But she is dead, she died from being too rich ... And my son, too, is dead, I don't know why ... I have to carry this burden all alone ... It's too much ... I should have a little cart that I could pull ... or that a dog could pull ... My God! How tired I am ...! There's no doubt that millionaires are miserable bastards sometimes ... and they weep, yes, they weep ... Oh, Lord Jesus, how they weep ...! So I, for my part, have ten million ... This is a fact, I can feel its weight inside my knapsack

... Oh, well! Just keep going, down the road ... like a vaga-bond ... Do not even try to understand ...'

"In the coolness of the damp grass he rubbed his bare feet, swollen from walking ... 'It's true!' he began again. 'There are times when I would rather be a poor man, like all the ones I met along the road ... a poor begging bastard ... without a sou to my name ... living from the charity of passersby ... My word—yes ...!'

"Jean Loqueteux was nearly naked, because his clothing was all in rags ... No, not even rags—shit-smeared strips, unrav-eled threads, held together by grime. His skin showed, beet-red and chapped, through the holes, the tatters of his coat. He had bits of straw, bits of wool, bits of feathers in his beard, which resembled the profusion of a sparrow's nest.

"Rummaging in his pocket, he took out a bread crust, as hard and black as a lump of coal, and chewed it slowly, thoughtfully. Between his teeth, the bread sounded like peb-bles being crunched.

"From time to time, he stopped eating and spoke, his mouth full, his gums bleeding: 'See ... I don't understand any-thing ... I have ten million ... It's right there, always in reach; I can draw on it whenever I want ... And I'd be a real idiot not to draw on it, since it replenishes itself as fast as I spend it ... Even when it's gone, it's still there, it's always there ... I've giv-en away vast sums to poor people on the road ... to lit-tle marching soldiers ... to old men weeping on their door-steps ... to pretty girls walking the docks and singing ... I hurl them to the four corners of the earth and sky ... I can never get rid of them ... Oh, well, all the same, I can never get any other bread than what I'm eating now, either ... True, it's not very good. It smells like outhouses and sewers ... It smells like shit ... I don't know what it smells like ... Even hogs wouldn't go near it ... It's something I just can't explain ... a misunder-standing that makes no sense at all ...'

"He shook his head and squeezed his knapsack, and, be-tween two chomps of his teeth, he went on: 'The bottom line

is, I've got ten million, that's a fact . . . There it is . . . I'm squeezing it in my hand . . . Being so rich . . . and not even being able
to eat when I'm hungry . . . ! That's very strange . . . Not having
a bed to sleep in anymore . . . inside a house, sheltered from the
sun and the cold . . . and always scorned by other men, and bit-
ten by dogs, whenever I even walk past a house . . . That, too, is
strange . . . I can hardly believe it . . . And yet it's true! The
world is not as it seems.'

"Having finished eating, he stretched out on the edge of the
ditch, his knapsack tucked between his legs, and he slept a
deep, peaceful sleep.

"That day, Jean Loqueteux was picked up by the local police patrolling the road where he slept, dreaming, no doubt, of
a fabulous palace and lavish tables laden with meats and fresh
bread. And since he had no identification papers, and since his
rambling speech indicated that he did not seem to realize he
was homeless, the police labeled him a drunk, judged him to
be dangerous, perhaps a killer, most certainly an arsonist, and
finally took him into town and tossed him unceremoniously
into a holding cell. After undergoing a series of interrogations,
and detailed inquiries about his past history, he was carted off
to prison, where he fell ill, and from there to a hospital, where
he nearly died. His health revived, the examining doctor asked
him a few standard questions, and thereby determined that the
poor bastard was completely deranged. The doctor immediately committed him to an insane asylum. Jean Loqueteux remained unassuming and polite; he tried to exonerate himself as
best he could, by talking about his ten million, humbly and
cautiously, and offering to pay a vast sum as a charitable contribution. They did not listen, and even shut him up with a good
deal more roughness than he deserved, and then, one morning,
the iron doors of the asylum clanged shut on him.

"In his new life as a lunatic—an official lunatic, that is—
Jean Loqueteux revealed himself to be endlessly kind, coopera-
tive, agreeable, and sensible. From the beginning he was
housed in a minimum security ward, and after two years of ob-

servation during which he did not once display any violent tendencies, they left him more or less to his own devices. They turned him into a sort of domestic, and made him do all the menial work. Sometimes they even sent him out to run errands, where he could have escaped or misbehaved at any time, and he handled himself beautifully, always with intelligence and good judgment—and he always returned to the asylum.

"In the early years of his incarceration, he often talked about his ten million, as if it were a well-established fact, taking people aside and making certain promises. Whenever he saw one of his wretched fellow inmates, or whenever he heard anyone at all complain about anything, he would say: 'Do not weep . . . Be brave . . . On the day I leave here, I will get my ten million, and I will give you one . . .'

"Just like that, he had given out one hundred or more . . . But after a while this mania of his diminished more and more, and finally disappeared altogether, to the point where he no longer snapped up the bait which the director of the asylum and I dangled before him. If the director slyly introduced the subject of money (the source of the mania), Jean Loquet-eux only smiled and shrugged, as if to say: 'Yes, I was insane once . . . I believed that ten million was real . . . Now I know it was really just pebbles.' Several years passed by, in which he did not once claim to be a millionaire.

"Everyone thought he was cured, and eventually we wondered if we might as well release him. He himself had often harped on precisely this possibility, seized by nostalgia for the open road, the barns where he used to sleep, the twilight, the grassy embankments where weariness overtook him, beneath the magic canopy of starry skies. But I still had my doubts.

"One morning I paid a visit to Jean Loqueteux, for a final test. The director assisted me, more solemn than usual, and a few asylum attendants were on hand. 'Jean Loqueteux,' I said, 'I am going to sign your exeat . . . But before I do, I have a few questions to ask you. Try to answer them as best you can . . .'

"Sometimes lunatics display uncanny powers of perception.

Jean Loqueteux noticed a certain resistance in my eyes, he sensed that all those people were gathered there to ambush him . . . Then he had an idea. 'Doctor,' he said to me, 'I wish to speak with you alone, for a moment . . .' And, when the others had gone away, he began again, 'Doctor, I must leave this place, and I feel that you do not want me to . . . Well, when I leave . . . mark my words . . . I will give you one million . . .'

"'Really . . . ?'

"'I swear to you, doctor . . . And if one million is not enough . . . well, then, I will give you two . . . !'

"'Where are they, your millions, my poor Loqueteux . . . ?'

"'They are safe, doctor, in a place I have marked . . . at the foot of a tree, beneath a large rock . . . And they must have multiplied a great deal in all this time . . . ! But hush now . . . ! Mr. Director is coming back . . . He will hear us . . .'

"And, that same evening, M. Loqueteux went back to the ward, and groaned to his comrades, 'I am too rich . . . They hold it against me. I am too rich . . .'"

Triceps stopped himself. "Sapristi . . . ! I forgot the patient I was supposed to see . . ."

He got up, turned around, put on his hat, and said, with a laugh like the ringing of an alarm clock, "Oh, well . . . ! They're always sedated, at least, at this time of day . . ."

Parodying the voice and gestures of M. Rouffat, he cried, "Long live the army! Kill the Jews!" Then he left in a dither.

XVII.

For the past few days, everyone has been talking about the Marquis de Portpierre. The baths have received a ton of publicity from his name alone ... The Marquis wins huge amounts of money at baccarat, poker, pigeon shooting ... His auto draws a crowd every time he takes it out ... Finally, his life of parties and high fashion is an endless source of thrills ... Clara Fistula tells me they are letting him stay at the hotel for free, and carrying him at the Casino.

"Such a big name ... just think!" he explains to me. "What a great political and social opportunity ...! And he's a good egg, too, if you can believe it ...! Not arrogant at all ..."

People also say that he has come to X in order to be close to Spain, where he is engaged in frequent and crucial diplomatic talks with Monsieur the Duke Philippe Robert d'Orléans, the monarchist pretender to the throne of France, now in Spanish exile ... And they are even buzzing about the imminent arrival of Monsieur Arthur Meyer, companion to the Marquis, and unofficial paymaster of his stock portfolio and his pleasures ...

Here is what I know about the Marquis de Portpierre ...

One Sunday morning I arrived at Norfleur, with a friend. Norfleur is a town in Normandy, the definition of "picturesque" — indeed, it has preserved its ancient character nearly intact. Built in a crescent at the bottom of the pretty Trille valley, and looking slightly down upon the vast, fevered prairies whose ever-green expanses roll out toward the west, Norfleur is itself looked down upon, to the east and north, by forest-covered hillsides which rise and fall in a series of gentle undulations. In Norfleur, you can still admire the ruins of a very old abbey—a long series of crumbling Gothic archways held in place by eons of ivy—and a beautiful, mostly unrestored church from the 15th century. The verdant Trille loosely girds the town with the breezy shivers of its trees (it is bordered all around by poplars) and the muted mirrors of its streams and lakes ... I saw the whole place again this morning, exactly as I had seen it some twenty years ago, the same narrow, dirty streets, the same houses with their peaked gables made of slate, only slightly more aged, only slightly more run-down, collapsing at the same, infinitely slow pace ... and even the very same people slumbering away, just as before, covered in the very same grime ... Norfleur has not made the slightest concession to the spirit of progress that has gradually rendered the surrounding cities and market towns unrecognizable ... With the exception of one gasping sawmill (left idle, anyway, for most of the year), no trace of industry has come to disturb the taciturn and monotonous existence of its stubborn, hard-working, independent farmers.

Nonetheless, on this day of all days, a throng of peasants, dressed in their Sunday clothes, had assembled on the square in front of the town hall, to hear mass and, afterwards, discuss their petty business deals. The crowd was more restless than usual, and more audible in its buzzing, for Norfleur was in the throes of election fever ... Merely by the passions they incited, and the financial interests they promoted or thwarted, the annual elections gave the town the fleeting illusion of motion and life. The walls were plastered with blue, yellow, red, and green posters, and here and there, clusters of townsfolk gathered around them, their chins jutting out and their eyes bulging wide, stymied into silence with their hands folded behind their backs, afraid of saying a single word or making a single gesture to betray any sort of opinion or preference ... In one corner of the square, some of the peasants waited for buyers, crouching behind baskets piled with plucked, scrawny hens, or sitting in front of little produce stalls full of vegetables wilting quickly under the blazing sun ... Meanwhile, hucksters pushed wheelbarrows loaded with unidentifiable odds and ends, prehistoric notions ...

My friend, who accompanied me, pointed out one of the

TWENTY-ONE DAYS OF A NEURASTHENIC

candidates holding forth, gesticulating, in the middle of the biggest, most animated crowd: it was the Marquis de Portpierre, a major landowner, famous throughout all of Normandy for his lavish lifestyle, and, in Paris, for the impeccable correctness of his livery, and his carriages. A member of the Jockey Club; well-known for training horses, dogs and young girls equally; a crack shot with pigeons; notorious anti-semite and militant royalist—he was, according to the society pages, the cream of French society . . .

Great was my surprise to see him dressed in a long blue smock and wearing a rabbit-skin cap on his head. Someone explained to me that this was what he always wore during elections, because it made him look like a holy man without having to profess an actual faith . . . In fact, he resembled a horse trader more than anything . . . and everything about his looks suggested he would not be out of place as one; for that matter, his physiognomy—leering and ruddy-cheeked, a beady-eyed jughead—suggested that he came from common peasant stock, rather than any vaunted "aristocratic pedigree" (as the columnists are wont to say).

I studied him closely. No one could have been sharper and more shrewd when it came to business deals, or more expert at palming off a broken-down nag or a sick cow; no one could have guzzled more liters of wine on market day, or been more well-versed in all the con-artist tricks of the carnival fairground . . . As I got up close to him, I heard him shout, while people laughed, "Of course . . . we all know . . . the government doesn't listen to the people. But you and I are going to take it back—that's my solution . . . Ah, yes, for the glory of God . . . ! My children . . ."

He was truly at ease in his peasant smock, and affected a boisterous friendliness, a kind of disheveled good nature, a wonderfully avuncular chumminess, laughing here, becoming indignant there . . . and always striking just the right note, lavishing lots of little love-taps with the side of his fist, lots of little familiarities, patting people on the shoulders and rubbing their tummies, making the rounds of the square again and again, pouring out tons of amusing stories all the way to the Hope Café, where he poured out tons of something else into the shot glasses ... And, the whole time, he dramatically brandished a thick Normandy club, made of knotty dogwood and tied into his right fist with a strong, black leather strap ... "Ah! For the glory of God ...!"

I must add that Norfleur was where the Marquis de Portpierre made his home—in fact, he considered it his fiefdom—and where his mischievous spirit, his flair for driving hard bargains, and his skill at winning people over, earned him enormous popularity. He had so thoroughly conquered that region through his brand of earthy directness (which also included the occasional unkind word) that no one would have ever thought to be shocked by the abrupt, moody changes which characterized the Marquis' day-to-day life—that is, during the months of the year when he was not running for election. On the contrary, everyone liked him, and always said, "Oh, he's a good egg, that Monsieur the Marquis. And you see, he's not too arrogant ...! And he's *good* to the farmers!"

No one was surprised, either, or at least not anymore, that he had kept up the tradition of certain privileges and honors set aside for great lords in olden days, such as, for example, this one ... Every Sunday, after mass, the verger took up his post at the door of the little chapel "reserved for the castle," and, when the Marquis left, followed by his family and his coachmen in full uniform, the verger, looking like he had stepped out of a painting with his feathered hat and red silk cape, preceded the Marquis at a solemn distance, clearing a path all the way to his coach, knocking over chairs and people, rapping the flagstones of the church with his gold-handled cane ... and screaming, "Let's go ...! Make way ... make way for Monsieur the Marquis ...!"

And everyone was happy, the Marquis, the verger, and the crowd ... "Ah, you'd have to search the whole world over to find another Marquis like that one ..."

They were also happy with his castle, whose white stone façade and high slate roof cast a shadow over the entire town,
from the hillside between the undulating beech trees; happy
with his automobile, which sometimes, on the roads, ran over
dogs, sheep, children, and baby calves—*splat*; happy with the
walls that surrounded his private gardens, and which were
studded with the broken ends of bottles; happy with his watch-
men who, on three occasions, opened fire on people hiding in
the bushes, killing despicable poachers before they could get
their hands on any more rabbits and hares. And I believe the
peasants would have been even happier if Monsieur the Marquis had deigned to bring back *all* the lovely aristocratic customs of yesteryear, such as, for example, beatings. But Monsieur the Marquis did not deign to do that ... He was too
moderne for that ... and then, let's face it, he was sometimes
heard to worry about his legal troubles, even though he was a
Marquis. In sum, the most honest man in the world, who
came by his popularity honestly ...

Peasants are generally known as shrewd and cunning; political
candidates, very often, as stupid. People have written novels,
farces, even sociological treatises about this, all of which con-
firm these two fundamental truths. Now, it happens that some
of these stupid candidates always manage to swindle the
shrewd peasants in the end. They have an infallible method for
doing this, which requires no intelligence, no preparatory research, no personal magnetism, nothing that you might expect
from even the most lowly menial worker or the most senile civil servant. This method can be summed up in two words: *make
promises* ... In order to win, a candidate need do nothing more
than exploit—and ruthlessly exploit—the most persistent,
stubborn, dogged mania of mankind: hope. Through hope, he
can evoke and control the things that matter most in people's
lives: their passions, vices, financial interests. Indeed, you could
pose the following axiom as an iron law: "That candidate is always elected, who, during a given election campaign, utters the

greatest number of promises *and* issues the greatest number of opinions—even, to some extent, opinions which he actually holds—no matter that these opinions, and the extent to which he holds them, are diametrically opposed to the voters' better interests." The form of surgery known as "pulling teeth"— demonstrated daily on the public squares, with less finesse, it's true, and certainly less rhetoric—goes by other names in the political arena: the constituents call it "voicing our will," and the politician, "listening to the will of the people . . ." And the newspaper writers use even more hallowed, burnished, glowing names for this same process . . . And such are the amazing workings of the political machine in all "democratic societies" that for several thousand years now, the will of the people has been continuously voiced yet never heard, while the machinery itself turns and turns without the tiniest crack in their gears, or the slightest pause in their smooth operation. Everyone is happy, and things appear to run smoothly.

What is most amazing about the workings of universal suffrage is this: because the people believe themselves to be sovereign, not subject to the authority of any masters above them, you can promise them benefits they will never enjoy, and you never have to keep promises which, anyway, are beyond your power to deliver. In a perfect world, you might think it would be better to never make such promises in the first place, since it violates the democratic and supremely human rights belonging inalienably (or so we are told) to these poor voters, who spend their entire lives chasing after these promises the way gamblers chase windfalls or lovers chase heartbreak. But we are all like that, whether we vote or not . . . When we get something we want, we lose the euphoria that comes from desiring it . . . And we love nothing so much as the dream itself, the eternal, vain aspiration toward a nirvana that we rationally know is unattainable.

Therefore, the essential thing in any election is to promise the world, to promise far and wide, promise more than any of the other candidates do. The more impossible these promises are to deliver, and the more profoundly they speak to what the voters really need, the more effective they will be. The peasant wants nothing more than to cast his vote—which is to say, to surrender his power of choice, his freedom, and his life savings into the hands of the first moron or the first crook who comes along—and again and again he demands only that the promises he is given, in exchange for these things, are worthy of all the pain that he suffers. What he gets from those promises is, finally, the ultimate certainty that he is destined to be swindled, a duped pawn on the chessboard of life.

"What does the little peasant really want?" a deputy said to me once, when we were discussing the subject of elections. "He wants promises, that's all. He wants them to be grandiose, unreasonable, and at the same time clear-cut and bold ... He doesn't care if you keep these promises, his well-documented greed does not think that far ahead; all he needs is to hear you make them. He is overjoyed if they have something to do with his cow, his acre of land, or his house. And as long as he can rehash it endlessly, in the evening or on Sundays, standing outside the church or in a bar, as something which might arrive or might never arrive—that's enough to satisfy him. Then, you can crush him with taxes, double his burden ... All the while, grinning his sneaky little grin at each new tax, each new administrative nuisance, he says to himself: 'It's all right ... It's all right ... I'll keep going ... My deputy will soon put an end to these underhanded dealings ... He *promised*!'"

This reminds me of a funny pre-election contretemps that happened once to the Marquis de Portpierre ...

A certain region far away from the Marquis' castle found itself assigned to his district, but because he never went there, he exerted little personal influence, needless to say, over the voters and their day-to-day lives. In fact, a strong faction had formed against him, which did not threaten his political office in the slightest, but was a blow to his ego nonetheless ... He defeated this opposition by promising to get the current administration in the capital city to build something that the region's voters had been asking for, in vain, for many years: a train stop. More years came and went, congresses as well, and the promised stop was never built ... which did not prevent the Marquis from always winning reelection.

With new elections coming up, and nervous about the fact that their deputy had stopped talking to them about the train stop, the peasants sent a delegation to politely ask for the latest word about the project, adding that the Marquis' opponent had also promised them one ...

"The train stop?" cried the Marquis. "How is it possible ...? You don't know ...? Why, it's being built, my good fellow citizens ... They are starting next week. They have had no end of difficulty getting underway ... with this scumbag government ... that doesn't want to do anything to help the farmers ..."

They countered that this did not seem to make sense ... nothing had been blocked out ... not one engineer had been seen in the region ... But such minor quibbles hardly shamed the Marquis. "A train stop ... you see, good people ... it's not a big deal ... it doesn't mean anything ... Engineers don't trouble themselves over easy jobs like that ... They have their blueprints ... they do all the blocking-out in their offices ... But I assure you, it's a fact ... they're starting next week ..."

In fact, five days later, at dawn, the peasants found a wagon full of gravel ... and next to it, a wagon full of sand ... "Ah! Ah! It's for our train stop," they said. "That settles it ... Monsieur the Marquis was right ..." And off they went to throw their usual ballots into the ballot box ...

Two days after the election, a municipal driver came and hauled away the wagon full of gravel, then the wagon full of sand ... And as he was leaving, the peasants shouted, "But that's our train stop ...!"

The driver whipped his horses, and said, "Seems to have been a mistake ... It was meant for a different department ..."

In the next elections, the region's voters clamored for their

train stop more violently than usual ... So, the Marquis pointed his finger and stared at them sternly ... "A train stop!" he
cried. "Who said 'a train stop'? What do you want with a god-
less stop ...? Bah! Stops were good enough for the past, but
not for us, today ... What you need is a *train station* ... Would
you like a station? Just say the word ...! A grand station ... a
beautiful station ... a station with wall-to-wall electric clocks
... snack bars ... book stalls ... Long live France ...! And if
you would like a few junctions, too, just say the word ... Long
live France ...!"

The peasants said, "A grand station ...? Of course! That
would be much better ..."

And once again, they carried the Marquis to victory ...

On the morning I am describing, the Marquis left the Hope
Café, followed by a band of peasants using the backs of their
hands to wipe away lingering drops of blue wine from their
lips, and at that very moment, his opponent happened to pass
by ... He was a pathetic, scrawny, pale, pimply-faced fellow,
who gave off a distinct odor of poverty, and who had had the
outrageous idea to run against the Marquis as a socialist candidate ... A former government schoolteacher, fired by M.
Georges Leygues for posting on his classroom wall—before the
vogue for it came back in fashion, that unlucky man!—the
Declaration of the Rights of Man ... he had been picked by
the Committee for Revolutionary Action as the candidate of
sweeping reforms, sweeping protests, and sweeping repara-
tions. A true intellectual, a true believer, devoutly committed
to "the cause," he did not, unfortunately, look the part. His
face did not match up, in any way, with the proud and fiery
slogans on his campaign posters ... To show his respect for the
voters, he had dressed up in his finest clothes ... a black frock
coat, rumpled, threadbare, fifty years out of date, reeking of
naphthalene, and eaten all over by starving colonies of moths
... A top hat, stained, yellowed, with a worn-out brim and
grease-smeared band, put the crowning touch on his ridiculous

outfit . . . He was all alone . . . absolutely alone . . . and, sensing
hostility, and looking fearful and ashamed, he scanned the
crowd for his friends, no doubt late in arriving . . .

The jeering Marquis immediately pointed him out to his
followers with his Normandy club . . . "See that dandy?" he
cried, with a loud laugh twisted by pure hate. "That, men, is
called a socialist . . . ! Ah, what a joke . . . !"

At first, some of the men snorted behind their hands, then
a few began to mutter . . . "Pretty little thing . . . ain't he?"

For his part, the Marquis de Portpierre appeared full of
himself in his big steel-toed boots and with his rabbit-skin cap
pushed back on his cranium, down to his nape . . . And as he
stuck out his chest, the wind billowed his smock, whose V-
shaped neckline exposed the knot in the red scarf tied around
his neck. He went on, "And he comes around here, playing the
gentleman . . . the elitist . . . taking his ease . . . insulting the
people by dressing like a prince . . . ! See that . . . ? Ah, for the
love of God . . . ! It's a disgrace . . ."

Two hundred stares smothered the poor candidate in mocking contempt . . . Emboldened, the Marquis decried even louder, "And where did he steal that frock coat from . . . ? And who
paid for that hat . . . ? I bet Germany knows something about it
. . . Those scoundrels . . . those dirty scoundrels . . . !"

The murmurs rose and swelled . . . A wheelwright, his arms
bare in a sleeveless shirt and his tree-trunk legs encased in a
leather apron, hollered, "It's plain to see . . . he's a traitor . . ."
Several other voices yelled, "Down with traitors . . . !"

The Marquis continued, pointing to his own blue smock,
rabbit-skin cap, steel-toed boots, and knotty club, "Do the
real friends of the people wear frock coats . . . like dirty foreigners . . . turncoats, Jews . . . ? Do I have a frock coat . . . and a top
hat shiny enough to reflect the sun . . . ? See that, you
men . . . ?"

"Long live Monsieur the Marquis!"

"I wear a peasant's smock . . . the smock of the good peasant
of France . . . the smock of honesty and hard work . . . the

smock of French thriftiness ..."

"Long live Monsieur the Marquis ...!"

"And I do not feel the slightest dishonor in that ... Isn't that so, men ...?"

"Long live ... long live Monsieur the Marquis ...!"

"While this scumbag elitist ... this cosmopolitan ... this socialist ..."

"Yes ...! Yes ...! Yes ...!"

"... dares to come here ... to mock the suffering of the people ..."

"Yes ... Yes ... It's true ..."

"... the suffering of the noble farmer ... who is the very soul of France ...! Ah, for the love of God ...!"

"Down with traitors ...!"

The unlucky candidate froze ... He could not fathom any of this hatred exploding against him ... First, he examined his frock coat to see if perhaps it really was an insult to the people. Then, he tried to speak up, to protest ... But the voices drowned him out ...

"Down with traitors ...!"

"Go back to Germany."

"To England ..."

"Yes ... Yes ... Down with crooks ...! Down with traitors ...!"

And as they shook their fists at him, he fled, pursued by the jeers and threats of the entire town. Then, the triumphant Marquis went back into the Hope Café, and, surrounded by cheers and acclamations, ordered fresh bottles, pounding the marble tables with his club and crying out, "How true it is ... for the love of God ...! A scumbag cosmopolitan ..." Then, he raised his brimming glass in the air ... "To the smock of France ... my friends ...! *Respect* the smock of France ...!"

This run-in with the socialist candidate gave me an even stronger desire to learn more about the Marquis ... I asked around, and was instantly inundated with entertaining stories ... In fact, I only had to mention his name to the locals, and then sit back and listen, for they were an inexhaustible fount of anecdotes about the Marquis; just as the Marquis himself, that perfect gentleman, was an inexhaustible fount of all sorts of exploits and scandals, sometimes funny, sometimes disturbing, and sometimes both at once, as the mood seemed to strike him ... And I discovered from these stories that the worse he behaved, the more they loved him ... Truly, his popularity increased with his corruption, which at least had the very French distinction of being enterprising and fun ...

The Marquis was very protective of his hunting grounds; to guard them, he hired brutes, bruisers, brawlers—thugs whom it was never good to run into in the woods at night. He chose them from among ex-petty officers and former secret police, trained in torture in the penal colonies, and who regarded a man's life as extremely cheap ... They inspired universal dread ... As a further incentive, he paid them well, awarding lavish bonuses for every kill, and, with a spirit of fatherly love, he saw to it that their barracks were always well-stocked with brandy. "You must keep them," he said, "in a constant state of drunken rage ... That way, they will not feel guilty about doing the dirty work, and when they have to, they will not hesitate to slaughter a man as if he were a rabbit ..."

For he judged no punishment too cruel and unusual for poachers. His principle was that you had to exterminate them, and treat them like polecats, martens, foxes, wolves and other predatory beasts ... Thus, after a string of brutal beatings and impromptu beheadings, which earned him even greater popularity and love throughout the region, hardly any poachers dared to venture onto his fearsomely, heroically guarded lands anymore ... They knew what lay in store for them.

"See ...!" the people said approvingly. "The rabbits, pheasants, deer, hares ... do they or do they not belong ... to the Marquis ...? Why don't the poachers leave those animals in peace ...? Serves them right ..."

Not all of the Marquis' exploits were Grand Guignol. He

was equally adept at broad comedy, and sometimes availed himself of the subtlest irony.

Every year, on the opening day of the hunting season, he sent out his guards before dawn to beat the underbrush in the public park, the community hunting grounds that bordered his own property, until the frightened game took refuge on his land and in his woods—those animals, thinking they had found a tranquil, friendly place, were completely off-guard when he himself came to shoot them, later that day ... And Norfleur's unlucky hunters—after running themselves ragged all day long in the clover and alfalfa of the public park, after walking around and around in circles, thrashing through acre after acre, trail after trail, through bush and brush, even the barren, fallow mudflats—dragged themselves home when evening came, defeated, exhausted, and muttering to themselves ... And, hanging up their empty game-bags next to their rifles, which they never got to fire, they groaned, "Bad year ... bad year ... There's nothing out there ... nothing ... nothing ..."

At market, the next day, when the Marquis heard them expressing their sorrow over this frustrating state of affairs, he solemnly explained, "What else do you expect ...? With this scumbag government ... and this bitch of a Republic ... nothing shocks me anymore ..."

Once a year, the Marquis invited the most prominent members of Norfleur's bourgeoisie to a great rabbit hunt, and they proudly accepted ... But on the morning of the hunt, he always had his guard root out all the burrows, and catch all the rabbits running free only the day before ... That evening, at the family-style dinner which traditionally ended the "great annual rabbit hunt," the Marquis made a point of apologizing to his disgruntled, demoralized guests. "I am disconsolate about this, truly I am ... And I cannot understand it at all ... But then again, the rabbit ... nothing is more whimsical than that little critter ... One day, you're wading through them in hip-boots ... and then ... the next day ... you go outside ... and there's not a single one in sight ... The rabbit is sly, if nothing else ... a well-known practical joker ... hee, hee ... that rat ..."

And the bourgeoisie forgot their sorrows a little, guzzling champagne ...

The Marquis turned out to be equally implacable when it came to his fishing, even though he never fished except to prove a point about the fundamental, sacred rights of authority and property, in an era where these rights were so neglected and abused ... On the other side of town, he owned three meadows, which did not abut his estate at any point, and were irrigated by the small tributary of a river. This stream of clear and singing water, free of any factory's pollution, was legendary for its large, sweet and plentiful crayfish ... So that no one could claim ignorance, huge, stern "No Trespassing" signs, one upstream and one down, marked off the forbidden zone to fishermen ... One afternoon, after shopping for cow manure, the Marquis was returning home to the castle through the valley, when he spotted old Franchart, sitting on the riverbank under a weeping willow and holding a crayfish scale ... His skin tanned and his hair pure white, old Franchart was a very gentle, elderly man, who had gotten his left arm pulverized in the gears of a mill, over fifteen years ago ... Disabled and unable to work, he cobbled together a living from odd menial jobs, public charity, and, when no other work was available, fishing for crayfish ... all in all, hardly a substantial living ...

The Marquis swooped down on old Franchart and greeted him joyously. "Hello there, old Franchart ... Still fit as a fiddle, eh ...? Things going your way ...?"

"Not at all ... Monsieur the Marquis ... not at all," replied the old man, quickly tipping his cap as a gesture of salute. "Ah, as I live and breathe, no ..."

"Come now!" retorted the Marquis. "You never stop complaining ... And yet, you're as hardy and robust as that oak tree over there ..."

Old Franchart shook his aged head. "Ah! That oak tree ...! Don't be deceived, Monsieur the Marquis ... Ah, Good Lord

... I should be so fortunate ..."

The Marquis planted his legs firmly apart, in their already wide buckskin chaps, and, standing with his left palm flat against his hip while he raked the grass around his feet with the cane in his right hand ... he cried out in a friendly voice, "Blessed old Franchart, come now!" Then: "And the fishing ... Is that going well?"

"You get straight to the point, Monsieur the Marquis ..." In a gently smiling tone, he added, "I am not too disappointed today ..."

"Ah ...! Ah ...! So much the better ... so much the better, sapristi ... Have you caught many crayfish?"

"As I live and breathe ...! Maybe two hundred, Monsieur the Marquis ... maybe more ..."

"Quite a morning ...! Nice big ones?"

"Nice enough, Monsieur the Marquis ..."

"And how much are they worth, these crayfish?"

"Crayfish ...? I'd say ... Monsieur the Marquis ... they'd go for one hundred sous per every hundred ... So, that'd come to around ... ten francs ..."

"Jesus ...! A banner day, old Franchart ... Really fills up your pot ... eh?"

"Aw, darn, Monsieur the Marquis ... It's been a long, long time since I was able to do *that*."

The Marquis prodded the old man's shoulder with the end of his cane ... and said, "Since they're so nice ... your crayfish ... I'd like to take them off your hands ..."

"I'd be delighted, Monsieur the Marquis ..."

"Show them to me ..."

Then, he noticed, half hidden in the grass and leaning against the willow, a gray canvas sack whose top was fastened with a bamboo tie ... Old Franchart picked up the sack, undid the tie, and opened it wide ... And a sun-shower of shimmering bronze crayfish swarmed and writhed among some freshly cut nettle leaves ... The Marquis cried, "Blessed old Franchart ...! How skillful he is, that old fart ...! They really are nice ones. Ah, well ... of course ... I'll take them ..."

He grabbed the sack and turned it upside down over the water, while giving it little shakes, and one by one, two by two, twenty by twenty, all the crayfish fell out ... fell out into the river with a splash ... For a few seconds, they flapped on the surface, then disappeared deep below the water ... Soon, there were only the nettle leaves, which the current swiftly carried away.

"Blessed old Franchart ...!" repeated the Marquis, tossing the empty sack against the willow, into the grass ...

Old Franchart was speechless, dumbfounded... Without a word, without a cry, without a gesture, he stared at the Marquis ... He stared at him with his bulging eyes ... where two tears ... two pathetic tears suddenly welled up and ran down the cracks of his old parchment face ...

Did the Marquis notice the tears running down ...? Perhaps. And here is what he said as he was leaving, in a half-threatening, half-playful tone, "You know, my dear old Franchart ... if I catch you here again, stealing any more of my crayfish, more than the fish will get thrown into the river ... You sainted old man ...! See you around ... Take care ..."

Before evening came, this anecdote had circulated all through Norfleur ... They were rolling on the ground with laughter ... "He's a real joker, that Monsieur the Marquis! A good egg!"

Several years before that, a worthy man named Chomassus came to Norfleur and bought a small piece of land next to the Marquis' estate. This Chomassus was a mailman from Les Halles in Paris, recently retired; in those days, they kept down the number of mailmen in Les Halles, because the commerce board allowed them to sell their positions for a profit, and private enterprise thrives on exclusivity. Chomassus wished to spend his last years with his wife amid the lyric beauty and tranquility of country life ... A big, stocky man, with a burgeoning stomach, he seemed both coarse and somewhat timid

at the same time. Smelling a potential sucker in this new neighbor of his, the Marquis immediately struck up a friendship
with the good-natured fellow . . .

One day, when the former mailman had gone out to super-
vise some reconstructions and renovations which he was making to his house, which was very old, the Marquis suddenly
came up out of nowhere and introduced himself. "My dear
sir," the Marquis said, "forgive my taking the liberty . . . but
you are going to be my neighbor . . . and perhaps my friend . . .
I swear to you I am most delighted about this . . . And I have
come, informally, to bid you welcome to our region . . . a very
famous region, did you know that?"

Chomassus was quite flattered by these remarks. Blushing
but grateful, he thanked the Marquis from the bottom of his
heart . . . The Marquis added, squeezing his hand so hard he
nearly broke it, "But please . . . get up off of your knees . . . sapristi . . . Count on me for *anything* you might need here . . .
And never be afraid that you are bothering me . . ."

And when the former mailman, moved by this somewhat
pushy but sincere friendliness (from a member of the nobility,
yet), went into a flurry of bewildered gratitude, the Marquis reassured him. "But it's the most natural thing in the world, my
friend, you see . . . between *gentlemen* such as ourselves, sapristi!"

Then, timidly, almost shamefacedly, the good-natured Chomassus said, "It's just that . . . I myself am not a gentleman . . .
Monsieur the Marquis . . . All the same, I really admire the nobility!"

To which the Marquis replied, "What is that you said, my
friend . . . ? Any man is a gentleman . . . when he possesses
heart . . . and you possess heart . . . by Jove . . . ! Why, it's obvious just to look at you . . ."

Throughout his visit, the Marquis wore Chomassus down
with friendly, intimate nudges and ecstatic exclamations,
meant to inspire trust. So, when he went back home that evening, the worthy tradesman enthused to his wife, "Things are

going well ... life is good ... We have a marquis for a neighbor, and he's not arrogant at all. Ah! Jesus ...! A good egg, in
fact. Makes you feel glad to know that a marquis can be like
that ..."

Every time Chomassus went out to check on the progress of
the renovations, he could count on the Marquis turning up, always with cheerful things to say, and bristling with handshakes
and backslaps. Not even plaster dust and paint fumes scared
him off. He wanted to be involved in everything. "It's looking
very chic here, my friend. It's coming together nicely. Ah! You
do have good taste ... You know, I am jealous of your castle.
It's making mine look bad ..."

"My castle! Oh, no!" Chomassus said, apologetically.

"Yes ... yes ... Sapristi, my friend, what else could it be but
a castle?"

He gave Chomassus advice on planting, recommended the
best decorators in town, and brought him up to date with the
customs and ways of the locals. "And you know ... the municipal elections are being held next year. I'm counting on you absolutely ... You are at the very top of my list ... If ... if ... I
remain in office ... we will turn the tables on this wicked, trea-
sonous government. For you people are the backbone of the
party, you, the real French, believers in the Good Lord ... Yes,
in the name of God ...! The Good Lord is *not* a cosmopolitan
... he is a *Frenchman* ..."

One day, the Marquis invited him to lunch at the castle.
Chomassus hesitated. The Marquis vehemently insisted, "Informally, my friend, informally. Sapristi! It's nothing at all, between gentlemen ... And then, the Marquise—to whom I
never stop raving about you—very much desires to make your
acquaintance."

In spite of his timidity, Chomassus finally said yes ... But
he was still very afraid, having never eaten at the home of a
marquis before ... How should he act at table? Would they
laugh at him? And what about the Marquise? And those bas-

tard servants? His heart was thumping out of his chest when he walked into the vestibule, covered wall to wall with antique tapestries . . .

Lunch was excellent, and more fun than the humble man had ever been exposed to before, a warm, friendly feeling of well-being all around and inside him. The Marquise displayed the down-to-earth charm of a perfect hostess, putting him at ease right away. She took an immediate interest in Mme. Chomassus, the Chomassus family, the friends of the Chomassus family, and their friends.

Everywhere he looked, he saw something that made him weak in the knees: the tapestries on the walls, the silverware on the buffet . . . a splendid trumeau, facing him, depicting a dazzling fairy made of flowers and fruit . . . And the two footmen who never stopped refilling his wine glass, pouring from ewers of chiseled silver. And, reeling through the heights of heaven itself, he thought, "Ah, when all is said and done, I'm a lucky man, having moved to this region . . . And it isn't so scary, dining at the home of a marquis . . . Hell, if anyone had ever told me that I, a simple mailman from Les Halles, would be spending my last years in castles, as the friend of nobility . . ."

His ego was already dreaming of being showered with luxuries and honors, and perhaps even getting to sleep with the Marquise.

Over coffee, the Marquis casually asked Chomassus, "Naturally, you brought your coaches here?"

"No," he replied, "I didn't . . . Didn't think I'd need them here . . ."

Scandalized, the Marquis jumped. "What?" he said. "You must have coaches . . ."

Instantly feeling ashamed, blushing, Chomassus explained, "A little cart, with a donkey . . . for provisions . . . That's enough for me."

"Impossible," the Marquis declared imperiously. "I won't allow it . . . You need a surrey and a roundabout . . ."

"But it's . . ."

"Look, my friend . . . You simply can't get by with any less . . ."

Shaken, Chomassus murmured, "You—you think so . . .?"

"Absolutely indispensable, my friend! I mean . . . by my honor, it's a disgrace! Look, I like you so much, and I am so very happy that you are my neighbor . . . that I would like to make a sacrifice for you."

"Oh! Monsieur the Marquis!"

"A very big sacrifice . . . I have a roundabout and a surrey, practically brand new, the current model, excellent craftsmanship . . . If the Marquise agrees, well, my friend, I will give them to you . . ." "Oh, Monsieur the Marquis!"

"Between gentlemen . . . what the hell! Those coaches cost me five thousand francs each. They have hardly ever been driven! And I will give them to you for two thousand francs each . . . It's crazy . . . Basta . . .! What am I doing . . .? But then again . . . whenever I see you out riding with Mme. Chomassus, I can pretend once again that they are mine . . . I will show them to you right away. No coaches, my friend . . .! Whatever will they say about you, in a region like this . . .? Please . . .! And I even have two excellent coachbuilders, which I will throw in for nothing . . . next to nothing . . ."

The Marquis squeezed Chomassus on the shoulder. "Yes, they're quite astonishing coaches, my friend . . .! But what can you do about it . . .? It will make me so happy to do it. That's how I am . . . In life . . . to be sure . . . you get too few opportunities to do something nice for a truly nice person." And then, with a beaming smile, pointing his finger and waving his hand magnanimously, he added, "Remember this well: giving gifts to one's friends is a hundred times sweeter than getting gifts from them . . . That is my motto."

Chomassus stopped arguing. He nodded . . . and agreed, "I suppose . . . Monsieur the Marquis . . . if you think so . . .?"

"Of course . . .! *If* I think so . . .? Ha! Another glass of this fine champagne . . . And when we get to the garage, my friend

... you are going to be *shocked* ... I promise you that ..." He suddenly looked worried ... and turned to his wife, who was leafing through a newspaper. "At least," he said, "if the Marquise does not mind ... You see, I set those two beautiful coaches aside for her use ..."

Friendly and smiling, the Marquise responded, "With anyone else ... I would say no ... without thinking twice ... But, for Monsieur Chomassus ... there is nothing I would not do ..."

Chomassus felt more and more uneasy ... Certainly, it worried him a little to burden himself with two such expensive coaches. It would mean having to hire a coachman ... keep and feed a pair of horses ... pay more in taxes ... It would probably be a huge burden for him, a real white elephant ... But how to refuse such an honor, so politely offered ...? It would make him look like the biggest, most ungrateful boor who ever lived ... "Truly, Madame the Marquise ... you *do* flatter me ..." Chomassus thanked her in a voice quavering lightly with emotion ... the urge to be gallant ... pride ... and faint lust ...

"Bah!" the Marquis cut in. "Between *gentlemen* ...!" Then: "Come, my friend ..." And the two men left the parlor, arm in arm ...

The Marquis owned an old roundabout and an even older surrey, which he had been trying to unload for more than a decade ... with no luck. They were outdated, ramshackle coaches, the kind you see in sporty engravings from the early years of the Empire. They did not run anymore. The worn-out, broken springs no longer held up the dilapidated chassis, themselves half rusted away. Indeed, it was a miracle that either one was still standing. At the slightest movement of their wheels, those old lopsided vehicles started wobbling to the left and right, like little old men whose heads bobble when they walk. With horses pulling them at a brisk trot, they would have gone up on two wheels at the turns, would have tipped over in spastic plunges, like drunkards. The upholstery of the seat cushions,

once a bright blue, had faded to a neutral color, going from
piss yellow to wilted green, and finally ending as a sort of
death-mask gray that seemed to be made of ageless dust and
chronic wear. The scorched leather had the darkened spots and
powdery crumbling of used kindling. The windowpanes were
all so cloudy that they were more like shades, constantly pulled
down, rather than glass. From having been brushed and
scrubbed with near-prehistoric tools, the trimmings had, so to
speak, melted away. The silk fringe was nothing but tatty
strings hanging down; the buttons, sewn into the seat cushions
when the coaches were new, as a mark of special craftsmanship,
were now dull, brittle bits that looked as if they had been
chewed up . . . The cheapest cab company would have refused
to use them as night-shift fiacres, lurking outside train stations
for desperate, stranded passengers, or rolling through slums
like ghastly, four-wheeled phantoms.

In vain, the Marquis had offered them to everyone he knew,
at rock-bottom prices. For several years, they had been featured
as "*amazing deals*" in the classified sections of specialty magazines, which, under the pretext of being about ranching, the
weather, or simply gourmet living, tempt their subscribers with
enterprising sales or the most outlandish trades . . . where you
see extremely wealthy people, the cream of the high aristocracy,
trying to swindle each other, pleading to trade a set of authentic Cochin china for an Érard piano, Larousse dictionaries for
tulip bulbs, old greasy scapulars for mandolins, rosaries blessed
by the Pope himself for Irish ponies, "flawless and well broken-
in," etc. Whenever a buyer or trader was lured by the raving
and always false descriptions in the ad, or by the fake, unreli-
able photos, and came to the castle to look at the coaches,
he ran off as soon as he saw them, sometimes cursing angrily— "Ah, no! Gentlemen do not play these tricks on one another . . . You cannot cheat the world . . . so shamelessly!" —
and seeming to be generally enraged.

So the Marquis, despairing of ever selling those accursed
coaches in the lamentable state they were in, had hired the lo-

cal wheelwright to polish their wheels, and a painter to give their chassis the cosmetic improvement of a light coat of paint. Thus, with his broken-down heaps somewhat disguised, the Marquis let them slumber away in a garage, waiting for the opportunity to match them up with an advantageous person. "For," as he so often said, "you will always get the opportunity to rob some sucker blind . . . The trick is not to give up while waiting for it." That worldly-wise aphorism was the actual motto by which he had lived his entire life, and it had served him well. Therefore, when he met the worthy Chomassus, he immediately sniffed out, with the sixth sense of a true gentleman, that this was exactly the opportunity he had been waiting for . . .

As they strolled arm in arm toward the garage, nearly skipping along tipsily, the Marquis began to lavish even more effusive words, gestures, shoulder-taps, and jokes, to hypnotize the former mailman from Les Halles, already primed to say yes to anything by the delicious meal, the Marquise's exquisite smile, the Marquis' charming, playful friendliness, and above all the three centuries of glory and honor which this modern perfect gentleman embodied so beautifully.

And, while walking and listening to the Marquis, Chomassus admired the vast undulating lawns; the mosaics of flowers; the enormous groves of trees; off in the distance, the quaint storehouses, white stone and pink brick, their sloping, lanterned roofs spread out prettily against the sky; and everything that such an estate summoned up, in his humble Parisian businessman's soul, of glory, splendor, and luxury . . . When they were walking past the tennis court, the Marquis asked him, "Do you like tennis . . . ? And Mme. Chomassus—no doubt she likes it, too . . . ? I warn you that the Marquise is incredibly good . . . You will not beat her without a fight."

Then, with the court behind them now, the Marquis cried, "Ah, my friend! I am truly happy that you will profit from this 'amazing deal' . . . It is right that it should be you, and no one else . . . Sapristi . . . Isn't it strange that you have hypnotized me in this way . . . ! What is it about you that you can bend me to your will . . . ? It's the art of seduction, it is . . . Blessed Chomassus . . . ! You give a person no time to clear out of the way . . . just . . . bang . . . that's it . . . ! And yet, for my own part, I have never been easily swayed . . . I'm no sucker . . . I know how to protect myself in the clinches . . . But with you . . . I am helpless, by Jove . . . !"

Chomassus interrupted from time to time to express his thanks. "Ah! Monsieur the Marquis . . . Monsieur the Marquis," he stammered . . .

And the Marquis replied, "It's true . . . You possess real charm . . . No one could refuse you anything . . . That's just how it is . . ." And a moment later, he said, "But one thing does worry me a little . . . Everyone in our region is going to be jealous of you, my friend . . ."

"Of—of me . . . ?"

"Well, who else? Naturally, of you . . . See . . . these beautiful coaches . . . I have turned down all other offers . . . even five thousand francs . . . and here I am, giving them away to you, for two thousand . . . ! They're going to be furious. After all, what a feather in your cap that will be . . . You will feel good about that, eh . . . ? And did you know, my friend . . . ? These are *historic* coaches."

The man's mouth dropped open as if struck by lockjaw . . . His eyes bulged. "Historic . . . ? You don't say . . ."

"Yes . . . they have been given that distinction . . . but swear to me you will not breathe a word to anyone . . . not to anyone . . . gracious me . . . !"

"Oh, I swear it . . ." He half-swallowed this vow in a weak, timid voice, not that he had the slightest thought of ever breaking it . . . But that word, "historic" . . . had such a mysterious, solemn ring that he became even more worried . . . Now the coaches took on a new dimension, of being sacred coaches.

The Marquis went on, in a confidential tone, "They were chosen for the distinction . . . five months ago . . . of being driven to Le Havre, to be shown to . . . M. the Duke d'Orléans

... Shush ...! Sapristi ... M. the Duke d'Orléans, who expressed a keen desire to come here and spend several days with me, in the utmost secrecy, of course ..."

Even more surprised now ... surprised to the point of panic, Chomassus stammered, "M. the Duke d'Orléans ...! Ah, I can't believe it ...! M. the Duke d'Orléans ...? Really?"

"Absolutely, my friend ... The one and only ..."

"But I thought the relatives of former kings were not allowed back into France, since the passing of that—that law ..."

"He is a true aristocrat, he doesn't let a little law stand in his way ... I will introduce you to him when he comes back through here ... But, not a word ...!"

"Oh, Monsieur the Marquis!"

"And do you know what he said to me, M. the Duke d'Orléans ...? He said to me, 'I love your magnificent coaches so much, my dear Marquis, that I do not want any others when I return to my people ...' And do you know what I said, then, to the Duke d'Orléans ...? I said to him, 'My lord ... my coaches would be eternally honored ... But you must not do that ... You must not return to your people in a coach ... You must be on horseback, my lord ... on horseback ...!' Isn't that how you feel about it, too, Chomassus?"

"Absolutely ... oh, absolutely ... Monsieur the Marquis ... On horseback ... That is the only way ..."

"Naturally ... I knew you would see it that way ..." He went on, "So, M. the Duke d'Orléans took my hand, squeezed it in his royal hand, and said to me ... his voice quavering with feeling ... 'Yes, yes ... that is how I must return to my people—on horseback ... You are right ... You are a loyal subject!' Hah! What do you think about that ...? Anyway, your coaches are over there ..."

They approached the garage ... The Marquis stopped and, placing his hand on Chomassus's shoulder, said, "Nearly *royal* coaches ... Doesn't that make you feel like a bigshot, my friend Chomassus ...?"

Chomassus felt himself spinning; where was he . . .? Thrones, empires, plumes, purple mantles, ermine furs . . . scepters . . . danced sarabandes of total abandon in his head . . . The thought of his retired mailman's buttocks sitting in the same coach seat as the buttocks of the royal-blooded Duke d'Orléans . . . ! And, as the Marquis continued to shake him by the shoulder, he sighed, "It wouldn't make me feel like a bigshot in the slightest, Monsieur the Marquis . . . I—I would never even dare to get into them . . ."

"Oh, come now, my friend . . . come now," the Marquis encouraged him. "You will be surprised . . . And Mme. Chomassus will also be surprised, eh . . . ? Do this for me . . . I want you to *knock out* this region with how chic you are . . ."

A groom stood up. "Open the garage," the Marquis commanded him, "the garage for the coaches of M. the Duke d'Orléans . . . !"

Chomassus's soul was deeply stirred. His heart was pounding violently. His soul was stirred, and his heart pounded at the thought that he would finally get to see and touch those famous coaches, which had carried away none other than a pretender to the throne, it was true, even if they failed to bring back a king. He tried to imagine what those coaches looked like, those coaches that were "almost a throne," those marvelous coaches which, for all he knew, could have rolled from Boulogne to Paris, through streets filled with clamoring hordes, the frenzied cheering of the entire French people . . . They must be magnificent, gilded all over, their paneling painted with fearsome crests . . . wide, high-backed seats, covered, like the bed of a queen, with quilts embroidered with fleur de lys . . . and, on the back, life-size statuary, polished, sculpted from gold, ablaze with gold, the heads adorned with dangling paper lanterns, the calves well-defined, the calves of a gladiator straining under the tender caress of silk leggings. And etched-glass lanterns, too, no doubt, like those exquisite pendulum clocks collected by that wealthy connoisseur, M. Isaac de Camondo . . . ! And the supple springs, agile, cradling, curving like a swan's neck . . . ! In their vehicular pomp and splendor, he likened those coaches to the Duke of Brunswick's dazzling equipage, which he had once admired at the Hippodrome, when his four prancing horses came trotting up, trailed by a band of circus tumblers in mauve tights, and hot-pink dwarf clowns spangled with silver sequins . . . Chomassus also thought of the imposing, architectural beauty of fancy hearses, laden with crosses and exotic flowers . . . carrying glorious generals and millionaire bankers to crypts sculpted by M. Charles-René de Saint-Marceaux himself, tomb-carver to the great!

And this mailman, who, up until now, had always thought of himself as a staunch republican, who had always voted for the reform candidate, suddenly discovered the heart of a monarchist beating within him. Yes, he longed to salute France . . . and French capitalism . . . He longed for that world of extravagant, festive traditions, courtyards decorated for parties, uniforms gleaming with all the gaudy trimmings of conspicuous wealth and vulgar luxury . . . that world of royalty . . . and even (goodness gracious!) . . . the Empire itself . . . In that moment, he felt a violent contempt for the way the new bourgeoisie had eradicated all vestiges of Republican ceremony and regalia . . . As a good Parisian patriot, he felt deeply pained by the ridiculous poverty . . . the drab, pseudo-communist poverty of M. Émile Loubet's baby-buggy coaches . . . Yes, Loubet, that weak, sniveling leftist who actually thanked Dreyfus and shook his hand after the Rennes trial . . . ! "Seemed like a shotgun wedding," Chomassus snickered to himself . . .

Wedding coaches, too — the ones he was going to see in a moment . . . But whose wedding . . . ? The reunion wedding, quite simply, of France and her bridegroom king . . .

In spite of his thoughts being driven to atypical heights of smugness by these coaches of the Marquis', Chomassus never lost his own feeling of humility. He was, by nature, susceptible to being awed by great things, nobility and luxury; but he was still a timid man, and he wrestled with himself . . . He said to himself, "The Marquis is being so nice to me . . . It's like a dream ... He gives me an absurdly low price—clearly—two thousand francs ... for historic coaches that would spark off a bidding war among all the great museums of Europe ... It's quite an honor, and it makes me feel very proud ... But I am a practical man ... I must look at the practical side of things ... What am I going to do with these coaches ...? I could never ... I would never dare to use them ... Well, perhaps I would ... but my wife ...? As ruddy-faced, fat and big-titted as Mme. Chomassus is ... I wouldn't be caught dead with her in such coaches ... It really has me worried ... Ah, if only this Marquis, who is so kind to me and treats me so well ... if only he would offer me an English cart ... or, better yet ... a small barrow ... made of polished wood ... with a little pony, who is very easy to drive ...? I would like that much better ... Yes, that would suit me much better ..."

Chomassus reflected on these matters, and, seeing him deep in thought, looking very serious, with his brow furrowed, the Marquis jostled him a little. "Well ... well ... what are you thinking about, Chomassus?"

Chomassus replied, "I'm thinking ... well, you see ... I'm thinking that, given our needs ... a small barrow of varnished wood, with a little pony who is very easy to drive ..."

But the Marquis cut him off with a loud burst of laughter, and shaking him by the shoulder with a friendly rudeness, said, "Blessed Chomassus ...! Is that a joke, a pony ...? A once-in-a-lifetime ... extraordinary ... opportunity ...? Hell ... just take my word on this, my friend ... I know what you really need ... Look ...! It's the moment of the unveiling ..."

And indeed, at that moment, everything truly was unveiled ... Stripped of their canvas coverings, there the coaches finally stood ... in all their historic majesty, before him ...

He could not believe his eyes ... "Surely the Marquis is playing a trick on me," he said to himself. "These old, broken-down crates ... these prehistoric fiacres that seem to have been run into the ground ... He cannot mean that these are ... the coaches ... the beautiful coaches of M. the Duke d'Orléans ...

No . . . it's not possible . . ."

His eyes wide, his mouth twisted in a grimace, Chomassus stared at the contraptions with mounting astonishment . . . And he turned, even more astonished, to stare at the Marquis next, as if seeking an indignant reaction, or, at the very least, an explanation of some sort . . . But the Marquis' own face expressed nothing of the kind . . . His legs firmly planted, his palms on his hips, his elbows sticking out, he puffed himself up with great satisfaction—a completely aristocratic satisfaction—and smiled, like someone delighted to find himself once again in the presence of a thing of great beauty. "Well, my friend Chomassus," the Marquis asked, "what do you think of my coaches . . . ? A real knockout, right . . . ?"

Since Chomassus did not reply as automatically as the Marquis expected, the Marquis asked again, "You *aren't* knocked out by them, Chomassus?"

"Very much . . . very much," the poor man quickly stammered, "knocked out flat . . . !"

"The current model, my friend . . . There are fewer than twenty of these in circulation . . ."

"Ah . . . ! You don't say . . . ?"

"Of course, I say . . . my friend . . ."

Chomassus worked up the nerve to grab the handle of a window, but when he tugged on it, the entire coach began to wobble back and forth . . . The springs creaked . . . the chassis cracked . . . It seemed to him that the coach was about to fall to pieces all around him, leaving him with the handle in his hand.

"Hmm . . . ? Those springs . . . ?" cried the Marquis. "Made of an amazing steel . . . It's bouncy . . . well-oiled . . . You know, my friend, inside there you feel as if you were lying in your very own bed . . ."

"Ah . . . ! You don't say . . . ?"

"Well, yes, I do say . . . !" Then, changing his tone: "Oh, what is it . . . Chomassus . . . why all these questions . . . ? Look at me for a second, face to face . . . Do I look like the kind of gentleman who swindles people like that . . . ? Gentlemen—

learn this well—do not play such tricks on one another ...
my friend ...”

Chomassus humbly begged the Marquis' pardon and, while
he was doing so, he finally got the window open ... The interior looked even more shabby and ruined than the exterior ...
And he murmured, “Is it just me, or are the linings extremely
faded ...?”

“Faded ...?!” exclaimed the Marquis. “You're crazy, my
friend ... It's all brand new ... It's just green ... that's all ...
Empire green ... the latest style ...”

“Ah ...!”

“All the rage ...”

“Ah ...!” Uttering this “Ah,” Chomassus lifted up the rug
that covered the floor of the roundabout ... That was when he
noticed two small iron rods, crudely forged, hammered into a
cross, and meant to hold the rotted, splintering wood together,
although the wood was still buckling and giving way ... “But
look, Monsieur the Marquis,” Chomassus beesched, “just look
at that ...”

The Marquis did not blush for even one second. “That ...?”
he said. “Well, that's the Binder cross ...”

“What ...?”

“... yes, the Binder cross, my ineffable Chomassus ... Don't
tell me you've never heard of the Binder cross ...?”

“Monsieur the Marquis ...?” pleaded the poor mailman
from Les Halles.

“Binder's greatest innovation ... the unmistakable mark ...
the craftsman's unforgeable signature! Ah ...! Ah, ah ...! Poor
Chomassus ... he has so many things to learn ...!” The Marquis closed the window again. “And you're in luck, you ...!”
he cried. “You know ... my coat of arms, there, on the paneling ... you may use it ... I grant you formal authorization ...
Ah, for Christ's sake ...! Blessed Chomassus ...! Come and
see the horses now ...”

Chomassus saw the horses, and bought them. He saw the
harnesses, too, and bought them. But the horses' knees explod-

ed as soon as they started up; the harnesses, whose leather was rotting, split open like the skin around a wound . . . When he finally got the coaches home, he had to replace everything, first the wheels, then the undercarriage, then the chassis. It ended up costing 9,500 francs . . . And he said to himself, "All the same . . . I would have preferred a small barrow of varnished wood, with a pony . . ."

Once again he became a moderate liberal, having had enough of the Marquis, enough of royal pomp . . . of luxury coaches . . . of Binder crosses . . . He daydreamed sweetly about reform candidates again. And, his heart broken by this misadventure, he often raged, "If that is how the monarchy does business . . . well, thanks but no thanks!"

His disgrace was made even worse when everyone in Norfleur laughed at him . . . "He's so funny, that Monsieur the Marquis . . . ! He's a good egg!"

It is the same exclamation I get, here, from the lips of Clara Fistula, Triceps, everyone; I hear it all over the hotel, which is putting up the Marquis de Portpierre for free, and at the Casino, which is footing the bill for his expensive pleasures . . . Silver trays laden with thousands of francs . . . And, watching him walk by, insolent in his happiness, his ease, his joy, I think again of that socialist candidate, so poor, so threadbare, so scrawny, and of the ugly scene that befell him in the middle of the town square in Norfleur, so deafening, so insulting, those shouts of "Down with the crooks!" led by that gentleman the Marquis himself, that con man, that swindler, that patriot . . .

XVIII.

Talked to two rather disturbing people yesterday: a Breton mayor, M. Jean Le Trégarec; and a Parisian clubman, M. Arthur Lebeau.

First, the mayor.

On the Breton coast, between Lorient and Concarneau, there is a village named Le Kernac.

Flat, shifting dunes, with patches of spindly dandelions and crown-shaped poppies, separate Le Kernac from the sea. A cove, well protected from southwestern winds by high walls made of square, red rocks, is filled with the same water as the nearby port, and serves as a natural harbor for fishing launches and small steamers seeking shelter from storms. Behind the village, beyond its steep, precipitous streets, the terrain is like a wasteland. In a sort of bowl, formed by the circular hills of moors, there are swampy prairies where oily, black water stands stagnant even throughout the most droughted summers. Pestilential fogs rise off those swamps. The people of Le Kernac, dwelling in slum-like hovels, choked by the stench of brine and rotting fish, are diseased and depressive: the men, wizened and puny; the women, wraiths as white as candle wax. You meet only hunchbacks, walking corpses; pale, wrinkled faces with their hair falling out; weak, sore eyes burned up by the glassy flame of fevers. While the men brave the sea in their ramshackle launches, in search of impossible sardines, the women farm the swamplands and hilly moors as best they can, wherever odd, sparse patches of loam appear, between clumps of gorsebush, like the chartreuse splotches on the bald heads of old people. It seems as though an unstoppable doom weighs on this little hell on earth, and, all through the gloomy, silent evenings, you think you can see death hovering in the air. In autumn especially, fever ravages this wretched populace. The creatures shrivel even more, fade, dry up and die, like sickly plants battered by an ill wind.

In this charnel-house atmosphere, this stifling air, there were only two men who lived well: the parish priest and the mayor.

The priest—or rather the rector, as they say in Brittany— was a small, dry and sanguine man, always bustling here and there, who took religion and his own priesthood very seriously. Unlike the majority of his Breton colleagues—whom you always find, whenever you visit them, in the middle of bottling wine or bagging a young girl—he was sober and chaste, and led an ascetic life ... And what an organizer ...! With the complicity of his friend, the mayor, and taking advantage of the wretched poverty of the people of Le Kernac every day, by means of clever charity drives and exorbitant tithes, he had managed to build, with the aid of the local government and the Church, a beautiful, white-stone cathedral, with a wrought-iron gate and a belfry, crowned with an enormous cross made of gold. The opulence of this temple made for an incongruous sight in the middle of that region's fathomless desolation ... But the priest did not stop there. Every week, in his sermon, he tirelessly stoked his parishioners' fervor, or played on their fears—for they saw him as vengeful and omnipotent—in order to demand new and ever more expensive sacrifices. One Sunday, he rose to the pulpit, brandishing the banner of the Holy Virgin ...

"Look at this banner!" he screamed in a furious voice. "Isn't this a disgrace? Look at this ...! Is this a banner ...? The silk is rotting, the fringe is unraveling, and the tassels are coming loose ... The rod is cracked ... Every one of the embroideries has fallen off ... And as for the image of the Holy Virgin ... disgusting...! You wouldn't use it—you, Charles Le Teur—to bandage your nag ... And you, Joséphine Briac, you wouldn't use it to scrub your pots ...! Ah! It makes no difference to you, you—while you live high on the hog, stuffing yourselves with abundance and luxuries, it makes no difference to you, wretched sinners, that on our high holy days of processionals and parish feasts, the Holy Mother of God walks among you in soiled rags, with her bare buttocks flapping in the air ...! Well, we must put a stop to this ... The Virgin *has had it* with your guilty indifference and your vile sins ... She wants a new banner, do you understand ...? A shining banner ... made from only the best of everything ... a banner costing, at the very least, two hundred francs ... Listen closely ... and memorize my words ... if you do not want anything but the most terrifying curses to fall upon you, upon your fields ... upon your boats ... if you do not want to be changed into jellyfish ... into toads ... into crabs ... into dogfish ... mark my words ... You, Yvonne Legonnec, you will give one hundred sous ... What did you say ...? You're broke ...? Very well, then ... You shall cut back on your boozing, pig ...! You, Rose Kerlaniou ... one hundred sous as well ... And if I catch you again behind the jetty, performing your obscene favors for the Kerlaur boy ... it won't be one hundred sous ... it will be ten francs ... You, old mother Milliner, you will give the calf that was born last night ... And don't give me that look, you old thief ... because if you resist, you will have to give more than that calf ... The cow, as well ... Jules, Pierre and Joseph Le Ker, you will bring me your next fishing haul ... and it had better be good ... No old ones, and no small fry, boys ... Nice big ones ... turbot and sole ... Is that understood, eh ...?"

And for a quarter of an hour or more, in this way, he assigned each person the contribution he or she would make, be it money, be it kitchen staples (slabs of butter, sacks of potatoes or grain), alternating his direct orders with the most outrageous insults ...

Leaning against a pillar, in the back, an old customs officer, who was a freethinker and believed that the fearsome rector did not notice him, began to chuckle discreetly into his thick mustache and his long beard, which were completely white ... But his laughter did not escape the priest, who suddenly pointed to the customs officer with his arm extended, at the end of which the banner shook and flapped like the sail of a dinghy in a storm. "You! Beardy ...!" he screamed. "How dare you laugh ...? And since you, insolent old fool, allow yourself to laugh in your insolent way, in the house of the Good Lord ... you will give twenty francs ..."

And, when the customs officer argued, the priest repeated in an even more booming voice, "Yes, twenty francs, Satan with a beard ...! And mark well what I say to you ... If you do not give me these twenty francs tonight, after vespers ... your fate is sealed ... I will denounce you to the public prosecutor ... for stealing—less than one week ago—the treasure from the shipwreck, found under the sea ... Ah-ha! You're not laughing anymore, old beard ... You weren't expecting that, were you ...? You beard from hell!"

And crossing himself, he intoned, "In nomine patris et filii et spiritus sancti ... Amen!" Then he got down from the pulpit and stood at the altar, whacking his dismayed congregation on their heads with the banner ...

That was Monsieur the Rector of Le Kernac ...

The mayor—M. Jean Le Trégarec—was also a rags-to-riches story.

A former sardine-fisherman from Concarneau, he had quickly amassed a nice fortune, and retired to Le Kernac, where he bought several acres of land and a luxurious house on the hill, the only pleasant place in the entire region, the only spot where there was anything resembling trees, greenery, flowers, a vague facsimile of life. The fatal malaria germs had not reached the height where that happy mansion stood, and the passing of the wide wind cleared away everything but the purity of its health-giving strength and its clean, bracing smell.

This mayor was a great and honorable man, or at least, he passed for one in that region. He wished only to dedicate himself to his constituents. And, in point of fact, he dedicated himself exhaustively. Just as the rector had built a beautiful, white-stone church, the mayor erected a magnificent Louis XIII town hall, followed by a superb Louis XIV schoolhouse, where no child ever attended school. But he had to halt the construction of an elegant Renaissance fountain in mid-progress, because the funds dried up, and so, they finally realized, did the water.

The community was up to its collective neck in debts, its collective back broken under the weight of them. The people were crushed by taxes, additional fees, multiple surcharges; but they thought of their mayor as a saint, a hero, and this assuaged their misery somewhat. He rejoiced in his good works, and dwelled at peace with his conscience, basking in the love of his fellow citizens.

Having no other building to erect for the joy and amazement of his people, he daydreamed about various catastrophes that would give him the opportunity to demonstrate the benevolence in his heart. "If only a horrible plague would wipe out the whole town overnight," he said to himself. "Oh, how I would nurse them, how I would massage them ...! They would die, though, it's true ... They would just keep dying, one after another, until it became monotonous ... If only they could die all at once, in groups of ten, twenty, thirty at a time ... Oh, what good use I could find for my energy, my organizational skills, my benevolence toward those rotten bastards!"

At moments like that, the heart of a Jules Simon truly seemed to beat inside his chest.

One day, his dream came true; it was in 1885, when cholera devastated Marseilles and Toulon. The mayor was out walking one morning on the quay of Le Kernac, and his thoughts crossed land and water, and roamed freely among the cholera sufferers in those distant cities. He pictured overrun hospitals, streets in mourning, the terror of the inhabitants, the corpses twisted by an agonizing death, the shortage of coffins, the great fires blazing on the public squares, and he said to himself, "How lucky they are, the mayors over there ...! I could never have such luck ... And yet, what do they do with it? Not a thing ...! They just go to pieces, that's all. They are not organizers. Ah, if only a great epidemic would come to me, then they'd see. They don't know the half of what I can do yet . . . And what do I ask in return . . . ? Absolutely nothing . . . I have no other ambition except to be of service . . . The Cross of the Legion of Honor would be thanks enough . . ."

At that moment, a schooner from Quiberon sailed into port and docked at the quay, against the pier where the mayor, transfixed, dreamed his charitable dreams. And all at once, he jumped. "Oh, my God!" he screamed.

On the schooner's deck, a sailor lay on a pile of nets, seemingly in the throes of some unspeakable illness. His legs twisted, his arms rigid, his whole head shaking with gasping hiccups, he let out strange moans and even stranger curses. Deeply moved, the mayor spoke with the captain of the schooner.

"Is this man ill . . . ? Does he have . . . cholera . . . ?"

"Cholera?" the captain said, shrugging. "Oh, yes . . . a funny sort of cholera . . . He's drunk, the pig . . ."

The sailor continued moaning. A spasm shook him all over. He raised himself a little on his wrists and, his mouth agape, his head lolling, his chest heaving with internal struggles, he projected a long stream of vomit.

"Hurry . . . hurry . . . help . . . !" roared the mayor. "It's cholera . . . I tell you it's cholera . . . Cholera has come to Le Kernac . . ."

Some men gathered around . . . Others ran away . . . The mayor gave orders: "Phenic acid . . . ! Steam heat . . . ! Light fires on the quay . . . !"

And, in spite of the objections of the captain, who continued to say, "But I'm telling you, he's drunk," the mayor leapt aboard the schooner. "Help me . . . help me . . . Have no fear . . ." They picked up the sailor and brought him ashore. Carried by three men (as supervised by the mayor), he was taken to the hospital by a roundabout route that led through every street in town.

"What is that . . . ? What is that . . . ?" the women asked, seeing that bizarre cortege pass by.

And the mayor answered, "It's nothing . . . Go back to

your homes ... It's nothing ... Have no fear ... It's just—
cholera ...!"

The women, turning pale at this news, ran through the
town, screaming and grimacing in fright. "Cholera ...! Cholera ...! Cholera is here ...!"

And while everyone was stampeding in all directions, the
mayor commanded in a booming voice, "Go and tell the rector
... Ring the bells ... Tell everyone cholera is in our streets ...
Have no fear ... Light fires, like they did in Marseille ..."

At the hospital, the mayor wanted to nurse the sick man
himself. He took off the sailor's pants and cleaned the diarrhea
that covered his body ... And when the nuns seemed a bit
faint, he comforted them: "Do you see ...? I have no fear ...
There is nothing to fear ... Everything is fine ... I am here ..."

Then he placed the man in a warmed bed, rubbing him for
a long time with a brush, and placing red-hot bricks along the
sides of his body, under his feet, under his armpits, and upon
his stomach.

The sailor groaned, thrashed about, threw off the bricks,
which were burning his skin, and let out angry curses mixed
with piercing cries.

"Cramps ... he's got cramps ... Rum ... Hurry ..." ordered the mayor. "Bring me a bottle of rum ... There's no time
to lose ... Have no fear ..." He placed the neck of the full bottle between the patient's lips. The old souse perked up immediately. A look of joy illuminated his face.

"There ... you see ...?" said the mayor. "He's coming
around again ... That's better ... It's the rum ... We will save
him ... Help me ..." And with a rapid movement, he tilted
the bottle straight up, the neck deep in the sailor's mouth.

Suddenly, the sailor began to choke. He flailed his arms
wildly. A spasm seized his throat. The excess liquid streamed
out of his mouth and his nose with a sound of rales and strange
whistles.

"Come on ... just drink ... swallow, sacred sailor," said the
mayor, pushing the bottle even deeper down his throat ... But

his eyes twitched and rolled back into his head. His stiffened members relaxed, his movements ceased . . . The sailor drowned in rum.

"Too late," the mayor pronounced in a grieving voice. "Sacred sailor!"

That evening, the town crier went drumming through the streets of Le Kernac. At every twenty paces, after a drum roll, he read the following proclamation:

> *TO THE INHABITANTS OF LE KERNAC,*
> *My dear fellow citizens,*
> *My dear constituents,*
>
> *Cholera has reached our town.*
> *It has already claimed countless victims.*
> *Rest assured. Your mayor will not abandon you. He has moved into the town hall permanently, prepared for any occurrence, and he is completely determined to fight this plague with you. Trust me.*
> *LONG LIVE LE KERNAC!*

But the streets were already deserted, and all of the citizens were huddling inside their hovels, with chattering teeth.

And now for M. Arthur Lebeau, Parisian clubman.

One night last winter, I was startled awake from a deep sleep by a loud noise, like furniture being knocked over in the next room. At the same moment, the clock struck four and my cat began to howl plaintively. I leapt out of bed and, quickly, rashly, with a courage that only showed how deeply convinced I was that danger was lurking, I threw open the door and dashed into the room. The lights were on, and all at once I saw a gentleman—very elegant, in evening dress, even sporting a few medals, for heaven's sake!—stuffing valuables into an antique valise of yellow leather. The valise was not mine, but the

valuables most certainly were, and something about this business struck me as contradictory and flat-out wrong, so I naturally wanted to stop it. Though I had never seen this particular gentleman before, his face was nonetheless vaguely familiar,
the type you see on the boulevards, at the theater, in restaurants at night, one of those proper, well-groomed faces that always make you say about their owners, "That must be a man
from some exclusive circle!" To pretend that I did not feel the
least surprise at seeing him in my home at four in the morning—a gentleman in formal attire, whom I had not invited to
be there—would be a lie. But it was only a certain surprise,
not compounded by any of the other emotions, such as terror or anger, which would ordinarily accompany a late-night
break-in. This clubman's elegance and good humor instantly
reassured me, for, I must confess, he was the last thing I had
expected to find; instead, I had been afraid of coming face to
face with some hulking, ruffian burglar, and having to fend
him off with some act of violence that was not in my nature,
and which could have turned out in any number of unforeseeable ways.

Seeing me, the elegant stranger stopped his work and, smiling at me in an ironic way that was not unfriendly, said, "Pardon me, sir, for awakening you so rudely . . . But it is not entirely my fault. You have very sensitive furnishings, truly; they
fall right to pieces at even the lightest touch of a crowbar . . ."

I saw, then, that the room had been completely ransacked:
drawers pulled out and emptied; windows shattered; a small
Empire desk, where I hid my stocks and bonds and my family jewels, pathetically up-ended on the carpet . . . In short, a
real pillage . . . And while I took note of these things, my un-
timely visitor continued, in a deep, authoritative voice, "Oh,
these modern furnishings . . . They're really not very durable,
are they? I have a theory that they suffer, as much as anything
else, from the sickness of our times, and that they are as neurasthenic as everyone . . ."

He gave a little laugh, low and infectious, which did not

hurt my feelings, and which revealed, when all was said and done, a man of the best education. I decided to introduce myself. "To whom do I have the honor of speaking?" I asked, no longer so suspicious of my nocturnal guest, even as a stray breeze from the open doors ludicrously blew up the hem of my nightshirt.

"My goodness," the perfect gentleman replied offhandedly, "at a moment such as this, my name might prove too great a shock for you . . . Besides, wouldn't you agree that it would be more suitable to wait until a less unusual occasion for an introduction, which I will be only too glad to make the next time I see you, I give you my word, and which, moreover, I would not want you to think I was angling for, by coming here tonight? I would prefer—with your permission—to maintain the strictest anonymity, at least until I have time to put things back in order."

"So be it, sir . . . But none of this makes it any clearer to me . . ."

"Why I am standing here inside your home, at such an ungodly hour, and surrounded by all this mess?"

"Exactly . . . I didn't think you'd be willing to tell me . . ."

"I should say not!" admitted the elegant gentleman. "Your curiosity is most understandable, and I would never dream of trying to avoid taking responsibility for my actions, here . . . But, pardon me . . .! Since you wish us to speak frankly in this little chat, wouldn't you agree that it might be more prudent for you to put on a robe . . .? Your state of undress worries me . . . It is cold in here . . . and one catches this damnable flu so easily, in this strange weather."

"Excellent thinking . . . Would you excuse me for a minute. . .?"

"By all means, sir, by all means . . ."

I went into my bathroom, where I quickly put on a robe, then I returned to the stranger, who, during my brief absence, had started trying to straighten up the room, demolished by his breaking and entering.

"Leave it, sir, please leave it ... My valet will clean all that up tomorrow ..."

I offered him a seat, I took one myself, and then, after lighting a cigar, I said to him in a friendly tone, "Sir, I am all ears ..."

Before telling his story, the clubman began to collect his thoughts, the way all heroes in novels do. But he quickly gave up on this cliché, and came out with it. "Sir, I am a thief ... a professional thief ... Let's call a spade a spade—a burglar, if you will ... No doubt you surmised this already?"

"Quite so ..."

"That is a credit to your intelligence ... So, I am a burglar. I did not choose to adopt this profession until I had completely proven to myself that, in these troubled times we live in, it was the truest, the most straightforward, the most honest of them all ... Thievery, sir—and I say 'thievery' the way I would say the law, literature, painting, medicine—was looked down upon, as a career, because the only people who went into it, until now, have been odious brutes, repugnant vagabonds, people lacking in elegance and education. Now, I claim to restore to thievery a certain luster, which it has by right, and to make of it a noble, honorable and enviable career. Let us not mince words, sir, and let us see life for what it is. Thievery is the sole preoccupation of mankind. A man chooses any profession—such as it is, please understand—simply because it allows him to more or less steal, and always to steal something from someone else. Your mind is too sharp, you see all too clearly what is hidden behind the deceptive décor of our 'virtues' and our 'honor,' so there is no need for me to support my theory with probing examples and decisive elaborations ..."

His flattery lodged, dead-on, in the area of my greatest vanity—well-earned, at any rate—my expertise in psychology and sociology, so I would never have cut him off with a peremptory and condescending "Well, obviously!" The elegant burglar relaxed a little, and when he spoke again, he was ready to pour out his heart to me. "I want to confine myself to telling you how this theory relates to my own personal experience ... I'll be very direct. I started out in big business ... But the dirty jobs I had to do as a matter of course, the heartless lies, the underhanded tricks, the cost-cutting, the red-lining ... the mergers and takeovers ... all of it quickly became distasteful to my innate good manners and my honest nature, so refined and so scrupulous ... I left business for high finance. High finance disgusted me ... Alas! I could not bring myself to leverage nonexistent companies, to forge fake deeds and fake money, to set up dummy mines, dummy isthmuses, dummy coal mills ... To think about nothing day and night except how to channel money from other people's coffers into my own, to make myself rich by slowly and steadily bankrupting my clients, thanks to hypnotic prospectuses and extortionist (but fully lawful) fees, was an unacceptable occupation to me, and one to which my scrupulous, lie-hating soul refused to yield ... Next, I thought of journalism ... It took me less than a month to see that, short of engaging in risky and complicated blackmail schemes, no one can make a decent living from journalism ... And then, on top of that, I was forced to deal with tainted sources and corrupt contacts every single day. When I think that, today, newspapers are run only by mercenary moguls and money-grubbing financiers, who believe that the power of the press will save them from spending the rest of their lives in prison—and who, moreover, are correct about that ... no, honestly, I could not live with that idea. You have no idea how deeply painful it is for a person such as I, who possesses a certain degree of culture, to be a slave to fat, ignorant fools, the majority of whom cannot read or write except to sign their names at the bottoms of bar tabs ... So, then, I ventured into politics ..."

Here, I could not hold back a burst of laughter which threatened to become a prolonged fit ...

"You guessed correctly," said the charming gentleman. "The less said about that, the better ... Next, I thought of becoming a man of the world ... a true man of the world ... I am a

good-looking young man; some of my attractive qualities are
natural and raw, while others have been refined by the kind of
life I have led ... personality ... an iron constitution ... endless elegance ... Nothing was easier for me than to become
the Boy Wonder of the Royal Street circle ... or to get invited
to Monsieur de Montesquiou's exclusive parties ... But, once
again, I have too many scruples ... Cheating at cards; shooting a horse at the track ... giving money and gifts to the debutantes ... while taking money and gifts from the dowagers ...
selling my name and my high society contacts to yet another
shady banker, popular fashion designer, automobile maker ...
a money-lender, or a pretty girl ...? Good heavens, no ...! In
sum, I ended up exhausting every respectable profession and
honorable career which public or private life can offer an ener-
getic, intelligent and sensitive young man such as I. I saw clearly that thievery (or whatever name you saddle it with) was the
single goal and the single motivation of all human activity—
but how distorted, how disguised, and, as a result, how much
more dangerous! That was when I proposed the following argument to myself: 'Since man cannot escape the iron law of
thievery, he would be far more honorable to practice it openly, and not muffle his natural desire, to appropriate others' pos-
sessions as his own, with pompous excuses, delusional vanities
and meaningless titles whose euphemistic folderol no longer
deceives anyone.' So, every day I stole; every night I broke
into wealthy homes; I took from the coffers of others whatever I needed to fulfill my own needs and human potential. This
took up only a few hours in the middle of every night, between
a chat at the club and a romantic fling at the ball. Apart from
those hours, I lived like everyone else ... I am a member of a
rather chic and well-regarded circle; I cherish my friends and
relations. Only recently, the minister awarded me this cross ...
And whenever I have a big haul, I give generously to everyone. When all is said and done, sir, I practice, openly and honestly, what everyone else practices with torturous detours and
shameful disguises ... In the end, my relieved conscience has

stopped nagging me about anything, because, of all the people I know, I am the only one who has courageously lived up to his own ideals, and rigorously adapted my individual nature to the very mysteries of life itself . . ."

The candles had burned out, and daylight streamed in through the Venetian blinds. I invited that elegant stranger to have breakfast with me, but he declined, saying that he was dressed for dinner, and did not want to offend me with such a faux pas.

Arthur Lebeau is a wonderful conversationalist . . . His personality and charm honestly make me very happy . . . Unfortunately, he is only staying at X briefly . . . barely a week. But he will stop here again, on his way back through . . .

"I am very busy . . . At this moment . . . I have no time," he said to me.

And when I asked him if he was plying his vocation here . . . he replied, "No . . . I am here to rest . . . While I'm here . . . I live off my trust fund."

XIX.

Yesterday we dined at Triceps' house, a dinner party given in honor of his friend and mentor, Doctor Trepan. There were ten guests, all rich and happy. Naturally, both during and after the meal, we spoke of nothing but the misery of the human condition. It is the sort of sadistic pleasure that makes rich people weep, after they have gotten drunk and gorged themselves on sauces, over the poor . . . There is nothing like a gourmet feast, expensive wines, succulent fruit, flower arrangements and good silverware, to inspire socialist feelings in us. The discussion began with questions of the loftiest and most abstract philosophy, but gradually degenerated into the anecdotal . . . And each guest told his story . . .

A well-known writer, a fat, ruddy, rubber-lipped man, with the pointy ears of a faun, said:

"Avenue de Clichy, at one o'clock in the morning. It's freezing rain. The sleet and thick grime on the pavement make it difficult and slippery to walk. The Avenue is nearly deserted. Only one or two other pedestrians pass by, their faces buried in the turned-up collars of their overcoats; only one or two fiacres roll by, empty, or bearing vague shadows to some shadowland; only one or two women pace the sidewalks, which give off a livid glow in the moonlight.

"'Sir . . . sir . . . come home with me . . .'

"Shouts, mingled with obscene curses and threats. Then silence . . . someone scurrying away . . . and back again. This noise gets closer, turns aside, hides, disappears, comes back and fades again, like crows above a battlefield strewn with rotting bodies.

"In every block, only the bars are still open, their blazing windows poking bright yellow holes in the black, dense mass of slumbering houses. And aromas of alcohol and musk—

crime and prostitution—waft through the air in little gusts, complementing and strengthening each other.

"'Sir . . . sir . . . come home with me . . .'

"For the past five minutes, a woman has been following me, whom I cannot see. I can only hear, at my back, her dogged footsteps and her voice whispering its monotonous, pleading refrain . . .

"'Sir . . . sir . . . come home with me . . .'

"I come to a stop under a streetlamp. The woman stops, too, just outside the lamp's circle of light. Nevertheless, I can see what she looks like. She is not beautiful at all—oh, no, too desperate, and her chronic pathetic lament drives away any idea of sin. For sin is ecstasy, silk, perfume, and glossy lips, and your eyes rolling back in your head, and dyed hair, and flesh decorated like altars, burnished like chalices, painted like icons. And it is also a pregnant melancholy, an opulent disgust, a sumptuous lie, gold and pearls half-buried in excrement. This wretched woman has none of that to offer me. Made old by misery more than age itself, enervated by hunger or hard drinking binges slept off in the gutter; deformed by the hideous work of her tragic profession; forced, in order to avoid getting stabbed to death, to keep walking, always walking, all night long, in search of the prowling desire always searching for her; sent reeling from a pimp who takes all her money to the equally extortionist cops, from coldwater flat to prison cell—she is a sad sight to behold. A light wool blouse loosely covers her breasts; muddy skirts flap and beat against her legs, an enormous hat tops her head, whose feathers melt in the rain; and across her stomach she holds her folded hands, two wretched hands red with frostbite, in worn-out fingerless gloves. At this hour, in this place, and given the way she looks and sounds, I take her at first for some charwoman who has been turned out by her employer with nowhere to go, rather than a streetwalker. I am certain she is insecure about her ugliness, self-conscious about the unattractiveness of her body, for she tries to hide her face from my sight even more, stepping farther back into the shadows, and seeming to be begging for alms rather than offering me a good time, repeating in a timid, trembling, nearly ashamed voice, 'Sir . . . Sir . . . come home with me . . . sir . . . I will do anything you want . . . Sir . . . Sir . . . !'

"Since I do not say anything, not because of disgust or disdain, but because I have just now noticed the sinister, red scar-necklace that surrounds her throat from ear to ear, and my heart goes out to her, she adds, in a very low whisper, and in an even more pitifully begging tone, 'Sir . . . if you would prefer it . . . Sir . . . ? I have a little girl at home . . . She is thirteen, sir . . . and very sweet . . . and she knows how to please a man the way a woman should . . . Sir . . . Sir . . . I am begging you . . . come home with me . . . Sir . . . Sir . . . !'

"I ask her, 'Where do you live?'

"And, quickly pointing to the next side street off the Avenue—a maw of shadow, a mouth of the abyss—she answers, 'Very close . . . See there . . . Just two steps away . . . You will be very pleased, let's go!'

"She runs across the street, so as not to give me time to change my mind, so as not to let my lust (or so she thinks) cool off . . . I follow her . . . Ah, that pathetic bitch . . . ! With every step she takes, she looks back at me, to make sure I have not slipped away from her, and she jumps from one enormous round puddle to the next, like some monstrous toad . . . A gang of men, leaving a striptease club, shout obscene comments at her as they pass . . . We disappear down the side street . . . The woman leading the way, me trailing behind, we trudge deeper and deeper into darkness . . .

"'Here we are,' she says. 'See, I wasn't lying . . .'

"She pushes through a door that has been left ajar. At the end of a narrow corridor, a small oil lamp, whose wick smokes and wavers, makes the walls flicker with lurid glimmers of crimes and shadows of death. We go in . . . I feel like I am walking on little furry creatures, like the viscous air itself is coating my arms in slime . . .

"'Be careful, honey . . . Some of these stairs are loose!'

"My being here has restored her confidence. She does not feel as if she has to apologize for herself anymore, perhaps she does not even feel ugly anymore, since I am here, she has me, she has won me over, she has brought home a man, all she has to do to get him to stay is to talk about sex, all she has to do to stimulate his generosity is to promise him love . . . Love . . . ! I am no longer that tentative 'Sir' whom she begged, only a few moments ago; now I am 'honey,' the expected windfall, the one who will, perhaps, provide her with what she will eat tomorrow, or the next sleazy drinking binge that will make her forget her hunger altogether, for a while, along with everything else, everything else, everything else . . . !

"By the oil lamp's flickering flame, she lights a candle and, motioning for me to follow her, leads me up the staircase. It is a long climb. The poor woman climbs with strain, with great effort; she huffs, puffs and gasps; she does not know what to do with her free hand, like a package that is too heavy. 'Not much longer, honey . . . Second floor . . .'

"And the candle drips wax, the walls sweat and suppurate, the wooden floorboards creak beneath our feet. I have to steel my stomach against the waves of nausea rising from the unbearable stench left by all the men who have been here, a rank, damp sweat stinging the nostrils, the smell of piss and shit and come and vomit in all the corners. Behind all the doors, I hear voices, laughing, sobbing, praying; bartering voices, threatening voices, voices giving orders, dirty voices, drunken voices, smothered voices . . . Oh, these voices! The sorrow of these voices in this night-town place of fear, depression and . . . sex!

"Finally we get there. The key creaks in the lock, the door creaks on its hinges, and here we are, inside a tiny room with only one green armchair, its upholstery ripped, missing a leg, and a sort of folding cot where an old lady screeches awake, bolting up like a ghost and staring at me with her bulging yellow eyes, staring strangely through me, like one of those forest birds who sleep all night with their eyes wide open ... In front of the window, underwear dries on a clothesline strung between the walls.

"'I told you about leaving those up,' the woman reproaches the old lady, who lets out some kind of grumble in reply as she takes down the underwear and throws it in a pile on the armchair.

"Another door, the bedroom ... We are alone now. I ask, 'Who is that old lady ...?'

"'She's the one who lets me use the little girl, honey ...'

"'Her mother?'

"'Oh, no! I don't know where she got her from. I only met her yesterday ... She hasn't told me, the poor thing ...! Ah, anyway! She's not very happy at all, not anymore ... Her son is in prison ... He used to be my lover ... He beat a guy to death over on Blanche Street, can you believe that, beat him to death ...? Her girls are in brothels ... and give her nothing ... I don't know how she manages to stay alive ...! Huh! Can you believe it ...?' Then: 'That's why she brought the little girl here ... to try to save her home ... Ah, if you can call it that ...! This place is a hole, a real hole ...!'

"The room is very sparsely furnished, and reveals unspeakable poverty ... The windows have no curtains, the fireplace no fire. The humidity peels the wallpaper from the walls here and there in flaps, like strips of dead skin ... It's so cold we can see our breath when we speak ... The woman apologizes. 'I have no firewood ... or coal ... Winter comes so quickly ...! And then, last month the cops came ... They arrested me ... They held me for three days before they let me go, can you believe it?' And she added, 'If only I had had twenty francs to give them, they would have left me in peace ... The sons of bitches ...! No, it's the truth! Some will let you go for a blowjob ... others want money ... With me, they always ask for money. These things shouldn't be permitted ...'

"At the back of the room, a big bed sprawls, with two pillows propped up against the bolster ... Beside it, another bed, narrower, smaller, where I see a ruffle of blonde hair peeking out from under the covers, and under this blonde ruffle, a thin pale face, asleep.

"'That's the little girl, honey ... Make yourself comfortable ... I'll wake her up ... Ah, you'll see how sexy and how skilled she is ... You will be very pleased ...'

"'No ... no ... let her be.'

"'Don't worry ... She doesn't do it with just anybody ... She only does it with gentlemen—generous gentlemen ...'

"'No ... let her sleep ...'

"'Whatever you say, honey ...'

"She is completely oblivious to the crime she is inviting me to commit; moreover, my refusal strikes her as rude ... When she offered to awaken the child, I watched her closely. Her hands did not tremble; she showed no signs of her blood pressure rising, making her veins throb or her face drain white. I ask her, 'And what if the police found her here, in your room ...? Do you realize you would be hauled into court and thrown into prison?'

"The woman sniffs vaguely, and says, 'Okay, I get it ... What do you want from me?' But when she sees the sad and solemn look in my eyes, she loses her confidence again. She does not dare to look at herself in the mirror; does not dare to show her face to me in the pale candle glow ... Rainwater drips from her hat, like the gutter on a roof ... She places the candle on the mantelpiece, and goes to stand beside the big bed, where she starts to undress in the darkness.

"'No,' I tell her. 'It's no use ... I don't want you, not now.'

"And I place two gold pieces in her hand, two gold pieces which she turns over and over again, weighing them and staring at them as if dazzled, hypnotized; she is speechless.

"I do not say anything, either. What could I say to her? Preach to her about repentance, the beauties of virtue? Words, words, words ...! She is not the guilty one. She is exactly what society has made of her, with its insatiable hunger that needs to be fed its giant daily helping of human souls ... Give her a

speech about rage and revolution ...? What would be the
point ...? More words ... Poverty makes you fearful and
weak; she lacks the strength to wield a knife, or shine a torch
on the selfish contentment of the rich ... Better just to keep
my mouth shut ...! Besides, I did not come here to hold forth
like a socialist. It's not the time for cheap speeches, which fix
nothing and only make us feel better about doing nothing ... I
came here to see, and I saw ... The only thing to do now is
leave ... Goodnight ...!

"The child is still asleep in her bed, with her blonde halo.
Her puberty is just beginning, and already her gums are infect-
ed, her breath is rotten, and there are deep crow's-feet at the
corners of her closed eyes. In the other room, I hear the old
lady pacing back and forth, dragging her slippers across the
creaking floorboards. The woman has hidden her two gold
pieces behind the bolster of her bed, and she whispers to me,
'The old lady will be furious that you did not do anything with
the little girl ... Give her something so she won't take everything you gave me ... She's a mean old lady, a real mean bitch
... Ah, it's true ...! Then wait for me to light your way, sir ...
There are a lot of loose stairs ...!'"

And here is what another dinner guest said:

"The other day, a carpenter came to my house to repair my
bookshelves. He is a very intelligent man who likes to talk.
While he worked, I asked him, 'Do you have any children?'

"'No,' he snapped harshly ... Then, after a pause, he said in
a gentler voice, 'I do not have any, anymore ... I had three
once ... They are all dead ...' He added, shaking his head, 'Ah,
as I live and breathe, when I think of what goes on ... and the
pain you suffer in this life ... perhaps they are better off, dead
... those poor little devils ... At least, they do not have to suffer.'

"I probed, a little cruelly, 'Is it long ago that the last one
died?'

"'Ten years,' he said. 'Ever since then, you see, neither I, nor my wife, wanted more ... No, never again ...'

"I explained to him the way the Piot Law works, that, being such a bad patriot as to have no children, or to no longer have any living children ... he would be subject to a special tax if this law gets voted in ...

"He did not seem very shocked, having gotten used to looking at life philosophically. 'I'm surprised anything's still legal,' he said to me, without a trace of bitterness. 'The law, of course ...! I know how that works ... I know it always works against us poor people ... Laws are what the rich people pass to keep the poor people down ... But, all the same ... what you are telling me about ... it truly is rather cruel ... because, if I have no more children ... it's really all their fault ...'

"'*Their fault* ...? Whose ...?'

"'The authorities ... the State ... I don't personally know the names of all the gentlemen responsible for passing the laws, and all of those responsible for enforcing them ... It's very simple ... and it's nothing new ... The State—we must at least give it credit where credit is due—protects hens, oxen, horses, dogs, and pigs, with a very sophisticated understanding of, and a very admirable eye toward following, scientific progress. They have found methods of raising all of these various, noteworthy animals in perfect hygiene. All throughout France—you can no longer count them all—there are societies for the protection of all the different species of livestock. There are beautiful stables ... beautiful pens ... beautiful henhouses ... beautiful kennels ... well ventilated ... well heated ... and provided not only with the bare necessities ... but with the utmost luxury as well ... They maintain them in a constant and rigorous state of cleanliness ... purified of all bacteria and fatal contagions by daily washings, medical disinfectants, phenic acid, boric acid, etc. I can tell you from personal experience, I have built chicken coops that are like palaces ... It's all well and good ... I am not jealous of the meticulous care that people lavish on animals ... Let us crown them in talent

shows ... let us give them awards ... let us subsidize organic
farms, I'm all for it ... The way I see it, every living being has
the right to be protected, and to be as happy as you can possibly make it ... But I would also like for children—the children of men—to not be, as they are, systematically denied ...
these very same rights ... provided to animals ... And yet, that
seems to be out of question. A child—a child counts for nothing ... Those human vermin can die out, and become extinct
... No one cares ... They even organize wholesale slaughter of
newborns ... as if we were threatened by a dangerous population explosion ... And the leaders, the bosses of this elite society—who are invariably, at the very least, the heartless per-
petuators of the same evils they denounce with such indignant
patriotic fervor—weep bitterly about the ever-decreasing number of children, which they make it so difficult for people to
have in the first place, or which they kill right out of the womb
by the surest and swiftest methods ... For the real child-killer
is this society, so harsh and unfair to young mothers who cannot feed their children ... They have to make it look as though
they are encouraging families to proliferate as much as ever, if
not more, and even threaten them with stiff fines when they finally take it upon themselves to remain childless, not wanting
to bring into the world more lives mercilessly predestined for
misery and death ... Well, I say nay ... it's the last straw ...'
    "He said all of this very calmly, while, high atop an exten-
sion ladder, he slowly and methodically sawed a small wooden
shelf ... The shelf finished, he folded his arms and looked at
me, while shaking his head. 'See, sir,' he said, 'isn't it true what
I am saying ...? When all of those fancy jokers examine their
conscience and recognize once and for all that the evil does
not just come from them ... but pervades the very structure
of this society ... in our barbarism and our greedy, capitalis-
tic laws which protect only the rich ... then, perhaps, we can
begin to change things ... Until then, we will merely continue
to scatter the seeds of human life to the very wind that obliter-
ates them ... What does this nation's wealth and glory matter

to me, when the only right I have here is to expire from sheer hardship, and to dwell in ignorance and servitude . . . ?'

"Then I asked him why and how his three children died.

"'All, or nearly all, died at home,' he answered me. 'Ah, it's a brief story, and it has happened to everyone I know . . . Case after case, suffering sometimes takes different forms, but the end result is always the same . . . I told you, just now, that I had three children . . . All three were healthy and strong, likely to live a good long life, I assure you . . . The first two, born thirteen months apart, died in the same way . . . Where I live, it is rare for the mother to be able to nurse her offspring with her own milk . . . Poor or insufficient nutrition . . . household worries . . . hard work, overwork . . . Well, I am sure you can imagine what happened next . . . The children were started on bottle-feeding . . . But they were already wasting away . . . Within four months, they had become puny and sickly enough for us to be worried . . . The doctor told me, 'Of course! It's always the same . . . All the milk is worthless . . . The milk itself is poisoning your children.' So I said to the doctor, 'Show me where there is good milk, and I will buy it.' But the doctor shook his head and said, 'There is no good milk in Paris . . . Send your surviving child to the country.' I turned the babe over to public assistance, who in turn entrusted him to a foster-mother in Percheron . . . Eight days later, he was dead . . . He died, the way they all die down there, from lack of care, from the savagery of the peasants . . . from filth . . . My third child, I kept him at home . . . He was doing very well . . . In those days, it is true, my wife and I had good jobs, and money was not lacking . . . He was fat and pink, and he never cried . . . Impossible to imagine a stronger, more beautiful boy . . . I do not know how he contracted that disease of the eyes which was spreading through our neighborhood back then . . . The doctor told me he had to be hospitalized . . . There was a special hospital for that disease. Oh, there was no shortage of hospitals . . . ! The little one recovered; but on the day when his mother was going to bring him home, she found him bawling and frown-

ing, convulsed with wracking coughs ... He had come down
with infantile diarrhea ... They would not treat him at the
hospital ... His mother was baffled ... Some kind of intern,
who happened to be there, said, 'We only treat eye diseases
here ... If you want him treated for diarrhea ... take him to a
different hospital.' His mother prayed, begged, threatened—
all in vain ... She picked up her ailing baby in her arms to take
him to a hospital which they had recommended ... He expired
on the way there ... And that was it ...! And now they come
back to give me the same speech: "Reproduce, for the glory of
God ...! Reproduce ...!" Ah, no thank you ... I'm done with
that ...'

"And, shrugging, he said, in a firmer voice, 'They are truly shameless, those fine gentlemen ... Instead of trying to find
tricks to increase the population, they would do better to find
some way of increasing the happiness and prosperity of the
people who are already born ... Yes, indeed ... But as far as
that goes ... they just don't give a damn ...!'

"When he had finished his work, he contemplated the
books arranged on my library shelves. 'Voltaire,' he said,
'Diderot ... Rousseau ... Michelet ... Tolstoy ... Kropot-
kin ... Anatole France ... Yes, that's all very nice ... But what
good does it do ...? Books are where ideas go to die ... Truth
and happiness never come from them ...'

"He packed up his tools, and left, very sadly ... very sadly ..."

A third, a landowner from Normandy, told us this:

"Old Man Rivoli owns a wall. This wall runs alongside a road.
And it is falling down. The rains and the road-workers' pick-
axes have eroded the foundations; loose stones barely stay in
place; and gaps open up. Nonetheless, it still looks pretty, with
the charm of an ancient ruin. Some iris crown the top of the
wall, some linaria, baby's-breath, jonquils sprout in the breach-
es; also, delicate poppies bobble in the breaks between the

stones. But Old Man Rivoli feels no appreciation for the lyric aspect of his wall, and, after looking at it for a long time, after pulling out the loose stones, like teeth in a poor man's jaw, he finally decides to fix it.

"He does not need to hire a mason, since he has been a jack of all trades, all his life. He knows how to mix mortar, just as he knows how to plane a wooden board, to forge an iron rod or raise a roof beam. Besides, a mason will be expensive, and will take longer to finish the job. So, Old Man Rivoli buys some lime, some sand; he finds several stones in his orchard and carries them out to the road, piling them at the base of his wall; and just like that, he gets to work.

"But, on the first morning, he has scarcely slapped on a half-full trowel of mortar to fill the first hole, scarcely installed the first stone, when he suddenly hears a harsh voice at his back. 'Well, now, Old Man Rivoli, what are you doing down on your knees there?'

"It's the road surveyor, on his morning rounds. He carries a pack on his back, crammed full of surveying tools, and two levels under his arm, painted black and red . . . 'Ah, ah!' he says again, taking up an imposing stance on the curb as the living embodiment of the bureaucratic regulatory commission . . . 'Ah, ah, at your age . . . you are still placing yourself in violation of the law . . . ? Tsk, tsk. So, let me repeat my question, what are you doing?'

"Old Man Rivoli turns and says, 'Well . . . I'm fixing my wall, what else . . . ? You can see how it's falling down everywhere . . .'

"'I do see that,' replies the surveyor. 'But, do you have a permit?'

"Old Man Rivoli becomes alarmed and stands up, holding his stiff, arthritic back with both hands. 'What do you mean, a permit . . . ? Isn't my own wall mine . . . ? I need a permit to do whatever I please with my own wall . . . ? Can't I bulldoze the thing and then build it again from the ground up, if I have a mind to . . . ?'

"'Don't get smart with me, you old reprobate . . . You know what that will get you if you do . . .'

"'When all is said and done,' persists Old Man Rivoli, 'is it mine, this wall—yes or no?'

"'This wall is yours . . . but it is on the public road . . . and you do not have the right to fix a wall that is yours, when it's on a public road . . .'

"'But you can clearly see that it's not staying up anymore, and if I don't fix it, it's just going to keel over like a dead man . . .'

"'That's very likely . . . but not my concern . . . I am citing you: primo, for fixing your wall without a permit; secundo, for placing, also without a permit, building materials on a public thoroughfare. You must pay a fine of fifty crowns, hee, hee, Old Man Rivoli . . .! That will teach you not to be ignorant of the law . . .'

"Old Man Rivoli's mouth drops open very wide, toothless and as coal-black as an oven . . . He is so stupefied, he cannot utter a single word. His eyes spin around in his head like little tops. After a minute, he tears off his cap and throws it onto the ground, moaning, 'Fifty crowns . . .! How is that possible . . .? Jesus, Lord God!'

"The surveyor continues, 'And that's not all . . . You will fix your wall . . .'

"'No, no . . . I will not fix it . . . It's not worth fifty crowns . . . It can do whatever it wants . . .'

"'You will fix your wall,' the bureaucrat insists in an imperious tone, 'because it's threatening to collapse, and if it falls it will damage the road . . . And remember this: if your wall does fall, I will cite you again, and this time you will have to pay a fine of one hundred crowns . . .'

"Old Man Rivoli panicked. 'One hundred crowns . . .! Ah, what awful luck! What kind of times am I living in?'

"'But, before you do anything, listen to me well . . . you must make a formal written request for a permit, get it notarized for a few guineas, and send it to the prefect . . .'

"'But I don't know how to write . . .'

"'Not my concern . . . That's what you have to do . . . And I've got my eye on you . . .'

"Old Man Rivoli goes back home. He does not know what to do about this problem; but the one thing he does know is that the government does not make idle threats. If he fixes his wall, it's a fine of fifty crowns; if he does not fix it, it's one hundred crowns . . . They are forcing him to fix his wall, and they are preventing him from doing so, at the same time. In any case, he is liable, and he must pay . . . His thoughts become jumbled. His head aches. And, feeling his powerlessness and his distress in all their extremity, he sighs, 'And just the other day, the President made a speech saying the will of the individual reigns supreme . . . that no decision can be made without my approval, and I can do whatever I want . . .'

"He asks advice from a neighbor who knows the law, being a municipal councilor. 'That's just how it is, Old Man Rivoli,' he tells him, in a pompous tone. 'You must go through proper channels . . . And since you don't know how to write at all, I would like to help you with this little task . . . I myself shall draft your request for a permit . . .'

"The request is mailed. Two months go by . . . The prefect does not reply . . . Prefects never reply . . . They are too busy composing verses, flirting with the court clerks' wives, or going off to Paris, where they spend their evenings at the Olympia, in the company of ambassadors. Every week, the surveyor stops by Old Man Rivoli's house. 'Well . . . what about that permit?'

"'Nothing yet.'

"'You must send a follow-up letter . . .'

"A whole series of follow-up letters end up joining the original notarized request inside the crypt of a desk drawer, buried under irremovable layers of dust. Every day, Old Man Rivoli watches for the mailman as he passes on his route. The mailman never comes to his door. And the gaps in the wall grow wider; more stones come loose and roll onto the curb, the wasted mortar dries up in the bucket and crumbles, hardening

more and more, because in the time that has passed, a bad frost
has come; and the gaps gain more and more ground, like lep-
rosy eating away that wretched, half-crumbled wall.

"One very windy night, it comes tumbling down all at
once. Old Man Rivoli sees the disaster in the morning, at
dawn. In its fall, the wall has brought down the espaliers of the
orchard, which produced such lovely fruit in autumn. Nothing
protects the unlucky man's property now; thieves and hobos
can come in whenever they like, chase the hens and steal the
eggs . . . And the road surveyor comes back, bullying, 'Ah . . . !
You see, I told you so . . . Naturally, it fell down . . . ! See! I am
going to cite you now . . .'

"Old Man Rivoli sobs like a baby, brokenly. 'How is it my
fault? How is it my fault? Since you prevented me from fixing
it!'

"'Come now, come now . . . it's not such a big deal, after all
. . . With the fifty crowns from the first fine, it will only be one
hundred and fifty crowns, plus damages . . . You can certainly
afford that.'

"But Old Man Rivoli can not afford that. His entire fortune was in his orchard, and in his two arms which kept the
orchard growing with continuous effort. The good-natured fellow turns gloomy . . . He does not leave his house anymore, remaining seated, all day long, in front of the cold, dead hearth,
his head in his hands . . . The bailiff comes, twice. He forecloses
on the house, then he forecloses on the orchard. In a week,
they are going to auction off everything . . . Then, one evening,
Old Man Rivoli gets up from his chair, and the cold, dead
hearth, and goes downstairs to the cellar, silent, unlit . . . Feeling his way in the dark, among his empty cider jugs, his work
tools, and his baskets, he looks for the thick rope that he uses
to wrap around his wine barrels . . . Then he climbs back up
the stairs, to his orchard.

"In the middle of the orchard, a massive old walnut tree
spreads its knotty, solid branches over the grass, up in the sky

turning pearly with the first moonbeams. He ties the rope around one of the highest branches, for he has glimpsed, in this tree, a means of escape. Bough by bough, he climbs even higher; then he ties the rope around his neck and jumps off, into empty space ... The spooling rope snaps taut around the branch, and the branch softly creaks ...

"The next day, the mailman brings the permit from the prefect ... He sees the hanged man swinging at the end of the rope, in the orchard, among the branches of the tree, where two birds are shrieking at the top of their lungs."

Then, a fourth guest tells us:

"Late one evening, after a fruitless, frustrating day, Johnny Rags decided to head for home ... Some home ...! That's what he called a certain bench he had picked out in the middle of Anvers Square, where he had been sleeping for more than a month, with the boughs of a chestnut tree for a canopy ... At that exact moment, he happened to be on the boulevard, standing in front of a burlesque house, where the competition for spare change, getting worse and worse as the night wore on (he was feeling out-of-sorts to begin with, and luck was not on his side), had left the beggar with a laughable haul ... only two pennies, and on top of that, two foreign pennies that were completely worthless ...

"'For a guy to palm off two bad pennies on a poor bastard like me ... And naturally, a millionaire to boot ...! Adding insult to injury ...'

"He pictured the gentleman again ... a handsome gent, dressed to the nines ... white tie ... a blindingly white shirt-front ... and a gold-handled walking stick ... Johnny Rags just shrugged it off, feeling no malice.

"What worried him most was getting back to Anvers Square ... It was very far away, and he was very attached to 'home,' his bench. It wasn't too bad there, when all was said and done;

at least he knew he would not be bothered . . . because he knew
the cops, who decided to take pity on him and let him sleep in
peace . . .

"'Heavens!' he said. 'This was one hell of a day . . . the worst
one I've had . . . in the past three weeks . . . And let's face it, the
begging business is at an all-time low . . . If the English have
any fault. . . and they like to think they don't . . . ! Ah, bless the
English . . . and may the devil take them . . . !'

"He set out walking, still holding out the hope of running
into another charity-minded gentleman along the way, or a
generous souse who might give him two pennies . . . two real
pennies this time, which he could use to buy some bread, tomorrow morning . . . 'Two pennies . . . two real pennies . . .
Who am I kidding? This isn't Peru . . . !' he kept saying to himself, while dragging his feet . . . for, on top of the fatigue he felt,
he also had a hernia, which was more painful than usual.

"And, when he had been walking for fifteen minutes, and
was losing all hope of running into a generous gent again, he
suddenly stepped on something soft . . . His first thought was
that it might be shit . . . Then, he thought it might be something good to eat . . . So often it's hard to tell the difference!
Chance is rarely kind to the poor, and does not usually have
pleasant surprises in store for them . . . Nevertheless, he remembered the evening when he found a leg of mutton on
Blanche Street, very fresh, a magnificent, enormous leg, fallen,
no doubt, from a butcher's cart . . . What he had stepped in, at
that moment, was not, of course, a leg . . . Perhaps it was a cut-
let . . . a goose liver, a veal heart . . . 'Gracious me!' he said to
himself. 'Let me just see for myself . . .'

"And he bent down to pick up whatever was under his
shoe . . . 'Huh!' he said. 'Well, now that I'm touching it . . . I
can tell it isn't something to eat . . . I've been robbed . . .'

"The street was empty . . . No bobby on the beat . . . He
went to a streetlamp to take stock of what he was holding in
his hand . . . 'Oh, well, now, what have we here . . . ? There,
that's better . . .' he muttered to himself, out loud.

"It was a black leather wallet with silver-capped corners ...
Johnny Rags opened it and looked inside ... In one of the
pockets, he found a wad of cash ... ten one-thousand dollar
bills, attached by a clip. 'Well now, would you look
at that ...!' he said ... And, shaking his head, he added,
'When I think that some people go around carrying wallets
like this in their pockets ... and inside the wallets, ten thousand dollars ...! What a shame ...'

"He went through the other pockets of the wallet ... There
was nothing else there ... no business card ... no photograph ... no letter ... nothing that gave any information about
the person who owned that fortune ... which he held now ...
in his own hand.

"And, closing up the wallet again, he said to himself, 'Well,
thanks a lot ...! Now I have to take this to a police station.
That's going to take me completely out of my way ... and I'm
already so very ... very tired ... No, truly ... I'm having the
worst luck tonight ...'

"The street was even emptier now ... No passerby passed
by ... No bobby on the beat ... Johnny Rags changed course,
and started walking to the nearest police station ...

"Johnny Rags had a hard time getting in to see the magistrate ... His raggedy clothes and gaunt, sooty face made them
immediately think he was a criminal. In fact, they were on the
verge of jumping on him ... and putting him in handcuffs ...
But, because of his gentle manner and his patient calmness, he
finally persuaded them to let him into the police commissioner's office ...

"'Mr. Police Commissioner,' greeted Johnny Rags, 'I have
something for you that I found just now, right under my foot,
out in the street ...'

"'What is it?'

"'It's this, Mr. Commissioner,' replied the poor wretch, letting the wallet dangle from the tips of his bony fingers ...

"'Okay ... okay ... and I suppose ... the wallet's empty, of
course?'

"'Look for yourself, Mr. Commissioner . . .'

"He opened the wallet, took out the wad of cash . . . counted it . . . and his eyes bulged with astonishment. 'Say, now . . . say, now!' he cried. 'There's ten thousand dollars here . . . ! Sapristi . . . ! This is a fortune . . . a fortune . . . Jesus Christ . . . !'

"Johnny Rags stayed completely calm. He said, 'When I think there are people going around with ten thousand dollars in their wallets . . . what a shame!'

"The commissioner could not take his eyes off this tramp, staring at him strangely . . . with astonishment more than admiration in his eyes. 'And you're the one who found this . . . ? But, sapristi . . . you are truly an honest man . . . an honorable man . . . You're a hero . . . That's the only word for it . . . A hero.'

"'Oh, no, Mr. Commissioner . . . !'

"'A hero . . . There's no doubt about it in my mind . . . because, when you get down to it . . . it would have been very easy for you to . . . Well, when all is said and done, my good man . . . you are a hero, that's all there is to it . . . ! You have performed a noble, selfless act here . . . the act of a hero . . . No, there's no other word for it . . . You deserve the Montyon Prize . . .'

"'Prize . . . Mr. Commissioner?'

"'Don't tell me you've never heard of the Montyon Prize . . . It's given every year to a poor person who shows himself capable of being good . . . by committing a virtuous act . . .'

"'Who came up with that prize?'

"'Why, naturally, a millionaire . . . The prize is named for him . . . Montyon. What you've done deserves it if anything does . . . What is your name?'

"'Johnny Rags . . . Mr. Commissioner.'

"The commissioner raised his arms to the smoke-filled ceiling of his office as if calling on God in heaven. 'And his name is Johnny Rags . . . ! That's just perfect . . . That's like something from a novel . . . Your profession?'

"'Alas!' replied the beggar. 'I don't have one . . .'

"'Why don't you have a profession ...? You live off a trust fund ...?'

"'Public charity, Mr. Commissioner ... And, indeed, can I say that I truly live?'

"'Ah, hell! Hell ...! I'm afraid that things are looking worse and worse for you ... Hell and damnation!' The commissioner made a kind of scowl, and, speaking in a far more dour tone of voice now, he said, 'So, what it comes down to is, you're a street beggar?'

"'Well, of course I am ... Mr. Commissioner.' "'Of course ...! Of course!' The commissioner became very solemn ... After a brief silence, he asked, 'Where do you live?'

"Johnny Rags replied, discouraged, 'How do you expect me to have a home?'

"'You have no home?'

"'Alas, no ...!'

"'You have no home ...? Say, are you making fun of me, my good man?'

"'I assure you ... not at all ...'

"'But you are legally required to have a home ... required under Article 269 of the penal code, which makes homelessness a felony offense.'

"'And through sheer bad luck ... I am required not to have one ... I have no job ... I have no money. And, when I hold out my hand ... people stick foreign pennies into it ... On top of everything else ... I am old and sick ... I have a hernia ...'

"'A hernia ... a hernia ...! That's all well and good ... I'm sure you do ... have a hernia ... But you have no home ... You are in a state of being homeless ... You are, quite simply, guilty of the felony offense of homelessness ... and subject to three to six months in prison, as a menace to society ... Ah, anyway ... anyway ... even if the laws do not apply to heroes ... they most certainly do apply to the homeless ... I am forced to arrest you ... This bothers me ... this disturbs me ... because ... what you have done ... is truly quite noble ... but ... what do you expect ...? Laws are laws ... We must uphold

them ... Poor unlucky heroic bastard ...! What an uncanny
thing ...!'

"While he spoke, he tossed the wallet up in the air and
caught in his hand, again and again ... Then he continued,
'Here's this wallet ... Okay ... In your place, and in your position, there are probably not very many who would have turned
it in ... I admit that ... I do not want to suggest that you were
a complete idiot to turn in this wallet ... No ... quite the opposite ... Your action is to be admired ... It is worthy of some
reward ... and that reward is ... the sum of one dollar ...
which we will have no trouble paying you once we find—if we
can ever find him—the owner of this wallet and the ten thousand dollars cash inside it ... Yes, but this does not take care of
the fact that you have no home ... And that is everything,
Johnny Rags ... Do you understand me ...? There isn't a single statute in the penal code, or anywhere else for that matter,
which requires you to find wallets stuffed with banknotes in
the street ... There is, on the contrary, a very definite statute
which requires you to have a home ... Ah, you would have
been better off, I assure you, finding yourself a home instead of
this wallet ...'

"'So, what happens now?' asked Johnny Rags.

"'So,' replied the commissioner. 'That's it ... You are going
to jail tonight ... And tomorrow, I will send you to a work
camp for beggars, for forced labor ...'

"And he pressed a buzzer ... Two sergeants came into the
room ... The magistrate motioned them with his hand ...
And while they dragged Johnny Rags off to a jail cell, the poor
man groaned, 'I can't believe it ...! Truly, today has been my
unlucky day ... These blessed bourgeoisie, I ask you, wouldn't
it be better for all of us if they kept their wallets in their pockets ...? What a shame ...!'"

And, finally, a fifth tale:

"I hope you will excuse me if my story is less amusing ... We have expounded on the comedy of pain . . . now it is time for the tragedy of pain . . . It's just as painful . . . albeit not at all funny . . ."

And he began: "One morning, a man of about fifty, very shabbily dressed, with a diseased, dilapidated look, gesticulating dramatically, babbling incoherently, rang my doorbell. After a few explanations, which terrified my maid and explained nothing, he asked to see me . . . Servants have no appreciation for a good mystery, they dislike poor people altogether, and they dread a wild, agonized face . . . She told him I was out . . . that I would not be coming home until quite late . . . even, possibly . . . no, definitely . . . I would not be coming home at all . . . The man seemed dismayed for a moment, but he did not press the point, and went away, saying nothing more . . .

"Half an hour later, he rang my doorbell again . . . His facial expression was, it seemed, completely changed . . . He looked calm, nearly beaming . . . He smiled at the maid, and his smile was filled with tenderness and kindness . . . In an extremely polite tone of voice, he said, 'Please give him these four pages, which I have just now written, down in the concierge's office . . . Please give them to him as soon as he comes home . . . Do not forget . . . It is a matter of life and death . . .' In a lower, more mysterious voice, he added, 'The fate of the entire human race is at stake. You can see how urgent this is . . . But, not a word . . . ! Especially to the cook . . . Cooks are imbeciles . . . They are sworn to destroy the human race . . .'

"Meanwhile, he handed them over one by one, those four sheets of paper covered in extremely large, spaced-out, feverish scrawl, very firm in places, very shaky in others . . . with nothing crossed out . . . In some places the ink was still wet. 'Not a word . . . !' he said again. 'I am counting on you . . .' And, without any other remarks, he dashed headlong down the stairs."

The guest reached into the pocket of his smoking jacket and took out a little roll of paper, which he unfolded. "If there is anyone here who is easily shocked and offended, I beg them to close their ears now . . . Here is the letter . . ." And he read:

"Sir,

"Ah! I know all too well the reason why ... why you do not understand me ... why you do not love me ... why you will never love me, and why everything in your being will abandon me to die on the gallows, or rot away in prison, freezing to death, with no one even to glance at me out of curiosity, let alone look upon me with compassion ...

"Others such as yourselves, sirs, you are strong and healthy boys ... You have clear skin, unclouded eyes, long arms ... And your bellies. Ah, yes, your bellies ...! But that doesn't matter at all ... I, too, need to eat ... God knows!

"Others such as yourselves, sirs, you are born ... and you grow up in charming countrysides where nourishment grows everywhere, where literally nothing grows that is not nourishing ... And, your muscles filled with strength, veins filled with hot blood, lungs filled with clean air, you tear yourself away from the joy and fecundity of your home towns, you come to Paris bringing this gorgeous ideal with you, this ideal which smells so sweetly of fresh meadow grass, freshwater springs, the tranquility and stillness of deep forests ... barns and hay ... Oh, hay! And when you come to Paris ... you conquer the city, even though (I hate to break this news to you!) you know virtually nothing about what Paris is really like.

"Parisian—ah, I would give everything I have (if I had anything) ... not to be, never to have been ... Perhaps then I would be less depressed ... Perhaps I would suffer slightly less and have slightly more hair on my head ... And most likely, too, if I was not from Paris, I would have been born somewhere else, like the rest of you ...! It is also possible I would never have been born, anywhere, which would have been the luckiest thing of all, for me ...

"For I myself am a son of Paris ... born from destitute thighs ... and degenerate people ... Crime was my father, poverty my mother ... My childhood friends were named Little Smokes, Garlic Breath, Kid Tramp, and The Death-Cheater ... Most of those unlucky bastards died in prison, the rest on the gallows ... And I feel certain that a similar death has been set aside for me ...! Until age eleven, I had never even seen a meadow ... a bubbling spring ... a lovely forest ... I had only seen knives, crazy eyes ... bloodstained hands ... (oh, wretched hands!) ... red from having killed ... and pale hands ... (oh, wretched hands!) ... pale from having stolen ...! And what else could they do?

"My eyes, in bouts of rage, in anger and in hunger ... and also in love ... have the same glint as those knives from my childhood, and remind you of the guillotine blade ... And my hands ... ah, my hands ... they have seen everything ... And having seen so many terrifying, sad or pathetic things ... they have remained savage hands ... clenched fists ... that can no longer do honest work.

"I did my time in the factories and sweatshops of Paris ... I did heavy lifting, and worked assembly lines ... I choked on smoke ... and I went down into mineshafts ... And I starved in my hunger, and I found, among my companions, no one to love me ... There was no time ... and work hardened our hearts ... and made us despise each other ...

"Later, at thirty, I came to a house where things were not as they seemed ... It was a bourgeois home ... No idling allowed, and no crime ... There was one master there ... instead of two hundred ... There, I was forced to obey ... I became resigned ... I learned self-control ... My days off helped ... Since the house was in the country, I relaxed by taking long strolls in the surrounding fields and woods ... And I spoke to bubbling springs ... to flowers along the roads and in the meadows ... And, although prematurely aged by suffering and worn out by work, I had youthful dreams again, as if I were sixteen ...

"Then, I went back to Paris ... And I wandered the streets every evening, going to bars ... to dives ... And I finally found some friends ... They were good-hearted, honest people, amateur drunks, veteran drunks ... amateur pimps, veteran pimps ... sad and funny ... generous and selfish ... And I loved them because they, at least, had a soul ...

"Yes, but this is not living . . .

"Feeling things and dragging one's sorrow from place to place, from evening to morning, from bars to prison, is not living . . .

"And now, here is all I want to do in life: make them despise me so much that they end up locking me away in a madhouse . . . prison . . . or clinic . . .

"When all is said and done, I want to become a menace to society . . .

"And I myself, for the people of Paris and for the peasants whom I love, I myself will go . . . yes . . . I will go and knock on the door of every deputy and every elector, even if there are one hundred million of them, and I will ask them to finally put us out of our misery, once and for all.

"For the people of Paris, and for the peasants whom I love, I will go . . . yes . . . I will go and find Loubet; and I will drag him to every single drugstore and opium den in Rue de la Roquette, Rue de Charonne, the Antoine slum, on a pay-day . . . Then I will take him to all the employment agencies where people gather, clamoring for jobs, and I will force him to go into the hovels where wasted, penniless wrecks are on the nod . . .

"For the people of Paris . . . and for the peasants whom I love . . . I will go . . . yes . . . I will go and invite the King of Belgium, the Prince of Wales, and all the kings, and all the rich and happy people, to come with me to the bars of Montmartre, the prisons, the work camps . . . until they learn to love prostitutes and cherish pimps, and all the other good-hearted people whom they hurt and destroy with their laws, their police dogs, and their gallows, and until they start erecting palaces and statues to them.

"For the people of Paris and for the peasants whom I love, I will go . . . yes, I will go and formally invite M. Georges Leygues and M. Henry Roujon to accompany me to the theaters of Paris, to the Louvre . . . and to the Academies, and to the Sorbonne . . . What a disgrace!

"And I will go to Rome and tell the Pope that the people of

Paris and the peasants, whom I love, do not want his Church anymore, his priests or his prayers . . . And I will go and tell the kings, the emperors, and the republics that their armies and their massacres are over . . . All of that blood and all of those tears, with which they flooded the entire universe, for no good reason . . .

"And I will wave my knife and my bloodstained hands in all of those faces, plunge them into all of those bellies.

"And that is how I will become a menace to society . . .

"I hold out the ardent hope of seeing you very soon, on a day when you will not be overburdened with work, when you return home at a decent hour, and when you are not in a hurry . . .

"I hate people who are in a hurry."

The speaker refolded the paper and put it back in his pocket . . . There was a silence, and I felt a chill run up my spine . . .

In keeping with his duties as master of the house, Triceps had not spoken a single word during all of these recitations . . . But he was never one to let scientific conclusions go undrawn. "My friends," he said, "I have listened attentively to your stories. And they have only confirmed me all the more strongly in the opinion I have held for a long time now—ever since the Congress of Folrath, specifically—that I myself have found the very heart of human misery. While you might argue that poverty is the result of a broken, unfair social order, I myself believe it is nothing other than an individual physiological degenerative disorder . . . While you might claim that the social question can only be resolved through political action, Marxism, or radical literature, I have screamed myself blue in the face that it can only be solved through a kind of therapy . . . It's obvious . . . There is no doubt about it . . . Ah, science, what a miracle . . . ! Did you know that, in the wake of certain rigorous, incontrovertible experiments, some scientists and I were led to declare that genius, for example, was nothing but a particularly grievous form of mental illness . . . ? Men

of genius . . . ? Maniacs, alcoholics, perverts, madmen all . . .
Thus, for a long time we were under the impression that Zola
had a very strong, healthy mind; all of his books seemed to
bear witness to this, to scream this truth . . . But not at all . . . !
Zola? An offender . . . a sick man in need of treatment, not
admiration . . . and someone whom I do not understand why
we haven't yet locked away in a madhouse . . . in the name of
public safety . . . Understand, my friends, that what I am saying about Zola is equally true of Homer, Shakespeare, Molière,
Pascal, Tolstoy . . . Madmen . . . madmen . . . madmen all . . .
Did you also know that the so-called spiritual faculties, the
so-called moral virtues of which man is so proud, and which
(oh idiocy!) we strive to develop through higher education . . .
yes, when all is said and done . . . intelligence, memory, courage, integrity, turning the other cheek, devotion, friendship,
etc., etc., are nothing but severe psychological defects . . . degenerative disorders . . . more or less dangerous symptoms of
the single most universal and terrible malady of our time: neurosis . . . ? Well, one day I asked myself the following question:
'What is poverty . . . ?' I began to reason, and I said to myself, 'Let's see . . . let's see now . . . let's throw out all the com-
monplaces, all the clichés which authors, poets, and philoso-
phers have bruited back and forth for centuries and centuries
. . . How is it possible, in a time of production and overpro-
duction such as ours, that there are still poor people . . . ? How
is it conceivable, how does it make sense that in an age where
we mass-produce too much linen, too much velvet, too much
cotton and silk, we still encounter people dressed in rags . . . ?
How can human beings die of famine and malnutrition when
food products and edible items of all varieties overflow all the
grocery stores in the universe . . . ? By what anomaly (inexplicable, it seems, at first glance) do we see—surrounded by so
many squandered resources, so much surplus literally going to
waste—men who actually strive to remain poor . . . ?' The answer was simple: 'Are they criminals . . . ? No . . . Maniacs, perverts, deviants, madmen . . . ? Yes . . . ! Sick people, when all is

said and done ... And I must cure them ...!'"

"Bravo ...! Bravo ...!" someone cheered.

Another cried, "Ah, ah ...! Here, here!"

Encouraged, Triceps began again. "Cure them ...? Once and for all ...? To do that, I would have had to take this theory of mine from the realm of hypothesis into that of rigorous experimentation ... from the swamplands of economic politics, the bogs of philosophy, into the fertile earth of science ... Child's play, for me, as you shall see ... I rounded up a dozen or so poor people, suffering, by all appearances, from the most harsh and extreme poverty ... I ran dozens of X-rays on them ... Listen to this ... They all showed—in their stomachs, their livers, their intestines—functional lesions, ulcers, none of which appeared sufficiently unusual and abnormal to me ... No, the decisive factor was a series of blackish spots which presented themselves all over their brains and up and down their cerebellums and their cerebral cortexes ... Never have I observed such spots on the brains of sick rich people, or healthy rich people for that matter ... That settled it for me, right then and there, and I no longer had a moment's doubt that the name of this mental and neuropathic dementia was: poverty itself ..."

"What were these spots like?" I asked.

"Like those spots that astronomers identify at the edges of the sun," replied Triceps, imperturbably. "With this one particularity, however ... they seemed to have a hooked shape ... And do you notice, my friend, how everything is interrelated ... one discovery leading to another ...? Stars or brains, you understand ...? From that moment forward, I held in my very hand not only the solution to the social question, but the equally important solution to a problem which I had been trying to solve for fifteen years: unifying the fields of all the scientific disciplines."

"Remarkable ...! What happened next ...?"

"I simply do not have the time to give you a complete physiological description of the spots ... It would be too technical

for you, anyway ... Be content with knowing that after analyz-
ing the subjects' X-rays, I determined the exact cause ... The
rest was standard treatment procedure for me ... I locked up
my ten impoverished subjects in efficient cells, fully stocked
with nothing but the tools I needed ... and I made them un-
dergo intensive fasting, caustic skin-peels around the face and
cranium, a daily battery of enemas administered like clockwork ... with the determination to keep up this course of
treatment until the final cure ... I mean, until these poor people became—*rich* ..."

"Well?"

"Well ...! After seven weeks ... one of those poor people
inherited two hundred thousand francs ... Another earned a
tidy fortune in a Panamian stock swindle ... A third was hired
by Poidatz, to write rave reviews in the morning paper about
the splendid performances of the popular theaters ... The other seven died ... I had started their treatment too late ...!"

Abruptly, he did an about-face, yelling, "Neurosis ...! Neurosis ...! Neurosis ...! All is neurosis ...! Wealth (remember
Dickson-Barnell) is also neurosis ... Of course ...! It's so obvious ... And to keep up our courage, then ...? Ah, my children ...! Beer ...? Absinthe ...? Cigars ...? Anyone ...?"

XX.

I've become pals with M. Le Trégarec, that Breton mayor whom I mentioned earlier. He comes to see me every day . . . He is a good man, whose unflagging cheerfulness makes me happy . . . He tells me stories about his country . . . And he truly has a way of saying things like, "*That was the year cholera came to Le Kernac* . . ." both sincerely and sarcastically, that never fails to get my attention. And why shouldn't he be sincere and sarcastic, since "that plague," which began, in fact, with the death of a drunken sailor, ended with my friend Le Trégarec receiving the Cross of the Legion of Honor?

Among the countless stories he has used to successfully cheer my morbid apathy, here are three which, I believe, really capture the unique flavor of Brittany . . .

First story:

Jean Kerkonaïc, a custom's house Captain on the verge of retiring and collecting his pension, longed to spend the last years of his life in his native Brittany, which he had left when he was very young but whose memory had remained alive in his heart, wherever he had dragged that uniform of his, the blue pants with the red stripe. He picked out a picturesque spot on the shore of the Goyen River, between Audierne and Pont-Croix, and built a cabin there. This cabin was solid white, and surrounded by pines, within sight of the river, which was a deep green from all the water plants which, at low tide, covered it like a meadow. At high tide, it was a wide, raging river, flowing between the high hills that were overgrown with stunted oaks here, and black pines there.

Moving into his new domain, the Captain said to himself, "Now I will finally be able to eat winkles to my heart's content."

It might be useful to remind the learned reader, here, that "winkle" is only a nickname for that tiny mollusk which our great Cuvier calls (who knows why?) "the coastal turbot." I would also add, for people who are ignorant of marine sea life and mock its etymologies, that the winkle is the little shellfish, a member of the gastropod and snail genuses, which is served on every hors-d'oeuvre platter on every table of every Breton hotel, and which you eat by ripping it out of its shell by quickly jabbing and twisting it with a miniature pick. It is easier to simply do it than to explain how it is done.

For a long time now, the thought of eating his fill of winkles had obsessed the noble Captain Kerkonaïc. According to those who knew him, it was the only vice of any kind that had ever preoccupied his thoughts, for he was a very upright man who consulted the Scriptures before he did anything.

He had always been "bowled over," as he put it, by the gastronomic delicacy of that species of mollusk, no less than by the fact that its meat was so puny and hard to get at, which made the difficult, exhausting ordeal of actually eating it all the more rewarding. It had become the Captain's dream that the winkle would not remain a mere local staple of the *table d'hôte*, but that it would become a delicacy sought after far and wide—such as, for example, the oyster, which was not nearly as delicious as the winkle, no, not nearly so! Ah! If only the winkle could truly become as popular—not at all unlikely, he imagined—as escargots or shrimp salad. What a revolution! It would bring everlasting fame, to put it plainly, and what else goes with fame . . . ? Ah yes, fortune. But how to make it happen?

And so, that noble customs' officer said to himself, while strolling at low tide on the shores, and wading among the flat-sided rocks where winkles cling—for he never ceased studying their behavior, at once itinerant and sedentary, examining them from the double physiological viewpoint of their shells' molecular elasticity and the organism's potential for genetic modification—he said to himself, "When all is said and done, we genetically modify beef, pork, poultry, oysters, and chrysan-themums. We grow them giant-sized, monstrous, abnormal mutations that shock Nature itself . . . How could the winkle, alone among farmable creatures, be unsuited to such hothouse conditions, and resistant to scientific progress . . . ? I don't be-lieve it."

Completely obsessed with breeding superior strains of win-kles, he became careless about patrolling the coastlines, and checking when ships unloaded their cargo or when the gun-boats docked every week. It got to the point where contraband was being brought through the customs' house in plain sight, and sailors made off with all the treasure from the shipwrecks found under the sea . . . The old days of piracy returned, and a new golden age of Edenic liberty joyously blossomed through-out the land.

One night he went down to the sea to watch the fishermen come in; in their trawl net, they dragged a man's corpse, par-tially devoured, his thoracic and abdominal cavities teeming with winkles. The winkles crawled like maggots in the decom-posing flesh, they swarmed the greenish remains in seething masses, and overran the skull, whose brains they had entirely devoured, and from which fresh armies of winkles continued to be spawned, spilling out through the holes where the nos-trils and eyes had been chewed out. And these were not tiny winkles, like the standard, scrawny, rachitic variety that you pick off the sides of algae-encrusted rocks. No, these were enor-mous, ample winkles, as plump as walnuts; fat, bloated winkles whose meaty bodies burst out of their nacreous shells, which glistened radiantly in the moonlight.

This gave the customs officer a sudden epiphany, and he ex-claimed wildly, "I see what they need . . . They need meat!"

The very next day, he brought home a supply of those mol-lusks, harvested from among the biggest, mainly the ones who had been feeding on that cadaver the longest. He cooked and ate them. They were tender as butter, melting in his mouth, absolutely delicious. He could slip them out of their shells by simply sucking at them a little with his lips—so easily as to render the tedious gouging of the pick obsolete.

"They need meat!" he repeated. "It's obvious . . ."

Captain Kerkonaïc was careful not to tell anyone about this discovery of his, and all night long he dreamed of gargantuan, priceless winkles, swimming and gamboling all along the shoreline, surfacing and diving again and again in the bubbling sea-foam, as big as whales.

He had to wait a few more years, until after his retirement, and after he built his house, to begin to make his dreams a reality. He chose a spot in the river that had a lot of rocky crevices, thickly padded with algae, and there he installed beds like the ones they invented in Holland for oysters, a series of rectangular corrals bordered by low cement walls, each one fitted with a sluice, to retain water when the tide was out, or to drain some off if the level got too high. Then, he filled these beds with baby winkles, strong and lively, with a beautiful sheen, hand-picked from among those which appeared to him to have "the most exciting future." And finally, every day, he fed them their meat.

To fatten up his winkles, he became a poacher. Going out hunting every night, he slaughtered rabbits, hares, partridges, and deer, then tossed their bloody carcasses into the winkle beds. He killed cats, stray dogs, all sorts of animals drawn by the scent of decay, whatever wandered into his rifle sights. Whenever a new horse or cow appeared in the region, he bought it up, butchered it, then crammed it—bones, sinew, skin and all—into the cement farm-beds, which quickly became an unbearable, suffocating charnel house. Every day the decay billowed, billowed, poisoning the air, blowing death over Pont-Croix and Audierne. Peasants dwelling within a few kilometers of the winkle farm suddenly fell ill with unknown diseases, and died in hideous agony. Flies spread the same death among the animals on the moors, up and down the hills, and across the meadows. Horses reared up, neighing, on the road, alarmed by that unmistakable stench of death, and would not keep going; they even ran away. No one strolled on the river-banks anymore.

People complained . . . in vain.

As for the Captain, he became as savage as a wild animal. Now, he never left his winkle beds, where, wading waist-deep in rotting meat, he lifted a hunk of carrion on hooks, swarming with winkles. Several weeks went by; not a soul saw him in Audierne, or in Pont-Croix, where he had the habit of going every Saturday to buy his groceries. But they did not worry about him. "He must be eating that rotting meat of his," they said, "to save money."

One day, nonetheless, someone decided to check out the winkle farm for himself. Surrounded by pines, the little white house stood with its door wide open. "Hey! Captain?" No one replied.

The visitor walked down toward the winkle beds, still shouting, "Hey! Captain?" Still, no one replied. But when he got close to that charnel house, the visitor recoiled in horror.

Atop a huge heap of greenish carrion, oozing viscous streams of pus, a man sprawled, his arms outflung in the shape of a cross, no longer recognizable, for his entire face had been eaten by winkles, turning the eyes into empty sockets and chewing away the nostrils and lips.

It turned out to be Captain Jean Kerkonaïc. He was right . . . They did need meat . . . !

Second story:

Mme. Lechanteur, the widow of a merchant with a good reputation in the neighborhood of Les Halles, left Paris at the beginning of summer with her daughter, a frail, delicate sixteen-year-old girl who was slightly depressed, perhaps even slightly ailing, and whose doctor had recommended a few months' rest in fresh air and open spaces; in short, country life.

"Preferably Brittany," he added. "But not smack dab on the coast . . . and not . . . smack dab . . . inland either . . . but somewhere in-between ..."

After searching high and low for a place that she liked, and which would also be right for her daughter, she ended up finding a very old, charming house, three kilometers outside the city of Auray, on the banks of the Loch. Surrounded by shrubbery, the house had a beautiful view of the estuary. What finally convinced her to take the house was the fact that there were no moors around it, none of those gloomy moors which she had seen everywhere in the Vannes and Gallo regions. Also, the caretaker who showed her the property opened the blinds in the parlor and remarked to her that, during high tide, you could see all the boats sailing by, all the launches from Bono, a little fishing port, located nearby at the confluence of the Loch and the Sainte-Avoye Rivers.

"And vegetables ...? Do lots of vegetables grow in the garden?" asked Mme. Lechanteur.

"Many types of beans, and some lettuce," the caretaker replied ...

In a matter of days, she moved into Toulmanach ... That was the name of the estate ...

Before leaving Paris, Mme. Lechanteur fired all of her servants, saying that in Brittany she could find as many as she wanted, all different varieties, at the cheapest rate. She had become convinced of this folk legend by reading several supposedly reliable history books. "They are loyal, virtuous, selfless people, who will work for next to nothing and do not expect to be fed ... They're a throwback to the days before the Revolution ... real gems ...!"

However, it only took a month to completely disillusion her ... She had gone through a dozen cleaning women, cooks and chambermaids, whom she had been forced to send away almost as soon as they got there ... Some stole sugar and coffee; others raided the wine and got drunk as sailors ... One woman had all the class of a fishwife; Mme. Lechanteur had walked in on her with a farm boy from next door ... And all of them demanded meat, at least for one of the day's meals

... Meat, in Brittany ...! The last one resigned voluntarily, belonging to a religious sect which forbid her, under pain of eternal damnation, to ever speak to any man, be he a mailman, a baker, or a butcher. Mme. Lechanteur fell into despair ... Obliged more and more often to cook her own meals and clean her own room, she could not stop sighing and repeating, "What a heartbreak, my God ...! What a heartbreak ...! So this is what Breton women are really like ...? Like this ...? Never in all my life ..."

She told her troubles to the grocer in Auray, where she went, every three days, to buy provisions ... And when she had run through her whole Suetonius history of the Twelve Maids, she asked, "Look, Madame, would you know of someone ...? A good girl ...? A *true* Breton woman ...?"

The grocer shook her head. "It's very tricky, Madame ... very tricky ... This country is very hard on domestics ..." And, humbly lowering her eyes, she added, "With the army stationed everywhere around here ... the army, you see ... it's not bad for business ... but, when it comes to the future of our young ladies ... ah, Madame, there's nothing more to say ...!"

"Who cares about that? I can't go without maids!" cried Mme. Lechanteur, at her breaking point.

"I understand ... I understand ... Madame ... It's a terrible spot to be in ... Wait ...! I did know of one, Mathurine Le Gorrec ... good maid ... excellent cook ... forty-four years old ... It's just that ... you see, she's not quite all there ... upstairs ...? Yes, right ... she's a little bit batty ... the way so many of the older women get, around here ... It's quite common at her age. It's just the way things are here. Ah ...! You're well within your rights to ask ... She worked for ten years in the home of Mme. de Créach'hadic ... your neighbor, on the river ..."

"But if she's crazy?" Mme. Lechanteur asked in a panic. "How can you expect me to have her in my house ...?"

"'Crazy' is not the right word," the grocer replied. "She's just weak ... a little bit weak in the head ... that's all ...

Sometimes she gets ... you see ... these ideas ... that do not make sense to anyone ... But she's a good girl ... very experienced ... and so very meek ... yes, meek as a lamb ... Madame can rest assured about her meekness ... There is no one meeker ..."

"All right ... but all the same, I'd prefer it if she wasn't crazy ... With crazy people ... you just never know ... Well, anyway ... send for her ... I'll judge her for myself ... How much does she charge ...?"

"Gosh ...! Fifteen francs ... I think ..."

"Ah, domestic help certainly does not come free here!"

And Mme. Lechanteur went back to Toulmanach, reassuring herself, "Weak in the head? That's not such a big deal ... And since she's so meek ... I bet I can bargain her down to ten francs ...!"

The next day, Mathurine Le Gorrec arrived at Toulmanach, at the very moment when Mme. Lechanteur and her daughter were sitting down to lunch.

"Hello, Madame ... Can this be your daughter, this beautiful young lady ...? It must be ...! Hello, Miss!"

Mme. Lechanteur studied Mathurine. She looked genial, pleasant and, indeed, very meek, with her big idiotic grin, but her eyes were somewhat strange and shifty. She wore her hair the way all the Auray women did, in a white, nun-like wimple; a little violet shawl was draped across her shoulders; a demure cloth guimpe covered her bodice. There was no doubt this examination went well, for Mme. Lechanteur asked warmly, "So, my girl, how would you like to become a cook here?"

"Very much indeed, Madame ... With a beautiful lady like you ... and a beautiful girl like her ... you would be wonderful masters to work for ... I always love working for wonderful masters ..."

"I understand you were with Mme. Créach'hadic for ten years?"

"Ten years, yes, Madame ... a very nice lady ... and very rich ... and so very pretty ... She had dentures made of gold ...! She kept them in a glass of water at night ... She was very pretty, very rich ... a very nice lady ... Does Madame also have gold dentures, like Mme. Créach'hadic? Madame *must!*"

"Oh, no, my girl," Mme. Lechanteur replied, smiling. "Tell me, what do you know about cooking?" Mathurine stared fixedly at the parquet floor. Suddenly, she bent down, nearly falling on her knees, and picked up the burnt end of a match with her fingertips, showing it to Mme. Lechanteur. "A *match*, Madame," she said. "This is very dangerous ... See, Madame, in Guémené, one day ... and this is absolutely true, what I'm telling you ... it's not a folk legend ... In Guémené, one day, a man put a match beside a pouch of tobacco ... The match caught fire, the pouch of tobacco caught fire, the man caught fire, the house caught fire ... And they found the man under all those ashes, with two fingers missing ... It's true ..."

"All right ... But what do you know about cooking?"

"Madame, I take two pig's ears, two pig's feet, chop up some parsley ... And I cook them for a long, long time ... It's a recipe I got from a sailor who'd been to Senegal, I learned it from him ... And it's so tender ... as tender, Madame, as butter ... as straw ...! Anyway, it is very, very tender ..."

She looked around the room with her shifty eyes. "Ah! Well ... this place is really quite lovely ... Lots of forest around ... It's just that, I must warn Madame that the forest is very dangerous ... There are animals in forests ... You see, Madame— what I am telling you, Madame, is absolutely true, it is not a folk legend ... You see, one evening my father saw an animal in the forest ... Oh, it was the most amazing creature ... It had a long, long snout like a roasting spit, a tail like a feather duster, and *legs*—legs, Madame, like steam shovels ...! My father stayed perfectly still, and the animal went away ... but if my father had moved a muscle, the animal would have eaten him up ... It's true ... And it's always like that, in the forest."

And she crossed herself, as if to wave away the evil spells of the forest, suggested by the tops of the bushes rustling in the breeze outside the window . . .

"Do you ever get ill?" asked Mme. Lechanteur, made nervous by these rambling, senseless remarks.

"Never, Madame . . . Once, Mme. de Créach'hadic's bell fell right on my head . . . It's absolutely true, what I am telling you . . . Well, nothing at all happened to my head . . . but that bell never rang again, no, it never ever rang again . . . And that's not a folk legend."

She spoke in a gentle, lilting voice. And this gentleness and this lilt calmed the poor widow a little, in spite of the fact that the words themselves were unhinged and incoherent . . . And then, Mme. Lechanteur had painted herself into a corner, so desperate was she to finally take advantage of the countryside and its pleasures, and needing someone to watch over the house in her absence, because she had already scheduled a river trip for exactly that afternoon, stopping at Port Navalo, visiting the dolmens of Gavrinis, the exciting Gulf of Morbihan, the Isle of Moines, the beach at Arradon. The boat she had chartered was already waiting, she was losing money . . . It was time to set sail. So she hired Mathurine on the spot. And, after telling her what to cook for dinner that night, she left in a rush — they would see her later!

It was eight in the evening when the ladies returned home from their expedition, with that pleasant feeling of being tired from having had fun, and they disembarked not far from their property, at a spot where the house itself was hidden by a particularly tall cluster of trees along the riverbank.

"I'm dying to know," Mme. Lechanteur said gaily, "what sort of dinner Mathurine made . . . I can't wait to taste some authentic Breton cooking!" Then, quickly sniffing the air, she said, "Oh, something smells burnt!"

At that moment, she saw the column of thick black smoke rising in the sky above the trees, and seemingly emitting shouts, alarmed yells, foreboding human voices calling out . . . "What's happening?" she asked, worried. "That looks like Toulmanach . . ."

She scrambled up the riverbank as fast as she could, and cut through the woods, running . . . The shouting grew louder, the yells more distinct . . . And all at once, blinded by smoke, choking, falling over, she realized she was standing in her own yard, and she screamed in horror . . . Nothing was left of Toulmanach, nothing but the foundations, some exposed beams, and smoldering embers.

Calm, smiling, in her white wimple, her little shawl and her demure guimpe, Mathurine came and stood beside her mistress. "It's very strange, Madame," she said. "It was a hornet's nest, can you imagine that . . . ? A hornet's nest . . . No lie!"

And, since Mme. Lechanteur just stood there, speechless, staring into space, Mathurine went on in her lilting voice: "Yes, it was a hornet's nest . . . Would Madame like me to tell the story? It's very strange . . . After Madame left, I took a little tour of the house . . . I went up to the attic . . . Madame had a very nice attic, by the way . . . And there, in a hole in the wall, was a hornets' nest. They are very bad, Madame—they sting, those little monsters . . . Whenever we found a hornets' nest at Guéméné, we smoked them out . . . And all the hornets die, and they don't sting anymore. So, I got a stick . . . and I lit the stick on fire . . . The stick set fire to the wall, which was made of wooden beams . . . The wall set fire to the house, which was very old. And so, the hornets' nest was gone, and so was the house, and so was everything . . . It's very strange . . ."

Mme. Lechanteur was not listening. Then, all at once, she gasped for breath, clawed the air with her hands, turned white as a ghost, and fainted in the arms of Mathurine.

Third story:

Because her baby was sickly, a mother did not want to wait the customary six weeks to get her baptized. At the same time, she

yearned intensely for that baptismal ceremony, and dreamed of
dolling up her daughter in white ribbons and taking her off to
church herself. But sickly babies like that are so fragile, every
breath could be their last; you never know if they will die from
one moment to the next. If they are going to die, at least let
them die Christian, so they can fly straight to heaven where the
angels are. And her daughter was most likely going to die. At
birth, she already had that gray, leaden cast of an elderly woman, wizened skin, deep furrows in her brow. She would not
drink, and cried all the time, a constant scowl on her face. The
family had to act quickly. They chose a kindly godfather and
godmother from the neighborhood, and one afternoon they all
set out for Saint Anne parish in Auray, where one of the vicars
had been informed by mail that same morning that they were
coming.

Indeed, it was a miserable baptism procession, as gloomy as
the burial of a homeless tramp. A helpful old neighbor-woman
carried the babe, bundled in her swaddling clothes and crying
behind a makeshift veil. The godfather in a blue jacket with
velvet trim, and the godmother in her nicest wimple, followed
behind; the father brought up the rear, looking uncomfortable
in his secondhand frock coat, too small on him and too glossy.
There were no relatives, no friends, no Breton bagpipes, no
pretty ribbons, no festive cortege parading across the moor. It
was not raining, but the sky was solid gray. A sadness beyond
words hovered over the dead gorse bushes and the red heaths.

The vicar had not yet arrived when they reached the church.
They had to wait for him. The godparents knelt at the altar of
Saint Anne and murmured prayers; the old woman rocked the
bawling infant, now and then interrupting her own prayers to
sing snatches of lullabies; the baby's father gawked at the col-
umns, the vaulted ceilings, all of that gold, all of that marble,
conjured from the impoverished land's slow and painful decay
as if some sprite had waved a magic wand. Prostrated before
the candles, women prayed, their noses pressed against the
floor's multicolored tiles. And the murmuring of lips, like the

songs of distant quails on twilit prairies, and the rustling of hymnals and clicking of rosaries, chimed to each other, called out and responded to each other across the echoing silence of the mournful, opulent basilica.

Finally, the vicar arrived, one hour late, as red as a beet and fumbling impatiently with the laces of his surplice . . . He was in a bad mood, like a man suffering a sudden attack of indigestion after a meal . . . Sneering contemptuously at the modest turnout, which did not promise to fill up the collection plate, he spoke angrily to the father. "What is your name?"

"Louis Morin . . ."

"Louis Morin . . . ? Morin . . . That's not a local name, is it . . . ? You're not from around here?"

"No, Monsieur Vicar."

"Are you a Christian, at least?"

"Yes, Monsieur Vicar . . ."

"You're a Christian . . . You're a Christian . . . And your name is Morin . . . And you're not from around here? Humpf! Humpf! It makes no sense . . . Where are you from?"

"I am from Anjou . . ."

"Well, at the end of the day, it's your own affair . . . What are you doing here?"

"For two months, I have been the caretaker at the estate of M. Le Lubec . . ."

The vicar rolled his eyes and groaned . . . "M. Le Lubec would do better to let people from around here look after his property . . . instead of poisoning our land with foreigners . . . people from God knows where . . . because, at the end of the day, I don't know you . . . ! And your wife . . . ? At least tell me you are married . . ."

"Of course we are married, Monsieur Vicar. I sent you my marriage license in the mail."

"You are married . . . married . . . So you say . . . ! And your license? That's easy to fake. At the end of the day, the truth will out . . . Why haven't we ever seen you at church . . . ? Not one of you has ever come to church, not you, not your wife, not anyone from your 'household' ... isn't that right?"

"My wife has been ill ever since we got here; she has been bedridden, Monsieur Vicar ... And there's always a ton of work to do, at home."

"You are a heathen, that's all there is to it ... a heretic ... a mountain man ... And so is your wife ...! If you had lit a dozen candles to our blessed mother Saint Anne, your wife would never have become ill. Are you the one who tends the cows at M. Le Lubec's?"

"Yes, Monsieur Vicar, if it pleases you."

"And the garden?"

"I do that, too, Monsieur Vicar."

"Good ... And your name's Morin ...? At the end of the day, that suits you." Then, he brusquely ordered the old woman to take off the baby's bonnet and bib ... "Is this a girl, a boy ...? What is this child?"

"It's a girl, the dear little one," quavered the old woman, whose clumsy fingers could not manage to unknot the bonnet's ties. "A daughter of the Good Lord, the poor little baby ...!"

"Why is she crying like that ...? She seems sick ... At the end of the day, it serves her right ... Hurry up ..."

With the bonnet off, the child's hairless, dented head appeared, with black-and-blue marks on each side of her brow. The vicar saw these two bruises, and cried, "This girl was not born naturally?"

The father explained, "No, Monsieur Vicar ... The mother nearly died ... They had to use forceps ... The doctor talked about delivering the baby in pieces ... For two whole days, we were beside ourselves with worry."

"Did someone baptize her in the womb, at least?"

"Of course, Monsier Vicar. We were afraid she would not be born alive."

"And who baptized her in the womb ...? The midwife?"

"Oh, no, Monsieur Vicar ...! It was Doctor Durand ..."

Hearing this name, the vicar went into a frenzy. "Doctor Durand? I suppose you don't know that Doctor Durand is a

heretic, a mountain man ...? That he drinks and lives in sin
with his maid ...? And you let Doctor Durand baptize your
daughter ...? How stupid can you get ...? Do you know what
he has done, that monster, that bandit, do you know ...? He
has let your daughter's body become possessed by Satan ...
Your daughter's body is possessed by Satan ... That's why she
cries ... I cannot baptize her ..."

He crossed himself and muttered some Latin words in a
tone seething with so much rage they sounded like curses.
Since the father stood there dumbfounded, his mouth agape,
his eyes bulging, speechless, the vicar asked, "Why are you staring at me so stupidly, like one of your cows? I am telling you,
I cannot baptize your daughter ... Do you understand ...?
Go back where you came from ... A daughter possessed by Satan ... That will teach you to call Doctor Beelzebub ... Go and
milk your cows ... Morin, Durand, Satan, and Company ..."

Louis Morin could only stammer out these words, while
absent-mindedly turning and turning his hat in his hands:
"It's unbelievable ... it's unbelievable ... How is this happening ...? My God, how is this happening ...?"

The vicar thought for a moment and said, his voice calmer,
"Listen. Perhaps ... there is a way ... I cannot baptize this girl
as long as she is possessed by Satan ... But I could, if you
would agree to it, exorcise Satan from her body ... There is
only one matter ... It costs ten francs ..."

"Ten francs ...?" Louis Morin exclaimed in dismay. "Ten
francs? That's very expensive ... Too expensive ..."

"Well, let us say five francs, since you are a poor man ...
You will give me five francs ... Then, at harvest time, you will
give me a bushel of potatoes, and, in the month of September,
twelve pounds of butter ... Is it a deal ...?"

Morin scratched his head for a few moments, perplexed ...
"And you will baptize her into the bargain?"

"And I will baptize her into the bargain ... All right?"

"It's very expensive," murmured Morin, "very expensive..."

"You accept the terms?"

"Well, yes ... It's just that, all the same, it's very expensive ..."

Then the vicar quickly passed his hands over the baby's
head, tapped her on the stomach, mumbled some Latin words,
and made a few strange gestures in the air. "There!" he said.
"Now Satan is gone ... We can baptize her ..." Then, saying a
few more Latin words, he sprinkled water on the baby's forehead, placed a grain of salt in her mouth, crossed himself, and
cheered gaily, "All right! Now she's a Christian, she can die ..."

They all walked back across the moor, their heads bowed,
silent, in the grip of nameless fears. The old woman walked out
in front, carrying the baby, who was still crying; the godfather
and godmother walked behind her; Morin trailed them at a
distance. Evening fell, a foggy evening filled with fleeting
shapes, a ghostly evening dominated by the statue of Saint
Anne, protector of the Breton people, giving her blessing from
the height of the church steeple.

And when my friend, the mayor of Le Kernac, leaves, I endeav-
or—to distract myself, and to escape my dread of the mountains for a little while—I endeavor to remain in this Brittany,
in my thoughts at least, no matter how gloomy, this Brittany
whose landscapes and faces come back to me, from when I
lived there myself, many years ago ... And more and more
landscapes flood my mind ... more and more faces ... I become lost in these thoughts for hours ...

It was in Vannes, one day when I was walking near the Jesuit
school, that I saw a short gentleman, about fifty years old,
sweetly walking hand in hand with a twelve-year-old boy.
Those were the ages I assigned them, anyway. I have this obsession with always guessing the ages of people I encounter
in passing and will, most likely, never see again. I pursue this
obsession to such an extent that, not content to do this guess-
work in my own head, I ask whatever friends are with me,
"Say, take a look at that guy passing by ... What age do you

think he is . . . ? I think he's such-and-such . . ."

We talk about it, back and forth. After establishing how old he is, I like to imagine particularly upsetting or dramatic events from his past, present and future. I use these "life thoughts" to make strangers seem less strange to me. That is how I pass the time.

The short, fifty-year-old gentleman was stooped, limping, scrawny, and slightly awkward in all of his movements. He seemed a little fearful, and very sad.

The twelve-year-old boy had a face that was pretty but closed off, beautiful eyes that had an evil glint; and he swayed his hips and wiggled his ass with the instinctual allure of a prostitute. In fact, he walked with such sly, fluid grace that he made the father's mannerisms seem all the more fearful, all the more awkward and — how should I put it? — pitiable. I assumed they must have been father and son, even though there was no physical resemblance between them, nor did they display the usual respect and restraint of the filial bond.

They were in mourning: the father, dressed all in black like a priest; the son, with a plain black armband around the sleeve of his school jacket.

I had no time to study them in detail. They were walking up the street that leads to the center of town; I was walking down, toward the harbor, to board a launch for Belle Isle. I was preoccupied with the thought that I was keeping the launch waiting, that I had missed the scheduled departure time. The man and boy passed me by, not noticing the way I was looking at them; they passed me by, like passersby will. And yet, watching them pass, I was seized by a feeling of melancholy, and very nearly physical pain; yes, physical pain I can still feel even now, when I think of it. I would not have been able to say why, and anyway, I never thought to wonder.

Often, in train stations or on ocean liners, and in hotel lobbies that are even more depressing than the ones in this tourist town I am stuck in now, I feel an inchoate, heart-rending sadness when I see the throngs of passing strangers, going God knows where, their lives, their paths crossing my own for a moment. But is it really sadness? Isn't it, instead, a sixth sense of curiosity, and a sort of pathological frustration at being on the outside, at not being able to find out everything I want to know about where all these nomads are going? And whatever I think I can read into the mystery of faces—ageless sorrows, interior dramas—isn't it quite simply ennui, that universal, unconscious ennui which all people feel far from home, drifters unable to recognize anything around them, and who seem even more panicked, more unnatural, and more lost than dumb animals who have wandered out of their familiar pastures?

At the same time, I felt something more intense, more heightened, stirring my soul when I saw that short gentleman and his son; there really was pain, which is to say an instantaneous, electric exchange of pain in him, pity in me. But what pain, what pity? I did not know.

When they had passed by and gone another thirty feet or so, I turned around to look at them again. The pedestrians who happened to be walking between them and me, hid them partially from my view, and in the gaps between these pedestrians' shoulders and hats, I could not see anything now but the short gentleman's back, an overburdened back sorrowfully bowed, with jutting shoulder blades; an imploring back, a pathetic back, the back of a man who has been weeping his whole life.

My heart ached for him.

At first, I thought of following them, drawn by some nameless spark of generic compassion—or perhaps it was a sadistic impulse. Then, without really making up my mind, I just kept walking down the street, mechanically. Soon, I began to see seamen scrubbing down blackish hulls; a pink schooner came into view, its masts waving in the air. Strong odors of coal tar met my nostrils, mixed with iodized vapors from the rising tide. And I stopped thinking about the short gentleman, swept away with all the rest into the great cyclone of oblivion. At that moment, I assumed it was lost forever, the shape of that back that had moved me so much . . .

Nevertheless, around evening, stretched out on the deck of the launch taking me to Belle Isle, my head resting against a sack of ropes, a vision of that short gentleman in mourning came back into my mind, but faraway now and foggy, and I satisfied myself with this explanation, neutral, without the slightest pang of conscience: "I'm sure he's a widower . . . And the boy resembles his dead wife . . . She must have been twenty . . ."

I did not wonder where he was now, what he was doing, if he was weeping all alone, in some hotel room or in the corner of a train car. And I fell asleep, pleasantly rocked by the waves of the sea, over which the moon seemed to have cast a vast net of light, with a tight, glittering mesh.

Three months later, I saw him again. It was on a train. I was going to Carnac. And where were they going? The little gentleman sat hunched in one corner of the car, to my right, and his son occupied the seat facing me. It seemed to me that the former was more stooped and broken than before, scrawnier, more awkward; and that the latter had blossomed, his eyes grown even more evil. I wanted to study the father's face more closely this time, but he turned away and pretended to be interested in the passing countryside: pines, pines, and still more pines, straits and wastelands, the flat, funereal moors. The boy squirmed restlessly and looked at me sidelong. Suddenly, he stood up on the seat cushions, opened the window, and leaned out of the train. Panicking, the father screamed, "Albert . . . ! Albert . . . ! Don't do that, my little boy . . . You could fall."

The child coldly replied, his lips twisted in a sinister rictus, "I'll do what I want . . . I'll do what I want . . . I'm bored with you."

The father got up, taking a black silk scarf from a little travel bag. "Well, my little boy," he purred softly, "at least put this scarf around your neck . . . The air is chilly today . . . I am begging you, on my knees, please put on this scarf . . ."

The boy shrugged. "Look . . . chickens," he said, pointing to a flock of crows flying through the gray sky.

"Those are not chickens," the short gentleman explained. "Those are crows."

The boy snapped harshly, "I say they're chickens, so that's what they are ...! Leave me alone ..." Then he made a rude, suggestive sound with his puckered lips.

Sighing, huffy, the short gentleman rummaged through the travel bag. "Albert ...! Your cough syrup, my little boy ... your syrup ... please drink your syrup ... You're making me tremble all over ..."

The boy took the bottle, hurled it out the window, and crowed, with an evil laugh, "There, there's your syrup ...! Go and fetch it for me, if you want ..."

Then, the father turned to me, his eyes beseeching—ah, what a martyr's face! Sunken cheeks; deep wrinkles; two big round pupils brimming with tears, encircled with red; and a stiff, gray, matted beard, the kind that grows on the rigid skin of the dead.

Now, I stood up in my turn, and slammed the window shut with a certain finality. The child scurried into the corner of the car, grumbling. The father's sad, kindly eyes radiated gratitude toward me ... We were standing so close that we were nearly touching, so I leaned into him and whispered, "He is all you have in the world?"

"Um, y-yes ..." he admitted, nervously.

"And ... he ... resembles ... your dead wife?"

The short gentleman blushed ... "Oh, er ... yes ... um, yes sir ... Oh, my poor dead wife!"

"She must have been twenty?"

I saw terror in his eyes; his poor frail bony limbs were shaking ... He did not reply.

We rode all the way to the Carnac depot in an uncomfortable silence. The train hurtled across an enormous barren expanse, a biblical plain, with Oriental shadows, an ineffable melancholy ... I wanted to say something to that gentleman, something consoling, something supportive—but what ...?

Knowing that someone in this world had sympathy for him, might have been a source of comfort. Perhaps he would have been better able to bear his difficult life!

In vain, I searched for the words . . .

I got off the train without looking back. And the train went on, carrying away the short gentleman, whom I never saw again . . . Oh, if only I had been able to find the right word that his grief needed to hear . . . ! But who, for that matter, has ever found it, that elusive word?

After walking on the moors and the beach for four hours, I went into a little inn, where I ate fresh oysters and drank a pot of cider. I was served by women, like the ones in the paintings of Van Eyck. They had the same tender gravitas, the same noble bearing, the same abundant beauty in their gestures . . . And so quiet!

The inn was very clean, the walls were whitewashed. There was antique paneling above the hearth, and, on the hearthside table, two large sea-urchin shells which reminded me of the Alhambra. I forgot what century I was in, forgot my life, human misery, I forgot everything, and I spent a sweet hour there, free from regrets.

That same year, I spent three days on the Isle of Sein.

Only a few miles separate the Isle of Sein from the continent. On clear days, from Cape Raz and the shore of Beuzec you can see its flat dunes, its thin yellow dash above the sea, and the gray menhir of its lighthouse. In this rather sinister watery realm, the Atlantic is sprinkled with treacherous reefs, whose crests shoot spray into the air even when the waves are calm; and those numberless currents, leaving undulating froth on the green surface of the water, make this area a dangerous passageway for ships. At low tide, the reefs, more visible, form a kind of chain of black rocks—from the steep cliffs along the shoreline to the coarse, pebbly sand of the isle itself—like an extended jetty covered, here and there, by choppy waves.

Wretched wreck of land, lost in that sea-sized sinkhole that they call the Iroise, and eroded by it more and more each day, the Isle of Sein, with its soil barren beyond words and its natives living nearly in a state of barbarism, strikes any traveler who lands there as more remote than the Pacific archipelagoes, and more desolate than the islands of the South Seas. Nevertheless, a population of nearly six hundred souls clings to life on this sand and these rocks, these pebbles and gravel, scattered throughout a handful of squalid villages. Agriculture on the island consists only of a few square acres of potatoes, malnourished cabbages, and some sparse buckwheat fields, bald as the head of an angry young thug; and it's left to the care of the women. No one here has ever seen a tree, and gorse bushes are the only shrub that can be made to grow in this iodized air, under the constant gusts of wind. When it blossoms, it gives off a vanilla scent, which masks the foul stench of unwashed bodies, rotting kelp and sun-drying fish, which stink up the air the entire year round.

Around the island, the tides teem with fish, and abound in eels and lobsters. Stunted and puny, wall-eyed and big-headed as porpoises, the men are all fishermen. Sometimes they go to Audierne and Douarnenez to sell what they catch. But mostly they trade it for tobacco and brandy from the English steamers. When bad weather forces them to stay on land, they get drunk. The men are often fearsome when they do, and are apt to pull knives for no reason. The women, who are in charge of most of the plantings and harvestings, and who do the best they can with what nature has to offer, make the fishing nets. Slow, tall and pale, they have been refined by generations of inbreeding into a kind of prettiness, but it is the deathly prettiness of consumption. Translucent complexions, complexions like wilted flowers, symptomatic of anemia and serous deficiencies, are very common here. In their rectangular shifts cut from black sackcloth, and the archaic wimples across their flat foreheads, with their long, bare necks and like thin, flexing stems rising out of folded shawls, they resemble stained-glass virgins.

Most of these women have never laid eyes on the continent. Many have never gone farther than the little harbor where the fishermen set out from, every day. When it comes to different ways of life, they know only what their poor island has to show; what washes up from the shipwrecks, so common on these reefs; what the ferry brings when it delivers the mail between Audierne and Sein three times a week: humble items of personal use, household amenities, cleaning supplies, which leave their knowledge of the wide world still more confused and woefully incomplete. Thirty years ago, when a man who had left the island alone, in the long-gone days of his youth, returned with a dog, it sent the women scurrying in panic. They believed it was the devil, and barricaded themselves in the church, screaming for help. The rector had to perform bizarre exorcisms, and nearly drowned the dog in holy water, before the women were willing to leave the church. But such random upheavals are extremely rare in the monotonous daily existence of this isle, where even the boldest colonists have never managed to introduce a cow or a horse—or a bicycle.

Ultimately, the women are always terrified when they look out across the strip of ocean that separates them from Life, and when they see, on clear days, that scraggly blue dot of mysterious terra incognita where there are cities, forests, meadows, flowers, and species of birds other than the indigenous gulls and the migratory petrels.

When the old men grow too old to fish, they spend all day every day sitting in the doorways of their houses, staring out to sea; sometimes they speak. In the days of their military service, they saw extraordinary things, scarcely conceivable: they saw horses, donkeys, cows, elephants, parrots and lions. By imitating different animal cries with wild abandon, they try hard to make the women understand. One of them said, "Picture a beast . . . a beast as huge as a thousand rats . . . Well, over there they call it a horse . . . A horse, remember that . . . They climb upon its back . . . or else they attach it to a kind of house with wheels, which is called a 'diligence' . . . And that carries you far, across very far distances . . . in no time at all . . ."

"Jesus, our Lord!" said the women, crossing themselves to dispel their terror of satanic images.

But those evolved forms never really took clear shape in the minds of those native women, incapable of imagining anything beyond the shapes and movements they already knew, and always being led back—like the half-distinct images constantly fading back into blur—to what they had seen with their own eyes, in their own daily lives.

One day, one of those women, whose chest was ravaged by cancer, decided, on the rector's advice, to go on a pilgrimage to Saint Anne of Auray. Even though the naval administration kept a military surgeon on the island, whose three-year tour of duty gave him experience from two distant countries and countless field wounds, the natives always turn to the rector when they need a doctor. Now, the rector had exhausted his entire battery of medicinal plasters, prayers and caustic herbs on the poor woman, and he pronounced his judgment, that Saint Anne and only Saint Anne had the power to cure this stubborn disease, if the Saint chose to do so. The sick woman set sail one morning on the little ferry, in so much panic about what she was going to see that she did not think once, during the entire journey, about the excruciating pains that racked her diseased body. She had hardly stepped onto the docks at Audierne, when she suddenly let out piercing screams and fell down with her face pressed flat against the ground, crying out, "Jesus, our Lord . . .! Devils . . . Devils . . .! They have horns . . . Holy Virgin, save me . . .!"

She had seen steers being loaded onto a schooner. In a herd, drool dribbling from their muzzles, they made moo-ing sounds, whipping the air with their tails . . . And the distressed woman repeated, "Jesus, our Lord! They have horns, like devils . . . they have horns . . .!"

They had a great deal of trouble making her understand that these were not devils, merely domesticated animals, such as there were everywhere on the continent, and that, as old

Milliner said, far from eating men, on the contrary it was men who ate them, with cabbage and potatoes ... She picked herself up, but was not yet reassured, and took a few cautious steps, shocked by the newness of the spectacle before her eyes. And there, on the other side of the port, on the hills of Poulgouazec, she noticed a windmill whose large paddles waved in a stiff breeze, spinning, spinning in the sky ... She turned pale, fell down again, and, with her forehead pressed against the ground and her arms and legs outspread, she beat the flagstones of the quay and screamed, "The Cross of Our Lord is spinning ... spinning ... The Cross of Our Lord has gone mad. I am in Hell ...! Oh, your grace ... your grace ... save me!"

Ever since that time, whenever she looks out across the blue or green or gray water, following the sinuous line of the Breton coast turning purple in the distance, she immediately crosses herself, kneels down on the pebble beach, and offers fervent thanks to Heaven for having delivered her from demons, from Hell, from that absurd, sinister Hell where Satan makes the Holy Cross of Our Lord ceaselessly spin in a constant wind of blasphemies and sin ...

XXI.

Bleak day today. But I got through it with nearly good cheer, because, as I keep repeating to myself over and over again, I only have to stay here for two more days. Also, the famous painter Barnez, Guillaume Barnez, came to see me ... His pompous stupidity, and his ego out of proportion to his talent, are always an endless source of amusement.

Barnez had the following episode happen to him ... Lucky for him, it happened late in his life, after he had already made his reputation.

One evening, Mme. Barnez had a last spasm, gave a final rattle, and expired ... And for a long time the famous painter remained prostrated before that pale cadaver, growing cold as ice—he was wild-eyed, refusing to comprehend, refusing to believe that death had truly come like that, so quickly, so suddenly, to take away his wife ... Carried off in only three days ...! In three days, a woman so beautiful, with such glorious skin, such a well-proportioned body, a perfect Renaissance figure ...! In only three days, that woman who had posed with such noteworthy, such classical poise, as empresses, courtesans, nymphs, martyrs ... She who had won him a Medal of Honor for her Death of Agrippina ...! In three days ... And yet, only one week before, she had been right there, recumbent on the model's plinth, among yellow silks and scarlet cushions, posing as Cleopatra ... yes, a Cleopatra that would have certainly won him a chair at the Institute ...! And Barnez thought again about the stiffness of her outstretched arms with their gold bracelets, the abundant thickness of her hair in disarray, her gleaming stomach, her dazzling breasts, the marvelous curve of her hips, her supple legs ... In three days, all of that had been extinguished, lost—it had disappeared ...! It was terrifying, unthinkable!

"Mathilde ...! My little Mathilde!" groaned the unlucky

man. "Say something ... Tell me you're not really dead ... You are merely posing for Ophelia, for Juliet—right ...? You are not dead, you are alive ... Ah, say something ..."

But when he touched her lips he felt the coldness of death, a coldness that burned him like a red-hot poker. So he sprawled across the bed, burying his head in the sheets and sobbing, "My God! My God ...! She is not posing!"

He did not want anyone to keep a vigil for his wife, and barred her door against annoying condolences. All alone, he set about preparing her for burial; all alone, he arranged flowers on the bed, fragrant bunches of white lilacs, white roses, giant white lilies, snowballs. Clad in a white gown and lying on her white bier, Mathilde seemed to be peacefully asleep.

The year before, Barnez had lost a child, his only son, a plump, pink, chubby, delightful child, who had posed, as a boy, for Cupids and Cherubs. And now his wife was being taken from him, too ...! Now, there was no one left to love him, and he was all alone, so alone that the thought of death became a fleeting consolation ... "What's the point in living? For whom, God? And why ...? Everything is slipping away ... everything ... even the ego gratifications of art, even the rapturous martyrdom of creation; even those divine frenzies, those sublime follies, which make the poetry of the eternal dream surge forth, surge forth, and quiver for a moment, breathing and alive, in a flesh tone, a shimmer of satin, a sunbeam on the sea, a lost shape receding in the mist ... Ah, everything is receding into the mist ... the medals, the commissions from heads of state, the decorations, the grand prizes ..." For a few minutes, he dwelled on the thought of building a double coffin in which he could lie forever beside his beloved wife ... "My beloved wife ... my Cleopatra ... my Agrippina ... my Niobe, my Queen of Sheba ...! My God! My God ...! And him, too, little Georges, in the nude, with curly blond hair, a little pink nose, a quiver of arrows on a long strap, gracefully stepping out onto an unrolling carpet of roses ... or even flying, against an ochre backdrop, with a pair of blue wings ...! My God ...! My God ...!"

Succumbing to exhaustion and despair in the middle of the night, he fell asleep ... When he awoke, the sun was flooding the death room with a brightness that was joyous ... vibrant. Barnez regretted letting himself give in to sleep. He even accused himself, "And here I was, sleeping ...! While *she* ... Ah, my beloved, forgive me ...! It's really true—she is dead ... What will become of me? I have nothing left, nothing ... Painting ...?" He shook his fist in rage. "Painting ... Oh, yes, painting ...! I have sacrificed to it the love of my wife and my son ... If only, instead of being a painter, I had been a lawyer, an accountant, a tailor, *anything* ... then those two beloved creatures whom I loved, whom I killed—because I did kill them!—would still be alive ... No, no, no more painting ... Never again ... I shall break my palette ..."

Very pale, his eyelids puffy, Barnez stared at his wife for a long time, with deep sadness. "What a wretch ...! What a wretch I am ...! I didn't know, didn't know ... how to love them," he sobbed.

But gradually, his eyes lost their sorrowful expression, and his gaze, anguished and tearful only a moment before, gained that intense concentration, that focus of all ocular energy, in one fierce flash—the unblinking focus of a painter, when he finds himself in the presence of a subject that inspires him. And he cried out, "What a skin tone ...! Ah, sacristi, what a tone!"

In the air, his index finger traced a slow circle around the forehead, the cheek and a portion of the ear, isolating them together, while he carried on the following discourse with himself. "Is it beautiful ... hmm ...? No ... and yet, how uncanny ... So exquisite, so unique, so ... *modern* ... It's something else all right ...! And I can't help thinking ... it's exactly like a Manet ...!"

He touched the nose, whose rigid, unbreathing nostrils were nothing but two small purple smudges. "The color of that ... Why, it's unprecedented!" He ran his thumb under the chin to indicate the shading, a translucent shading, just a suggestion of bluish pink, hardly there at all. "And that ...? Ah,

Christ . . . ! Isn't that extraordinary . . . ? Like a cloud, I swear!"
His finger returned to the forehead, the hair, the ear. "And the
harmony of all that together . . . and that . . . ! And the composition . . . ? No, it's too striking for words!"

Moving in ever more sweeping circles, his hand roved over
the gown and the sheet laden down with flowers . . . "And those
whites . . . ? Ah, God . . . ! How superb! And yes, how modern!
What a splash this will make at the next Salon . . . !"

A flower, slipping from the edge of the bed, fell onto the
carpet. Barnez picked it up, put it back in its place, and added
a few more flowers here and there . . . Then, he stepped back,
closed one eye, and measured with his hands the space which
the scene would take up on the canvas, concluding, "A thirty
foot canvas . . . That would fit it like a glove . . . like a glove . . ."

His foot beat time; his head, swaying from right to left like
a metronome, clicked off a jaunty tempo, while he sang in a
sing-song style: "*Like a glove, like a glove, Carolus-Duran would
love . . . !*"

Erecting an easel in the room, he began to work in earnest,
with real devotion. All day long, an unearthly stillness surrounded the lifeless body, starting to decay among the flowers,
a stillness broken only by the brush tapping on the canvas,
and, from time to time, the monotonous little nonsense song
that Barnez had gotten into the habit of singing whenever he
worked:

> Monsieur Bonnat said to Monsieur Gérôme,
> Monsieur Bonnat said to Monsieur Gérôme:
> Yel-low chrome . . . !
> And tra deree, tra dera . . . Tra la la, la la, la la!

The following morning, as soon as daylight broke, he was back
at work again, hurried, feverish, grumbling about Mathilde's
chin, whose exact tone he could not seem to capture. "But
what tone is it, that fucking chin . . . ? Once again, everything's
slipping away from me . . . Yesterday it was lilac—today, or-
ange-ish . . . The harmonies are gone . . . Come on, quickly . . . !

Some green there ... Ah, my poor Mathilde ... You don't pose
like you used to ... Poor darling ... Your left cheek doesn't stay
turned ... and you've gotten stiff all over ... Jesus, it's frustrating ... These things ... I must hold a séance and ask you about
these things ... But wait a minute ...! I don't want to get
mixed up with the occult, it's evil ...! Shit ...! I've run out of
cadmium ..."

And rummaging in his paint box, he began to sing again at
the top of his lungs:

> Monsieur Bonnat said to Monsieur Gérôme,
> Monsieur Bonnat said to Monsieur Gérôme:
> Yel-low chrome ...!
> And tra deree, tra dera ...

Barnez was interrupted by the sudden entrance of his valet.
"Well ...? What is it ...? I told you not to disturb me ..."

The valet replied solemnly, "Sir, the morticians are here!"

Barnez exclaimed, "Morticians ...? What morticians?"

"Master made the arrangements ..."

"Ah! Yes, I did ... Well, tell them to go to hell ..."

"But, Sir," replied the servant, "it's for Madame!"

"Well, who cares ...? Madame ...! I'm not finished yet.
I need two more hours ... Keep the morticians busy, will
you ...? Give them something to drink ... Give them a tour
of the studio ... Or rather, no ... listen to me ..."

Barnez motioned his servant to come closer, and then, his
face gaily breaking into a crooked grin—a grin that seemed to
summon up some lost bohemian prowess of better days, that
kingdom that had once been his—he ordered, "You shall tell
those morticians they've got the wrong house; it's the next
street over."

And he went back to painting.

That evening, coming home from the funeral, Barnez
locked himself in the bedroom. And for a long time, weeping,
his brow furrowed, his head in his hands, he remained prostrated before the canvas, all that was left to him now of his be-

loved Mathilde. After an hour, as night began to fall, he got up and looked again at the unfinished work. "Ah! How far off I was," he sighed, "and how much more I would have had to do. I couldn't capture it . . . Hell!"

And turning back to the bed, empty now except for a few forgotten flowers withering forlornly, he became triumphant, and said, "Well . . . I'll just do a still life!"

Since that time, Guillaume Barnez has been very sad. He confided his feeling of discouragement to me. "I can't paint anymore," he said. "And if I didn't have old paintings in my studio, I really don't know what I would live on . . . You remember my Supper at Nero's . . . ? Yes . . . ? Well, before coming here, I sold it to the Sacred Heart Church of Montmartre, as *Cana's Wedding Night* . . . ! But then . . . what do you expect . . . ? Art is dead now . . . It is only for the Monets . . . the Renoirs . . . the Cézannes . . . It's a disgrace . . . ! Ah, my poor Mathilde was right to die . . ."

I tried to console him. "How can you complain . . . ? You are still the famous painter, Guillaume Barnez. And you are about to be named to the Institute!"

"Famous . . . ? Of course! Naturally, I am famous . . . I am more famous than ever . . . But whenever one of my paintings happens to come up for sale, at the Drouot Hotel . . . well, it's priced at seventeen francs . . . the frame included . . . I tell you, Art is dead . . . dead . . . dead . . . !"

And, with this melancholy prophecy, he left me . . .

I still felt moved, in spite of myself, by the predicament of Guillaume Barnez (so brilliant, back when I used to know him), even moments later, as I went up to dress for dinner. Someone behind me on the stairs called to me, "Monsieur Georges . . . ? Hey . . . ! Monsieur Georges . . . May I have a word with you . . . ?"

I turned around. It was M. Tarte, M. Tarte himself, still dressed from horseback riding, just returning from an excursion to Port Vénasque, in high spirits, humming a tune, an ar-

nica flower in the boutonnière of his cream overcoat. "Hey!
Good evening . . ." he greeted me. "I am very pleased to see
you, dear Monsieur Georges . . . Very pleased, indeed . . ."

And squeezing my hand in his dogskin-gloved hands, as
if to break it, he kept smiling and repeating, "Yes, very pleased . . . very pleased . . . Ah! You cannot imagine how much I
like you, my dear Monsieur Georges . . . No, indeed . . . You are
a friend of mine . . . a real friend . . . Besides, today . . . I love
everyone . . . Do you hear me . . . I love everyone . . . !"

Coming from M. Tarte, such effusions shocked me greatly,
since it was never his habit to say things like that. Quite the
opposite, in fact.

He was a dry little man, nervous, maniacal, with fluttery
gestures and a whiny sneer in his voice—someone who fussed
about everything and nothing. He was, so to speak, the hotel's
nightmare guest. Not a single meal was allowed to pass without
being spoiled by his criticisms, his endless nitpicking commen-
taries. He never found anything to his satisfaction, nothing
was right, he complained about the bread, the wine, the beef-
steak, the waiters, the people at the next table. His spiteful demands extended even to the water closet system, which, according to him, had fundamental mechanical defects. He was a
daily torment to us all. And all of a sudden, there he was, dis-
playing an affectionate cheerfulness, overflowing with it, even,
and his face, usually scowling with wrath, glowed like that of a
lover, or a recent heir . . .

What had happened to him . . . ? Did his excursion to some
black, cavernous mountain lower his standards at last . . . ? I
was curious to know the cause of this abrupt transformation.
"So—a pleasant excursion, Monsieur Tarte?" I asked.

"Excellent, dear Monsieur Georges . . . Excellent . . . Oh,
excellent!"

And since, at that moment, we were stopped in front of his
room, M. Tarte said to me, "Would you care to do me a great,
great favor . . . ? Come to my room for a minute . . . Oh, just
a minute, my dear Monsieur Georges . . . For I must tell you

about my excursion ... I must tell *someone* about my excursion
... a friend ... like you ... Please, I am begging you!"

I happen to love eccentrics, the quirky, what doctors call
"the degenerate type" ... They, at least, possess the cardinal
and all-important virtue of not being like everyone else ... A
madman, for example ... I mean a madman who roams about
freely in the world, as we sometimes encounter them ... too
rarely, alas, in life ...! Such a man, however, provides an oasis
in this gloomy, regulated desert that is bourgeois life ... Oh,
dear madmen, heroic madmen, gods of consolation and luxury, whom we should worship with fervent cults, for they alone,
in our slavish society, keep alive the traditions of spiritual free-
thinking and creative fulfillment ... They alone, now, know
what it is like to be God ...

So, ask yourself whether I accepted the offer which M. Tarte
made to me. "Why not ...? Delighted, Monsieur Tarte ..."
And into his room with him I went.

He immediately pointed me to a chair, as comfortable as
the current state of civilization and Pyrenean furniture permitted. Then, he made himself comfortable, swallowed up in an
armchair. "Ah! Monsieur, my dear Monsieur Georges," he exclaimed, sensuously stretching his limbs ... "You would never
believe how happy I am ... happy ... happy ...! I can finally
breathe ... I've had a weight lifted from my mind, from my
heart, from my conscience ... Yes, I have had the weight of all
these mountains, Maladetta and the whole chain of the Monts-
Maudits, removed from my mind. I am free—when all is said
and done I feel lighter, utterly weightless, I daresay ... I feel as
though I am beginning to awaken from a long, agonizing, hellish nightmare, and all around me, above me, inside me, I see
light ... light ... light ... That is what has really happened—
I've found my way back to the light ..."

"So, what extraordinary occurrence happened to you? What
wondrous event? What miracle?"

His face radiantly happy, his arms flung out over the arm-
rests of the chair, stretching all his limbs in sensual relaxation

like a cat, M. Tarte replied, "My dear Monsieur Georges ...
Ah, my dear Monsieur Georges ...! I killed a man!" On his
face and in his voice, there was an expression of relief, of deliv-
erance, the intoxication of a cleansed, purified soul. "I killed a
man ... I killed a man ...!"

I could not keep myself from starting up in fright, but M.
Tarte silenced me with a wave of his hand. "Do not scream,"
he said, "and do not interrupt me ... Allow me to tell you
about the liberating euphoria which came to me today, from
having killed—ah, compare the sweetness of that word to a
bubbling fountain—having killed ... a man ...!"

Then, in clipped, short, staccato sentences, he spoke the
following: "My dear Monsieur Georges, I suffer from chronic
pharyngitis ... Until now, it has been resistant to all forms of
treatment ... This year, my doctor prescribed the steam room
here at X, for me ... Do you know what that is ...? It seemed
like a miracle ... In short, I came here to breathe at last ... But
the first time I went to the steam room, the breathing appara-
tus prescribed for me was already in use ... There was a gentleman there ... With his entire nose, mouth and chin buried in
the opening of this tube, he was inhaling deeply, passionately. I
could not see much of him at all ... I saw him only as a massive, bulbous forehead, with a receding hairline, so that he
looked like a road of yellow sand between two bushy embankments of shocking red hair ... From what I could see, he
looked like a circus clown or a carnival geek ... Well, I had to
wait three quarters of an hour ... I became very impatient, and
vowed to get there earlier the next day ... The next day, when I
got there, the same gentleman was already there ... The day after that, I came even earlier still, by one hour ... And again,
there he was ... 'Ah, this is unbelievable!' I cried. 'Does he ever
leave that tube?' And that was when I felt a violent hatred
against this man ... A seething hatred ... You just can't imagine it ... My hatred grew, getting worse by the day, because—
you will not believe me, though every word I'm saying is absolutely true—not once, in the course of twenty-five days, no,

not once did I find the equipment free . . . The first thing I saw when I went into that room was that forehead—bulging, breathing, pulsating . . . And that forehead seemed to mock me . . . to laugh at me . . . Yes, indeed, it was convulsed with laughter, at me . . . Never would I have thought that the bare forehead of a balding man could make up in sheer insults what it lacked in hair . . . That forehead obsessed me . . . I saw that forehead everywhere, everything I looked at turned into that forehead . . . Many times, I had to talk to myself, to restrain myself from grabbing a hammer, a club, and bashing in that ubiquitously ironic, snickering forehead . . . My life became unbearable. Ah! My dear Monsieur Georges, during those twenty-five days I experienced the strange, aching torture of thinking only about killing that man, and yet not daring to . . . I committed that murder again and again, inside me . . . in the realm of vague desire rather than realized action . . . Nonetheless, it was an excruciating thing to endure . . . It was because of this state of psychological distress, and also to escape, if only for a few hours, from my disturbing obsession to kill, that I decided to go along on the excursion to Port Vénasque . . . I left this morning, with a good guide . . . a good horse . . . The sky was slightly overcast; the fogs cleared, the higher I climbed . . . It became sunny . . . dazzling . . . But the mountain is a fearsome thing . . . It provokes only thoughts of desolation and death . . . Far from distracting me from my preocccupations, it seemed to use its own diabolical power to make them grow . . . At a certain spot, I was struck by the truly lucky idea of getting off the marked road, the tourists' route, and reaching a high enough peak where the snow would glitter in the sun . . . I left my horse in the care of the guide, and all alone, driven by blind rage, I attacked a sort of trail in the rock, rising straight up to the very lip of an abyss . . . A very steep climb . . . Twenty times, I thought I would tumble into that abyss . . . I was struggling onward . . . when I suddenly found myself head to head and shoulder to shoulder with a man descending the same narrow trail . . . Ah, fateful day . . . ! It was

my man ... the man in the breathing tube ... My blood
pounded in my veins ... At the exact point where I recognized
him, the way was so narrow that it was impossible for two men
to pass abreast of each other without jostling, and without taking great care not to knock each other off ...! 'Give me your
hand,' I said to that man, 'and be careful ... for the strait is
dangerous, and the abyss is bottomless ... You'd never climb
out again!' And, as he held out his hand to me, that moron,
that first-rate moron, I gave him a shove, a flick, that made
him lose his balance. He fell ... 'Ah, my God!' he screamed.
'Goodbye, goodbye, goodbye!' I yelled, watching him plum-
met, bouncing from one craggy rock to the next ... He disappeared into that abyss, I never saw him land ... It is entirely true to say that landscapes are really nothing but states of
mind ... because, all at once, the mountain appeared resplendent to me, shining with unknown beauties ... Oh, the intoxi-
cating sunlight ...! What satisfaction ...! What serenity ...!
And an otherworldly, glorious, beautiful music seemed to rise
from that abyss."

M. Tarte stood up. "Doing it like that, you see," he said after a brief silence, "it's clean, it's perfect ... I have no blood on
my fingers, no brains splattered on my clothes ... And the
abyss tells no tales ... It won't tell its little stories to a soul. I
am happy ... happy ... I can breathe ... Ahhhh ...!" Then,
looking at his watch: "It's getting late ... Go and get dressed,
for I am planning to celebrate tonight ... celebrate like a king
... Yes, my dear Monsieur Georges, tonight ... champagne
flowing like water ... pretty girls ... Oyez ...! Oyez ...!"

"And tomorrow ...?" I asked.

"Tomorrow ...? Oh, well, tomorrow, I won't have to see
that forehead anymore ... And I will take the breathing cure in
peace ... See you later ...!"

And M. Tarte, that friendly, smiling, honorable man,
walked me to the door.

XXII.

I will never disclose the chain of strange circumstances that led to my hearing, today, this bizarre confession, which I am printing solely for its great dramatic interest. I am not a snitch; I have always lived by the belief—and I have always felt good about believing this—that justice should be left to take its own course, completely on its own, when it comes to investigating and punishing criminals. I have no intention of becoming its procurer ... quite the opposite ... Let it take its own course, then, with Ives Lagoannec, as much as with M. Jean-Jules-Joseph Lagoffin ... It goes without saying that I have changed the names in this testimony ... an unnecessary precaution, however, because the man who told it to me has been moved to a safe place outside the country, thanks to me ...

Here, then, is the confession:

My name is Ives Lagoannec. With a name like that, what other country could you imagine me coming from, besides Brittany? I was born near Vannes, in Morbihan—heehaw, heehaw!—the most Breton place in all of Brittany. My father and mother were small-time farmers, very sad, very religious and very dirty. Drunks too, but that goes with the territory. On market days, I was always finding my parents by the side of the road, in quite a state ... Good Lord ...! And many times they spent the night sleeping it off and vomiting in the bottom of some ditch. According to local custom, I grew up in the stable with the pigs and cows, like baby Jesus. I suppose I was always considered so filthy, always covered in so much shit, that when my father came to wake us up in the morning, the animals and me, it took him a long time before he could find me amidst all the cow dung. My parents raised me with all sorts of superstitions. I knew the names of all the devils of the moor, and all the fairies of the lake and the shore. Besides the Pater and the Ave, a

few canticles in honor of Saint Anne, and the miracle tale of
Saint Tugen (who was said to cure bad temper and violent
rage), those were the only things I did know. I was also taught
to honor the Reverend Father Maunoir, a Quimper Jesuit who,
simply by putting his foot down on all the foreign tongues,
gave the Bretons the gift of their own Breton language, plus a
remarkable fresco that everyone can see in the cathedral of
Quimper-Corentin ... I can say, not without pride, that I was
one of the best educated and smartest children in the whole
country!

Each and every day until I turned fifteen, I spent the whole
day out on the moor, watching over a little red horse, a little
ghost horse whose muzzle grew two long gray mustaches from
rubbing against gorse bushes. And three ewes, as black as demons, with the red eyes and long pointy beards of old billy
goats, followed me around, hobbling and bleating. Do not ask
me what those animals found to live on. Air, no doubt ... and
the grace of God, probably, because eating the grass did not
make *anything* grow on that moor, I assure you.

When all is said and done, I was a very polite, obedient lad,
fearing God, respecting the Devil—a loner always. Unlike so
many other children, an evil thought never entered my mind.
To be completely fair, I should say that no thought of any kind
ever entered my mind ... not even at night when, with my
mother being dead, my father used to go and get into bed with
my sister, who was older than me ... Don't scream at me about
that, and do not think that there was anything sick about it,
any unnatural perversion ... No ... it's just the way with us,
and it does not stop us from being good people, saying our
prayers and going on pilgrimages ... Just the opposite ...
We're very big on family, you see ... My father got my sister
with two more children, who were my brothers *and* my neph-
ews ... Neither one lived longer than a month ... But I don't
know why I am telling you this, since it has nothing to do with
the rest of my story ... And why would you want to hear about
it ...?

Like all the guys, I did my military duty, and I ran into a lot of trouble trying to learn a little bit of French, since I only spoke Breton ... which caused me many humiliations and got me into a lot of fist fights. When it came to reading and writing, for instance, in spite of all my efforts and my hard work, I just had to give it up ... By persisting in all that studying, all I got, in the final reckoning, was a type of brain fever that nearly killed me and which I sometimes feel has left my thinking forever twisted and defective. But I did recover, in the hospital at Brest, with a certain Sister Marie-Angèle, whose white hands touched my very soul and made it long to come bursting out of my skin and fly around the room, a very sweet, tender memory that gives me goose bumps whenever I think about her. And I think about her often, like that big swan I saw once, one winter evening, fluttering over the moor ... A fairy perhaps ... or perhaps the soul of a saint, like that very pretty Sister Marie-Angèle, who saved me from dying ...

Getting out of the army, when he finds himself in the circumstances I was in, there is no young Breton man who does not go on to become a domestic. Brittany is the classic land of service. She serves God, the fatherland and the middle class ... So I became a servant, too.

I went to work as a second carter on a big farm near Quimper. That was where a rather unusual incident happened to me, which I might as well call "The Incident of the Little Hare." I always had an idea that it might have had something to do with how my life turned out, later ... Might have even been the whole reason *why* my life turned out the way it did. But here is what happened.

One evening, Jean, a worker at the farm like me, came back from the fields where he had been working hard all day long. Carrying his tools upon his shoulder, he entered the courtyard like some kind of conqueror, holding out this wriggling thing and waving it in his hands. Night was falling; you couldn't see what it was very clearly.

"What have you got there?" asked the overseer, washing his hands at the pump.

"It's a little hare I caught in the hedge of Clos-Sorbier," replied Jean.

"Blessed Jean ...!" said the overseer. "And what are you planning to do with this hare?"

"I want to raise him!" Then he asked, "Will you allow me, boss, to put my little hare in the rabbit hutch, along with the rabbits ... and to fetch a drop of milk in the morning, for him to drink?"

"That's up to the housekeeper, my boy ..."

"Oh, she won't mind ...!"

I was unhitching the horses in the shed. I muttered in a mean, sarcastic tone, "Yes, right ...! We'll all be turned into werewolves, or even gulls, thanks to that little devil-rat ... If it was up to me ...? Thumbs down!" I shoved my horses, and spat a thick clump of phlegm at them.

"Come on!" said the overseer. "There's Ives, jealous again ... Pipe down, you brute. You know I don't like that, and I'm starting to get fed up with your rudeness."

I became angry, and said, harshly, "*My* rudeness ... What I am saying is true, and I'm not afraid of you ..."

The overseer shrugged and did not answer me, and, while I continued to grumble in the shed, he went inside the house, where the evening soup waited on the table, steaming. I quickly put my horses back in their stalls and hurried inside to get my share ... Jean came next, after preparing an empty corner of the rabbit hutch for his little hare. We were all quiet while we ate. I was in a vicious, savage mood ... Jean had a pleasant, faraway look, daydreaming, no doubt, about the gentleness of furry little animals ... When we were going off to our beds, I took Jean aside and whispered to him, through my clenched teeth, "I'm going to fix you once and for all ... Just watch ... You'll see ..."

Jean replied very calmly, "I am not afraid of you ..."

And I finally understood why I despised Jean ... I despised

him because he liked everyone on the farm and in the region. Gentle, obliging, his gestures lighter than most men's, yet brave and strong when he worked—both men and women liked him. I could not stand his superiority, I who was hated by everyone, I don't know why ... Every good word, every compliment struck deaf thuds of hatred in my heart ... I was always picking fights with him, which he always talked his way out of, pretending to be nice to me and be my friend. Every Sunday evening, when he was coming back from town, I lay in wait for him, to jump on him and smash his face with a rock ... But I was afraid of actually going through with killing him. And I did not even dare to insult him too much anymore, seeing how the overseer would not hesitate to take Jean's side over mine.

That night, I lay down on my pallet in the stable, tortured more than ever by hate. My chest thumped like an overheated machine, and I tore the sheets from my bed, strangling them with my bare hands ... Visions of murder haunted me all night long, and I could not sleep ... Oh, to kill Jean ...! I felt as though all the sorrow would suddenly vanish from my soul ... To kill Jean ...! Oh, to kill Jean ...! I felt as though, after doing that, I could love other people, perhaps I could love my horses, my good horses whom I had been punching and shoving ever since Jean poured the poison of universal hate into my heart. Oh! To kill Jean ...! Instead of driving away those red visions, those red, fleeting visions of death passing before my eyes in the shadowy darkness of the stable, I forced myself to see them more and more clearly, to give them a hateful shape and body, Jean's shape, Jean's body lying at my feet with his throat cut, gasping and gurgling ... Then, I felt instant relief ... It was like the drop of cool water on the lips of a desert traveler dying of thirst ... Oh, to kill Jean!

The little hare got bigger ... Every time Jean came back from the fields, he went to fetch some milk for the animal and put fresh straw in the hutch. He talked baby talk to it and sang little folk songs to it, as if it were a child ... They loved that hare around the farm because they loved Jean ... Everyone asked Jean, "Well . . . ? How's your little hare?"

Jean replied with a sweet smile, "He's doing well . . . He drinks a lot . . . His eyes are nice and bright . . ."

As for me, I detested the hare because I detested Jean. Every time they talked about the hare in front of me, I felt a terrible fire blazing in my chest . . . And when I went to bed on those evenings, I said to Jean, "You crook! I'll fix you once and for all . . ."

One night, I could not stand to stay in bed, so I got up, lit the lantern in the stable, and went out into the courtyard . . . I was barefoot, in a nightshirt . . . I walked past the building where Jean was sleeping at that hour, I stopped for a few moments under Jean's window, then I kept walking. The guard dogs came sniffing around me and, recognizing my scent, did not bark. I would have loved to give them a few strong kicks with my foot, but I was afraid of someone hearing them yelp in the night. Why? I have no idea . . . I did not know where I was going or what I planned to do. When I got to the rabbit hutch, I stopped again . . . then I got down on my knees . . . I stretched out flat on the ground, eye level with the little screen on the hutch, with bits of straw sticking out, and tufts of grass lit up by the lantern . . . And I hissed between my clenched teeth, to keep my voice from being heard, "You crook . . . ! You dirty crook . . . !"

I opened the screen, pushed aside the straw and grass, and stuck my hand deep inside . . . "I'll find you . . . Go on . . . ! You're smart to hide . . . I will find you, you dirty crook . . . !"

My hand groped around awhile, then finally clutched something soft and warm, a squirming ball I dragged out into the lantern light . . . The little hare . . . "Ah-ha . . . ! It's you . . . ! It's really you . . ." My voice was choked, very hushed, very hoarse . . . "Yes, it is really you . . . at last . . . ! Tell me you are Jean, you filthy beast . . . !"

The little hare had its ears back . . . In its ruffled fur, I saw only the tip of its wiggling nose, and its black eye, where life seemed to capsize under a lashing wind of terror. "Tell me, are

you Jean?" I repeated. "Jean ... Jean ... Jean ...!" I brought the
lantern even closer to the hare. "How long I have wanted to
watch you ... How long I have wanted to watch you die ...!
Jean ... Jean ... Because you really are Jean, right ...? I recognize you. You *are* Jean ... And I want to watch you die ...!"

I picked up the hare by its throat. "Ah-ha ...! For a long
time now I have wanted to torture you ... For a long time now
I have wanted to kill you ... For you are Jean ... You are his
soul, his soul that I hate ... *I hate* ...!" And I squeezed the
hare by its throat.

The animal's head seemed to swell up as if it would burst
... Its eyeball popped out in a gushing ooze ... It tried to slash
my hand with its claws ... It fought hard and long under my
fingers ... And the more its life drained away, and the weaker
its movements became, the more I cried out, "Ah, at last! I've
got you ... Jean! I've got your pathetic life in my hand ... You
cannot hurt me anymore ... and no one will ever love you
again ... Never again ..."

Spasms of ecstasy ran through my whole body ... I truly
thought I was dying, flooded by a sudden wave of overpowering bliss ...

When the little hare was dead, I threw it back into the
hutch, closed the screen and went back to the stable and got
into bed ... My limbs exhausted, my mind blank, I slept deeply, like a baby without guilt ... like a man set free.

The following day, I could look at Jean calmly, without hatred ... And ever since that night, I was never rough and mean
to my horses again, at least as long as I remained at the farm.

But I did not remain there long.

Next I went to work for a notary in Vannes ... then a doctor in Rennes ... Nothing special to say, except that they were
pleased with me. Indeed, I was punctual, sober, obedient, well-
behaved ... and I made up for my complete ignorance of how
to serve the middle-class by using ingenious mnemonic tricks.
Not once was I seized by a crisis of hatred and murder, like the
one that had driven me to such agony on the farm at Quimper.

I came to believe that little hare was none other than the Devil himself, and when I strangled the Devil, I killed off, at the same time, the evil urges he had put into my head ... But I earned very little, and I had only one thought, of going to Paris, where they said there are places where you can just bend down and scoop up gold—whole fistfuls of gold ...

After the Rennes doctor, who, in his capacity as president of the congregation of Saint Yves, prescribed more prayers than purgatives for his patients, there was a wealthy widow in Laval. I lived there for only one month, because, being very stingy and very religious, she let us die of starvation, "fasting for the Lord" ... From Laval, about which I have nothing else to tell, I went to Mans, to an engineer's—ah, the poor man, he really got cuckolded!—and from Mans, to Chartres, to a bishop's ... You will not believe what I'm about to tell you, and yet it's true. All during this time I was still a virgin ... Women left me alone, and I did the same with them. But the bishop's cook, a big fat sow with three chins and four bellies, set herself the task of teaching me about love, one stormy night, after making me drink five shots of absinthe, one right after the other, which made me feel so ill I thought I would die ... That was when she went to work on me, the old vampire, as if she had not eaten anything in weeks, and I would surely have had the very life sucked out of me if I had not decided to run away, one fine morning ... She had a very cheap trick that she liked to do ... Before making love, she crossed herself three times, and she made me cross myself, too, as if we were going inside some blessed chapel ... Can you believe that? After Chartres, I finally went to Paris, through an employment agency ... I felt as though I had conquered the world.

You see, I had stuck to my original plan, and made a straight line, never swerving to either the left or the right, straight toward the ultimate goal, where Fortune gleamed ...

In the various stages of my journey, I gathered and learned my knowledge of my profession, to such an extent that, when I arrived in Paris, I could serve, I won't claim in the homes of princes and dukes, but in nice middle-class homes, as well as being a coachman and a valet.

The day after my triumphant entrance into the capital, I was introduced to a little old gentleman, in mourning from head to toe, the victim of a terrible misfortune. His coachman—the coachman whom I was supposed to replace—had just killed this gentleman's wife, under mysterious circumstances, and for reasons still unknown to the magistrates at that time. He told me about this tragic event with great discretion and sorrow. He had a very wrinkled, very sneaky face, a long overcoat quilted and puffy like a priest's *douillette*, and whenever they moved, his snow-white hands made soft sounds of bones cracking. As he read through my references, which were excellent, he shook his head and said to me, with a panicked look, "But his were perfect, too ..." Then, he added timidly, "You understand, I must make precise and serious investigations into any servant I hire from now on ... because I am all alone now ... and if I get another killer, it would not be my wife now ... I'd be the one he would kill ... Ah! Ah ...! You understand ... I can't just take whoever comes along like this ..." "The gentleman can rest assured that I am not 'whoever comes along,'" I declared. "'Whoever comes along' would not have served in the home of a bishop ..."

"No doubt ... no doubt ... But how can I really be sure?" And his eyes seemed as if they were trying to slip under my skin ... to sound my depths ... down to the very bottom of my soul ... "And then again, there's something else," he said, after a silence. "You are Breton. The other one was also Breton ... You must admit, that's hardly encouraging."

"But the gentleman knows," I replied with a reassuring voice that took even me completely by surprise, "the gentleman knows that even if all Bretons are not servants ... all servants are Bretons ..."

"Yes ... yes ... but that's still not a reason ... I am all alone, now; I am very old ... I have ... I have ... a lot of valuables here ... Show me your hands."

I held out my hands to him. He studied them closely, measuring, so to speak, the length of my fingers and the reach of my thumb, and testing the flexibility of my joints ... Then he said, "They don't seem too bad ... They don't seem too terrible ... They are the hands of ..."

"The hands of a laborer," I declared proudly.

"Yes ... yes ... yes ... What it comes down to is this: let's wait and see ... Let's sleep on it ..."

No references, no medical exams, and none of the long interrogations that he forced me to submit to, satisfied him. The little gentleman wanted to send a very detailed questionnaire to all the homes where I had served, about my character, my state of mind, my obvious qualities, my possible defects, my homicidal tendencies, atavistic or otherwise, etc. I had nothing to fear from this inquiry, and I agreed to it with the best grace in the world, because, as you can well imagine, I had neglected to include that Quimper farmer among my references ... And yet, deep down inside, unnerved by all of these suspicions, exasperated by this sort of psychological espionage—which I was being forced to submit to, like some criminal—I felt dark thoughts and disturbing urges rise inside me for the second time, seeming to give off a strong, bitter odor, exhilarating and fearsome.

A week after our first interview, the little gentleman made me promise to bring my baggage to his home and immediately take up my position as coachman.

I went right away ...

My new master lived in Rue du Cherche-Midi, in a very old house that, in spite of annual renovations, never looked any less ruined and rundown. He himself was an old maniac. He collected—if you can believe this—candlesnuffers!

Have I told you that my master's name was Baron Bombyx? I immediately noticed that he was miserly and extremely picky. Although his household consisted of a governess, a valet and a cook, he did not trust anyone else to help me move in. He showed me the stable and the old white mare, a completely broken-down nag, shaking on her bowed legs ... "Her name is Faithful," he said to me. "Ho! Ho there! Faithful ... Ho! Ho!" And, caressing her croup, he went into her stall. "She is a good mare ... She is very gentle ... I've had her for nineteen years ... Ho, Faithful ...! Isn't that right, Faithful?"

Faithful turned her head toward her master and licked the collar of his overcoat.

"See ...? A real lamb ... It's just that, she does have one quirk ... She doesn't like it when you brush her from right to left ... She only likes to be brushed from left to right ... like that, see ...?" Rubbing his hand across the belly of the animal, he imitated the movement of the brush. "It's a quirk ... That's the only thing you need to know ... Left to right—will you re-member that?"

I examined Faithful's legs, gnarled and arthritic. "Doesn't she limp, this mare?" I asked.

"A little," replied the Baron. "She limps a little, it's true ... Hell, she's no longer young ... But she does not have much work to do ... I drive her ..."

I scowled and snarled at him, "It's obvious ... She can bare-ly stand up ... She's an old bag ... And then, when she hits the ground some day, Monsieur the Baron will say it's my fault ... Ah, I'm wise to that trick ...!"

My master looked at me sidelong, squinting, and said, "That is not going to happen ... She never stumbles ..."

"No ... I might be the one who stumbles," I muttered be-tween my clenched teeth ...

I felt very free, very much at ease, around that pathetic man who had made himself so completely vulnerable to me the very first time we met. And it aroused me, in a brutal way, to domi-nate him with back talk and threats. I saw a look of anger flick-er into his eyes ... but he did not dare to stand up to my rude-ness. He left the stall, closing it again. "Ho! Ho ...! Faithful ... Ho ...! Ho ...!"

We went back into the shed.

Under a gray oilcloth slipcover, an antique berlin slum-

bered, like the ones I recalled seeing, now and then, in my
childhood back home, in cartoons of Marquises driving on the
road . . . In one corner, empty grocery-store crates were stacked
up, and cans of tinned food, also empty and dented. I blushed
in shame. Of course, I had not expected to get my first job,
straightaway, in some ultra-chic household, to have sumptuous, fashionable liveries fall right into my lap, and earn twenty
thousand francs driving around some pair of bluebloods; but
at the same time, I did not expect to come to Paris and bury
myself alive under all this ancient dust, to get consigned to a
past growing ever more extinct. For the first week or so, I had
walked around the city, going to all the most elegant places,
and overflowing with ideas and ambitions; I felt the heart of a
modern man beating inside me . . .

I consoled myself with the thought that everyone has to
start out somewhere . . . in terms of getting my feet wet, so to
speak, in this new world, and I promised myself I would not
remain too long in that dump . . . I lifted up the oilcloth and
sneered contemptuously at the coach. "It's not exactly a young
man's car," I said. "Ah! Goodness, no . . ."

Old Bombyx pretended not to hear this observation. He
opened a door. "Here is the saddlery," he said.

It was a very cramped room, with brick floor and walls,
paneled with polished pine, or unpolished, rather . . . The harnesses, draped on sawhorses, seemed to babble senilely, to each
other, of long-gone better days. The humid air had blackened
the leathers and tarnished the metal buckles . . . A little stove,
which could not be lit, and whose busted pipe ran the length
of the whole wall, made a perfectly ridiculous complement to a
chair whose seat had the straw coming out of it, and whose
back was missing all its wooden slats. On a shelf, covered with
tarmac paper, the former coachman's uniform lay neatly folded.

"Please, try it on," my master said to me.

"It's just that," I objected, "I do not like to wear another
man's clothing."

"A uniform," declared the Baron, "is not clothing . . . It belongs to everyone and to no one . . . Besides, this one is practically brand new. He couldn't have worn it more than ten times, before . . ." But he did not finish that sentence, which knifed his mouth into a twisted grimace . . .

"Makes no difference!" I argued. "I don't like it, especially when . . ."

"But I had it steam-cleaned . . ." And, after a few seconds of silence, he added, in a less fearful voice, "I want you to wear it . . . You can't even see the blood stains anymore . . . Anyway, I can't buy new uniforms every day . . . Each man lives according to his means . . ."

"Enough! So be it," I gave in. "But Monsieur the Baron must understand that this is not very inviting . . . I mean, if only it hadn't been a killer . . . !"

"As killers go, he was very clean," replied the Baron. "Come on . . . Try it on . . . I'll bet it fits you to a tee . . ." Feeling my waist, and the breadth of my shoulders, he said, "Yes, I'll bet it fits . . . I'm sure it will . . ."

I took down the uniform and unfolded it. It was a very plain style—actually, "style" is too pretentious a word for that uniform: a jacket of blue drugget, a blue vest, blue pants with red piping, and a varnished leather cap adorned with a gold stripe. There was also a vest for stable-work, with red and black stripes. Indeed, it was all very clean and looked like new. I could barely see any worn places anywhere on the linen, on the elbows of the jacket or the knees of the pants, as hard as I checked.

I tried on the uniform.

"I told you!" the Baron cried. "It fits you beautifully . . . It looks much better on you than on him . . . It seems to have been tailored just for you."

"I don't think so . . ." I said.

"What don't you like about it? It fits you perfectly . . . Just look at yourself in the mirror . . . The jacket does not have a single wrinkle . . . It's like a second skin . . . The seaming of the pants is very nice, very straight . . . It's marvelous . . ."

Then, in a slow, solemn voice, I said, "I don't need to look at myself in the mirror . . . It may be true that this uniform fits my body very well . . . but it does not fit my soul at all . . . !"

The old Baron fought off the shock that suddenly flashed into his eyes. "What do you mean by that . . . ? Tell me what you mean by that . . . Your words have no meaning . . ."

"Words always have meaning, Monsieur the Baron . . . And if mine did not, you wouldn't be quivering in fright, the way you are right now . . . Huh . . . ?"

"Me . . . ? Tsk, tsk, tsk . . . ! I think all Bretons are slightly batty . . ." He had resolved to close his ears to the voice that, at that very moment (I was sure of it), was echoing inside him, saying to him, screaming at him, "This man is right . . . Buy him a brand new uniform . . . Burn this one, which, in spite of the steam cleaning and the dyer's acid baths, harbors a demon . . . Don't even look at the ashes . . ." And, brusquely, with nervous gestures, which made the joints of his long white hands crack, he said to me, "Come, now, let me show you your room."

The room was located above the stable, and next to the hayloft. You reached it by a little wooden staircase, covered with twigs of straw and hayseed pollen. A real hole in the wall, that attic room—a stray dog wouldn't even have seen fit to mark it as his territory. As soon as I saw it, I said to myself, "Just wait and see if I bring some pretty little chambermaid from the neighborhood up here . . . some pretty little fruit-seller . . . some pretty little who-cares-what . . . and see if I hang around for very long in this place!" A metal cot with a stained mattress, two rattan stools, a whitewashed wooden table holding a chipped bowl—that was all there was for furniture. No cupboard: just a simple closet with an iron rod above it, and, attached to the rod by rings and hanging down, a curtain of old rotting, moth-eaten calico, with a red palm-leaf print. On top of a stepstool, near the bed, stood a rusty gray chamber pot that had once been, I think, a butter-tin. And the stench of horse-dung rose up through the cracks in the floorboards.

"Well, this is your room," Baron Bombyx said to me. "It's not luxurious, but you have everything you need." He was about to leave, when he suddenly said, "Ah! I forgot to tell you ... I'm the one who makes the purchases of oats, straw and hay ... You do not have to worry about doing that ... You don't get an extra five percent for supplies and keeping up the stable ... You just get your flat wage ... It's the way we've always done things ... here ..." Then he left the room.

I threw myself down on the cot. Something bizarre and terrible was happening inside me. As soon as I had put on the former coachman's uniform, I felt something itching all over my skin ... And little by little, this itch was seeping into me, taking hold of me, penetrating my flesh to my deepest insides, and burning there ... At the same time, strange thoughts, disturbing thoughts, rose in my brain, which seemed to teem with crimson fogs and blood-tinged mists ...

"Old skinflint," I shouted, "you're the one that should have been killed ..."

I got up ... I violently tore off my clothes and paced, stark naked, around the room for a long time ... Then, my fever finally subsided ... I hung up the uniform on coat-hangers in the closet ... put my own clothes back on ... and went to the stable to look for Faithful. "Ho! Ho! Faithful ...! Ho! Ho ...!"

It was under these unusual conditions that I began my service in the home of old Baron Bombyx ... an easy service, very undemanding, which left me, I must say, with a lot of free time. I only had to care for Faithful, wash the coach, and polish the harnesses. Twice a week, in the morning, I took the governess to market, to the furnishers, and, on Sunday, to mass. It was rare that we ever left the neighborhood. During the eight months that I lived in that place, we only crossed a bridge eight times.

Out of revenge for the week, I took them riding for three long hours every Saturday, the governess and the Baron, on foot, in the Bois des Sceaux ...

I got very little pleasure out of those rides, at least not enough to make up for all the humiliations I had to endure. That old limping mare, who seemed to come right out of some church painting of the Apocalypse; that antiquated coach even more apocalyptic than the mare; also my uniform, whose cap was too big and came down over my ears and into my eyes; and, against the grayish background of the coach's flower-print upholstery, those two strange faces, one (the governess) bloated and puffy, a runny cheese, caked in make-up and smothered in the doodads of a clownish, outmoded style, and the other (the Baron) completely dried-up and ghost-white, always looking around with panicky eyes, sticking up from the old-fashioned velvet collar of his *douillette*, like a tooth sticking up from a blackened gum, a tooth yellowed and eroded by the ages . . . All of this made people in the street laugh at us. They ran along behind us, shouting ugly insults at us . . . Those insulting pranksters rained down on us, like masks on the street on the last day of Carnival . . . I didn't feel like a man, being laughed at like that, but the laughter was nothing compared to the uniform itself; and I despised the Baron, for being so cruel as to make me wear it.

I had never been inside Monsieur the Baron's house. His living quarters, it seemed, were filled with glass cases in which he carefully and methodically arranged, by their era and their native country, his candlesnuffers. To hear the people in the neighborhood talk about it, there must have been several thousand of them . . . Thousands of candlesnuffers . . . ! And he bought new ones all the time . . . ! He spent all morning at the pawnshops and secondhand stores. And at noon, after his lunch, the Baron went back out, always alone, always on foot, and spent the next six hours making the rounds of the ironworks emporiums, the novelty shops . . . I only saw him at seven o'clock every morning . . . when he came down to inspect the stable and see for himself "how the oats were holding out." Then, he caressed the mare's croup—"Ho! Ho . . . ! Faithful . . . Ho! Ho . . . !"—and went away again without ever speaking a single word to me ... not out of contempt but out of fear, and so as to avoid looking into my eyes, which—I had noticed—made him blush and act flustered.

The cook and the valet had given me the cold shoulder from the very start. They were old, with their heads bowed and their backs bowed even lower, always crossing themselves and praying. As soon as I saw them, I had the instant impression that they were big crooks, waiting for their right moment to rob the boss blind and liquidate the whole house—let alone the candlesnuffers—like clockwork. Mealtimes were an ordeal ... We ate in silence, in a hurry, fighting over the food and the bottle of wine like three rival animals squaring off over a kill. And when, every once in a while, they did look up at me with their faces as worm-eaten and dusty as the paneling, the joists and the banisters of that house, they glared at me with pure hatred, a hatred so bitter and, at the same time, so thick that I could barely stand to see it ...

But more than anything, it was my uniform that drove me crazy and filled me with the greatest rage. Whenever I wore it next to my skin—and, by a strange turn of events, a sort of unstoppable perversity, I had started wearing it all the time, even on my days off—I became someone else. An other took my place, an other slipped inside me, penetrated all the pores of my skin, pervaded my entire being like a corrosive substance, undetectable but burning like a poison ... And this other was, no doubt, the former coachman, the killer coachman, whose murderous soul was trapped in the clothes I wore. What was this soul made of? I tried to figure it out, in vain ... Was it a gas ...? A liquid ...? A sticky secretion ...? A mixture of tiny creatures—too tiny to be seen ...? I tried everything I could to exterminate it ...! I spent all the money I had on benzene, camphor, powder insecticide; I wore myself out scrubbing it with gasoline, with solutions of the most potent antiseptics. Nothing worked. That soul resisted everything I tried. In fact (oh fearsome wonder, oh terrible mystery!) the linen was not even singed after I soaked it overnight in sulfuric

acid—that is how much that obstinate soul had impregnated
the fabric with his immortal essence. Not only didn't the material burn, but the soul seemed to absorb the acid and become
stronger, more hateful and restless. What was meant to kill it
had nourished it and made it grow ... At that moment, I gave
up and placed myself at its command.

And yet, I did try to put up one more fight. The Baron had
come at his usual time to inspect the stable and caress the mare
in her stall, saying, "Ho! Ho ...! Faithful ...! Ho! ... Ho!"
Using a firm, calm voice, I told him, "Monsieur the Baron was
wrong not to buy me another uniform ..." And even as I spoke
these words, my hand moved to clutch my own throat, as if
trying to strangle myself. "He was wrong ... I wanted the Baron to know that, when all is said and done, he was wrong ..."

"Is it worn out already?" he asked me.

I stared at old Bombyx, and shook my head. "No," I replied. "This uniform will never wear out ... It *cannot* wear
out ..."

I thought I noticed an involuntary shudder running under-
neath his long *douillette*. His eyelids fluttered like Persian
blinds shaken by the wind ... He said, "What does that mean ...? Why are you saying this to me ...?"

"I say this to Monsieur the Baron because Monsieur the
Baron needs to know ... There is a spirit in this uniform. A
spirit is trapped in this uniform."

"Trapped ...? What ...? What ...?"

"A spirit, I tell you, a spirit ... It's plain enough ..."

"You're crazy ..."

"If Monsieur the Baron will permit me to answer him with
all due respect ... Monsieur the Baron is the one who is crazy ..."

I spoke calmly and convincingly, while trying to dominate
the old man with sneers and mean looks. The Baron turned
away and, starting to have one of his trembling fits, he clutched
the open throat of his *douillette* to his scrawny chest. Then he
said, timidly, "Let's not talk about this anymore, my friend. It's

pointless ... When it gets worn out, I will buy you a new one."
He smiled a pale smile and added, "Seems like you're getting
vain about your looks ... I won't be able to afford you ... My,
my!"

So I stopped insisting. But, scowling again, I cried, "So be
it! As Monsieur the Baron wishes ... And if some misfortune
befalls us, it is Monsieur the Baron who will have brought it on
... by the Devil!"

I grabbed the broom and violently swept the straw in the
stall ... "Ho! Ho! Out of the way, Faithful ...! Ho! Ho ...!
Faithful ...! Ho! Ho ...! Goddamn nag!"

Straws flew from the broom; some bits of fresh horseshit
splattered the Baron's *douillette*. And poor Faithful, startled by
my display of anger, stomped her bony hooves against the hard
flagstones of the stable's floor, and backed herself into a corner
of the trough, while watching me with alarm, the way you look
at madmen in asylums ...

The Baron stopped me, and asked, "What misfortune are
you speaking of?"

Although petrified with fright, he forced himself to shrug,
somehow. I replied, "How would I know ...? Could anyone even hazard a guess ...? With the soul of a demon like
that ...! By the Devil ...! By the Devil ...!"

Old Bombyx decided it would be safest just to leave the stable. He was right about that. At that very moment, I actually
felt the soul of the old coachman physically moving inside me,
sinking into my deepest parts, running through my arms and
legs, running down through my hands into the handle of the
broom itself, which it lifted above my head like a long third
arm, invincible and shaking with the violent, torturous desire
to kill ...

Feard by my master, rejected by my coworkers, and disgusted with myself, I took very little time, and even less effort, in
turning into a complete criminal. I did not wrestle with myself
at all about it, it felt so natural. Too lazy to even scratch myself,
a barefaced liar, a thief, a drunk, a womanizer, I acquired all

the vices, all the sins, and practiced them with an expert knowledge of their worst, most shameful secrets, as if I had been doing them all my life. Indeed, I felt as though I had been born with those base, atrocious instincts, even though I actually inherited them from wearing the other man's uniform. Ah, I could barely remember the days when I was an eager, zealous servant, in the home of that worthy notary in Vannes, deathly afraid of not performing any of my duties well enough, killing myself over a single speck of dust on the pony's hide, working with the strength of a longshoreman to polish the brass, to make the rusted metal of the horse's bit, for instance, shine like new again. But now, nothing was left of that vigorous, hardworking, devout, shy young man that I was, when I was still myself.

By this point, no matter how easy my duties were, and how well paid I was for them, far beyond anything I had ever hoped, I nonetheless neglected them completely. Faithful was badly tended, dirty, her legs never washed, her head filthy, like someone who goes without bathing for a week. Countless batteries of lice and ticks lived in her mane and tail, which I had decided to never comb or wash again. Most of the time, I forgot to feed her. It was not rare for a week to go by without me making the vaguest attempt to care for her. I even managed to sprain her knee by hitting it with the brush, for no reason. Her knee swelled up. The veterinarian called it a very serious accident, and prescribed a series of treatments, none of which I performed. And it was lucky I didn't, for the poor animal ended up healing quickly, no doubt from me leaving her alone. It's always best to let Nature take her course, you see . . . She alone knows the secrets of an old mare's knee, just like the willful stubbornness of old Bombyx or even, especially, the mysterious uniforms of coachmen . . .

You can tell what happened in my life after this, I suppose, without me having to go through all the details. At night, knowing instinctively and without any prior experience how best to use them to make remarkable profits, I pimped out a few girls; by day, I was at the bars, spending my time playing dice games for drinks with immigrants, barflies, suburban scum, fairly mild types, really, who came to the neighborhood to see if there were any good burglaries to pull. Good sports, besides, generous in their way, and full of fun, they never failed to keep me amused with their jokes and impersonations, their brightly colored caps pulled down on one side, and their jewelry, all of which had either a war story or a love story behind it. They immediately saw that I was "their kind" of person. And they talked to me very openheartedly, like friends, like brothers.

"This neighborhood's a gem," they said. "It's got more hidden treasures than most. It's overflowing with lonely old maids, biddies and widows, alone or virtually alone, and so mean no one can stand to be around them—you get a job in their homes doing 'honest work,' and just make off with fat sacks and stacks of money, and no one asks any questions. It's also full of very antisocial old men, loaded with more cash than they know what to do with, collectors, misers and maniacs of all kinds—you can get a real nice haul out of them. The only thing about these old people is, they're harder to kill than they look ... Your blackjack just breaks on their backs ... Their leathery skin is blessed somehow, they just go on and on forever. It's murder to murder them!"

They told me grisly stories, the slow agonies of old people with a knife twisting in their guts; shocking butcheries, atrocious crimes, told in cheeky, snickering voices, and which, far from making me shudder with horror, exalted me more than poems and music exalt an artist, intoxicated me more than booze does a drunk, and made the hot steam of blood lust rise in my brain.

Many nights, our elbows on the table, our wine-stained chins resting in our hands, we discussed, seriously and calmly, the best way to break into old Bombyx's house some night ...

"I know him ... *His* skin must be thicker than an elephant's! Ah, bad luck has tanned it raw ...!" one said.

"We should bring the valet in on this . . . He's got a dishonest face if I've ever seen one . . ." said another.

"Might be good . . . might be bad . . .!" said a third. "It's risky."

And a fourth one said, "His candlesnuffers . . .! What do you think we could get for those candlesnuffers?"

These plans kept me smiling when nothing else did. Twenty times or more I brought them up for discussion, when absinthe flamed in my good friends' eyes. And yet, they stayed at the planning stage.

Whenever that old Baron, as maniacal and meticulous as he was, appeared pleased with my work—ah, how can I explain this?—it only enraged me. However, he did not dare to make the slightest complaint. During his little regulation tour of the stable in the morning, I always had the feeling that he had promised himself he would criticize me, criticize me from top to bottom . . . But as soon as he entered, I gave him such a mean stare that I immediately took the words right from the tip of his tongue and shoved them back down his throat. Then, he paced around the stall in circles, very uncomfortable, with pathetic, awkward gestures, and stammering a few meaningless words in a trembling voice: "Very good . . . It's very good . . . Ah! Ah . . .! Good bowel movements . . . A little dry . . . But good all the same . . . Good, good bowel movements . . ."

To add to his disturbance, I yelled, "We're out of oats . . .!"

"What? Out of oats . . .? Are you sure . . .? We should have enough left for twelve days . . ."

I muttered, "Ah! Ah . . .! Does Monsieur the Baron think I am eating his oats?"

"Okay . . . Okay . . . Okay . . . I suppose I'm mistaken, after all . . . I shall order some more, today . . . Good bowel movements . . . Very good bowel movements . . . A little black . . . But good . . . Good."

Finally, caressing the croup of the mare, as was his custom, he said, "Poor Faithful . . .! Ho! Ho! Faithful!" Then he left, his steps halting and uncertain . . .

One morning, I came home drunk, and I had a laugh—
funny story—painting Faithful's mane and tail red. The boss
came in. Getting over his initial moment of shock, he had the
guts to ask me, "What did you do to her?"

"What I wanted," I said back to him. "And what business is
it of yours, you old skinflint . . . ? I've got my stable . . . you've
got your candlesnuffers . . . ! Is that understood? Now go . . .
Get out!"

The old Baron summoned up all his courage and said to me
solemnly, "I am not happy with your service . . . I am giving you one week's notice . . . You will leave here within the
week . . ."

"What . . . ? What . . . ? Say that again . . . No, wait . . . I
want to see if you can say that again." I looked around for my
broom . . . But Bombyx had disappeared. I screamed at him,
while he ran across the courtyard, "Fine . . . Fine . . . I've had
enough of this dump, too . . . I've had enough of your filthy
mug . . . Do you hear me . . . ? Hey! Hey . . . ! Do you hear me,
you old asshole?"

Then I left the stable, got dressed quickly, and went out . . .
It was a real bender, lasting three days and three nights . . .

It wasn't until the fourth day that—very drunk, hardly able
to stand on my own two legs—I went back to the house on
Rue du Cherche-Midi, in the wee hours . . . I had to wait, sitting on the sidewalk with the garbage, for the door to open . . .
I had no other thought except lying down and sleeping off my
wine, sleeping for hours and hours . . . And what other idea
could I have had, when I was so drunk that my brain was
liquefied and my stomach turned over in heavy waves of nausea . . . ?

I found the door of my room locked, but the hayloft door
was open . . . I climbed in through there and let myself fall
with a thud onto the bales of hay, which seemed to me like a
soft, pleasant bed.

I wasn't there ten minutes when old Bombyx appeared in
the rectangle of the doorway, his silhouette hunched over,

twisted into strange angles. He was fetching a bale of hay for Faithful, and I understood that, during those three days I was gone, he had been doing my job . . . It amused me to see this.

He did not see me, he did not know I had come back . . . And, thinking he was by himself and mumbling out loud about damages I had done to his property, no doubt, he said, "That thief . . . ! That drunken scum . . . ! That killer . . . !" He came close to me, so close that his hand brushed against me.

I was sober in a flash . . . I felt an overwhelming, almost sexual bliss stab into me and flow all through me, I don't know what power gave my arms and legs such agility and strength. I grabbed the old man's hand and pulled him toward me so violently that he fell down, screaming . . . With my free hand, I clutched a fistful of hay and shoved it into his mouth. And, jumping up and straddling the scrawny old man, holding him down with my knees, I squeezed him around the throat with both my hands, which felt as though they were channeling all the scattered, far-flung forces in the universe, funneling into me, flowing in a rush . . .

I stayed that way for a long, long time, because all I could think of were my friends' words: "Old people, they're harder to kill than they look!" When it was done, I piled lots of hay-bales on top of the corpse, and mounds of loose hay . . . And then, relieved and happy, I stretched out on top of the pile, where I slept a very sweet, deep sleep . . . without dreams.

XXIII.

Before leaving the Pyrenees and Clara Fistula, and Robert Hagueman, and Triceps, and all those poor, ridiculous or miserable bastards who did not distract me from my ennui for one second, I wanted to see my friend Roger Fresselou, who has lived for years now in a small village in the Ariège mountain, the Castérat.

A long, arduous voyage. After six days of steep, backbreaking climbs, I arrived, aching and exhausted, at the Castérat, at nightfall. Picture thirty or so houses bunched together on a narrow plateau, surrounded on all sides by a pressing horizon of black mountains and snowy peaks. In a flash, the view can become spectacular, especially if the fog recedes from the horizon a little, turning it opal, and covering it in gold dust. But this impression quickly fades, and in the shadow of these towering walls, you immediately feel invaded by a gloomy melancholy, the inexpressible anguish of a prisoner.

At the altitude where the village stands, trees stop growing, and no other bird appears except the cumbersome lagopode with its feathered claws. Made of schist, the soil nurtures only a few scrawny clumps of rhododendrons and, here and there, carlinas opening their large yellow flowers, with pointy, wounding quills, only at noon when the sun is at its brightest. On the slopes of the plateau, toward the north, a short, round, grayish grass sprouts in the summer months, feeding the flocks of cows, goats and sheep, whose little bells can be heard ringing constantly, like the constant tolling, in our countrysides, of the little bell of the priest, who goes out every evening to give last rites to the sick. Nothing is sadder, nothing is less like a flower, than those rare flowers that do venture to live in this ungrateful, joyless environment; poor sickly plants, with hairy, whitened leaves, and whose misshapen corollas have a discolored shade, the clouded glaze of dead eyeballs. Winter—with its huge, drifted mounds of snow, bulging over and bursting through the belt of snow-packed precipices — cuts off the village from the rest of the world, the rest of life. The flocks have all fled to the lower valleys; the healthy men have gone elsewhere, sometimes very far away, to look for work or a little excitement; even the mail stops coming ... For months and months, you get no news of anything happening beyond this impassable snow. Nothing remains alive except a few old men and their wives and children (and barely alive at that), hiding inside their houses like marmots in their burrows. They hardly ever go out except on Sunday, to hear mass in the church, a sort of little squared-off tower sticking up out of nowhere, with a wooden lean-to in the shape of a barn attached to one side. Ah, the sound of the bell muted by the snow!

Nonetheless, this is where my friend Roger Fresselou has lived for the past twenty years. A little flat-roofed house, a little rock garden, and rude, taciturn, jealous men for his neighbors, sad and muttering, wearing hats and dressed in plain and pious sackcloth, and with whom Roger rarely ever communicates.

How did he end up here? How could he, of all people, live *here*?

In truth I have no idea, and he himself doesn't know any better than I do, I imagine. Every time I've asked him the reason for this exile, he shakes his head and answers, "What do you expect ... ? What do you expect ... ?" without explaining himself further.

The strange part is: Roger is not that old. He has only one gray hair, and not one wrinkle on his face. But I hardly recognized him, wearing his mountain-man clothes. His eyes are flat and dull; they never light up, ever. And his face has taken on the same ashen color as the rocky soil. He is a different man, no longer resembling the one I used to know. A completely different life, which I know nothing about. I try to figure him out, in vain.

In younger days, I knew him as an enthusiast, with lively and delightful passions. Still, he was never someone who displayed much exuberance in either words or actions; his was the chronic melancholy of all young people weaned on the poison of metaphysics. In our little cenacle, in Paris, we had high hopes for his future. He had published literary essays in new journals, which, while not being flat-out masterpieces, nonetheless attested to serious qualities, a curiosity about life, a visible striving toward greatness. With his bright mind and robust, four-square physique, and with his prose style, he was one of those who would have no difficulty sailing right through the narrow straits and reefs, where talents often founder, and no difficulty eventually conquering a wide public. In art, literature, philosophy, and politics, he was never rigidly locked into sectarian ideologies, although he disapproved of both revolution and beauty. Nothing morbid in him, no abnormal hobbyhorses, no intellectual perversions. His intelligence was rooted in solid ground ... Then we learned, only a few months later, that he was living on a mountaintop.

Since I have been here with Roger, we have not once spoken of literature. Several times, I have tried to steer the conversation back to this subject that he used to love, but he has immediately changed the subject in a grouchy way. He has not kept current; when I pronounce certain names with conviction—names once held dear, now burnished by the stuff of legend—he has not shown the slightest internal flinching, not even a furtive blink. Nor has he displayed the bitterness of any regrets. He seems to have forgotten that entire life, and his former passions, his former kinships are only dreams now, erased forever! About my work, my hopes partly realized, partly frustrated, he has not breathed a word to me. Moreover, I have scoured his house for a book, a magazine, a cheap picture clipped out and nailed to the wall—and found nothing. There is nothing here, his shack is as bare of intellectual life as that of any mountain man.

Yesterday, as I pestered him once more to tell me the secret of this inexplicable renunciation, he said to me, "What do you expect . . . ? What do you expect . . . ? Fate brought me here, on a summer vacation . . . The landscape pleased me because of its inexpressible misery . . . or at least, I thought it pleased me . . . I came back here the following year, with no plans . . . I intended to only spend a few days . . . I ended up staying here for twenty years . . . ! And that's it . . . ! That's all there is to it . . . It's very simple, as you see . . ."

This evening, Roger asked me, "Do you ever think about death?"

"Yes," I replied. "And it frightens me . . . so I force myself to think about other, less frightening things . . ."

"It frightens you . . . ?" He shrugged, and went on, "You think about death . . . and you run around . . . and you chase your own tail . . . and you spin in all directions . . . ? And you slave away at fleeting things . . . ? And you dream of pleasure, perhaps—perhaps glory . . . ? Poor boy . . . !"

"Ideas are not fleeting things," I argued, "since they're what pave way for the future, they're what lead to progress . . ."

With a slow wave, he pointed out the circle of black mountains. "Future . . . progress . . . ! How can you utter such words in the face of *this*, such meaningless words . . . ?" Then, after a brief pause, he continued, "Ideas . . . ! They're just like the wind, that's all . . . It passes over, the tree shakes for a moment . . . the leaves quiver . . . and then, it's gone . . . and the tree becomes still again, like before . . . Nothing has changed . . ."

"You are wrong . . . The wind is filled with germs, it carries pollen, sows seeds . . . It fertilizes . . ."

"Yes, it creates monsters . . ."

We remained silent for a moment . . .

From the circle of black mountains facing us, around us, from those implacable walls of rock and schist, I felt something like a deadly oppression, a suffocation . . . I literally felt the heaviness of those mountains in my chest, on my skull . . . Roger Fresselou began again, "When the idea of death struck me all at once, I felt, simultaneously, all the pettiness, all the vanity of those strivings with which I had stupidly let my life become consumed ... But I was still dragging my feet ... I said to myself, 'I chose the wrong path ... Perhaps there is a different path to *choose*, something else to *do* ... Art is corrupt ... literature, a lie ... philosophy, a mystification ... I shall go in search of simple people, unsophisticated, virgin hearts ... Surely there must be, somewhere, in pure places, far away from cities, a raw human material that I could sculpt into beauty ...! Let's go there ... Let's look for that place ...!' Well, no—men are the same everywhere ... Their only differences are cultural ... And from the lofty, wordless peak where I looked down on them, even those differences vanished ... It was only a squirming, swarming, faceless horde, whatever it was, wherever it was going, dragging itself closer and closer to death ... Progress, you say ...? But the faster and more conscious progress is, the closer it takes you to the ineluctable end ... Thus, I remained here, where there is nothing left but ashes, scorched rocks, dried-up sap ... where everything has already gone back to the endless silence of the world of the dead ...!"

"Why didn't you just kill yourself?" I screamed, unnerved by the calm in my friend's voice, and seduced, also, by the horrible, morbid obsession with death floating over the mountains and around the peaks, hovering above the gulfs and sounding its toll in my ears, the chiming of those little bells echoing across the slopes of the plateau ...

Roger spoke again, with that same hypnotic, hypnotized serenity, "You cannot kill what is already dead ... I died twenty years ago, when I came here ... And now you, too—how many years ago did you die ...? Why do you keep moving around from place to place ...? Remain in the spot where you fall ...!"

I ordered the guide to take me back, back to people, light, and life ... At dawn, tomorrow, I'm going away ...

Appendix:
A Member of the Academy?

It had been ages since I saw my friend Georges Leygues, and I was unbelievably sad ... when, yesterday evening, in the wings of the Opera, suddenly leaping out at me from behind a cardboard stage-set, his noble dome shinier than ever, his mustache even more imperial, that expansive and gesticulating devil of a minister threw himself right into my arms ... At first I thought, because the hug had been so abrupt and rude, that I had been attacked by a theatrical prop ... My delusion was short-lived ... and I quickly realized that I had only been waylaid by a government factotum ... That's not quite so dangerous ...

"Ah! Finally ...! It's you ...!" cried Georges Leygues. "We never see you anymore! What have you turned into, a kind of savage ...? I've missed you a lot, you know ...!"

"Well, now, look at you ..." I said, trying to out-enthuse his southern effusiveness ... "What on earth are you doing here?"

The minister smiled and stroked his handsome mustaches, comma-shaped and slippery with pomade. "Well, old boy," he replied, "I'm double-checking ... the budgetary specifications ... It's not really a minister's official duty ... But I must *earn* the responsibilities France has given me ..."

He did not stop eyeballing me ... and, smacking me familiarly on the shoulder, he shouted, "Strange ...! You haven't changed one bit ... Not one bit ..."

"Nor you," I replied. "I find you the same charming lad."

"It's my career ...! What do you expect? Since the irony of life has chosen me to teach beauty to the masses, I have to set a good example ...! It's all in a day's work ... I am very happy ... You have no idea how much I've missed you ... I've been saying that every morning to Pol Neveux: 'That bastard, I miss

him . . . ! Every day I don't see him, I feel less and less like a
minister . . . !'"

He was so happy to see me again that I recalled the moment when he was going to give me a medal, right then and
there. He had noticed that this caused me some anxiety and,
very amiably, like a good chap, he had reassured me. "What an
idiot you are," he had said to me. "I'd never play such a trick
on you as that . . . ! No . . . ! It's like our friend Rodin. I promised him . . . this would be his year . . . Well . . . I decorated
Grenet-Dancourt, you understand . . . ? Friends are friends, sapristi . . . ! I hope you won't hold it against me . . . !"

We strolled out onto the cluttered stage. The minister took
me by the arm to steer me through the rocks, the seas, the temples, which descended from the flies with a clatter, or ascended
there . . . And while he was leading me, he took up the same
train of thought, telling me, "Nevertheless, I would like to do
something for you . . . Would you like me to commission a bust
of you from Denys Puech . . . ? Now there's a marvelous sculptor . . . ! Three gouges with his thumb . . . and it looks just like
you . . . He missed his calling, that boy . . . ! He should have
made busts for the homey restaurants and the luxury bars of
the seaside resorts . . . He would have taken the cake in no time
flat . . . ! I dream of taking him along with me during the next
election campaign. He'll do a bust of everyone who votes for
me . . . What—you don't want that?"

I asked him, "What would you do with my bust?"

My friend quickly replied, "But, old boy, I would donate it,
on behalf of the State, to the Goncourt Academy . . . and Bernheim, in my name, would deliver one of those speeches that
guarantee a man's place in posterity . . . !"

I thanked him warmly . . . and, not wanting to offend such
a generous minister with a discourteous refusal, I declared,
"We'll see . . . we'll see . . . ! All in good time . . . !"

He was insistent.

"I'd really like to do this, you know! I have, in my marble
sculpture warehouse, an old bust of Changarnier . . . With

two or three retouches by Puech . . . it would be a perfect like-
ness . . . ! Take advantage while I'm still in power . . . !"

And since I protested violently against the unthinkable idea
of power languishing without Georges Leygues somewhere in
it, he said, shaking his head, "One never knows! One never
knows! Stranger things have happened . . . !"

But this supposition, which had never occurred to him, this
supposition so unlikely and yet with such a ring of prophecy
. . . made him somewhat sad. He dreamed of impossible cata-
clysms. Two young dancing girls wandered past us, smiling,
risqué and flouncy. Their skirts of pink gauze brushed the
minister's frock coat . . . He did not even pay them the slightest
attention . . . Out of habit I changed the subject (we'd exhausted it anyway) so as to change my friend's gloomy thoughts.
"But, speaking of the Academy . . . ! Is it true what they are saying . . . ? You nominated yourself?"

My friend's physiognomy relaxed . . . His eyes filled with
fresh glimmers . . . His mustache quivered . . . He replied,
"That's how things are done . . . I simply expressed . . . or rather
. . . I let it be known . . . through discreet and cunning friends
. . . that I would certainly not decline to nominate myself to
the Academy . . . That's true enough. It seemed to me that that
would get the job done . . ."

He studied my face for any reaction his words might have
caused . . . Then: "What's *your* opinion on the matter?"

I pretended to think, to seem as though I took such a question seriously . . . And gravely, affectionately, I asked him, "Do
you have any claims to fame?"

"What . . . claims to fame . . . ? How comical you are . . . ! I
have any and all. I'm a minister."

"Yes, but what else?"

"What better claim to fame *could* I have, than this position
I am in, unique in the history of the world, of a perfectly medi-
ocre man, ignorant beyond words, who has always been, is,
and will always be a minister?"

"I'm not arguing with you there . . . But do you have any

others? Do you have any claims that you have really earned, and which do not come from the post that you hold ... so, ah, permanently?"

"How would I have any others, and how could I have earned them, since I do not have any reason to be anything except the minister that I am ... and who, at any rate, lays claim to everything? Deschanel ... case in point ...! Has *he* ever been minister?"

My friend expressed his contempt with a meaningful shrug.

"Deschanel ..." I replied. "That's not the same thing ... He throws great dinner parties ..."

"Ah! You want to know the truth? That's the joke of the century ...! I have never eaten a bite at his home without getting a stomachache!"

"He's elegant!"

"As for me, I never strive for elegance ... but then, I have natural chic."

"He is friends with bishops!"

"Well ... and I'm not?"

"Are you rich?"

"Comfortable ..."

"That's not good enough ... Are you a Duke?"

"Not yet ... But Méline promised me a duchy, when he comes back into power ..."

"Have you written any verse ...?"

Poor Leygues suddenly stopped cold ... The only reason he did not turn white was because he could not have gotten any whiter if he tried ... and looking at me with beseeching eyes, he stammered, "Let's not mention that."

The two dancing girls came back toward us ... "M'sieu Minister ... we have something to tell you ..."

But "M'sieu Minister" was not listening to them. He was dreaming of Albin Valabrégue.

Le Journal, February 3, 1901

Translator's Notes

p. 4 *M. Guillaume Dubufe... so beloved by M. Leygues*: Guillaume Dubufe (1853–1909) was an Academic, allegorical painter. Georges Leygues (1857–1933), who rose to even greater political heights later in his career—including Minister of the Navy and President of the Counsel of Ministers—earned Mirbeau's lasting enmity during the former's tenure as Minister of Education (*ministre de l'Instruction publique*). Mirbeau saw him as demagoguery and mediocrity incarnate.

p. 7 *Deschanel*: Paul Eugène Louis Deschanel (1855–1922) was elected President of the Chamber of Deputies in 1898, and later was elected President of France, a position he only retained for a few months due to ill health. He was known for having the best chef (and also the best hairdresser) in all of Parisian politics.

p. 26 *Lancereaux, Pozzi, Bouchard, Robin, Dumontpallier*: Étienne Lancereaux (1829–1910) was a physician who did research on alcoholism, syphilis, and diabetes; he became President of the French Academy of Medicine. Samuel-Jean Pozzi (1846–1918) was a gynecological clinician and surgeon. Charles Bouchard (1837–1905) was a bacteriologist. Albert Robin (1847–1928), a specialist in stomach disorders, was Mirbeau's personal doctor. Victor-Amédée Dumontpallier (1826–1899) was a gynecologist with a special interest in the occult.

p. 42 *M. du Buit, Esquire... M. Émile Ollivier*: Charles-Henri du Buit (1837–1919) was a high-profile attorney, what we would call today a "corporate lawyer," mainly representing the interests of a French multinational metals conglomerate. He later sued Mirbeau in 1908 to prevent the performance of Mirbeau's play *Le Foyer* (*Charity*); this controversial work exposed the social problem of ostensibly charitable "homes for wayward youths," in which the adolescent charges were economically exploited and sexually abused. Mirbeau won the case and the play was performed in 1908. Émile Ollivier (1825–1913) was a republican delegate during the Second Empire and later served as President of the Council of Ministers (Prime Minister). He was longstanding figurehead of French imperialism; in 1870 he made a speech in which he welcomed war "with a light heart."

p. 54 *Bazaine*: Marshal François Achille Bazaine (1811–1888) was condemned to death for refusing to obey orders to surrender the city of Metz to the Prussians in 1870; later, this sentence was commuted to twenty years in prison. Bazaine escaped from the Saint Marguerite prison island in 1874, and spent the rest of his life in Spanish exile.

p. 62 *Galliffet*: Gaston Alexandre Auguste de Galliffet, Marquis de Galliffet (1830–1909) carried out the massacre of the Paris Commune in 1871. In 1899, he was appointed Minister of War by the Waldeck-Rousseau administration. Socialist deputies greeted the announcement of his appointment with shouts of "Killer!" to which Galliffet calmly replied: "Killer? Here I am!"

p. 80 *Mun and Mackau*: Adrien Albert Marie, comte de Mun (1841–1914) and Ange-Ferdinand-Armand, baron de Mackau (1832–1918), were leaders of the right-wing faction of the French parliament.

p. 99 *M. Paul Bourget, M. René Doumic, and M. Melchior de Vogüé*: Paul Bourget (1852–1935) was a novelist and socialite psychiatrist, the author of such novels as *Le Disciple* (1889) and *Cosmopolis* (1892); he and Mirbeau were friends at one time. René Doumic (1860–1937) was a conservative literary critic, frequently hostile to Mirbeau. The Vicomte Marie-Eugène-Melchior de Vogüé (1848–1910) was also a literary critic, a neo-Christian reactionary.

p. 110 *Frédéric Febvre*: Febvre (1833–1916) was an actor as well as a sociétaire and vice-doyen of the Comédie-Française; he gave his last performance in 1893. Mirbeau often lampooned "the great Frédéric" in his writings, especially in his "imaginary interviews."

p. 110 *a Russian Lafont*: Pierre-Chéri Lafont (1797–1873) was a vaudeville actor who specialized in playing romantic leads.

p. 111 *Sarcey*: Francisque Sarcey (1827–1899) was a theater critic for the *Le Temps*, and stood for everything Mirbeau despised: the cult of the well-made play that does nothing to outrage "respectable" middle-class sensibilities.

p. 114 *M. Guitry*: Lucien Guitry (1860–1925) was one of the great actors of his day; Mirbeau wrote the part of Jean Roule, in *Les Mauvais Bergers* (*The Bad Shepherds*), for him. He was the father of Sacha Guitry, the twentieth-century actor, playwright, and film director.

p. 123 *Frédéric Lemaître, Mélingue, Dumaine, Mounet-Sully, Coquelin*: Frédéric Lemaître (1800–1876) was the greatest actor of the romantic era. Étienne Marin Mélingue (1808–1875) was a popular boulevard actor, as was Louis-François Dumaine (1831–1893). Jean Mounet-Sulley (1841–1916) was a tragic actor of the Comédie-Française. Benoît-Constant Coquelin (1841–1909) also hailed from the Comédie-Française; Mirbeau regarded Coquelin as the definition of a ham.

p. 124 *Poidatz is letting me in on that popular theater scheme . . . Rouvier*: Henry Poidatz (1854–1905) was a banker, publicist, and newspaper magnate. He attempted to launch a doomed public subscription to drum up support for the official, traditional, state-run, and generally conservative lyric theaters then (and now) in existence, and predominantly serving the upper classes. Thus, despite Mirbeau's sarcastic comments to the contrary, the sort of theater he espoused wasn't especially popular, at least in the sense of a broad appeal to the people. Mirbeau, for his part, promoted a more working-class, demotic French theater. Maurice Rouvier (1842–1911), a statesman belonging to the political faction known as the *Républicains opportunistes* (Republican Opportunists) served several terms as Minister of Finance and President of the Counsel of Ministers; he had ties to big business and was implicated in the Panama scandal.

p. 127 *Arton's squealing again*: Born Léopold Émile Aron, Arton (1849–1905) was one of the central figures in the Panama scandal. In 1893, he was sentenced to prison in absentia for bribing public officials (known as the *chéquards*). Having fled to England, he took the name of "Newman" and set himself up as a tea merchant.

Found and arrested, he was eventually extradited back to France despite claims that he ought to be considered a political refugee and not a common criminal. Brought back to Paris, he was retried and finally acquitted in 1897. His testimony lead to charges being levelled against several other figures involved in the Canal corruption, all of whom were nonetheless acquitted as well.

p. 128 *a monument to Floquet*: Charles Floquet (1828–1896) was a French statesman, elected to the Assemblée nationale in 1871 and serving in a variety of posts throughout his life, including President of the Counsel of Ministers. The subscription referred to in *21 Days* was meant to fund a monument in Floquet's honor, a move which Mirbeau mocked in *Le Journal*, writing that Floquet's "insignificant, universal-suffragist" soul made the man "a perfect model for a state-sponsored sculptor."

p. 129 *Félix Faure . . . Méline and Madame Adam*: Faure (1841–1899) was elected President of France in 1895; Mirbeau criticized him for his anti-Dreyfus stance, as indeed he criticized Jules Méline (1838–1925)—who served as President of the Council of Ministers and Minister of Agriculture, with a staunchly conservative, protectionist agenda—for the same reason. Juliette Adam (1836–1936) was the founder and first editor of *La Nouvelle Revue*; she also appears as Mme. Hervé (de la Moselle) in Mirbeau's 1884 Zola-by-way-of-negritude novel *La Belle Madame Le Vassart*, published under the pseudonym Alain Bauquenne.

p. 150 *Crime and Madness*: Refers to a collection of articles, published in French translation under the title *Le Crime et la Folie* in 1873, authored by the British psychologist

Henry Maudsley (1835–1918), a pioneer in the study of psychopathy and the criminally insane.

p. 157 *Monsieur Arthur Meyer*: Arthur Meyer (1844–1924) was the editor of *Le Gaulois*, a monarchist, socialite daily. Mirbeau worked for a time as Meyer's secretary in 1879, and later made this "Jewish anti-Semite" one of his favorite targets during the Dreyfus Affair.

p. 183 *the Duke of Brunswick*: Charles II, Duke of Brunswick (Charles Frederick Augustus William, 1804–1873) was chased off his own lands by his subjects in 1830, and spent the rest of his life traveling back and forth between Paris and London.

p. 192 *Jules Simon:* Jules François Simon (1814–1896) was a conservative politician and Republican Opportunist who engaged in acts of fake philanthropy, exposed and attacked numerous times by Mirbeau.

p. 197 *his damnable flu*: This is a reference to the flu epidemic that claimed hundreds of lives throughout France from December 1891 to January 1892, and caused a breakdown of the social order.

p. 200 *Monsieur de Montesquiou*: Robert de Montesquiou (1855–1921) was a poet and socialite, famous for his dandyism and his lavish dinner parties. He served as the model for two celebrated literary characters, Huysmans's Des Esseintes and Proust's Charlus. Mirbeau befriended him in 1892.

p. 226 *M. Henry Roujon*: At the time when *21 Days* was written, Henry Roujon (1853–1914) was the director of the Musée des Beaux Arts; earlier in his career, however, he had been a contributor to *La République des Lettres* under the pseudonym Henry Laujol, at which stage Mirbeau and he were on good terms. Later, Mirbeau accused him of having betrayed his youthful ideals and thinking like "a bureaucrat"—one indication of which was Roujon's refusal to use his post to advance the careers of the artists of whom Mirbeau approved.

p. 259 *like a glove, Carolus-Duran would love. . . . Monsieur Bonnat said to Monsieur Gérôme*: Charles Auguste Émile Durand (1837–1917), known as Carolus-Duran, was an Academic painter who specialized in high-society portraits, among them the noted *La Dame au gant* (*The Lady with the Glove*, 1869), a painting of his wife. Mirbeau often criticized him, seeing him as nothing more than a vulgar "decorator." Léon Joseph Florentin Bonnat (1833–1922) and Jean-Léon Gérôme (1824–1904) were two of the leading lights of the Institut de France, and, for this reason, were often mocked by Mirbeau. Bonnat painted photorealistic portraits, while Gérôme, who was exrremely hostile to the Impressionists, worked in an Academic and classical mode.

p. 297 *I've been saying that every morning to Pol Neveux*: Pol-Louis Neveux (1865–1939) was a writer and member of the Académie Goncourt, and held a post as secretary to Georges Leygues's cabinet.

p. 298 *Denys Puech*: A successful sculptor, Puech (1854–1942) received numerous government commissions during the Third Republic. He was elected to the Académie des Beaux-Arts in 1905.

p. 298 *to the Goncourt Academy . . . and Bernheim. . . . an old bust of Changarnier*: Mirbeau was eventually elected to the Académie Goncourt in 1907. Adrien Bernheim (1861–

1914) was the Inspector of Theaters for the Ministère des Beaux-Arts.
Nicolas Anne Théodule Changarnier (1793–1877) was a royalist general and statesman who, in his military capacity, participated in the conquest of Algeria and the Franco-Prussian War.

p. 300 *friends with bishops*: This might allude to the fact that, in 1894, during his tenure as Minister of Education, Leygues acted in concert with the Church and the correspondingly reactionary clerical contingent of the government to dismiss Paul Robin (1837–1912) from his post as head of the Prévost Orphanage in Cempuis. This progressive educator espoused, among other things, a liberal, atheistic, experiential, and coeducational program for underprivileged children in his care. Mirbeau vigorously denounced Robin's removal; Robin later committed suicide.

p. 300 *Albin Valabrégue*: An enormously prolific and successful playwright, Valabrégue (1853–1936) wasn't much respected by Mirbeau.

OCTAVE MIRBEAU (1848–1917) was a leader of the "Decadent" movement. Producing works in reportage, art and literary criticism, travel writing, fiction, and drama, he inspired everything from surrealism to gonzo journalism.

JUSTIN VICARI is the author of several books of literary and film theory. His first book of poems, *The Professional Weepers*, won the Transcontinental Award. He has also translated Paul Eluard, François Emmanuel, and Joris-Karl Huysmans.